Burning Embers

MATED BY FIRE
BOOK ONE

KATIE MAY

EXPRESSO PUBLISHING, LLC

Edited by Lindsey Loucks of Midnight Library

Cover by Laura Social-Clarke of Covers by Aura

To my supporters on Ream. Thank you.

Foreword

This is book one of a why choose/reverse harem series where the FMC won't have to choose between her love interests at the end. Though this book takes place in high school, all characters will be over the age of eighteen before any sexy times commence. Triggers include sexual assault (not a main character), hints of past abuse, and death. There will absolutely be NO cheating. All of the guys are one hundred percent devoted to the FMC from the second they see her (though some may need to get their heads out of their asses first).

One

IZZY

All of my belongings can fit into one duffel bag.

It's sad, really, when you think about it. How can an entire lifetime of items be confined to a bag only half the size of me?

I never allowed myself to overly think about my belongings—or lack thereof—until now. Even I have to admit the sight is pitiful. At least it's better than the garbage bag I carried around when I was first put into the foster care system years ago.

Amanda Highland taps her manicured fingers against the steering wheel as she stares at me out of the corner of her eye. That red lipstick she likes to wear so much looks like a bloody slash across her face. I've never seen her do anything but scowl before—usually at me—so this impassive front has a tendril of *something* crawling through my chest.

Guilt?

Regret?

Fear?

I absently finger the strap of the bag resting on my lap.

"This might be your last chance, kid," she murmurs, her jaw clenching in a way that has me quickly looking away.

I hate the anger splayed across her face. It makes me feel as if I did something wrong...which I didn't. All I did was defend myself.

I ignore Amanda's condescending tone as I turn to stare out the window, watching the rippling green hills shift into woodsy forests. Interspersed amongst the trees are cottages. Some are small—the type of home you would expect a wilderness survival expert to stay in —while others are large and extravagant.

It takes everything I have within me not to gawk.

I don't *gawk*.

At the end of the road, the asphalt transitions into dirt, broken apart by tire tracks. The ride is unsurprisingly bumpy, and I have to grip the handle above my head to keep from banging my skull against the window. After what feels like hours, but I know to only be minutes later, we arrive at the largest house I've seen so far.

Though calling this monstrosity a house or even a cabin is a grave insult.

A gazebo rests directly before the front entrance—

six pillars holding up a hexagonal roof with a swinging bench underneath. The mansion itself is constructed out of both mismatched stones and wooden pillars, somehow seamlessly blending modern and ancient architecture together.

There are so many windows that I wonder how this family ever receives any privacy…but then I remember that they live in the middle of nowhere. The closest town is over fifteen miles away.

Towering trees surround the home from all sides, though it doesn't make the building appear gloomy or desolate. The ambient lighting trickling out through the open windows ensures that.

"Damn, kid," Amanda murmurs under her breath and whistles fondly.

I ignore her.

The house may be pretty, but that means nothing when it comes to the people inside.

I know very little about the couple who chose to foster me—only their names.

Gerry and Hale Prince.

Amanda assured me that they've been extensively checked out, but she also said that about the last few homes I've been placed with.

Extensively checked out my ass.

If it comes to it, I'll do what I did the last time things went badly—stab first, ask for forgiveness later, and run like hell. It's what I'm best at, after all.

Amanda slides out of the car, and I don't waste any

time doing so as well. Slinging the duffel bag over my shoulder, I stare up at the place I'll be forced to call "home" for the next year.

Home. Scoff.

That's one word that has never been associated with me. I've had places I slept in, places I lived in, and places I survived in. None of them could be considered a "home," and I doubt this will be any different.

I nibble on my lower lip as the front door opens, and a tall, broad-shouldered man steps out. He's handsome for an older guy, with dark hair peppered religiously with gray streaks. A few wrinkles bracket his eyes, but I have the distinct impression they're not from old age. When he smiles, unveiling sparkling white teeth, those creases deepen even further.

"Hale!" A smile I've never seen before on Amanda's face—at least not directed at me—makes an unexpected appearance as she strides forward with her hand extended. "Where's Gerry?"

"He's away for a few days doing some business," Hale explains, though he doesn't take his gaze off of me, even as he shakes her hand. His eyes ignite with an excited gleam that immediately sets me on edge.

Because that gleam? It's not a malicious or cruel one.

And I don't know what to do with people who are genuinely nice.

In my world, they don't survive long.

I resist the urge to palm the blade I always keep hidden up my sleeve.

The longer Hale stares at me, the more unnerved I feel. Ice fuses my joints together until I'm unable to move a muscle, even if I wanted to.

"You must be Isabella." Another wide, beguiling smile unfurls on his face as he takes a few steps away from Amanda to stand in front of me.

He doesn't move to hug or even touch me, something I appreciate immensely. I don't allow my gratitude to show on my face as I give him a slow once-over, searching for any indication he's not what he seems.

When he allows my perusal of him, not flinching or even seeming offended, I shift my duffel bag to my opposite shoulder and say, "Izzy."

"Excuse me?"

"Most people call me Izzy." I shuffle from foot to foot as I wait for him to respond.

His beatific smile broadens. "Izzy."

He says the name reverently, and a pang of self-consciousness reverberates through me. I love my name —it's one I chose for myself—but I can't help but think it's almost childish. Isabella is a woman. Izzy is a scared child, a street rat, an orphan. And Bella? She's just an idiotic girl obsessed with a sparkly, virgin vampire who watches her sleep.

We continue to stare at each other for what feels like an obscenely long amount of time.

Finally, Hale clears his throat and nods towards the car. "Can I get your other luggage?"

"I don't have any other luggage." I once again shift my weight, suddenly unable to meet his penetrating stare.

The ground... The ground is definitely more alluring. Ohhh. What a pretty pebble. It's all...gray and boring and pebbly.

"What do you mean?" There's a tightness in Hale's voice that has me jerking my head up. His lips are compressed in a grim line, and his eyes are flinty. It's so unlike his kind demeanor from only a few minutes earlier that I resist the urge to gape like a lunatic.

Oh fuck.

Is he pissed that he may have to buy me new supplies? I should tell him that he needn't bother. I've made do with what I possess for the last ten years. I don't need any handouts.

The state may provide these foster houses with a generous sum of cash each month to take care of their charges, but I'm not an idiot. I know the system can, and will, be abused.

I've experienced the world's wickedness firsthand.

"It's fine," I rush to say, desperately trying to quell the anger brewing in his eyes, wanting him to direct it anywhere but at me. "You don't need to—"

"As soon as you're settled in, we can head to the mall," Hale interrupts, his tone succinct and firm.

The hardness in his eyes tells me that arguing will

be futile. He turns the force of his glare onto Amanda, and I find myself breathing easier now that I'm no longer suffocating under the weight of his stare.

"How can these types of things happen? Why isn't the system protecting these kids better?" Anger infuses every word—anger...on my behalf.

An odd, fluttering sensation unfurls in my chest.

Amanda sighs tiredly and absently scratches at the bun she pinned her hair up in.

"You know that people take advantage of the system, Hale. We do what we can for these children, but so many foster parents are in it for the benefits, not for the kids themselves."

Hale huffs and folds his large arms over his chest. His gaze slides in my direction, and the ice in his eyes melts marginally, softening his entire exterior.

"Don't worry about a thing, kiddo," he says in a gentle voice that makes me instantly want to relax.

I don't, though. Not yet. Still, I find myself hanging on to every word he says.

"I don't want you to worry about things like clothing and food. We'll take care of that. Just focus on schooling and your classes."

School.

Fuck.

It's always hard being the new kid, but it's even harder when you're the *foster child* new kid. And in small towns like this? People talk. By the end of my first day, everyone will know exactly where I came from and who I am.

The mere thought has an infestation of fire ants scampering directly underneath my skin.

Pushing all thoughts of new schools and classmates to the back of my mind, I focus on what else Hale said.

We'll take care of that.

Normally when I hear those words, I automatically assume I'm indebted to someone. Or multiple someones.

Why don't I feel that way with Hale?

Why does the sincerity dripping from his voice calm me and untangle the huge knot in my stomach I hadn't realized existed?

Still, I can't help but argue. "You don't have to. I can get a job and—"

Once again, Hale cuts me off with a negligent wave of his hand. I can't help but note a strange birthmark marring his pale skin. It almost appears to be in the shape of a tree.

"Don't be silly. You can get a job if you want to, of course, but don't think it's necessary." He shoves his hands into his front pockets and flicks his gaze towards Amanda. "Shall I show you two around?"

"Is it different from the last time I visited?" Amanda jests with a teasing grin. Her high heels click against the asphalt as she moves towards the front entrance.

Hale chuckles and says something to Amanda I

can't quite hear, not over the sudden roaring between my ears.

Has Amanda visited this home before?

Does she come often?

And if so...does that mean Hale has other foster children staying with him?

A chill that has nothing to do with the wind cascades through me.

Who exactly will I meet inside of this house?

Two

IZZY

The inside of the house is just as extravagant as the outside.

Hale leads us through the kitchen, dining room, sitting room, living room, and eventually into the library. I can't help but gape in disbelief as I take in the towering stacks full of every type of book imaginable—nonfiction, fantasy, horror, and even romance. A three-tiered chandelier dangles from the ceiling, providing just enough lighting for someone to sit on one of the recliners and read comfortably. An unlit fireplace completes the eighteenth-century gothic look.

"Can I just live here?" I murmur to no one in particular as I spin on my heel, trying my damnedest not to swoon.

My life changed constantly as a child—one second, I would be sitting on a bunk bed in a small town in

Ohio; the next, I would be in the city next door, starting all over again. New house. New family. New school. New friends. New life.

However, my one constant throughout all of that was my love for books. My first foster mom—one of the good ones—bought me my first chapter book when I was nine years old. I fell in love instantly with the world, relishing the way I could be transported into a kingdom far, far away just by flipping through some dusty, old pages.

But real life? It isn't some stupid fairy tale. The monsters aren't big and green and covered in spikes. No, these monsters wear human faces and pleasant smiles. They speak in cordial tones and make you feel cherished and wanted—all before they stab a knife through your back.

"You're a fan of reading?" Hale's question tugs my attention back to him. A bright smile lights up his face, making him look years younger than he probably is.

I try to tamp down my initial enthusiasm over the beautiful room. If there's one thing I've learned from my time in the foster care system, it's that people use your likes against you. They wield them as weapons, ones capable of slicing at your skin more keenly than any bullet or blade can.

"I didn't really have much else to do," I confess with a half-hearted shrug.

Hale's face falls at my nonchalant answer before he clears his throat.

"Yes...well...feel free to use this room at any time." A more genuine smile teeters at the edges of his lips, though it doesn't fully form. "You may not be able to live here, but you can use it as often as you please." In a conspiratorial whisper, he adds, "Besides, if you stayed here twenty-four seven, where would you even shit if you had to go to the bathroom?"

A snort of surprised laughter escapes me entirely unbidden. I can't help but gape at him.

He merely grins and flashes me a wink before gesturing towards the door. "Come on, kiddo. Let me show you where you'll be staying."

He leads us down another long hallway with peach-painted walls and mahogany floorboards. The only sound is the click-clack of Amanda's heels and the repetitive tick-tick-tick of some unseen clock.

"I sleep with my husband on the floor above," Hale begins. "That floor isn't off limits by any means, but there's only our bedroom up there. And the adjoining bathroom." He points towards the very first door in the hallway we're currently in. "This is where Jake and Seth sleep. Jake's actually in your grade; hopefully, he'll be able to help you acclimate to the new school."

Hale sounds so optimistic by the prospect that he completely misses the way my body shivers.

A strange man living a few doors down from me?

Prickles of unease race up and down my spine like scuttling spiders. My joints seem to be frozen; it's physically painful for me to move forward, as if I'm the Tin Man in Oz.

Hale seems like a kind man, but what about this Jake person? Would he hurt me? Would Hale even care if he did?

Instinctively, I palm my knife once more, taking comfort in the familiarity of the metal against my suddenly slick skin, before allowing it to slide back up my sleeve.

"Seth's twelve and in seventh grade. That kid's a genius, I tell you. He's either going to develop the cure for cancer...or blow up the world with one of his failed experiments," Hale continues, shaking his head with a fond chuckle. He then gestures towards another door opposite the first one. "That's the bathroom Seth and Jake share. Of course, you're allowed to use it if there's no one in there, but that's predominantly where the guys will get ready in the morning and at night."

Hale stops in front of the door farthest down the hall. Tension lines his wiry body, and he seems to be holding his breath.

"Is this...?" I gesture towards the still-closed door.

"Your room. Well, the room that you'll share with Vasilissa. But don't call her that. She hates it." Hale sighs deeply and finally pushes open the door to the bedroom.

The first thing that I note is the pungent scent contaminating the air—I can't quite put my finger on what it is, but I can tell it's some sort of flower.

The next thing I notice is the barrage of *pink*.

It's everywhere.

The bedspread, the walls, the rug, the clothes. One side of the room appears to be Barbie's wet dream, while the other is much more modestly decorated with a black and purple comforter and a simple wooden dresser.

"I really hope you like pink," Amanda murmurs with a chuckle, no doubt eyeing my all-black attire.

I shrug. "Don't mind it."

It's definitely not my favorite color, but I'm not one of those girls who believes you're somehow "lesser" because you enjoy it. If magenta gets your rocks off, then more power to you. I'm personally more of a green chick myself.

"Lissa is going through a pink phase," Hale confesses somewhat sheepishly. He distractedly scratches at the nape of his neck. "She's a freshman in high school and is still trying to find herself and all that fun teenage stuff."

He shudders—something I can relate to.

I sometimes hate being a teenage girl.

"And she's okay with me sharing her room?" I ask, feeling inexplicably timid.

I move towards the bed on the left side of the room and set down my duffel bag. The farther inside the room I get, the stronger the scent becomes. It's like I'm standing inside a giant-sized bouquet made up of every flower imaginable. I wrinkle my nose instinctively and try to hide the cough bubbling up my mouth.

Please don't tell me I'm allergic to whatever...*this* is.

Pink?

Am I allergic to pink?

The absurd thought brings a reluctant smile to my lips.

"*Is she okay with this*?" Hale repeats my question in a mocking tone and then scoffs. "Honey, she's the one who purchased your bedspread and most of the furniture for you. She would be here now if she didn't have school."

"Oh."

I really don't know what else to say to that strange revelation.

Why would she take such an interest in me? I already know I'll disappoint her. That seems to be my MO. There's no way I can live up to her expectations—whatever they may be.

I'm too skittish, too rough, too cruel. Life hasn't been kind to me, and in turn, I haven't been kind to it.

"Okay, Hale." Amanda claps her hands together from behind me. "I have a few things I need to discuss with you in the kitchen, if that's okay."

"Of course." Hale places a hand on my shoulder, and I try not to wince or pull away.

The longer it stays there, however, the more comfortable I become. I don't know how to articulate it with words. Something about Hale drains the tension from my body and puts me at ease. He seems to radiate a kind, fatherly vibe unlike anything I've ever felt before.

"Let me just take care of this with Amanda, and then we can head out and do some shopping."

That same arrow of trepidation I felt earlier pierces my chest yet again.

I try to tell myself that normal people give things to others without wanting anything in return.

I try to tell myself that Hale has done nothing to make me so wary of him—the exact opposite, in fact.

I try to tell myself that everyone is innocent until proven guilty.

All of that doesn't stop the icy claws of terror from gripping my heart and squeezing.

I blame all of those turbulent emotions for what happens next.

Hale releases me just as an exuberant voice exclaims, "Holy shit! It's the new girl!"

Arms wrap around me from behind, and my fight-or-flight instincts kick in. It feels as if I'm breathing vinegar instead of air. Razor blades take up residence in my throat.

Before I can even think through my actions, the stranger has been flipped over my shoulder.

And my knife? Yeah, that fucker is pressed against the intruder's throat.

Three

IZZY

"Izzy!" Hale yells in alarm, just as Amanda exclaims, "Isabella!"

The man underneath me lets out an "oomph" of pain, though the noise quickly transitions into a bark of breathless laughter.

I don't move or even breathe as I hold the dagger against the man's skin, the blade applying just enough pressure to draw a tiny droplet of blood.

"I take it that somebody doesn't like hugs," an amused voice says, slightly raspy from being manhandled by me.

He doesn't seem at all perturbed or even frightened by the very real threat quite literally caressing his jugular.

"Izzy!" Hale's voice is urgent and pleading. "You're safe, honey. That's just Jake. He was just playing with you. You're safe."

The name penetrates my defenses.

Jake...

Jake. Jake. Jake.

One of Hale's foster children.

Slowly, I lower my gaze to the boy—man—I'm straddling.

Jake weakly offers me a wave, his face flushed and his eyes comically wide.

The first thing I note is that he's cute in the all-American, boy-next-door kind of way. Blond, tousled hair frames a face constructed out of sharp lines and dimpled cheeks. Brilliant hazel eyes stare back at me beneath that mop of amber curls, devoid of any fear or malice. They simply glimmer with amusement.

Oh...fuck.

Fuck. Fuck. Fuck.

This isn't the first time I...ahem...prematurely tackled someone and threatened to murder them. I doubt it'll be the last. I have a tendency to act before I can think through the consequences.

Quickly—and with my heart somewhere in the vicinity of my throat—I scramble off my new foster brother.

"Shit, shit, shit," I curse, forking my fingers through my tangled blonde hair, a few shades darker than Jake's. "I'm sorry. You scared me. I didn't... I mean... I don't..."

"It's okay, Izzy," Hale says in a soft, soothing voice.

He takes a step closer to me, his hand hovering just

above my shoulder. But he doesn't touch me like he did only moments before. For some reason, that hurts more keenly than any blade could've.

Did I scare him?

Is he going to kick me out already?

This will be a new record for me—not even an hour and I'm already changing homes.

"Jake." Hale's voice takes on a scolding, reprimanding tone. He levels a penetrating glare in the other boy's direction. "What did I say about personal space?"

Jake doesn't move from where he's sprawled on the ground, though I do see him roll his hazel eyes. "Respect it."

"Yes." Hale nods decisively before heaving out a breath and extending a hand for Jake to take. "You totally deserved that ass kicking."

"I think I broke my bumhole," Jake whines playfully as he allows Hale to haul him to his feet.

Now that I'm no longer...um...straddling him, I see that Jake's nearly an entire head taller than me. His lean, muscular body is encased in blue jeans and a brown and gold football jersey. I'm honestly not surprised that he's on the football team. It fits his golden god image. I wouldn't be surprised if he's one of the most popular guys in school.

And...I just tackled him to the ground.

And held a knife to his throat.

Hello, social suicide.

But Jake doesn't seem upset by what I just did. If anything, his eyes crinkle and his smile broadens when he stares at me. He sheepishly shoves his hands into his pockets and rocks back on his heels.

"Sorry for startling you, new girl." Jake flicks his gaze towards Hale before focusing once more on me. "Hale always says that I need to stop being so…" He flounders for an appropriate word.

"Touchy feely?" Hale supplies.

Jake rolls his eyes. "Yeah, yeah. What he said." He removes one of his hands from his pocket and extends it to me. "I'm Jacob, but you can call me Jake."

Tentatively, I venture a step closer. The knot in my chest gradually loosens the longer I study his genuine smile and twinkling eyes. Just like with Hale, something about Jake puts me at ease. The tension always coiling my muscles ebbs away the longer I hold his hazel gaze.

"I'm sorry for…you know…flipping you," I say, my cheeks flushing. "And putting a knife to your throat."

Hale begins to chuckle from behind me, and Jake winces.

"Yeah…maybe we never tell anyone about that. Ever. I have an image to maintain." He gives my hand a firm shake before releasing it. "But it is good to meet you."

I try for a smile, though it feels foreign on my face. My lips don't quite know how to move the way I want them to. "Yeah. Likewise."

Jake's smile widens at my feeble attempt at civility before it abruptly straightens out. His lips press together, and he turns his head to stare at something over my shoulder. "I have to warn you, though, that if you think I'm a... How did you put it, Hale? If you think I'm a touchy-feely person, then that's nothing on—"

"Oh. My. God. She's here! SHE'S HERE!" The loud, exuberant, shrill voice sounds from directly behind me.

Instinctively, I wince, sure that scientists haven't even discovered a pitch as high as this yet.

"Lissa," Jake finishes lamely.

Every muscle in my body locks together when something rams into me from behind. This time, however, I'm prepared for it, and I don't flip her over my shoulder.

Or put a knife to her throat.

Despite that, I can't quite get my joints to unfreeze. My heart slams against my rib cage like a bowling ball knocking down pins. The air seems to be made of tiny daggers.

"Lissa!" Hale reprimands, his voice stern.

The newcomer—Lissa, apparently—ignores her foster dad and squeezes me tighter. All I can see are thin arms wrapped tightly around my waist, each of the wrists covered in bracelets.

"Oh my gosh! I'm so excited you're here! When Hale told me that a new girl was coming to the house, I was over the moon! It's been just me for so long. And boys are stinky! Do you like your bedspread? I wasn't sure what color to get you. I was going to go with pink for obvious reasons, but Jake said I should choose something a little more modest, whatever the hell that means. Do you like it?

"I also chose your dresser, though Hale didn't allow me to pick out any clothes for you. We didn't know your sizes. But I can totally go shopping with you, if you want. I'm a super good shopper! I think you would look amazing in pink. It would really complement your hair. Is that your real hair color? I love it! I always wanted blonde hair, but Hale and Gerry told me that I have to wait until I'm older to dye it. Maybe I'll dye it pink! Ohhhh! Rainbow! No, purple! I can't decide."

As the verbal freight train that is Lissa continues her long, drawn-out monologue, Jake reaches forward to untangle me from the iron vises around my waist. He flashes me a sympathetic smile as I'm finally able to free myself from the tiny girl.

Spinning, I take in my roommate for the first time.

She's incredibly short—so short, that I half believe that she's under four foot. That, combined with her cherubic, dainty features, makes her look years younger than her actual age. Dark brown hair cascades down her back in perfect ringlets, held away from her face by a pink headband. She wears a pink skirt, a white- and pink-striped shirt, and pink knee-high socks.

Is this what Barbie's child would look like if she had an affair with GI Joe?

Lissa squeals again, as if she's pleased to have my attention, and rushes forward to give me another hug. Just like before, I go rigid in her embrace, reminding myself to breathe.

"This is going to be so much fun!" she squeaks. "It'll be like a sleepover every day. I've always wanted a sister."

"Lissa..." Hale warns, sounding exasperated.

I imagine this is a daily occurrence with the tiny girl.

"We're still going to the mall, right? To buy you clothes? Do you need anything else? A phone? A computer?"

I open my mouth to respond that I don't need any of that stuff, when Hale butts in.

"We'll stop at the technology store in the mall. Ethan still works there, correct?" He directs this question at Jake, who nods once.

"Yeah, I think so." To me, Jake explains, "Ethan's one of my buddies."

"Oh."

Really, what else is there to say to that?

"I'm going to be in the car!" Lissa screeches, and then she races out of the bedroom, her brown hair trailing behind her.

"Lissa! We're not leaving for another half hour!" Hale calls, but it's too late for Hurricane Lissa.

She has come, demolished everything in sight, and then retreated without a backwards glance.

"I'll keep an eye on her," Jake murmurs to Hale. When Hale nods in approval, Jake turns to me, smiles, and gives my shoulder a reassuring squeeze. "See you in a bit."

And then he's gone.

Amanda clears her throat uncomfortably from where she still stands in the doorway. She moves a hand down her pencil skirt before glancing at Hale.

"I still have a few things I need to discuss with you in private, Hale," she says.

Hale nods. "Yes, I'll meet you in the kitchen."

Amanda hesitates, her eyes flicking towards me, before she nods once and strides away in the direction Lissa and Jake went.

Leaving me alone...with Hale.

The older man blows out a weary breath and runs his fingers through his hair, salt-colored strands seasoning the dark locks. He studies me with keen, all-seeing eyes, though he doesn't say anything. I have the distinct feeling I'm a tiny butterfly pinned between two glass slides, just waiting for him to analyze beneath a microscope.

"You've had a tough life, kiddo," Hale begins softly. "I can't even imagine the things you've been through."

Indignation heats my cheeks.

I'm not stupid. I know that Hale and his husband would've had access to my case file, but I suppose a part of me hoped that he hadn't read it. Or if he had, he wouldn't bring it up. I don't want my life to be a carnival show for the town folks to laugh at and mock. I'm not saying Hale would make light of all I've been through, but...

Pinpricks of ice race up and down my arms. I'm suddenly freezing, though I'm not sure if that's from the roaring air conditioner unit above me or my own trepidation.

"But I can't have you carrying a weapon in my house," Hale continues, his eyes shining with both regret and resolve. He jerks his chin towards my jacket sleeve, where I have the blade hidden away in a tiny sheath I created. "I trust you, kiddo. I do. But what if you had cut Jake's throat in your panic? Or stabbed at Lissa when she grabbed you? I want you to feel safe, but I have to think about my other charges as well."

I want to argue with him, mount a protest, scream and yell at the unfairness of it all.

If I wanted Jake or Lissa to be dead, they'd be dead.

I know my skills with a knife.

However, I can see things from Hale's point of view, too. All he wants to do is protect his foster children. And who am I to argue with that? Hale has been nothing but kind to me since I arrived, and yes, that could change at the drop of a hat, but I don't believe it will. He seems to radiate sincerity and compassion the same way my last foster dad reeked of stale cigarettes and alcohol.

Biting down on the thousands of protests I want to make, I reach inside my sleeve and grab the tiny knife. It feels as if I'm giving up a part of myself—one of my limbs—but I know I have to give in.

Hale must see the struggle in my eyes, because his own significantly soften, a feat I didn't think was possible.

"You're safe here, Izzy. I promise. I know it'll take time for you to believe that." He grabs the blade from me. "You're safe."

I don't know if I necessarily believe him—how could I, when I just met him an hour ago?—but it feels as if a heavy weight lifts from my shoulders the second the blade leaves my hand.

But what Hale doesn't know is that I don't need a knife to be a lethal weapon.

I can be that all on my own.

Four

IZZY

The nearest mall is a thirty-five minute drive from Hale's house.

Lissa takes the opportunity to point out every building and shop we pass, with Jake interjecting whenever he deems it necessary.

"That's the *best* ice cream shop in town. They seriously have, like, a thousand different flavors. I'm personally partial to chocolate strawberry cheesecake." Lissa jabs a finger at the window yet again, leaving behind a smudge print. "And that's Rory's Diner. They serve delicious burgers. You can put tomatoes on them. And every type of cheese imaginable. And lettuce. And onions. Ohhh! Don't forget the best ketchup and mustard that ever existed. And that... That's the high school!"

We're driving so fast that all I see is a brick, cube-like building. It doesn't appear particularly impressive, though I know better than to judge something based on appearance alone.

The thought of attending a new school in just a few days' time has bile scorching the back of my throat like fingers of fire. A cold chill that has nothing to do with the air conditioning sends goose bumps skittering up and down both of my arms.

If only Hale's home had been fifteen miles to the east. Then, I could've remained at the school I just started to grow familiar with. Sure, I may not have the most friends, but the few I had were loyal to a fault. They sat by me at lunch when all of the other kids spurned the weird new girl. Hell, I was even beginning to believe Royce DeMore would ask me to homecoming.

But that's a different life—one I'll never get to live again.

Just a few more months until you're eighteen. Then, you can escape this state and everyone in it.

I listen but don't contribute to the conversation as Hale drives the remaining ten minutes to the closest mall—a mammoth structure holding more stores than I've ever seen in my life. The lot is so full that Hale's forced to park near the back exit, though that doesn't seem to perturb Lissa, who immediately jumps out of the car and begins skipping towards the glass doors.

Hale snaps at her to watch for traffic. When she doesn't seem to hear him, he huffs and races to catch up with her. Jake remains beside me, flashing me a tentative smile and knocking his shoulder against my own.

"Don't look so down, new girl. I thought most women loved shopping."

I instinctively wrap my arms around my waist as I keep pace with the striking football player.

"I guess it's just the prospect of..." I struggle to find the words, but fortunately, Jake grasps at the thread I left dangling from my fingertips and weaves it into something coherent.

"Owing someone?" he guesses correctly.

I shrug. "That hasn't worked out so well for me in the past."

Jake shoves his hands into his front jeans pockets as he squints against the blinding sun. I can't help but note he refuses to make eye contact with me, no matter how long I stare at him. It's almost as if he's deep in thought, a million miles away despite physically standing directly beside me.

"Hale and Gerry are good men." Jake's voice is resolute and sincere, holding no room for argument.

The conviction in that one statement nearly takes my breath away. I suppose it's because I never allowed myself to believe that *anyone* is inherently good, not when I know firsthand how many shades of gray paint this dreary world.

"They took me in when I was fifteen, and I've been living with them for about three and a half years now."

That...

That takes me by surprise.

I gape at him, my feet momentarily stalling, forcing Jake to stop walking as well or risk leaving me behind. "You're over eighteen?"

A wry smirk touches the edges of his lips. "That surprises you?"

Um...yes. Absolutely.

Most kids, as soon as they age out of the foster system, pave their own way in life, whether or not it's by their own volition. The majority of foster parents don't want an eighteen-year-old kid living in their house when they're not getting paid for them. Besides, there's a whole plethora of rules foster parents have to follow in regards to non-family member adults living in their house.

"Were you adopted?" I question, before immediately clamping my lips together. Of all the intrusive questions...

But Jake doesn't seem offended as he chuckles, tossing a strand of golden hair away from his face.

"Not officially. There were some...issues." His nose scrunches, but he doesn't elaborate.

I half wonder if it has to do with the fact Hale and Gerry are a same-sex couple. This fucked-up system would rather have kids suffer traveling from home to home than place them in the custody of a loving couple who just so happens to be the same sex.

Our conversation ceases when we finally reach Lissa and Hale, who are standing by the entrance, waiting for us to arrive. Lissa beams as soon as she sees me and reaches for my hand.

"Hale said we could go clothes shopping first!" she practically squeals, tugging me forward. "This is going to be so much fun! We can see all of my favorite stores and meet all of my favorite clerks and try on all of my favorite styles—"

"Yay," I deadpan as she drags me inside.

Hale and Jake both chuckle from behind me, the latter's voice reaching my ears a second later.

"At least this time it's not me she's trying to dress in pink skirts."

* * *

Two hours later—and fifteen stores later—I heave my tired body down on the nearest chair in the food court. My stomach rumbles as the enticing smells of greasy burgers, pizza, and pasta bombard me from every direction. I can't even remember when I last ate, but I know shopping with Lissa was the equivalent of running five miles in a marathon.

I. Am. Exhausted.

Whatever expression Hale sees on my face makes him chuckle, that traitor.

My new foster dad simply stood by while Hurricane Lissa cocooned me in her whirlwind of energy and then spit me back out in a pink, dazed heap.

Jake nudges my shoulder with his. "You still alive there, new girl?"

"Is it possible to die from too much pink? Is that a thing?" I lament dramatically, eliciting chuckles from both Hale and Jake and a pout from Lissa.

"You only bought, like, two pink articles of clothing," my new roommate protests, sounding slightly indignant. "You didn't even get the sparkly pink dress that looked *amazing* on you."

"It was transparent," I reply in a deadened voice, ignoring the way Jake attempts to smother his laughter with the back of his hand. "And, technically, lingerie."

"I'm so happy I wasn't there to see *that*," Hale mumbles, causing me to instinctively smile.

"And I'm bummed I wasn't there to see that," Jake counters.

I playfully hit at his shoulder as he smirks at me. While Jake has spent our time at the mall half-heartedly flirting with me, I know he doesn't mean anything by it. He's handsome, sure, but the attraction I should feel for him just...isn't there.

"Ha. Ha. Ha. You're a regular comedian, aren't you?"

Jake winks. "If I say yes, will you try back on that pink, translucent underwear set?"

This time, it's Hale who hits Jake across the back of the head.

"Ow!" Jake clutches his scalp dramatically. "Are you trying to get me concussed?"

"If it stops you from being a shameless flirt, then yes." Hale doesn't even blink at Jake's exaggerated pout.

"That's child abuse."

"You're eighteen."

"That's adult abuse."

Hale rolls his eyes and then moves to stand, turning his piercing gaze onto me. I immediately wince and begin to shake my head.

I know that look.

It's the same one Lissa speared me with as she dragged me from store to store despite my protests, filling my arms with more clothing than I've ever seen in my life.

"Shopping. Done. No. Shopping. No more," I whine, clunking my head against the table as if I can't keep it up a second longer.

"You're just like Jake." Hale chuckles.

"Oh my god. There's two of them now?" Lissa says in a mock whisper.

I squint my eyes at her in a glare, but she simply flashes me an unrepentant grin. With a huff of irritation, I roll my eyes and allow Hale to haul me to my feet.

"Jake, Lissa, grab the bags for me, please," he instructs.

Jake and Lissa don't even complain as they sling the numerous shopping bags over their arms, though I can't help but feel a twinge of guilt.

Both because they're carrying my new clothes…

And because Hale bought me all of this stuff to begin with.

Whenever I tried to protest I didn't need anything, he simply shook his head and jabbed a finger at my face.

"You're getting it," he would say firmly.

Anytime I even stared at something longer than a second, he would add it to the cart—aka Jake's arms.

"Where are we going now? Haven't you tortured me enough?" I'm only half teasing.

Yes, I'm incredibly grateful for everything Hale has bought me with seemingly no strings attached—though I still can't help but be wary over his intentions—but my legs hurt, my toes ache from being shoved into too-small shoes, and I swear I have a perpetual wedgie from the trip to Victoria's Secret.

"You'll need a phone and a new laptop before classes on Monday," Hale says, his tone as nonchalant as if he's discussing the weather instead of a few hundred dollars' worth of merchandise I've never had before in my life.

I gape at him, momentarily speechless. The breath quite literally is siphoned from my body.

I know he said it before but…

"No." I shake my head adamantly. "I don't need that stuff. It's too much."

"You're turning eighteen in a few months." Hale wraps an arm around my shoulders and begins to steer me towards a store I hadn't noticed before.

I don't recognize the name, but from the number of gadgets displayed in the window, I reason it's an electronic store.

"You have the freedom to do what you want to do. However, Gerry and I simply ask that you check in from time to time, which you'll need a phone to do. We worry. There'll be rules, of course, and a set curfew, but we can discuss that later. And a laptop is mandatory for all seniors. I would allow you to use Jake's old one, but he shattered it—"

"*Accidentally*," Jake pipes in.

Hale nods. "Right. He *accidentally* tried to throw it at a bat that had somehow made its way into the house. And he *accidentally* missed the bat and sent it sailing out the window."

Jake leans forward to stage-whisper to me, "The bat was trying to eat my face."

"The *bat*," Lissa interjects, "was actually a butterfly. But Jake just likes to change the story to keep his street cred."

"I named him Perriwrinkle," Hale adds.

A chuckle slips free unbidden, and an unfamiliar warmth unfurls in my stomach. God, what would it be like to be a part of this family? Truly a part of it? To have inside jokes and a camaraderie that only come from innately knowing the people you're with?

A desperate, gaping *need* cracks my chest open.

A need to be a part of this group.

A need to be loved and wanted.

A need to not be shoved aside like trash the second someone gets tired of me.

"Ethan's working, correct?" Hale says, tugging me out of my internal reverie.

"Yeah." Jake dips his chin towards the window, where I see a man crouched behind the counter, sifting through a box of cords.

"He's your friend from school, right?" I ask.

"Sort of. I mean, I'm friends with the guy, but we're not super close. His brother's on the football team with me, though, and he's pretty cool. But Ethan's one of the smartest guys around. I fucking love it when I get paired up with him for a class assignment. Him and Ansel have been battling it out for valedictorian all four years now."

"Language," Hale chastises half-heartedly.

"Sorry, boss." Jake gives him a mock salute. "Him and *fuck face* have been battling it out for valedictorian all four years now."

I choke on my laughter as Hale clicks his tongue and sighs.

"I take it you don't like this Ansel person?" I ask.

"He's a douchebag." Jake shrugs. "He could be one of the most popular guys in school if he actually made an effort with anyone. But he'd rather spend his days alone in the library or in the corner of the cafeteria by himself."

"Maybe he's just shy," I suggest.

"Trust me." Lissa places her chin on my shoulder

from behind, causing me to startle. "That's definitely not why he has no friends. I like everyone...except for him."

"He's a real asshole," Jake adds.

This time, Hale doesn't even comment on Jake's language. A tentative smile plays on the older man's lips. I wonder if he agrees with Jake's assessment of this Ansel person. Does Hale know him?

"Who's the asshole?" an unfamiliar voice calls from just below the counter.

Almost immediately, heat gushes through my veins, infusing me with more warmth than I've ever felt before. It's a strange, disembodied sensation that seems to imprint itself on my very soul. Shock rattles through me.

What the fuck *was* that?

As quickly as the heat arrived, it dissipates, leaving me feeling oddly bereft.

The man behind the counter stands up from his crouched position so suddenly I actually stagger back a step in fright.

Sweet Mother Mary...

To say this man is sexy is an understatement if I've ever heard one. His skin is deeply tanned, as if he spends a lot of time out in the sun, and contrasts beautifully with his dark golden locks that are cut just below his ears. Even dressed in a hideous red shirt and khakis, he exudes confidence and sexuality.

With his sleeves rolled up the way they are, I can see

the beginnings of tattoos creeping underneath the fabric and disappearing from view. A strange birthmark rests on the inside of his wrist, almost resembling a flame. The sexy stranger wears a pair of dark-framed glasses, expertly weaving sexy nerd and bad-boy surfer together into one enticing package.

"Ethan! Hey, man!" Jake calls, but this man... Ethan... He doesn't take his eyes off of me.

And as I watch, my heart hammering against my rib cage like a sledgehammer, Ethan takes a step forward...

And promptly knocks over a display case of new phones before landing face-first in the pile of crushed electronics.

Five

ETHAN

What in the ever-loving snickerdoodle fuck is happening?

That one thought plays on a continuous loop in my head as I remain face down in a pile of Apple products. For a long, *long* moment, I don't move, half believing that this is nothing but a horrible nightmare, and I'll wake up at any second to laugh at the ridiculousness of it all.

But...nope.

The woman's sweet scent cocoons me in a rippling blanket of fire, engulfing me in heat.

Mine, my wolf snarls in the back of my head. The possessiveness in that one word makes me wince.

How can this be happening?

This girl is...human. There's no doubt about that.

Yet every fiber of my being wants to howl to the moon and declare her as my own. It's an intricate need inside of me—this primitive facet of my personality that I didn't even know existed until just now.

Mine. Mine. Mine.

Mine.

"Shit, man. Do you need help?" Jake extends a hand, and it only takes me a second to accept his proffered limb.

I allow the other male to haul me to my feet as I attempt to regain at least some of my lost dignity. I brush my hand down the store-issued, hideous red shirt, ironing out imaginary wrinkles. Anything is better than meeting the gaze penetrating the side of my head.

The gaze...of my fated mate.

No. That can't be true, can it? She's human, and I'm...not.

Even as I think that, another wave of heat washes over me. It feels as if a thousand pinpricks of blazing swords are being jabbed into my skin simultaneously.

"I suppose it's too much to hope that both brothers got the athleticism in the family," Jake teases, drawing my attention back to the grinning football player.

I try to laugh, but it comes out forced and jittery. "Yeah. Sports are definitely more Emery's thing."

Though it's not like I would know.

Emery didn't even tell me that he decided to join the football team. I had to hear it from Ashton the night before the first game.

Grief arrows through my chest. It's not the first time I felt this emotion in regards to my very much alive brother, and I'm sure it won't be the last. I can't help but remember late nights laughing with him, exploring the woods with Ashton and Reid, swapping places to confuse our parents. But that was a different life, one I doubt we'll ever return to.

We may be pack, but we're no longer brothers. My twin is just as much a stranger to me as the woman standing in front of me.

The woman...

My mate.

Our mate.

Slowly, cautiously, I allow my gaze to drift to her, studying her truly for the first time since she stepped inside the store. I've seen a lot of beautiful women over the years, but none compare to this goddess standing before me. And I'm not just saying that because she may or may not be my fated mate. Everything about her calls to not only the wolf inside of me but the man as well.

Golden hair, highlighted with darker amber strands, cascades around her shoulders in loose waves. Her brown eyebrows arch over chocolatey eyes that ensnare me as effectively as any trap hidden beneath the foliage in the forest would if I were in my wolf form. She wears a simple pair of jeans and a green sweater that accentuates the generous swells of her breasts.

She's perfection personified, and I've never wanted

a woman as badly as I want her. My skin quite literally prickles as if tiny fingers are poking and prodding at me.

Am I gawking? Fuck, I'm gawking, aren't I?

Stop being a creep, Ethan! Say something!

"We sell phones," I blurt like a total fucking dumb-ass, gesturing towards the pile of toppled devices at my feet.

Jake snorts from somewhere behind me, and his foster sister, Lissa, gives me a strange look. Hale is also staring at me curiously, but I try my best to ignore his inquiring gaze. If anyone is capable of seeing right through me, it's him.

The beautiful girl shoves her hands into her pockets and rolls back on her heels. One of her dark brows arches.

"I can see that." Her smoky voice skates over my skin like a physical caress.

"We're actually here to get Izzy a phone." Jake moves to walk around me and then slings an arm around the beautiful woman's shoulders.

And I. See. Red.

Jealousy thrums through my veins—white-hot and potent—and my claws lengthen and my fangs begin to elongate.

Why is this man touching my mate?

Putting his arm around her?

And why the fuck is she smiling up at him?

Ice tumbles through my veins and immobilizes me,

momentarily dampening the fire from before. I'm going to kill him. I'm going to rip him apart and cut out his heart and—

What the cotton candy fuck, Ethan?

I quickly turn away before any of them can see the change taking over me, distorting my features.

"Ethan?" Hale's voice is both cautious and suspicious.

I detect a hint of a warning as well, one that reminds me what will happen if anyone ever discovers the truth about what we are.

But what can I tell him?

That I believe this human female he's with is my fated mate? That my wolf is going positively berserk seeing another male drape himself over her, even knowing it's someone as harmless as Jake? That I want to rip her jeans down and drop to my knees before her and lick her—

"We phones have. I mean, phones have. We. Have them. Yes." I grab at the nearest object I can find—which is most definitely *not* a phone—and toss it back at them. I don't even need to look to know the headphones have landed with a soft thump at the girl's feet.

Fuck. Get ahold of yourself, Ethan!

"What's his problem?" I hear my mate whisper to that soon-to-be-dead football player. Wait. No! No murder. "Is he always like this?"

Jake chuckles. "I promise he's cool. I swear. He's probably just stressed from work."

Well, damn. Now I don't want to kill Jake too terribly. He just stood up for me when he totally could've thrown me under the bus to win the attention and affection of this gorgeous bombshell.

Maybe instead of murder, I can do a little light maiming...

What the fuck?

I'm beginning to sound like Ashton. And Reid. And even Emery. I'm supposed to be the level-headed one of the pack.

How did this become my day? One second, I'm teaching old lady Beatrice how to turn on and off her computer. Next, I'm face-to-face—or back-to-face, as the case may be—with my mate.

She probably thinks I'm such a freak.

Hale clears his throat, but I don't immediately turn to face them, pretending instead to peruse the shelves for random phone cases. I'm not quite sure I have myself under control. I haven't felt this out of sorts since I was a wee pup.

"We need to pick up Izzy a new phone and a laptop for school. Do you have any suggestions?" Hale asks.

Izzy.

What a beautiful name.

Iz-zy.

Izzzzz-y.

Izz-yyyy.

"Um...yes...of course. Right on it. Pew. Pew." I fire

my finger gun off at him over my shoulder and then inwardly curse.

What the fuck is my problem? I may not be the star of the football team, but I'm popular in my own right. I'm the class president, the founder of the robotics club, a member of National Honors Society, and one of the most sought-after bachelors at Saint Views High.

Not that you'd be able to tell from my less-than-spectacular first impression.

I finally deem myself ready to turn around. Now that I know I won't go on a...ahem...killing spree, it seems prudent that I see my mate a second time. That I memorize the sharp curves of her cheeks and the cleft in her chin. That I daydream about those perfect, cupid-bow lips that commandeer my attention.

Just now, those lips are quirked in a half smile, one that makes her dark eyes glitter.

That smile...is directed at me.

Me.

Fuck.

Focus, Ethan! Do your damn job!

"Right. Let me show you some of the newest models..." I lose myself in all of the tech talk, momentarily forgetting that the woman standing before me is my mate.

Okay. That's a lie. It's impossible to forget completely. Her sweet scent funnels through me like a tornado, but instead of leaving behind nothing but destruction and chaos, I feel an innate sense of serenity.

We settle on the newest iPhone—much to Izzy's displeasure—and a rose-gold MacBook. At first, I think it's because she's not a fan of the Apple brand, but then I realize it's because of the cost. I hear her whispered conversation with Hale, even from where I stand on the opposite side of the store, installing a few programs for her.

"It's too much," she says.

If I were a normal human, I wouldn't be able to hear their hushed voices. But I'm not normal, and I'm certainly not human.

Should I feel guilty for eavesdropping? Probably.

Do I stop? Unfortunately, I don't.

What is this girl doing to me?

"Nonsense." Hale places a hand on her shoulder and gives it a squeeze.

Unlike when Jake touched her, I don't feel the need to race across the room and rip him limb from limb. Maybe it's because Hale is already mated and old enough to be her father. Jake, on the other hand...

A growl slips free unbidden, and I immediately clamp my lips together to stop the sound.

Fuck.

"I don't have any money to pay you back." Izzy sounds tired.

Out of my periphery, I watch her run her fingers through her blonde locks.

What I wouldn't give to wrap those lambent gold strands around my fist and—

What? No! Focus!

"You don't need to, kid." He gives her shoulder another squeeze before releasing her. "We're a family. And this is what families do."

My heart thuds strangely at his words.

Family.

I used to have a family.

And now...

I shake my head to clear it.

Izzy and Hale meet me at the counter, the former shuffling from foot to foot and the latter smiling warmly. I've always liked Hale. He may be in a different pack than my own, but he never allowed such petty rivalries to impact his behavior towards me and the others. It's for that reason alone that everyone adores him and his husband.

Without asking for the total, Hale hands over his credit card, ignoring Izzy's tight-lipped frown.

Another strange pang reverberates through me.

I should be the one providing for my mate.

Me.

Not Hale. Not Jake. Not anyone else.

How barbaric can I possibly be? This is the twenty-first century, for fuck's sake. I don't need to *provide* for Izzy. She's a strong, independent woman who can take care of herself. And yet...

Fuck my wolf.

Seriously, fuck him and his primitive tendencies.

"There's...um...actually a sale going on today," I lie,

keeping my head lowered so no one can see my expression.

Emery once told me I was an open book. It's nearly impossible for me to lie without the truth splaying across my face.

"A sale," Hale repeats dryly, not buying my bullshit for even a second.

He doesn't call me out on it, however. He couldn't possibly know the truth. More than likely, he thinks that I'm hypnotized by a pretty face—which I am.

He can't ever know the full story, though.

"Yes. A sale." I rack my brain for something reasonable. "Half off."

"Half off?" Izzy flashes me a confused look, and my heart beats like a war drum in my chest.

My hands are suddenly clammy, then sweaty, and then clammy yet again.

"Yup." I hurriedly swipe Hale's credit card and then plug in the machine half the total. "Just for these two...um...products."

Can I be any more stupid?

Hale continues to eye me strangely, but he doesn't mount a protest as he signs the receipt.

As soon as they leave the store, I'll have to grab my own credit card to finalize the payment. I could use the pack credit card that Ashton set up, but that would lead to questions.

And I'm not quite sure I'm ready to reveal the truth to my packmates yet.

God, I feel like a selfish asshole for admitting that out loud, but a part of me fears how they'll react, especially once they discover she's human.

And then there's Desiree to consider...

No, it'll be best if I keep this to myself, if only for a few more days. I can look more into Izzy and discover where she came from, why she's here, and how she fits into this fucked-up puzzle. She's obviously a missing piece, but what that means for all of us eludes me.

"Thank you, Hale." Izzy flashes the older man a timid smile, and envy shoots through me like lightning.

I want her to be smiling at me like that—all flushed cheeks, batting lashes, and plump, pink lips.

Focus, Ethan. You can't lose control.

I grip the countertop so tightly that my knuckles bleach white.

"I'm assuming this means I'll see you at school on Monday?" I query, grateful when I don't growl the words out like an animal.

Izzy smiles at me shyly and tucks a strand of golden hair behind her ear. "Yeah. I'll be there."

"Maybe I can sit by you at lunch?"

The smile slips from her face, and she begins to blink owlishly at me. Her perfect pink lips open, shut, and then open again. She seems at a loss for words.

"I...um... You? With me? Um." She continues to blink, not finishing her stuttered statement.

What the fuck?

Is that a no?

Jake chuckles and once again wraps an arm around her shoulder, steering her towards the door.

"Come on, new girl. Before you begin drooling all over the store's floor." He chuckles wanly, stealthily sidestepping the elbow she throws at his stomach.

Drooling?

What the toaster-loving fuck just happened?

And what am I going to do now?

Six

IZZY

Jake continues to tease me the entire drive home, much to my chagrin and Lissa's amusement. I'm not the type of girl to blush easily, but even I can admit that my cheeks lit to an inferno when I set eyes upon the striking man in the technology store.

To say Ethan's cute is a fucking understatement. The man is sex on a stick, all rippling, chiseled muscles, tousled blond hair a few shades lighter than my own, and dreamy green eyes that reel me in. I've never had such an attractive guy talk to me before, let alone ask to sit by me at lunch. Most of the students at my old schools gave me a wide berth, unwilling to associate with the freaky new girl who bounced around from home to home.

Gossip and rumors persisted, following me everywhere I went. Most thought I was a troubled kid who beat the shit out of her foster parents or stole from them. Others assumed I was a slut who tried to seduce every man within sight. Those reasons *must* be why I bounce around so often.

Cue the sarcastic roll of my eyes.

Anyway, all of those rumors stemmed back to one thing and one thing alone—I was a social pariah. Even when guys found me attractive, they kept their distance, only flirting with me when they thought no one was in view. The one guy I dated seriously kept me as his dirty, little secret.

Look how well that relationship ended.

So to have Ethan suggest I sit with him at lunch? It's a new and slightly unnerving experience for me. I can't help but wonder if he'll change his mind the second the rumor mill begins working its malicious magic.

"Do you need a napkin to wipe all of that drool from your chin?" Jake asks now, jabbing a finger at my face. A teasing glint lights up his eyes.

"She'll probably need a bucket to catch all of it," Lissa chimes in.

"Okay, okay. I see what this is. Tease the new girl." I roll my eyes exaggeratedly, but I'm not too upset by their lighthearted jabs.

If anything, it makes me feel like I...belong. There's a sense of kinship in the air that has been noticeably absent from all of my other foster homes over the years.

"Jake, Lissa, knock it off," Hale chastises from the front of the car.

In the rearview mirror, I watch his lips twitch in the beginnings of a smile.

I know he's up to mischief a mere second before he says, "When we get home, we'll need to set a tarp down to catch all the drool."

"Hale!" I gasp in mock outrage as Lissa and Jake fall apart in laughter.

"You couldn't be any more obvious if you tried," Jake teases. "You practically had heart eyes."

"I did not!"

"Did too," Lissa interjects, bouncing up and down eagerly. "You totally find Ethan attractive! Eeep! Just wait until you see his brother and friends—"

"All right, all right." Hale turns the car into his long driveway. "That's enough teasing for one day. Lissa, Jake, help Izzy take in all of her bags. Izzy? If you don't mind, can I talk to you for a second?"

A wave of trepidation rushes over me at his words.

Hale wants to talk to me...alone?

An icy chill, like the breath of winter itself, skates down my spine.

Jake and Lissa don't seem surprised by Hale's declaration as they jump out of the car, pushing and shoving each other as they race to carry the most bags inside. Jake, of course, wins, but Lissa definitely gives him a run for his money.

Once the two of them disappear inside of the

house, Hale releases a heavy breath. Then, without a word, he exits the car and moves to lean against it. I take my own cue and clamor out of the back seat, making sure to leave ample distance between the two of us.

A part of me wants to trust him—especially since he's been nothing but kind since I arrived—but years of ingrained fear activate my fight-or-flight response. I'm just not sure which one will win this time around.

Hale folds his arms over his chest and keeps his gaze on the horizon, where the setting sun is dipping low behind his house, painting the world in shades of palest pink and red.

"I wanted to check in and see how you're doing," Hale begins, not pulling his attention off the horizon.

I appreciate that immensely. I'm not sure how comfortable I'd be if he were looking directly at me.

"I'm doing great," I say quickly.

One of Hale's brows quirks. "Be honest with me now."

A chuckle escapes me. "Am I being that obvious?"

"You're not the first foster kid to pass through these doors, and I guarantee you won't be the last. Talk to me, kid."

I debate what to say, nibbling on my lower lip as words evade me, before I settle on, "It's a lot to take in, if I'm being completely honest."

"It doesn't bother you, does it? The fact that I'm married to a man—"

"No," I rush to reassure him. "It's not that at all. It's just..." I once again struggle to find the right wording to articulate the thoughts percolating in my head. "I don't have the best track record with foster homes. I'm not saying they were all horrible or I was abused in all of them or anything like that, but—"

"You don't need to explain yourself to me if you don't want to." Hale finally turns to face me, his eyes earnest, his features grave. "I just want you to be comfortable here." He chuckles and brushes a hand through his dark hair, streaked liberally with gray. "Jake was a lot like you when he first arrived. He refused to accept anything we purchased for him. He was definitely a grumpy little shit."

"Really?" That surprises me. From what little I know of the football player, he seems jovial and down-to-earth.

And he definitely worships the ground Hale walks on.

"This world is a fucked-up place, kid, and my only goal is to make it a little less fucked up for the few kids I'm fortunate enough to take in."

I swallow around the lump in my throat. "That's... noble of you."

"I'm not sure that's the right word." Hale once again turns to stare off into the distance, squinting against the sun, which is still bright enough to be blinding. "A lot of us here have shitty pasts. I think that's how we became a family in the first place. We understand each other in a way no one else does."

Once again, Hale seems to be considering his words, his expression contemplative as he tilts his head to the side. "I just want you to feel comfortable, kid. If that means you want to pay me back for everything we purchased today, then do it. I don't expect you to, but I know what it's like to feel as if you owe someone something.

"I want to be someone you can look up to, a father figure, so to speak, but if you just want a friend, I can be that too. You don't have to decide anything right now, but I just want you to know I have your back. Jake, Lissa, and my husband do too. We're a family, and we would love for you to join it, if you want to."

I don't know what to say to that. It's as if a bomb went off in my head, and shrapnel is flowing everywhere, cutting me up and making me bleed.

For years, all I wanted was for someone to say exactly that—to refer to me as a member of their family. When I realized that would never happen, or that there would be conditions involved that I couldn't achieve, I created a new goal.

Survive.

All I wanted to do was survive.

Now, if Hale's being sincere, he's offering me more than just the chance to survive. He's suggesting I may be able to *live* as well.

"I...um... Thank you, Hale." That's all I can think

of to say. The anvil in my chest is making it hard to breathe.

Hale offers me a small smile, one that reaches his eyes and emphasizes the crinkles surrounding each of them.

"Why don't you go inside and start unpacking before Lissa does it for you? Because trust me, if you allow that spitfire to organize your room, you'll never wear anything but dresses and skirts for as long as you live." His eyes shadowed with horror, he adds, "I still pull out dresses from my closet to this day."

Hale's words reverberate in my head all throughout the rest of the day and far into the night, when the moon glistens in the dark sky like a pearl in a velvet box.

Family.

Trust.

Comfortable.

Safe.

A migraine threatens to rip my head to pieces.

Fuck, is he right? Could I potentially find a home here, with him and the others? Do I even want to?

Those questions battle for dominance inside of me as I turn to stare at my reflection.

Black sports bra covered by a currently unzipped hoodie.

Black, skin-tight leggings.

Sneakers tied tight.

A sliver of guilt embeds itself beneath my skin at what I'm about to do tonight, but common sense eclipses it.

I don't know Hale, and despite how sincere he sounded, I can't trust him. Not yet. Trust is earned, not presumed, and it'll take more than a day to acquire mine.

The house is eerily silent—almost unusually so. I'm used to hearing the crackle of the television and the guffaw of old men and women from my previous homes. Trepidation curdles in my gut like a tendril of electricity.

Is everyone asleep already?

I risk a glance at the clock to see that it's just after two in the morning.

If anyone were to be looking out their windows...

But no. I need to do this. I'm not sure I'll be able to settle until I do.

Moving on silent feet, I pad to the window and push it open, wincing when it squeaks. I hold my breath, half expecting Hale to charge down the hallway and kick open my bedroom door to demand answers, but the house remains quiet. Serene.

Outside, crickets chirp, and a tree branch snaps as a critter scurries by. The familiar sounds of traffic are noticeably absent.

Still, I find I can't release the breath trapped in my lungs as I sling my leg over the sill.

At my previous foster house, I lived on the third floor, which made it a bitch to enter and exit. I got quite used to scaling the walls. It's almost strange for this—sneaking out of the house—to be so damn easy.

My feet touch down.

I brace myself for a light to turn on in a different room, for Hale to ask where I'm going, for Jake to quirk his eyebrow or glare at me suspiciously, for Lissa to scream my name.

But there's only silence.

I keep my head lowered as I skirt around the edge of the forest, traveling towards where I know the street to be.

A strange chill skates down the back of my neck, a familiar sensation like when you're in a crowded room and swear you feel a pair of eyes on you.

I freeze in mid step, glancing from side to side, but there's not another person in sight.

Probably just an animal, I think, feeling ridiculous.

Still, I find that my pace quickens as I head towards the road.

Fifteen minutes later, I'm standing on the side of the street, the darkness both cloying and suffocating. A truck idles a few feet ahead of me, its windows tinted.

I've just taken another step forward when a giant of a man ventures out of the forest.

I don't even get the chance to scream before his hand is over my mouth, stifling the sound.

Seven

IZZY

Almost as soon as the hand touches my mouth, capturing my impending screech, it releases me.

Bright-blue eyes, framed by the thickest lashes I've ever seen, peer back at me from inside the hood of his sweatshirt. A devious smile spreads across his face.

"Jesus Christ, Grayson!" I glare. "Don't sneak up on me like that!"

Grayson—my closest friend for the better part of ten years—simply chuckles, the low, husky sound reverberating through me.

He tugs down his hood, revealing a mane of pitch-black hair that has grown longer over the months. A few strands sweep forward and hide his eyebrow piercings from view. His large, muscular body is encased in a pair of dark jeans and a similarly colored hoodie.

He taps my nose mockingly, and I swat his hand away with a scowl.

"You're an ass." I push past him to move towards the truck left idling.

Another one of Grayson's low laughs reaches me as I swing myself into the passenger seat. A second later, he joins me, his cinnamon scent surrounding me. It takes every ounce of will I possess not to breathe him in deeply, to lose myself in a smell I've grown to associate with comfort and security.

Muttering under my breath, I lean forward to mess with the buttons on his truck. Cold air wafts from the vents, and soft classical music begins to fill the cabin. Once I'm satisfied, I lean back in the seat with a heavy sigh.

Grayson stares at me out of the corner of his eye as he guides the car down the twining streets. His pierced brow cocks upwards, a question glimmering in his blue gaze.

"Long day," I grouse, shifting my head so I can maintain eye contact. "I, apparently, have an over-enthusiastic foster sister."

He chuckles in amusement and then returns to silence, waiting for me to finish speaking.

"But my new foster family seems...okay, if I'm being honest. But god, I can't wait until I'm eighteen and can just move on with my life." I absently fiddle with the ends of my blonde hair, gauging Gray's reaction out of the corner of my eye.

The two of us met in one of my first foster homes. He's one year older than me, and he exuded a confidence and lethal savagery I yearned to emulate, even at that age. He must've seen something in my eyes—a peek into the broken soul of a girl who has been knocked down one too many times—because he immediately took me under his wing.

Even when he got kicked out of that foster home and put into a new one, he maintained contact with me. First, it was sneaking to my various foster homes in the dead of night. Then, it was buying me a cheap flip phone so he could check up on me. Now, it's something...darker than either of those.

I actually believe that Grayson may be stalking me.

And I don't feel an ounce of fear over the fact.

"Ohhh! That reminds me!" I reach into my sports bra and grab out my brand-new phone.

His eyes flick to me momentarily, lowering to my chest, before immediately snapping back to my face.

"I got a phone! A real phone! A big-girl phone!" I teasingly swing the iPhone in front of his face.

He shakes his head with a wry smile twisting up the corners of his lips. He then jerks his chin towards his own phone sitting in the cup holder, indicating for me to place my new number into his.

I grab it with a happy hum and plug in his passcode. I search for my contact name—and instantly groan when I see what name he saved me under.

"Gracie? Really?" I wrinkle my nose at him. "My middle name?"

Grayson chuckles yet again. He knows more than anyone how much I hate my middle name.

Isabella Gracie.

Ugh.

I plug in my new phone number and am just about to hand it back to him when it buzzes with an incoming notification. Instinctively, I click on it, and the smile slips from my face at the barrage of text messages.

> SYDNEY
>
> Why aren't you calling me back, baby?
>
> SYDNEY
>
> I'm waiting for you.
>
> SYDNEY
>
> Grayson, why aren't you answering?

Those text messages are followed by a plethora of photos. The first few show a brunette woman in a pair of lacy underwear. And the last few show the same girl in nothing at all.

I drop the phone with an almost blistering speed, cringing when it falls to the floor and then slides beneath my seat.

Grayson throws me a disbelieving look, his brows furrowing.

"The vibrations startled me," I lie, forcing an easy-going smile back on my face, though it wilts at the edges like a rose sprayed in pesticide. "Also, your girlfriend texted." I try to keep my voice calm and nonchalant, not allowing him to hear any of the hidden emotions percolating inside of me.

Grayson's frown deepens.

"You know...Sydney." I shift uncomfortably in the passenger seat. "She was sending you a lot of texts and pictures." I try for a laugh and pray it doesn't sound as forced to his ears as it does my own.

In all the years I've known Grayson, he never once indicated he was interested in me like *that*. Even when I tried to kiss him, back when I was a confused fifteen-year-old and he was sixteen, he simply grabbed my shoulders and pushed me away with a frown on his face. I was so embarrassed that I refused to talk to him for over a week, afraid I ruined our friendship, but he found me at my foster home, held me against his chest, and silently assured me that everything will be all right. That *we'll* be all right.

But then everything became confusing yet again when I lost my virginity a few months later. I'd been dating the guy off and on for a few weeks and, naïvely, thought he was the one. However, after we did the deed, he left me abandoned in the middle of the woods with a sneer on his lips, telling me how "easy" I was. How I was a desperate foster girl who would suck any dick for money. Tears streamed down my face, and that was how Gray found me—a few of my shirt buttons missing, blood and cum still staining my legs, and my eyes swollen.

My ex's broken body was found in the park the very next day. He suffered three broken ribs, two broken fingers, and a bruised and bloody cock. He told the police that he was mugged but couldn't identify the attacker.

I knew in the darkest recesses of my soul that Grayson was involved.

Ever since then, Gray has watched me like a hawk, following me from town to town, keeping in the shadows, this silent, immovable mountain of muscle. Whenever I even flirt with a boy, he's there, his eyes glacial, his jaw clenched.

I assumed...

Well, I stupidly assumed he returned my crush.

Apparently, I was wrong.

He probably only sees me as a little sister.

The thought twists my stomach into a dozen tight, intricate knots.

Grayson runs a hand over his clenched jaw as he turns down a rather familiar side road. The huge, red barn in the distance is surrounded by cars. Music, shouts, and laughter can be heard even through the doors of the truck.

Gray pulls into an empty parking space but doesn't make a move to get out of the vehicle. He simply sits there, his fingers moving across the stubble on his chin, his eyes unfocused, his lips pursed.

I knock my shoulder against his with a teasing smile. "Come on, big guy. Let's go. Is your new girlfriend going to be here? I'd love to meet her." I try for a chuckle, but it comes out strained. "Maybe I'll even find a dick of my own to ride tonight."

If anything, Gray's scowl deepens even further before he forces his expression to smooth over. Well, *I* thought I was funny.

He tugs the keys out of the ignition, reaches behind him for his duffel bag, and then jumps out of the truck.

I recognize the glint in his eyes tonight—insidious in nature, with an unspoken threat lingering in the air.

Someone's going to die tonight.

And I can't help but think that my offhanded joke about finding a dick of my own had a part to play in that.

Eight

UNKNOWN

I relax against the silver Aston Martin, take a long drag of my cigarette, and exhale, allowing plumes of smoke to permeate the air.

The moon is high in the sky, bathing the rustic red barn in silver ribbons. A copious amount of light emanates from the various windows lining the perimeter of the building, though they're too far up for me to see inside from my current position. Either way, music blares, drowning out all other sounds.

Finished with my cigarette, I drop it to the ground and stomp on it with my boot.

What the fuck is taking him so long?

"Hey, sexy," a low voice purrs, a mere second before manicured fingers grasp my forearm.

I stiffen at the unwanted contact before forcing my features to relax, to adopt a sultry expression.

"What's a young lass like you doing out here all on your own?" I ask, giving her a slow once-over.

She appears to be about twenty, maybe twenty-one, and has chestnut-colored hair that cascades around her shoulders. Her nose is just a little too long and thin to be considered traditionally attractive, but she has the largest rack I've ever fucking seen. They strain against her thin tank top, her nipples poking through the material.

My cock immediately twitches in my pants. I can't remember the last time I got laid by anyone who wasn't my bitch of a wife. She's been becoming more aggravated by the "whores" I've been bringing home. Her words.

At first, she was fine with our little arrangement, as long as I maintained discretion. But when I caught that bitch on her back with some low-ranking fuck rutting into her pussy, all rational thought fled.

Fuck her. And fuck discretion.

If I want to bring a younger babe home, then so be it, so long as my children never catch me in the act.

The woman places her ample breasts against my arm and begins to giggle coyishly. I smirk at her indulgently as I fiddle with the strap of her shirt, pulling it down her arm so her breast can spring free.

Not the best pair of tits I've ever seen but definitely not bad. Her pink nipple is already as hard as a diamond.

I consider fucking her right here and now, taking

her against the hood of my car, when something golden catches my attention in the distance.

Isabella Gracie Martin moves confidently towards the entrance of the barn, her hips swaying in a way that draws my attention to her firm ass. My cock becomes even harder, practically bulging against my zipper, and I have to hold in the desperate groan that threatens to escape.

I've always had a thing for blondes.

Soon, she disappears inside of the barn, not even sparing a look to the shadow in the distance, watching her intensely. I lick my lower lip as hunger flares in my chest.

"Wow. Someone's excited," the woman coos, dragging her fingernails down my chest and stopping at the bulge in my pants.

She bats her eyelashes incessantly at me, no doubt thinking the cause of my arousal is her. Still, a mouth around my cock is better than my own hand.

I grab her nipple and give it a hard pinch, eliciting a gasp of surprise from the woman. Pain splays across her face, and my arousal amplifies tenfold. Before she can change her mind and try to run, I grab her hair and force her to her knees at my feet. With my free hand, I unzip my pants and pull my cock out, allowing the tip to drag along her lips.

"What are you doing?" she asks in alarm, struggling against my hold on her. Her tits bounce in a way that draws my eye.

"Shut up," I bark.

When she opens her mouth to protest, I feed my cock into her mouth, one inch at a time. She gags around me, tears filling her eyes, but I simply force myself deeper inside of her. She's nothing but a vessel for me, after all. A little slut for me to use and discard.

And, when I close my eyes, I can picture her hair is golden blonde.

I begin to fuck her mouth as she cries around my length, trying to pull herself free, but the dumb slut should've known what she was getting herself into when she propositioned me.

My phone buzzes in my pocket, and I fumble to grab it while still pistoning in and out of her mouth.

"Yes?" I grunt as my balls grow unbelievably heavy.

All I can hear is stuttered breathing, nearly inaudible amongst the raucous crowd, and then a raspy voice says, "She's here."

"You know what you need to do." I pull my phone away from my ear and throw it onto the hood of the car.

At the same time, my pleasure races through me like lava, and I come with a groan, spilling my seed inside the woman's mouth. She chokes and sobs and struggles to pull herself away from me, but I continue holding on to her hair.

"Shhh. Shhh. Shhh." I reach down to grab both of her cheeks and pull her back to her feet. I can't help but think of how beautiful she looks like this—her face stained with tears, her cheeks puffy, her mouth coated in my arousal, and her perky breast on display. "Don't cry. Everything will be okay soon."

She sniffles. "What are you—"

I grab her neck between both of my hands and give it a twist, causing her body to fall to the ground dead at my feet.

Frowning, I pull my pants back up and tuck my dick away before grabbing my discarded phone. I then turn towards one of my men, who has been waiting by the doorway of the car, surveying the surroundings with a cold, detached look he's perfected.

He doesn't even glance my way as I slide into the passenger seat and snap, "Get rid of it!"

Once I'm settled comfortably in my seat, belatedly aware that two of my men are grabbing the arms and legs of the unnamed whore, I turn back to my phone.

No updates yet.

It's no matter.

With Isabella in town, everything is going as planned.

Nine

IZZY

The need to fight is an almost physical force within me—it curls my hands into fists, creates tension in my shoulders, and paints the room in a bloodred sheen.

I can't remember the last time I've been in the ring. Too long, that's for damn sure. It was probably when I stayed at my last foster home with Mrs. Penya and her delinquent son.

If I thought it was loud outside the barn, that's nothing compared to the inside. I can barely hear myself think over the raucous crowd all gathered around a makeshift circle in the center of the room. A few bodies jostle me as I move through the throng of people, but Grayson's intimidating size keeps them from getting too close.

In the ring, two men are fighting savagely, blood spurting in every direction and bruises already beginning to pepper their skin. The blond-haired one is on the ground while the brunette pummels his face with ruthless abandon.

The designated announcer—a sleazy fucker by the name of Dennis—calls an end to the match as the crowd roars. Money is exchanged. Unofficial fights break out. Someone in the distance screams.

It's fucking paradise.

I'm so preoccupied with the fight that it takes me a second too long to realize I lost Grayson in the crowd. I push up on my tiptoes, attempting to see over all of the heads, but I can't seem to pin down his shock of dark hair.

I wonder if he's with Sydney.

The thought sits like acid in my stomach, though I quickly try to smother my instinctive reaction.

"Hey, gorgeous," a sly voice purrs in my ear a mere second before arms curl around my waist.

I recognize the voice almost instantly.

Justin Miller.

"Let me go, Justin," I say, not even bothering to look over my shoulder. "Before I break every finger in your hands."

"Don't be like that, babe." His cheek nuzzles against mine.

Justin was...a mistake. A big fucking mistake. It was a mistake that involved one too many drinks, a bedroom, and a subpar orgasm. I try my hardest to only sleep with guys I'm positive I'll never see again, but then I met Justin.

He's handsome in a pretty-boy type of way, with sun-kissed skin and Justin Bieber-styled hair, as ironic as that sounds given his name. I was feeling depressed after I saw Grayson walking out of the barn with a different girl, so I allowed Justin to take me home.

And now, he never lets me hear the end of it.

I'm just grateful that he always chooses to engage with me when Grayson is preoccupied. I'm not sure what my overprotective best friend will do if he discovers I fucked some trust-fund rich kid from the good part of town.

"Bella..." He probably thinks he sounds sexy, but anyone who calls me "Bella" is an automatic nope in my book. "You're so tense, babe. Let me help you with that."

His hands travel to my shoulders as he begins to knead the muscles there.

"You're right." I stealthily slip out of his embrace and flash him a saccharine-sweet smile over my shoulder. "I am tense. Which is why I'm here."

Without waiting for him to respond, I hurry through the crowd, focusing only on Dennis's luminescent bald spot. When he sees me, his eyes flare with excitement, and he steps away from whomever he was talking to.

"Isabella! It's so good to see you today!" His

booming voice reverberates through the room, even over the blaring music, chatter, and laughter.

"You got anyone for me today?" I ask, already unzipping my sweatshirt.

If there's one thing I can appreciate about Dennis, it's the fact that he never ogles me. He's sleazy, sure, and looks as if he eats puppies for dinner, but never once has he done anything inappropriate with me. Here I am, in nothing but a sports bra and leggings, and his gaze doesn't stray from my face for even a second.

"Have a new girl. Larissa or something. She signed up an hour ago, but we haven't been able to find someone for her to compete against."

"Put me down." I jerk my chin towards his clipboard.

His eyes glimmer with unfettered excitement. "You good to go in ten?"

The smile that carves itself onto my face is cold, full of pent-up rage and aggression that demands an outlet. "Of course."

Dennis nods and moves through the crowd, no doubt to find this Larissa person and tell her that the next fight will be ours.

I move to an empty corner of the room and begin to run through my pre-fight exercises. It's there Grayson finds me, his brow furrowed in confusion and a silent question in his gaze.

"I couldn't find you," I explain with an eye roll. "Were you busy with your new girlfriend?"

I try to sound teasing, but even I can detect the tinge of hurt in my voice. Dammit.

Grayson's expression clouds over, becoming unreadable as he watches me complete my stretches.

After a moment of continued silence, at least between the two of us, he tosses his bag at my feet.

"Thanks," I murmur as I unzip it and begin to tape up my hands.

Through it all, Grayson watches me, one of his dark brows quirked. I ignore his penetrating gaze as I use my teeth to rip the tape. Satisfied, I throw it back inside his bag and move around him.

His hands land on my shoulders, the warmth of his palms seeping through my skin and migrating straight to my lower belly, but I shrug him off. The last thing I need right now is to be distracted by my unreciprocated crush on my best friend.

Dennis moves towards an overturned box and steps on top of it, making sure he's slightly higher than the rest of the crowd. He has a megaphone that he presses to his mouth. "Tonight we have a real treat for you! What is sexier than two women fighting it out?"

He laughs jovially as the crowd joins in, and I have to rein in my eye roll. I wonder if he and the rest of the men here would still find it sexy if they knew I was only seventeen. Alas, when I first started fighting here almost two years ago, I lied and said I was eighteen, hence the vulgar comments.

No matter.

As long as I can pound my fist into someone's face, I'm a happy camper.

I jump on the balls of my feet as Dennis continues his introductions.

Everything has been changing so quickly I can barely wrap my head around it. One second, I was in a small home shoving a bookcase against the door to keep my pervy foster brother out. The next, I'm...safe? I think? Maybe? It's just so hard to put your trust in someone when you've been burned as often as I have.

Because every time shit hits the fan, *I'm* the problem. Not him or her. Me. The social workers don't care that the only reason I stabbed my foster brother was because he snuck into my bedroom. They don't care that I kicked my old foster dad in the dick because he was being a perv. They don't care that my foster mom slapped me, so I slapped her right the fuck back.

I'm the problem.

Me.

Always me.

Fighting in the ring is the only way I know how to release all of this rage inside of me. This fury... It burns me alive, eating at my skin like teeth made of fire. Only fighting dampens the flames and allows me to just breathe easily.

I take a moment to study the girl across from me—my opponent.

She's tall and willowy and appears to be in her late twenties. Her hair is cut in a stylish bob that stops just below her chin, red streaks scattered throughout. She wears a lime-green sports bra that strains against her ample cleavage—an intentional outfit choice on her part, I presume. The men are already ogling her and screaming for her to win.

"Good luck," she tells me when she catches my eye.

I can tell she actually means it.

"You too." I give her a nod of respect that she returns.

Sometimes, it's hard being one of the few women in a male-dominated sport, especially when that sport is done illegally in the barn on the outskirts of town. I've quickly become friends with a lot of the women here, despite the bloodshed.

"AND GOOO!" Dennis hollers, and then he quickly moves out of the circle.

The men and women present begin to scream, but their words filter through one ear and immediately exit the other. I can't focus on them. Only my opponent matters.

I study her quickly, searching for any weaknesses, but she seems to know what she's doing. Her stance is loose and casual, allowing her to be nimble on her feet, and her eyes are hyper-focused on my face. This is obviously a woman who has fought before.

Good.

I like a challenge.

A cunning smirk tugs up my lips as I feign to the left. When she moves to counter my attack, I dive to the right and throw an uppercut at her jaw. She immediately punches at my stomach, and I'm not quick enough to move out of the way. I instinctively keel forward—which is my first mistake.

She slams a punch at my face that has me seeing stars and then follows that with two quick jabs to my shoulder.

Fuck.

She dances out of my way before I can return her blows.

"I don't want to hurt you, little girl," she says, her tone halfway between teasing and serious. "Just bow out now."

I charge at her while she's speaking, my head lowered like a ram's, but fling myself to the ground a second before I reach her, sliding through her legs. She stumbles, and I quickly roll myself back to my feet and kick her in the shins from behind.

She falls to the ground on her hands and knees, and I jump on her back, hugging her neck with one hand and raining punches on her face with my other. She wiggles from side to side, desperately trying to buck me off of her, but I'm a stubborn bitch when I want to be.

She suddenly pauses, and I realize why a second too late.

With a yelp, she throws herself backwards, crushing me beneath her. Pain reverberates through my spine as I ricochet off the wooden floorboards.

Larissa attempts to roll off of me—probably so she can straddle me—but I perform a backwards roll to get away from her. Then, while she's on her knees struggling to her feet, I jump at her and wrap both of my legs around her neck, forcing her to the ground. I find myself straddling her shoulders as she lies on her back, peering up at me with one swollen eye.

She knows as well as I do that there's no escaping this position. I can see the defeat in her gaze...as well as her begrudging respect.

Keeping her eyes trained on me, she taps her fingers against the ground, signaling that she yields.

"And that's the end of the match!" Dennis rushes over and all but pulls me to my feet, holding my arm up in the air. "Isabella is our winner!"

There's a mixture of boos and cheers from the crowd, but I drown them all out as the high of my victory sweeps through my veins like a drug, potent and intoxicating. Sure, my body aches fiercely, and I'll need to cover up all of my bruises with makeup before I see anyone, but there's nothing quite like winning to put everything into perspective.

Larissa stumbles clumsily to her feet and extends a hand for me to shake.

"Good match," she says with a smile.

I grip her hand. "You're definitely going to give me

a run for my money. Are you new here? I don't think I've seen you before."

"Yeah. Just arrived a few days ago." She wipes at a blood rivulet on her cheek.

"And the first thing you did was find an illegal fight ring in town?" I smirk at her, and her eyes glimmer with mirth.

"You know it." Someone over my shoulder seems to capture her attention. She turns back to me with a smile. "See you again?"

"Of course."

Dennis grabs my shoulder to garner my attention as Larissa disappears into the crowd. He holds out a wad of cash.

"Your winnings for tonight," he says as I eye the bundle of one-hundred-dollar bills.

This could almost be enough to pay back Hale for the computer, phone, and clothes. Almost. I just need to find a way to give it to him without him believing I'm a prostitute or something.

"Thanks, Dennis." I take the money and shove it into the back pocket of my leggings.

No one here would be stupid enough to try to steal from me. There's a plethora of unspoken rules regarding Dennis's fight club.

Don't talk about fight club.

Respect the fighters.

And don't ever, not ever, steal what doesn't belong to you.

I've seen firsthand what happens to someone who breaks those rules. His mutilated body still haunts me to this day.

I return to my corner of the room to see that Grayson has left, though my sweatshirt and his duffel bag remain. I unwrap my hands and throw the tape away before using a towel to wipe the blood and sweat off my face and arms. Quickly, I shove the sweatshirt back on over my sports bra and scan the crowd for Grayson.

I find him almost instantly.

He leans against the long table that serves as a bar, his back to me. In front of him is a rather familiar girl with light-brown hair, smokey eyes, and bright-red lips. The shirt she wears is unbuttoned far enough to show a hint of her black bra.

Sydney.

Grayson's...girlfriend.

Something inside of my heart cracks and splinters, slicing my insides up along the way. I know I shouldn't care—I've learned my lesson long ago—but the pain persists, regardless.

The beautiful woman places her hand on Grayson's bicep and steps even closer, invading his space. She pushes up on her tiptoes...

I can't watch this.

I refuse to.

I hurry in the direction of the exit, no thought in my mind except for "escape."

"Bella! Where are you going?" Justin grabs at my arm, but I shake him off of me with a snarl.

As soon as I'm outside, I take desperate lungfuls of sweet, fresh air. I thought it would clear the cobwebs from my head, but it seems to do the opposite. Each breath I take sends razor blades slicing down my throat.

Fuck.

Why do I allow Grayson to hold such power over me? I need to get over this stupid crush on him, and fast.

I debate going back inside, finding Justin, and asking him to take me back to his parents' pool house to fuck me senseless, but the thought of him touching me has unease skittering down my spine.

Briefly, Ethan's face appears in my mind, his flushed cheeks, disheveled blond hair, and thick-framed glasses. Heat percolates low in my stomach.

My reaction to the strange man takes me by surprise.

I don't even know him, yet I'm lusting after him like a bitch in heat. What is wrong with me? Sure, he's sexy, but after what happened with Justin, I swore off sex with men I'll have to see on numerous occasions. And since Ethan's attending the same school as me... he's off-limits.

Even if he is one of the sexiest men I've ever laid eyes upon in my life.

With an annoyed huff aimed at myself, I move towards the road. It'll be a long walk back to my house, but there's no way in hell I'm waiting for Grayson. Besides, a little fresh air and exercise will do me good. I'm not afraid of the darkness and the secrets it holds. It's the light that terrifies me—I don't want to see the face of my attacker.

As I begin the trek home, I can't help but feel as if there's a pair of eyes on me.

Watching me.

Stalking me.

Hunting me.

Ten

IZZY

My phone buzzes on my bed for the twentieth time this morning, but I ignore it. I know, without a shadow of doubt, that it's Gray demanding to know why I left without him.

And he's probably a little pissed at me that I locked the window to my new bedroom, refusing to allow him entry.

Well, sucks to be him.

Shoving all thoughts of Gray to the back corner of my mind, I consider my reflection in the full-length mirror.

I decided to go with the "comfortable but stylish" route for my first day of school. They're already a few weeks into the semester, so I want to make sure I don't stand out too much. The last thing I need is a blazing beacon on my back, declaring me to be a new foster kid in the area. However, I don't want to look like a hobo either.

The red sweater slides off one shoulder, revealing the strap of my bra. I paired the shirt with tight skinny jeans that mold to my legs. I kept my makeup minimal —a little bit of blush, a dab of mascara, and red lipstick. I debated what to do with my shock of blonde waves before deciding to keep my hair down.

Satisfied with my appearance, I reach for the backpack Hale gifted me this morning. It used to belong to Jake before he purchased a new one for himself.

Hale assured me that he'll stop at the store and get me a different one, but I told him that I was completely fine with Jake's old one. The ratty backpack with the duct tape on the side reminds me a little of...me— broken and haphazardly stitched back together.

"Izzy! Are you coming?" Jake calls from farther down the hall.

I stare at myself one more time in the mirror before nodding in satisfaction. Perfect.

Quickly, I move towards my mattress and lift it just enough to reveal the tiny slit on the bottom. It wouldn't be noticeable unless you knew explicitly where to look. I stick my hand inside, grab two twenties, and shove the money into my backpack. I don't know what I'll need to pay for, but I found that it's always better to keep just a little bit of change on you rather than nothing at all.

"Coming!" I hurry out of the room and race to the kitchen.

Hale's standing at the stove, seemingly juggling two pans at once. The left one is filled with fluffy scrambled eggs, while the right pan has a pancake bubbling in the center. A stack of already cooked pancakes rests beside it on a plate.

Jake leans against the counter, nibbling on a piece of bacon, but he straightens when he sees me.

"Damn." He offers me a bright, toothy grin. "I didn't think it was possible for you to *not* look like a homeless person."

"Ha, ha, ha, very funny," I deadpan as I move towards him and snag a piece of crunchy bacon off the plate he's hoarding.

He glares at me in mock disapproval and swats at my hand.

"I think you look nice," Lissa interjects. She sits at the center island with a single pancake in front of her, and she grabs the syrup and begins to pour it over top. "The sweater would look better if it was pink, of course. But then again, everything looks better as pink. Sweaters, pants, dresses, shoes, socks..."

She sighs wistfully, seemingly oblivious to the syrup that's still continually trickling over her single pancake.

Jake, however, reaches for the bottle. "You're gonna give yourself a cavity," he chastises.

She simply sticks her tongue out at him and resumes eating.

"What do you want to eat, Izzy?" Hale asks, drawing my attention back to him. "It's your first day at a new school, so I decided to go all out."

"The pancakes are really good," Lissa says around a mouthful.

I wince nearly imperceptibly and blow out a breath. I'm not the biggest breakfast eater, having not had the option at most of my old foster homes. I've gotten used to coffee and nothing else, except for the occasional granola bar. Still, Hale went through all this effort...

"Eggs, please?"

"Right on it." Hale expertly scoops a spoonful of scrambled eggs onto a plate and hands it to me.

I take it and return to my position beside Jake, who's still protecting his damn bacon like it's an Infinity Stone.

Jake catches the direction of my stare and scowls. "Don't even think about it, new girl."

"Jake, share," Hale reprimands.

Lissa chuckles.

"I share a lot of things in life," Jake retorts haughtily. "But not my bacon. Never my bacon. A man shouldn't be forced to."

"That sounded oddly sexual," I murmur, too low for Hale or Lissa to hear.

Jake does, however, and snickers.

"Head out of gutter, new girl." He jostles me with his shoulder.

"What about you, Seth?" Hale says. "We have eggs, pancakes, and baco—"

"No bacon!" Jake all but growls.

I turn slightly, coming face-to-face with the third foster kid I have yet to be introduced to.

He's young. I can tell that just by looking at him. He's probably a few years younger than even Lissa. His brown hair flops in front of his face, obscuring his right eye from view, but his left eye studies the room with an astute intensity I've never seen on such a young face before. He wears an oversized gray hoodie, loose jeans, and a pair of huge red headphones that rest around his neck.

His gaze flicks to me for a fraction of a second before he dismisses me, focusing back on Hale. Instead of answering, he simply places his headphones over his ears, grabs his backpack off the floor, and heads out of the kitchen.

Hale sighs heavily.

"Don't mind Seth," Jake tells me, waving a piece of bacon in front of my face. I have to rein in the urge to lean forward and bite down on it, stealing it from his hands. "He's a sweet kid, but..."

"Seth sees the world differently than we do," Hale cuts in when it's apparent Jake isn't going to continue.

"Change is always hard on him, so your appearance here is something he'll have to get used to."

"I'm sorry," I say immediately, wincing.

I know *exactly* how hard change can be.

"Don't be sorry, new girl." Jake gives my shoulder a squeeze before pushing away from the counter. "You just need to give him a chance to open up to you." He glances at his watch before turning his attention back to me. "You almost done? We need to leave now if we're going to make it to school early enough for you to find your classes."

"We have to drop Seth off at his private school first," Lissa says as she shovels the last of her sugar-drenched pancake into her mouth.

School.

Classes.

The familiar tendrils of terror wrap around my heart and squeeze. I've gotten good at thinking about school in conceptual terms. But to be hit in the face with the full reality of my situation? Yeah, I think I may pass out.

Hale was sent my class schedule a day before I even arrived at his house, and Jake did his best to give me a rundown of where each class was. Unfortunately, I only have one class with my foster brother. The other five...I'm on my own.

"Don't be anxious, Izzy." Hale flashes me an encouraging smile. "You'll do great."

"What could go wrong about starting my senior year weeks after school already began in a place I know absolutely nobody?" My voice borders on hysteria.

"You're panicking," Jake points out dryly.

"Totally panicking," Lissa agrees.

"Everything will be fine," Hale reassures me again. "And you have my number if you need anything."

"Mine too," Jake says. "And I already said I'll sit with you at lunch, so don't worry about that." He adopts an imperious tone and hefts his chin into the air. "Anyone who sits by me will automatically become popular. It's the unspoken rule."

I snort at his antics, even as my stomach twists itself into a dozen tight knots. I can't help but remember Ethan's offer to sit by me at lunch…

But no. Surely he already forgot about me, the strange new girl. There's no way a guy like him would ever be interested in a girl like me. There seems to be a neon sign dangling above my head that screams, "WARNING—PRODUCT IS DAMAGED."

I wish I weren't pissed at Grayson. He always knows what to say when I'm freaking out about starting a new school. A lot of times, he'll come visit me on campus or find me in the parking lot after school ends.

I miss him, and I hate the fact that I do.

But I can't focus on Grayson or Ethan or anything except putting one foot in front of the other. Who cares if the ground I'm walking on is cracked and weak, threatening to shatter at any moment? Who cares that I may fall through the floor into the abyss below?

One foot in front of the other.

That's my mantra.

Steeling my spine, I glance at Jake. "Let's go."

Eleven

IZZY

After dropping Seth off at his school, Jake drives us to the local high school—an unassuming brick building that's three stories high. The parking lot is surprisingly crowded for this early in the morning, but Jake tells me it's because most of the sports teams are required to do some weight training before classes begin.

Thank goodness I don't play on any teams.

I tried gymnastics when I was younger before I realized that I wasn't a fan of the skin-tight, revealing leotards. Then I joined the cheer team for a couple of years, though I quickly discovered I wasn't "peppy" enough for the coach's liking.

Besides, I found that it was hard to join a sport when I was constantly moving from school to school. The second I started making friends, I had the rug ripped out from underneath me and had to start all over again.

It was better for everyone if I just kept to myself.

As soon as the car is put into park, Lissa flings open her door without a backwards glance and races across the lot, nothing but a flurry of pink clothing and brown hair. She joins a group of similar-looking girls, a wide, beguiling smile on her pretty face.

"You ready for today?" Jake questions as he grabs his backpack from behind him.

"Not at all," I answer honestly, stepping out of the car and waiting for him to join me.

"You'll be fine, new girl." He hits my shoulder with his own and releases a genuine chuckle. "Remember what I said before... If you're friends with me, then you're popular."

"How did I get stuck with such a modest foster brother?" I tease.

"God's gift to you." He hikes his bag farther up his shoulder and then waves to a few people we pass.

"Why didn't you have to head in early for weight training or whatever?" I query as he claps hands with another bulky man—no doubt a fellow football player.

"You can choose to weight train either in the morning before school or in the afternoon after prac-tice," he explains as we move up the steps towards the entrance of the school. He holds the door open for me and waits for me to step inside before following in behind me. "Most choose to do it in the morning. I chose after practice."

The interior is exactly what I would expect from a school that's located in the middle of nowhere. It's so stereotypical that I have to hold in the laugh that threatens to burst free.

The white tiles are polished so meticulously that I can see my reflection on the surface. Lockers line either side of the hall, interspersed with doors that lead to classrooms. I don't see a stairwell leading to the upper levels of the school, but I assume that's because it's in a different hall.

"Do you have your schedule? I can't remember your classes," Jake says, and I immediately reach into my backpack pocket to hand it to him.

He smooths out the wrinkles on his knee before holding it up to his face and studying it intently.

"So you already know that you have AP Literature with me. That's going to be on the second floor. I can meet you at your classroom before that, and we can walk together. Let me show you where your first few classes are, as well as the cafeteria."

The layout of the school proves to be rather simple. The majority of the senior classes are on the first floor —a benefit of being older, according to Jake. All of my AP classes are on the second floor. The only class I have on the third floor is Art, a requirement I desperately wish I didn't have to take. I have the artistic ability of a turtle with both of its fins cut off. The last time I tried to "craft," I superglued my hand to my face.

As we move through the halls, I can't help but inconspicuously survey every student present. Everybody seems to know everyone, and the familiar pangs of isolation bombard me. I'm used to feeling like this—alone, even when I'm in a crowded room—but it's never felt so pronounced before.

There's a certain ease and companionship amongst the other students in the hall that I long to emulate. I wish I could walk up to that random girl, say hi, and have her smile back at me. I wish I could high-five that burly football player with the easy-going smile and sparkling eyes.

Jake tries to introduce me to everyone we come across, but after the tenth name, I begin to feel dizzy. What was her name again? Rachel? Rebecca? Raina? Fuck.

It's only as we move to the cafeteria and claim a table near the center of the room do I realize who I'm actually looking for.

A certain gorgeous nerd with mussy blond hair, glasses, and a timid smile...

A wave of heat rushes through me, causing my cheeks to burn.

Jake remains oblivious to my thoughts as he chats with one of his friends—some football player named Dec, a man with spiked red hair and laughing green eyes.

"Don't look now," Dec whispers suddenly, the words uttered from the corner of his mouth as he attempts to remain inconspicuous.

"What?" Jake's head whips up, and almost immediately, his cheeks turn crimson. He ducks his head with a noncommittal grunt.

"I told you not to look," Dec chastises, though I detect amusement in his voice.

"Fuck off," Jake growls.

"Who aren't we supposed to look at?" I keep my voice low, though Jake still feels the need to shush me, going so far as to place his hand over my mouth.

Dec smirks. "Desiree, Emilia, and Mimi." He jerks his head towards something over my shoulder. "Otherwise known as the love of Jake's life."

"Shut the fuck up," Jake snaps scathingly, glaring at his friend.

I try to turn towards where Dec's staring, but Jake places his hand on my knee, providing just enough pressure to elicit a tiny gasp from me.

"Don't you dare," he warns me.

I grin at his obvious embarrassment. "What do you think I'm going to do? Jump up on the bench and declare that you have a crush on...?" I look to Dec to finish that sentence.

"Desiree," he answers with a shit-eating grin.

"Desiree." Ignoring his hand still on my knee, I flick my hair over my shoulder to get a better glimpse of the three girls.

I can't see them clearly from so far away, but I can tell that they're beautiful. Flawless, even. One girl stands in front of the other two, and her chestnut-colored hair falls in perfect ringlets down her back. She moves with a grace that suggests she knows how beautiful she truly is...and relishes in the fact. She's definitely not the type of girl I thought Jake would be interested in.

But to each their own.

The ringleader—Desiree, more than likely—says something to the other two that has them both giggling. She then tosses a perfect curl over her shoulder and sashays away, not sparing a glance towards anyone in the cafeteria.

As soon as she's out of sight, Jake drops his forehead to the table with a groan.

"I'm pathetic, aren't I?" he murmurs, his voice muffled from where his mouth is squished against the wood.

"She seems...nice?" I try.

Dec snorts. "She's the devil incarnate. I honestly don't know why you're into her, man."

"Because I hate myself," Jake huffs out forlornly, still keeping his forehead pressed to the table.

"Besides, you know that girl has her sights on Ashton and his friends...not that they give her the time of day."

"I know, I know, okay? I'm a pathetic excuse for a human being in love with a literal demoness." Jake reluctantly pulls his head up from the table and levels Dec with a frosty glare. "Happy?"

"Very." Dec slides his gaze towards something just over my shoulder. "And speaking of the devils…"

"Hey! Izzy, right?" a familiar voice exclaims from directly behind me.

The rush of heat from before returns with a vengeance, liquifying my veins.

"Ethan." I try to play it cool, but I'm sure my cheeks are an even brighter shade of red than Jake's.

I don't want to admit even to myself how desperately I wanted to see Ethan. I can't say for certain why, though. Sure, he's sexy, but I've known a lot of hot guys over the years. There's just something about him that seems to innately reel me in…

Today, he's dressed in a simple blue T-shirt that conforms to his muscular physique. His blond hair has been styled away from his face, emphasizing his sharp cheekbones, plush lips, and vibrant green eyes.

He absently pushes his glasses farther up his nose as he slides onto the bench opposite me and beside Dec.

"Hey, man," Jake greets, extending his hand to do a bro fist-bump thing.

"Hey." Ethan's gaze shifts to me, and I swear a blush creeps along his cheeks.

Is he just as nervous as I am? No. I find that hard to believe. Not when he looks like that.

"So how's your first day treating you, Izzy?"

"I didn't get lost, so I call that a win."

Jake snorts. "You've also been following me around like a besotted puppy. Do you think you can find your way back to your locker if I wasn't here to guide you?"

I playfully swat at his arm. "Are you accusing me of being directionally challenged?"

"If the shoe fits..."

"Oh. Jake gave you a tour of the school already?" Ethan questions.

Something in his tone has another flood of liquid heat cascading through my veins. Am I mistaken, or does he almost sound jealous?

However, when I meet his gaze, his timid grin is firmly in place, not a single hint of malice in his sparkling eyes.

"He attempted to." I smirk at Jake before returning my attention to Ethan. "He got distracted more than once talking to people."

"It's not my fault I'm a popular god," he huffs petulantly.

Ethan snickers. "Keep telling yourself that, man." Turning towards me, he smiles sweetly and extends a hand. "Can I see your schedule?"

"Oh, yeah, sure." I slide it over to him, and he immediately lowers his head to look it over.

I take the moment to study him. The mussy blond hair, impeccably styled. The sharp features chiseled from limestone. His voice, as smooth as cognac and just as addicting.

Ugh.

I seriously need to get over this stupid crush. I barely know the guy. Sure, he seems sweet, if a little shy, but that doesn't mean I can start picturing him naked.

Though the thought of Ethan naked...

Bad, Izzy! Bad!

"You have first period with me!" Ethan flashes me a happy smile. "And third. And lunch. You have second with my friend Ashton, third with me and Emery, fourth with Reid and Emery, and fifth with just Reid. You're unfortunately all on your own for sixth."

"Who are Emery, Ashton, and Reid?" I query, canting my head to the side.

Didn't Dec mention something about Desiree and Ashton? And didn't Jake mention Ethan having a brother?

"Oh, um..." Ethan's cheeks flash crimson yet again. "My friends. And my, um, twin."

Something desolate passes over his features, like a bloated storm cloud moving in front of the sun. Just as quickly, he shakes his head and plasters his signature smile back into place.

"I can walk you to first period, if you want? But no pressure. You don't have to if you don't want to. I mean, I can walk behind you, if you want. Or in front of you." He agitatedly forks his fingers through his hair, disarranging the meticulous strands.

"I need to stop by the office first to get some forms signed," I say, standing from the bench and grabbing my backpack off the ground. "But if you're okay to wait for me to finish—"

"Yes!" he blurts...and then immediately facepalms himself. "I mean, yeah. That's fine. I can do that. I don't play any sports, so I have nothing I need to do this morning." He pauses, flushes, and then says, "Well, I do play baseball, but they don't start their season until the spring. But I doubt you want to know about that..."

I wave goodbye to Jake and Dec and follow Ethan down the hall towards the administrative offices.

"I actually know a little bit about baseball," I confess.

One of my old foster dads—my favorite—watched it almost religiously. I don't think he missed a single game. Even when he was diagnosed with cancer and spent most of his days in the hospital, he still found a way to watch the sport.

"You do?" A blush tinges his cheeks pink.

"I'm not an expert or anything, but I went to a few games."

We turn at a fork in the hall, and I start going straight when Ethan places a hand on my lower back. Heat immediately migrates from where he touches me, traveling south, but I work to keep my expression impassive. Ethan guides me towards the right and then instantly releases me.

"The office is over here," he explains, his cheeks still bright with color.

"Thanks." I flash him a timid smile, one he returns, before his own freezes on his face.

His gaze lifts to something over my shoulder, and his entire body seems to vibrate with tension. Surprise is written into every line of his visage.

"Ethan?" I turn to face him fully, but his focus isn't on me. "You okay?"

As soon as those words leave my mouth, a cold chill passes over me. It's a similar sensation to when you're in a room full of people and feel a set of eyes burning a hole in your back.

"Why don't we go this way instead?" Ethan babbles, grabbing for my wrist and attempting to lead me the way we came from. "It'll be easier to…"

As he talks, I slowly turn to stare over my shoulder…and immediately clash eyes with a pair of verdant ones, so similar to the man touching me that I think I'm seeing double. But then I remember that Ethan claimed to have a twin.

Slowly, the man wearing Ethan's face begins to smile—a wicked, nightmarish, lurid, *lazy* smile that has chills of unease skating down my spine.

"Oh, fuck," Ethan murmurs just as the stranger peels away from his locker—and the girl he was talking to—and storms in our direction.

Twelve

EMERY

Sweat trickles down my forehead as I move out of the weight room and to the locker room. The rest of my team follows behind me, jostling and laughing amongst themselves as they discuss the upcoming game against our biggest rivals—the Vipers.

But I can't focus on any of that, though. Not when I have a goddamn Calculus test in exactly two hours that I need to pass or risk getting benched for the rest of the season.

School has never been my strong suit, not like it is for Ethan and even Ashton. I honestly don't see the fucking point of learning about X and Y and imaginary numbers. Teach me something that will benefit me in the future, like how to calculate taxes and apply for loans. Don't teach me how to do multiplication with numbers that don't truly exist. What's the goddamn point in that?

Irritation thrums through my veins as I move towards my locker, grab a change of clothes, and then head towards the showers. I want to take my time under the spray of blistering water, but I know I need to head to my first period early if I have any hope in hell of studying before my second period test.

Cursing, I shut off the shower and quickly change into a fresh pair of clothes. I don't bother to brush my blond hair. Instead, I simply fork my fingers through the disheveled strands, frowning when they flop back into place in front of my eyes.

Ashton's waiting for me outside of the locker room, his arms crossed over his chest and his expression carefully blank. A frown tugs at his brows when he catches a glimpse of my face. Almost immediately, he grabs his phone out of his back pocket and begins to type on it.

"I'll take care of it," he tells me firmly, not even glancing up from the screen as we maneuver the now-crowded halls, heading towards our lockers.

I scowl. "You don't need to do this for me, Ash. It's not fucking worth it. It's just one test."

"And if you fail, you're going to be benched," he points out, his tone almost absent as he continues to keep his gaze glued to his phone.

Somehow, he's able to traverse the halls without bumping into anyone, despite his attention elsewhere. I wonder if it's his skills as a wolf...or the bright neon sign that seems to hang above his head, warning everyone to stay clear of him. The other students part around him like a boulder resting in the middle of a roaring river. Fear, awe, and caution splay across their faces as they eye him with barely veiled curiosity.

I've seen firsthand what Ashton can do just with that damn phone of his. He could probably take over the world if he felt so inclined to, all while never leaving our cozy town in the middle of nowhere. I don't know who he plans to blackmail, bribe, or threaten now, but it's a pointless endeavor. Ashton can't fix all of my problems for me just because I'm a stupid moth-erfucker.

Maybe if I ask Ethan for help...

Almost as soon as that thought enters my mind, I dismiss it in a tidal wave of anger. Hell would sooner freeze over than I'll ever ask that piece of shit for help.

Ethan may be my twin brother. He may be my packmate. He may be the other half of my soul...but he's also the man I hate most in the world.

I wrench open my locker with more force than necessary and quickly sift through the textbooks there, deciding which ones I'll need for the day. Ashton watches me with cold, calculating eyes, his phone now dangling loosely in his grip. One of his dark brows quirks upwards in a silent question, but I shake my head.

"No. I don't want your help with this." I grab my

enormous Calculus textbook and glare at the cover—a smiling woman holding a calculator like she's having the time of her goddamn life. "Fucking math."

Ashton's lips purse, but he chooses not to argue with me. Yet, despite his silence, I know that he'll intervene if I do fail and find myself benched during the next game. It's in his blood to help the members of his pack, regardless of what we say or do.

"Have you talked to Ethan at all today?" Ashton's quiet voice has a chill skating down my spine, like the Grim Reaper himself is hovering behind me and whispering in my ear.

My jaw clenches, and tension reverberates through my body. My knuckles turn almost white from how hard I grip the textbook.

"Why the fuck would you ask me that?" I snarl..

Ashton ignores my outburst. "He's been acting weird. And he hasn't returned any of my texts."

"He always acts fucking weird."

Once again, Ashton chooses not to acknowledge my outburst. Both Reid and Ashton are keenly aware of the tension between me and my twin, but they've made it clear time and time again that they'll be Switzerland in this battle between the two of us. I don't know how they can be so goddamn calm knowing what Ethan did, but then again, they *are* his packmates, just as they are mine. The brown mark on all of our skins—the one that looks like a roaring flame—proves as much.

At one point, I wanted nothing more than to be in a pack with my twin brother. He was my best friend, my confidant, my partner in crime…

Until everything changed and he became my enemy.

I squeeze my eyelids shut to hold back the onslaught of emotions that threaten to drown me. That seems to be an ever-present constant in my life whenever I even *think* his name.

Because of him, my life has been forever changed.

Because of him, our pack no longer has control of our future.

Because of him, we're tied to someone we can't stand.

As if the universe has heard my silent fuming, the she-devil herself appears at the end of the hallway, her two flunkies trailing a few steps behind her.

Ashton doesn't even bother to say goodbye to me as he hightails it out of there, his gaze never straying to the woman striding towards us. I quickly try to slam my locker shut and follow after my best friend, but I'm too damn slow.

A second later, she's on me like damn mold, her manicured hand grasping my bicep and pulling me to a stop.

"Ethan," Desiree greets with barely veiled disdain.

She stares at me like I'm the shit under her boot, and I can say with utter confidence that the feeling's mutual.

"It's Emery," I growl, despite the fact she knows that already. She just likes to purposely mix up our names to prove to us time and time again that we'll never be anything to her.

Bitch.

There was a time long, long ago when I thought Desiree was attractive. But then again, volcanoes are hot, and I don't want to stick my dick in any of those.

Her brown hair cascades in perfect ringlets down her back, held in place by a white headband with a similarly colored rose on the side. She wears a pleated skirt that stops just above her knees, a white blouse, and a dark blazer. I've heard more than one student claim that she's the epitome of schoolgirl porn.

That mere thought makes me want to gag.

What self-respecting man or woman would want to fuck the devil herself?

"How's my favorite wolf shifter doing?" she asks with a saccharine-sweet grin, brushing a strand of perfectly curled hair behind her ear.

"What do you want, she-bitch?" I lean against my locker with a scowl. "Did you just want to spend time in my company?"

All at once, her fake smile fades, replaced by her trademark glower that has lesser men pissing themselves. Fortunately for both of us, I'm immune to her ire.

"Oh please." She scoffs and rolls her eyes. "Don't go thinking that I'll ever develop feelings for you and the rest of the Lost Boys. Honestly, it's insulting. I'd rather fuck a rusty spoon for the rest of my life than have any of you ever touching me."

She smooths a hand down her blouse, ironing out imaginary wrinkles, as I grimace.

That was one visual I really, really didn't need in my head.

She absently glances over her shoulder at Mimi and Emilia, who are watching our exchange like it's the most exciting tennis match they've ever seen. Desiree flicks her fingers lazily, and the two girls immediately step out of earshot.

How the fuck is Desiree able to do that? Innately command other wolves without so much as a word? I know it's not because Mimi and Emilia respect her. I mean, who the hell can respect a two-legged goat who sucks the blood out of children every full moon?

Yeah, yeah, I may be exaggerating just a little bit, but it wouldn't surprise me if Desiree partook in such rituals.

Only when Desiree's sure that she won't be over-heard does she focus back on me, crossing her arms over her chest and glaring. "We need to talk."

"Isn't that what we're doing?" I quirk an eyebrow. "Or are the words coming out of your mouth the screech of a banshee announcing the death of everyone in the immediate vicinity?"

She doesn't even blink at my insult. "Is this your attempt at humor, Elias? Because let me be honest... It stinks. Or maybe that's just your body odor. Hard to tell."

I grit my teeth together and work to modulate my breathing.

Fucking Desiree.

She continues talking before I can get a word in edgewise.

"We need to talk about how we're going to behave this year." She straightens her spine almost imperceptibly and runs a hand down her skirt. "I want you to officially announce our mating. And I want you four to be my boyfriends at school."

For a moment, all I can do is stare at her in slack-jawed disbelief. Then a bark of dry, humorless laughter escapes me, the noise slipping past my lips unbidden.

"What type of weed have you been smoking?" I shake my head at her in disgust. "There's no way in hell we're doing that."

All of that was stipulated in the deal we made with Desiree's father. We have until we graduate high school to savor our freedom before we'll be forced to tie ourselves down to Desiree for the rest of our miserable lives.

Fuck, how things have changed...

When Ethan, Ashton, Reid, and I were revealed to be pack members once we reached puberty, we were ecstatic. The four of us have been best friends for as long as I can remember. Everyone knew we would be connected together in a way that defies all logic.

There are over fifty packs in the town, all of them ranging from a few members to a dozen or so. Most wolves know who will be in their pack by the time they reach puberty, but some never receive a marking.

Some...like Desiree.

Everyone assumed that meant she was a pack's Heart—the members' fated mate who will help tie them all together in a way that can't be articulated with words. Fated mates are immensely rare, which makes it all the more exciting when someone is suspected of being one.

But when Desiree's eighteenth birthday came around and she didn't receive any mark—and no packs felt the mating bond with her—the truth became abundantly clear.

She wasn't a pack member or a Heart.

She was a lone wolf.

Of course, her millionaire daddy couldn't handle his precious baby being without a pack and potentially turning feral. Because of Ethan's actions a few months prior, Daddy Desiree made a deal with our pack—aka, the bastard blackmailed us.

We were to pretend to be Desiree's fated mates, since it was apparent none of us were to have a fated mate of our own.

Even just thinking about the lie has bile scorching my throat and the taste of ash settling on my tongue.

Not only is Desiree the queen bitch, but she's also one of the few wolves with a special gift. Hers just happens to be the sight. As in, she can see into the future when she touches someone.

It was only a few months ago when she grazed my hand and told me in no uncertain terms that she'll never love any of us and we'll never love her. If we were to continue this sham of a "mating," we would be miserable for the rest of our lives.

When Ethan innocently asked her why she didn't just break this off, she responded with a flippant, "I don't have a choice."

And that was that.

We're chained to her irrevocably now because of a decision Ethan made.

"People are going to get suspicious," Desiree insists with a scowl. "Everybody knows that my eighteenth birthday was months ago. And they know that I met my so-called fated mates. When they discover it was you four all along, they're going to wonder why you behaved so coldly to me."

"Maybe it's because we hate you?" I suggest with a smile that's more of a baring of teeth.

Desiree simply narrows her eyes at me. "I get what I want, Enoch. And I also get what I *don't* want but need. That just so happens to be you and your brothers. We have a deal—"

The sweetest scent hits my nose then, and I tense. Fire rushes through my veins, and I have to bite back the cry of pain that threatens to escape me.

What the fuck?

My veins are burning. Lava is scorching my skin. My blood is boiling. I swear a thousand needles are being jammed into my brain, and each one has been lit on fire.

At first, all I can do is gape at Desiree, wondering if she's the one eliciting such a reaction from me.

But then I hear a soft, lyrical voice, and the world goes still around me.

"Ethan? Are you okay?"

Mate.

My wolf perks his head up inside of me, ambling to his feet and beginning to prowl. A stabbing pain takes up residence in my chest, and I half wonder if I'm dying. But if this is death, then I'll embrace it with open arms.

Mate.

The woman...is my mate.

"Emery." Desiree's scowl deepens as she stares at me in confusion, but I'm already dismissing her and turning towards the voice.

I briefly register the appearance of my goddamn brother, but I force him out of my mind. For now.

I can't focus on anything but the blonde beauty before me.

Our eyes lock, and another bolt of heat slashes at my chest.

Before I realize what I'm doing, I'm stalking after her, ignoring Desiree's annoyed voice from behind me.

This woman's face is all I can see, the sharp curves

of her cheekbones and the dusting of mascara on her lashes dominating my attention. She's fucking breathtaking, and I find myself hypnotized by the way her breasts brush against her shirt with every inhale and exhale she takes.

Mate.

My mate.

Our mate.

My gaze briefly snaps to Ethan's, who dons a sheepish smile, and I feel my eyes instinctively narrow.

Did he…*know* about her? And kept it from us?

Questions rattle around in my head, each one demanding my attention, but I find that I can't voice any of them. I don't dare to.

Because this woman is *human*.

I can tell that almost immediately as her sweet scent funnels around me.

Human.

My mate is human.

I've always heard stories about packs finding their fated mates, but when my eighteenth birthday came and went without feeling any connection to another wolf, I knew that I would have to accept that I'll never find the one meant for me and my packmates. I'll never find my Heart.

But now, I'm staring into the eyes of the woman I know is the missing piece of my soul…

And she's staring at me as if I'm a goddamn stranger.

Her gaze volleys between me and my brother, and I find that I don't like that. I want her attention to be on me, only me. Not him. Never him.

I allow a cold smile to tug up my lips as I survey her from head to toe. I lick my upper lip, and my tongue catches on the piercing there. "Hello, pretty lady. What's your name?"

Thirteen

IZZY

There's no denying the similarities between Ethan and this new guy. For one, they're both unfairly attractive, with blond hair and verdant-green eyes. For two, they're built like running backs, all tight muscles and strong forearms that leave my knees weak.

Ethan, however, wears a pair of glasses that give him a chic, almost nerdy look that contrasts greatly with his muscles and tattoos. He embodies the "boy next door" persona down to a T. Everything about him is warm and inviting, calmness seeming to radiate from his pores.

This new guy, on the other hand...

Well... I'm not certain he has a calm bone in his body. His strong, muscular frame is rigid with tension, and his eyes are hard, rife with some indecipherable emotion. He's dressed entirely in black—a skin-tight black shirt and black jeans—and has more piercings than any person I've ever met before. I count at least three in his ear, two in his right eyebrow, one in his left brow, a hoop through his upper lip, and a ball in his tongue.

It's that tongue piercing that captivates my attention. I can't help but gape as he slowly, almost leisurely, traces his lips with that damn silver bulb.

Mocking me.

Enticing me.

Fuck.

My stomach tightens and flutters like a horde of butterflies has just been unleashed.

Ethan, on the other hand, has gone stiff beside me. The same tension that seems to emanate from his brother in almost palpable waves ripples from Ethan's frame now. Both men regard each other with barely veiled distaste.

Didn't Ethan tell me he has a twin brother? Or was that Jake? Either way, I know for certain that these men must be identical twins. There's no other explanation. If they were to wear the same clothes and style their hair the same way, they would be impossible to tell apart.

Wait. No.

I stare into Ethan's pained eyes before flicking my gaze towards the stranger's hard face, hewn from stone.

No, I'm not sure I'll ever mistake them for one another.

The stranger says something to me, but for the life of me, I can't hear a single word that leaves his plush, pierced lips. Or maybe I can hear but choose not to comprehend. His words seem to go through one ear and then immediately drift out the other.

What's his name again? I could've sworn someone told me.

Fortunately, I don't have to think too long about it because Ethan heaves out a breath. "Emery, what are you—"

"I'm not talking to you, brother," Emery snipes, saying the word "brother" like it leaves a particularly foul taste in his mouth.

His face pinches, and he forces his gaze off of his brother and onto me. Intrigue lightens the green of his eyes. Intrigue...and something else. Something I can't quite name or even articulate. Whatever that elusive emotion is makes those damn butterflies flutter around once more in my stomach. I tell those butterflies to leave me the fuck alone and get a life.

I don't *get* fluttery butterflies.

Okay, that's not entirely true. What I meant to say is that I don't get damn fluttery butterflies for anyone but Grayson.

"It's...you," the new guy, Emery, breathes.

And then, to my utter astonishment, he leans

forward. His gold-flecked eyes consume the entirety of my vision as his nostrils flare.

"Are you...sniffing me?" Incredulity bleeds into my voice as I gape at him.

What the fuck?

Discreetly, I try to smell myself to see if I forgot to put on deodorant or perfume. But no. I smell as fresh as a damn daisy.

Is that why this weirdo's sniffing me? Because he likes my body wash or whatever?

"Emery," Ethan barks, his tone harsher than I've ever heard it.

Not that I've heard it a lot, mind you, but I have the distinct impression that it's rare to get a rise out of the smiling, somewhat timid twin.

Then again, maybe I'm wrong. There has to be a reason why Emery stares at Ethan like he's a piece of shit he accidentally stepped on and now can't scrape off of his boot.

"How long have you known?" Emery's voice borders on a growl as he glares at his brother.

How long has he known about what?

I feel as if I'm missing something, something important...

His hands curl into fists and then uncurl by his sides. The sudden hostility and aggression radiating from him have me instinctively backing up a step. Emery catches the movement, and his eyes widen.

"Emery," Ethan warns again.

Emery doesn't pull his attention from me even as he addresses his brother. "Fuck you, Ethan."

I clear my throat and try to think of what to say. "Um, obviously I arrived at a very bad time. It appears as if you two have...um...things you want to discuss." I gesture between the two of them with a flippant hand wave. "I can practically cut the tension between you two with a butter knife."

"There's no tension," Ethan insists at the same time Emery snaps, "He didn't tell me!"

Okay...

The two men glare at each other as I take another step back.

The halls are already beginning to thin out, and I still need to head to the office to retrieve whatever paperwork they have for me. Or fill out paperwork. Or something. Honestly, I have no idea why I'm even heading to the office in the first place.

"What's your name?" Emery turns to face me completely, as if trying to ignore that Ethan even exists.

That theory's only confirmed when Emery shifts his muscular body so he's nudging his twin out of the way.

"Isabella."

"But she likes to go by Izzy," Ethan interjects from just over Emery's shoulder, sounding more resigned than angry.

When I glance at his face, his lips are curved into a tight frown and his eyes are pained. A sort of wistful desperation distorts his features as he stares at his twin before he masks it.

Emery's jaw clenches at his brother's interruption before he nods once. "Izzy. That's a beautiful name."

He shoves his hands into his front pockets and offers me a charming smile—one so wicked and salacious that it's capable of setting me aflame.

It's also a practiced smile that looks all too natural on his face.

I can't help but wonder how many women he's flashed this particular smile at. That thought is completely irrational...as is the sudden burst of jealousy in my chest.

I shake my head to clear it of such outrageous thoughts before extending a hand in greeting. "And you must be Emery. I've heard a lot about you."

Emery's face falls instantly, a scowl replacing his cocky smirk. "What exactly has this asshole—?"

"You don't look like the type of guy who eats sand for lunch," I say innocently. "But maybe you add some seasoning to make it taste better?" He gapes at me, at a loss for words, so I continue. "I also can't see you as the type of man to pretend your basketball is your girlfriend and cuddle her at night. But then again, to each their own."

"What...?" His brows furrow together, but when he sees the blossoming smile on my face, they smooth out. "You're fucking with me, aren't you?"

"Maybe." I give him a gentle smile to show that I'm

only teasing. "But it truly is nice to meet you. I hate to cut this short—"

"You have to leave?" Emery asks briskly.

"I have to go to the office," I explain. "Paperwork."

I wrinkle my nose to show him just how much I *love* that prospect. Honestly, you would think that all of this would've been taken care of beforehand. This seems like a waste of time, if you ask me.

"Well, I can show you the way, if you want..." He bites down on his bottom lip and gives me a slow, lust-filled once-over.

God, this is the type of man who will drag me into a closet, rip down my pants, and fuck me against the janitor's shelf. And I can't say I would mind. Everything about him just screams "sex."

Ugh.

Damn hormones.

It's been only a few minutes at this new school, and already, I'm imagining having sex with not one but *two* of my classmates. Twins!

"Let the girl be, Emery." The cold voice drags my attention off of Emery and Ethan and towards the girl who has now joined us—the same girl Emery was talking to only moments before. "You don't need to add another notch to your bedpost. Honestly, I don't even understand how that thing is still standing. Haven't you chipped away enough of it yet?"

Emery's eyes flare with anger as the girl subtly

moves in between us and stops when she's directly in front of me.

She extends a hand with a sugary-sweet smile. "I'm Desiree. And you are...?"

I take a moment to survey her, my heart transforming into cement with every second that passes. I'm not one to compare myself to another girl, but with Desiree...it's really hard not to. She's beautiful. And she obviously knows Emery, if their interaction is anything to go by.

Her brown hair hangs in perfect ringlets just to her breasts, which strain against her white blouse. The skirt she wears stops in the middle of her thighs and shows long, slender legs I would kill for. Her makeup looks to have been applied by a professional. I can't spot a single blemish or blotch.

But I shove all of my insecurities away and force myself to smile, force myself to take a step closer with my own hand extended.

There's always this stigma in the world that women need to compete against each other. For men, for jobs, for respect. I refuse to be someone who puts another person down to make myself feel better. So what if Desiree is beauty personified? So what if she seems to be familiar with Emery and even Ethan, if her smug grin is any indication?

If this were a romantic comedy, the beautiful mean girl would tug my hair and warn me to stay away from her man. But this isn't a movie or a book. This is real life. And in real life, not every beautiful girl is a bully.

Keeping a smile firmly plastered on my face, I reach forward and clasp her hand with mine.

She immediately goes ramrod straight, her eyes widening before turning glazed. She teeters on her feet, and Emery instinctively reaches out a hand to steady her.

"Desiree?" he asks, his tone somewhere between alarm and annoyance. It's like he can't decide on which emotion to feel.

Desiree's grip in mine is almost painful. What the fuck is her problem? I try to pull away from her, try to free my hand from her iron-like grip, but she refuses to release me.

"Is she okay?" I ask Emery and Ethan. "Is she having a seizure or something?"

One of my old foster sisters had a seizure disorder. A lot of times, she would stare blankly into space, forgetting where she was and what she was doing until she came out of it.

"Do we need to get the nurse?" I'm not even sure if this school has a nurse, if I'm being honest. The majority of my previous public schools didn't. But I don't know what else to do or say.

"No. No nurse." Desiree's grip tightens on mine once more before she releases me. "I'm fine."

But she doesn't sound or even look fine. She's staring at me with a quizzical expression that has the hairs on the back of my neck standing at attention. That look... It's almost like she's blaming me for whatever the fuck just happened to her.

Which is crazy.

"Desiree..." Emery's voice is a warning as he glares down at her, but she ignores him and keeps her focus on me.

I shift underneath her scrutiny.

"Interesting," she says at last. "Very interesting."

She seems to be speaking more to herself than to any of us. Abruptly, she smiles, one that makes her eyes glimmer and somehow enhances her already ethereal beauty.

"I suppose I'll be seeing you around, Izzy." She wiggles her fingers in a wave before stepping around me.

Immediately, the two girls I noticed earlier, standing farther down the hall, move to join her, remaining a few steps behind her.

"Beast. Machine." Desiree directs the first insult at Emery and then the second at Ethan.

Without another word, she flounces away, her brown curls practically bobbing with every step she takes as if the strands have a life of their own.

I can't help but gape at the two brothers. "What the fuck was that about?"

Emery's jaw clenches. "No idea."

I can tell he's being honest.

Reluctantly, he pulls his gaze off of Desiree's retreating back and focuses on me once more. His nostrils flare a second time, and he inhales deeply, like he's trying to suck in my scent. A little weird, but who am I to judge?

Okay. I'm totally judging.

That was weird as shit.

"Do you want us to walk you to...?" Ethan begins tentatively, and I notice the way Emery stiffens at the word "we" leaving his twin's mouth.

I hurry to dismiss his words before an argument can brew. "Don't worry. I know where it is. Down there, right?"

I point farther down the hall, where glass-paneled windows peer into a large room.

"We can bring you," Ethan presses, just as the bell rings overhead.

Dammit. Now there's no way I'm not going to be late for my first period class. At least I have that with Ethan.

"Don't worry. I'll be fine. Save me a seat?" I flash Ethan a nervous smile.

His face brightens. "Of course."

"You have first hour with her?" Emery looks as if he's cracking a tooth with how tightly his jaw is clenched. "So you guys must've had a lot of time to go over your class schedules, huh?"

There's an accusation in his tone that I can't understand.

Ethan obviously does, though, because his face flames with what looks like shame.

"Emery..." he begins, his voice pleading.

Emery ignores him.

"Let me see your schedule," he says to me. When I simply stare at him, he pushes out his lips in a pout and bats his eyelashes. "Pretty, pretty please?"

"With a cherry on top?" I say, but I'm already pulling out my schedule and handing it to him.

He surprises the shit out of me by grabbing out his phone and snapping a picture of it before shoving his cell back into his pocket.

"I'll text you the classes we have together. Now I just need your number..." He waggles his eyebrows suggestively, and I can't help but laugh.

Why do I have a feeling that *this* is the real Emery? Not the broody man he seems to transform into whenever he talks to Ethan. But someone who's carefree and silly, if not a little flirty.

"Is this your way of getting every girl's number?" But fuck me, I can't help but recite it to him, watching his ringed fingers move across his phone's screen.

"Do you plan to steal my top-secret strategy for your own gain?" he asks seriously, not bothering to glance up from his phone.

"Maybe..."

Emery's smile abruptly fades as if something just occurred to him, and he turns towards Ethan with a quirked brow.

"Does Ashton and Reid also know her *schedule*…?" His lips pinch.

"No." Ethan's teeth grind together. "Not yet. I was planning on giving them her"—he flicks his gaze to me—"*schedule* at lunch."

"Interesting." Emery's eyes narrow before he focuses on me. A smile once again stamps itself onto his handsome face. "From just a glance, I know for sure we have lunch together, so if I don't see you earlier, then I'll see you then."

"You also have second period with her," Ethan points out. When Emery glares at him for speaking, Ethan flushes red and takes a step away. "You might have more, but I don't remember."

"Okay, okay. Text me your schedule or whatever. But I need to get to the office, and you guys need to get to class."

"So bossy." Emery places a hand over his chest in mock offense. "Is this how it's going to be when we enter a relationship?"

Those damn butterflies return with a vengeance, and I have to take pesticide to them to stop the irrational fluttery sensation in my stomach.

"What relationship?"

"The one where you fall desperately in love with me." He winks, and a burst of heat shoots down my spine.

I snort and roll my eyes, already stepping past him in the direction of the office. I don't bother to turn around as I call over my shoulder, "Maybe it's the one where *you* fall desperately in love with *me*."

I could be mistaken—I probably am—but I could've sworn I heard Emery mutter, "Probably," under his breath.

But when I turn around, all I see are the twins' backs.

Heading in opposite directions of each other without a word of goodbye.

Fourteen

IZZY

The fluttery sensation in my stomach refuses to dissipate, even after I step into the office. I have to put my hand over my belly in a futile attempt to...

To *what?* Beat the butterflies to death? Quell the rising nausea?

I can say with certainty that I've never had a crush before—outside of Grayson, at the very least. I've been to dozens of schools, and probably had just as many boyfriends and partners, but I can't remember ever having these so-called "butterflies." My hands have never turned damp with anxiety. And my heart has certainly never raced like it wanted to break free of my chest.

What is it about those twins that elicits such a reaction from me? Sure, they're good-looking, but I've met a lot of handsome men over the years. They're so different from each other, though. You would think I would like one more than the other, but—

I mentally shove all thoughts of Emery and Ethan to the back of my mind. Then, to ensure they won't creep back to the forefront unbidden, I erect a concrete wall between my current thoughts and them. I refuse to continue fantasizing about two guys I've only just met.

Talk about creepy.

I take a deep breath, fiddle with the strap of my backpack, and then step farther into the office.

It's like every other office I've seen throughout the years. A single desk rests in the very center of the room, which I assume belongs to the school's secretary. Right now, though, it's empty, though I see a mug of still-steaming coffee beside the computer. Behind the desk is a long hallway that more than likely branches out into smaller offices and meeting rooms. To the right of the desk is the principal's office—a Mrs. Hendricks— and to the left is the vice principal's office, though I'm unable to see that name plaque.

Mainly because a tall man is leaning against the wall beside the open doorway, watching me.

No, not a man.

A student. Probably a senior. He's certainly too young to work in the school, at least at first glance.

I try to ignore the feel of his gaze on me as I stand in front of the abandoned desk, shifting uncomfortably from foot to foot.

Where is the secretary? In a meeting? Should I knock on the principal's door? Should I sit in one of the chairs against the far wall and wait for her to return?

I settle on the latter, claiming a seat as far away from the man as possible and taking out the new phone Hale bought me. Already, there's a text blinking on the screen from an unknown number.

UNKNOWN

> We have third and fourth period together! Woot!

UNKNOWN

> This is Emery, btw.

UNKNOWN

> From the hallway.

UNKNOWN

> But of course, it's impossible to forget my handsome face.

This last text is followed up by a flurry of winky and heart emojis.

I stifle my laughter as I respond.

IZZY

> Huh. I think I know who you are. Are you that guy with the red mullet and beard that touches his ankles?

EMERY

Nah. My hair's actually white, and I
wear a robe and have a magic
wand.

IZZY

Dumbledore?

EMERY

Merlin, actually. But you seem to
know your wizards.

IZZY

This is a really random conversation.

EMERY

Random is my middle name.

EMERY

Actually, that's a lie. It's Micah. But
don't tell anyone that. It's a safely
guarded secret.

IZZY

Why would that be a secret? Micah
is a normal name. At least it's not
Leslie or Patricia or Anus or anything
like that.

EMERY

Ethan's middle name is Anus.

This time, I can't quite keep my snort in, though I try to smother it when I feel that whisper of a stare ghosting across my skin.

My phone dings again, indicating that Emery has sent another text message.

EMERY

I'm sure you figured out by now that
the two of us are related.

IZZY

Nooo. I never would've guessed. Are
you distant cousins?

EMERY

He's my fifth cousin twice removed.

IZZY

Good genes must run in the family,
then.

EMERY

Good genes, you say?

This text is proceeded by a flurry of jean GIFs.

EMERY

Am I mistaken, or are you trying to
hit on me, Iz? You want to get into
my jeans, don't you?

I roll my eyes, even as a tiny smile flutters at the corners of my lips.

I'm just about to reply to his text when a throat begins to clear obnoxiously from across the room.

I tense, my muscles locking tight, as I straighten in the chair. I don't even have to look to know he's still watching me.

"Why are you staring at me?" I finally explode, swiveling in the uncomfortable plastic chair to face him completely.

And oh my god.

What the fuck is it with the guys at this school? Is being sexy as sin a requirement for enrolling here?

The man looks as if he stepped off the pages of a *Peoples'* "Top 100 Sexiest Men Alive" article.

His dark hair is slightly spiked, but in a way that feels natural, not as if he spent time styling it. The color is slightly lighter than the dusting of stubble on his strong jaw. He wears a fitted, light-blue dress shirt that clings to his muscular figure and emphasizes his biceps and forearms. His shirt is tucked into a pair of khakis that look just as fucking good—if not better. I'm pretty sure ninety percent of the female population would cut off their right arm to be reincarnated as his pants. The firm line of his lips is juxtaposed by the twinkle in his eyes that suggests that he's about to get into trouble. Or maybe he's already in trouble.

Or maybe he simply *is* trouble.

The stranger folds his arms over his chest and surveys me.

When he doesn't immediately speak, I find myself filling the silence, my irritation at his blatant perusal thrumming through me. "What are you even doing here? Do you have a meeting too?"

Yes, Izzy. Because you're the office police. My god. Can you be any more of a weirdo?

His lips twitch in the makings of a smile. "Is that why you're here? Do you have a meeting? Or are you in trouble?" He tsks his tongue in a way that sounds almost mocking. "I haven't seen you around, which means you must be our new student. In trouble on your first day? Rough."

I roll my eyes at him. Of course the sexy guy is a jerk.

Aren't they all?

"I'm not in trouble," I snap, feeling unnaturally defensive. "I have some forms I need to fill out before I can start. I got an email telling me to come here before classes." As an afterthought, I add, "Can you stop staring at me like some sort of creep?"

His smirk broadens, transforming into what may be considered a smile if it wasn't all sharp edges and serrated blades, as he pushes away from the wall. Without a word, he stalks into the office and begins to rummage beneath the vice principal's desk.

My heart picks up speed as he returns, two soda cans in his hands. He tosses one to me with a sly wink, and I just barely catch it before it can whack me in the face.

I gape at him in stunned disbelief, but he simply shrugs a shoulder.

"What?" He feigns innocence. "I heard that the vice principal keeps a bunch of goodies in his office."

A part of me wants to throw the can back at his stupidly handsome face. But a tiny voice in my head screams, "That's assault, dipshit." I settle for shoving the soda in my backpack, hoping that no one will see it. The last thing I need is to get caught stealing from the vice principal on my first day of school—even if I wasn't the one who actually stole anything.

"What's your name?" the stranger asks, watching me with barely veiled amusement.

He resumes his position against the wall, his arms once again crossed over his chest as if he hasn't a care in the world.

"Why?" I quip. "So you can get me in trouble?"

"My name's Christian. Christian Montgomery. There. Now it's mutually assured destruction." He opens his own can of pop and takes a sip, staring at me over the rim. "Are you going to drink yours?" Lowering his voice to a conspiratorial whisper, he adds, "It might get a little fizzy rolling around in your backpack all day."

"Isabella," I reply after a moment, ignoring his comment about the soda.

"Like that chick from *Twilight*?"

I wrinkle my nose. "God, no. And don't even think about calling me Bella."

I once again glance at the secretary's desk, wondering where she is and when she'll return. I just want to sign whatever paperwork she has for me and get started on my day. And maybe a part of me wants to meet up with Ethan and Emery as well...

Nope. Bad brain.

No thoughts of Ethan or Emery allowed.

Desperate to distract myself, I blurt the first thing

that comes to mind. "Why are you here? Are you in trouble?"

Christian's eyebrows arch upwards, as if he's surprised by my boldness, before he grins.

"I actually have a meeting with the principal scheduled in a few minutes. If you must know." The last statement is said almost as an afterthought, dripping with so much sarcasm that an acerbic taste coats even *my* tongue.

I fold my arms over my chest. "Fair's fair, after all. You asked me, so I asked you."

"Isn't that middle school mentality?" He cocks his head to the side curiously. "You show me yours, and I'll show you mine?"

"I believe that's elementary school," I respond, watching as he takes another sip of his pop. "Speaking of elementary school...I can't believe you stole from the vice principal."

"I didn't know stealing was 'elementary school.'" His smile broadens, unveiling a row of perfectly straight and white teeth.

Damn him. Why does he have to look like he was plucked directly from a dental ad?

"What type of schools were you going to?" he asks.

An uneasy feeling settles in my stomach at his question—despite the fact he asked it rhetorically.

Ignoring his retort, I sit up straighter and say, "If you get in trouble, I'm not covering for you. I can't afford to get any disciplinary action on my first day of school."

The last thing I need is for Hale to believe me to be more trouble than I'm worth. I don't think I can survive being thrust back into the system again, forced to fend off wandering hands and sneaking food from the cabinets at night to stave off my rising hunger.

"Are you going to snitch on me?" Laughter dances in his eyes.

"Of course not," I snap. "Besides, I'm sort of an unintentional accomplice."

"I didn't know accomplices could be unintentional."

"Haven't you ever watched an episode of *Criminal Minds* or *SVU*?" I squint at him. "Accomplices can totally be unintentional."

Christian opens his mouth...but immediately snaps it shut when a door down the hall opens and a petite woman with graying hair and a kind smile hurries out. Her eyes widen when she sees me.

"Hello, dear. Can I help you?" She claims the vacated receptionist seat and takes a sip of her coffee.

"Um...yes." Instinctively, I flick my gaze to Christian, who continues watching me curiously from his spot against the wall. "I was told I needed to come here before my classes this morning."

I give her my name, and she tells me that there are a few forms my foster parents forgot to fill out. I'm to bring them home to have them looked over and signed before returning them tomorrow.

I take the freshly printed papers from her and shove them into my backpack just as the secretary's gaze finally flits to the man standing like a silent sentry beside me.

"Good morning, Mr. Montgomery." Her cheeks turn crimson, and she ducks her head with a lilting giggle, despite the fact she's old enough to be his mother.

Wait...Mr. Montgomery?

"Good morning, Olive," Christian greets, none of his cocky arrogance from earlier making an appearance in his tone. He sounds cordial and almost...respectful.

What the fuck?

I stare at Christian in disbelief as he backs into the office. I can tell he feels my gaze on him—his shoulders stiffen—but he doesn't turn to stare at me, keeping his attention pinned on Olive.

"Can you tell Mrs. Hendricks to meet me in my office as soon as she's done with her meeting?" Without bothering to wait for the secretary to respond, he begins to shut the office door—slowly enough for me to see the smirk playing at the edges of his lips.

It's only when the door is completely closed do I see the nameplate on the wall beside the office.

Mr. Montgomery.

Vice Principal.

Fuck.

Fifteen

IZZY

I can't stop thinking about the sexy vice principal, even as I head to my first period and take the empty seat beside Ethan.

Class is already in session, but thankfully, my teacher doesn't do more than give me a passing glance and a tiny nod of acknowledgment. I might've just died if she made me stand on a chair and introduce myself.

Who the fuck is Christian Montgomery? How is he the vice principal of a high school when he looks as if he just graduated himself? He looks to be twenty-five at the oldest. And why haven't I heard anything about him from the other students? Surely, they would gossip about the sexy staff member if he's been here a while... and even if he hasn't.

I make a mental note to ask Lissa about him as soon as I see her. If anyone were to know the details surrounding the elusive vice principal, it'd be her.

Shoving all thoughts of Mr. Montgomery out of my head, I focus on my first class of the day, grateful that the curriculum seems to be following a similar setup to the one at my old school. The last thing I need is to get behind on my first day of school. It's hard enough being the new kid. It's even harder being the new kid who's failing five of her classes.

Been there. Done that. Got the T-shirt.

I'm not dumb. Not at all, actually. But it's more difficult than one would think it'd be to transfer from school to school, all moving at different paces. One day, I would be studying molecular biology. The next, I would need to quickly brush up on the water properties of lakes. I probably try harder than any other student around, desperately trying not to fall too far behind.

I don't get the chance to talk to Ethan during our first class, though I can feel his penetrating gaze on me throughout the lesson. I will my cheeks not to burst into flames at the gentle caress of his gaze. I refuse to freaking blush.

When our teacher finally dismisses us, Ethan is at my table before I can even blink, an easy smile on his face as he fiddles with his glasses.

"You have AP Lit next period, right? With Ashton?"

"I don't know who this Ashton person is, but I do know Jake is in that class with me." I shove my textbook back into my bag and then stand, swinging my backpack over my shoulder in the process.

Ethan's hand is slightly extended, almost as if he wishes to take my bag from me, but when I quirk a brow at him, he casts me a sheepish smile and quickly lowers his arm.

"You remember where all the AP classes are, right?" He opens the door to the classroom for me and steps aside to let me pass.

Butterflies erupt in my stomach before I can squash them. "Second floor, correct?"

"Yeah. The Lit class should be on the right side of the hallway. I would take you there myself, but I have to get to gym class on the opposite side of the school." He rolls his eyes, but that easygoing smile never fades from his face.

"I'm lucky that I'm not required to take gym class this semester." I shudder dramatically. "Running and me? We don't get along too well."

Fighting and me, on the other hand...

But thinking of fighting always inevitably makes me think of Grayson, and that's something I refuse to do. I know I have no right whatsoever to be pissed at him—we're not together, and he's never shown any inclination that he wants to be more than just my friend—but jealousy and unrequited love are fickle things. They defy all logic and common sense, reverting you to a primordial cavewoman who bangs on her chest and screams, "MINE!"

"Yeah, I'm not the biggest fan of gym class either. I took it to have another class with Emery, but..." A frown overtakes his face as he rubs his hand through his messy golden locks. Just as quickly, he smiles, though it doesn't reach his eyes. "Anyway, you'll like AP Literature. I took it last year, and the teacher is hilarious. And my friend Ashton will be there too."

"You keep talking about this Ashton guy...and another one. What was his name again?"

"Reid." Ethan nervously fiddles with the straps of his backpack. "You'll meet him later today. I think." The last two words are said almost under his breath. Then louder, he adds, "Reid's a good man. Promise. It's not what you think."

I give him a quizzical look. "I don't think anything. I don't even know him."

"Yeah, well..." Once again, Ethan agitatedly runs his fingers through his hair, disrupting the strands even further. I'm beginning to believe that's a nervous habit of his. "Things with him are complicated, okay? And things aren't always as they seem."

"That's not ominous at all..." I chuckle and roll my eyes.

I make a mental note to search for Reid and Ashton in my next few classes, maybe introduce myself. But if they're as hot as the twins, I might just self-combust before I can even get a word in.

We stop walking at the stairwell, though it doesn't appear as if either one of us is in a hurry to get to our next class. Unlike my other schools that gave us only three minutes between class times, we have a solid ten minutes to traverse these halls. That's enough time to go to the bathroom, grab a drink from the cafeteria, and even talk to your friends. I feel almost spoiled, truly.

"Sorry. I don't mean to be weird." Ethan's nose crinkles in a way I shouldn't find adorable.

Nope. Most definitely not. Ugh. I blame my over-active libido and my long-suppressed hormones.

"It's just..." Whatever Ethan's about to say tapers off when his phone buzzes.

He flashes me an apologetic smile and then reaches into his pocket to retrieve his cell.

A frown distorts his handsome features.

"Is everything okay?" I lean my shoulder against the wall and cross my arms over my chest.

The halls are still pretty crowded—numerous groups are conversing against their lockers—but I want to head to my second period early to speak with the teacher and discuss my missed reading assignments.

Ethan's frown deepens, causing creases to manifest around both of his eyes. "Yeah." He tries for a smile, but it's forced. "It seems as if Ashton isn't actually going to be joining you today in class. And I don't think Emery and I will be in Chemistry today either." The ticking of his jaw momentarily commandeers my attention. "But we'll definitely meet you at lunch."

"Are you sure everything's okay?" I can't help but feel concerned for my new friend. What reason would he and his friends have to skip class in the middle of the day? Is that something they do often? Is something wrong? At the same time, I know it's not my place to press for answers. I don't know them. Not truly.

"Everything's perfectly fine," he rushes to reassure me, but I note that his voice is a little higher pitched than normal. Proof that he's lying? "But I need to go." He hesitates, though, staring at me as if he wishes to say something else. After a long moment, he heaves out a breath and says, "I'll see you at lunch."

Without another word, he hurries down the hallway, stealthily sidestepping students who dare walk into his path. I watch him go with no small amount of confusion.

What the fuck is going on?

Even as I think that, I tell myself it's not my problem.

But at the same time...why does it feel like it is?

I've just turned towards the doorway leading to the stairwell when an arm links with mine. I startle, my muscles tensing, as rose-scented perfume barrages me.

I glance to the side to see Desiree standing there, looking as meticulous and perfect as ever. She doesn't even acknowledge my presence as she tosses a strand of hair over her shoulder and begins to walk me up the metal staircase.

"Um..."

"We have second period together," Desiree says in lieu of explanation or greeting, her tone light and airy. "We need to hurry if we want to get a seat together."

Um...okay?

What the fuck?

Sixteen

ASHTON

I duck beneath the bright-yellow police tape and do a quick scan of my surroundings.

Father was right—this place is a dump. Calling it a shed is too generous of a term for the dilapidated, crumbling building barely able to hold two people, let alone two wolf shifters.

And a dead body.

My gaze homes in on the female sprawled on the ground, her body twisted at an unnatural angle.

She's naked, which makes the entire scene even more macabre and nauseating. I can clearly see the stab wound in the center of her chest, the hole surrounded by dry, crusted blood. Her mouth is open in a silent scream, one she'll no longer be able to release, and her vacant eyes are staring sightlessly at the ceiling above, where numerous holes riddle the vaulted roof.

Father's thinning lips are pursed as he stares down at the shifter dispassionately.

"What happened?" I ask, though I already know the answer to that question, even before he speaks.

"Hunters." The word is practically a growl, and it ripples through the air before settling on my tongue, chalky in flavor and tasting oddly of battery acid.

Bile scorches my throat as I crouch down beside the corpse and give her a slow once-over, searching for any clues my father may have missed. I inhale deeply, trying not to gag as the stench of blood and decay overwhelms me.

"She died a day ago," I conclude. My stomach weaves itself into a dozen tight knots.

"Yes," my father agrees in that cold, no-nonsense voice of his. "Anything else?"

I move around the body until I finally see the strange symbol painted onto the back of her neck—a single red X inside of a small circle.

The Hunters' symbol.

"Her name's Larissa," Father begins as I continue to scan the body and small shed. "She moved here a few weeks ago with her pack. They reported her missing late last night. Apparently, her last known location was an unofficial fight club run by a human."

"And how far away is the fight club from here?" I finally reach into my pockets and tug on a pair of gloves. Then, I move her blood-streaked hair away from her face so I can study her for injuries.

There are no bruises around her neck, indicating that her attacker didn't choke her. I wonder how he got the jump on her, then. Shifters are significantly stronger than any human, both male and female alike. It seems strange to me that someone would be able to overpower her.

"About fifteen miles to the north," Father tells me.

"So he must've brought her body here," I deduce. "Was she dead before or after she entered this shed?"

My question is aimed more at myself than at my father. I know he won't respond to me, even if he does know the answer.

Not when he's training me and my pack to take over for him.

There are over one hundred packs in the town, each one ranging from two members to ten, sometimes even more. Father is a part of the Council—a group of wolf shifters who maintain the peace between all of the varying packs. Originally, that position was held by my father, his Heart, and his packmates. But when my mother and my other fathers passed away...

I swallow around the razor blade that seems to have become lodged in my throat.

Shoving all thoughts of my parents to the back of my mind, I focus instead on the female before me. I've never met her before, but that doesn't mean her death doesn't hurt. Any loss of life stings like a bitch. I can't even imagine what her packmates must be going through. If I were to find my fated mate and lose her, I'd go insane.

I inhale yet again and squeeze my eyelids shut. After a moment, I open them and pierce my father with a look.

"She was moved here after death," I say at last.

The blood in the shed isn't fresh, and the stench of decay is nearly overwhelming.

My father's lips twitch, though they don't ever grow into a full-fledged smile. "Very good."

I straighten and follow my father out of the shed. Father gives a brief nod to the police officer on the scene—a fellow wolf shifter—before leading me towards the black SUV parked nearby.

The shed Larissa was found in is directly beside a large, nondescript farmhouse in the middle of nowhere. The couple who owns the house—a retired husband and wife in their late sixties—has been in Florida the last two months on an extended vacation. Obviously whoever stashed the body here knew that fact and hoped Larissa wouldn't be discovered for a few extra weeks. And the murderer might've gotten away with it if the gardener hadn't stopped by the shed to retrieve the hedge clippers he left behind.

"Isn't this the second person to be killed at this fighting ring?" I query as I fold my arms over my chest and stare at my father.

He gives a derisive snort. "Are you talking about

that human girl?" He shakes his head. "You know we don't worry about matters that involve the humans."

"You don't think they're related?" I furrow my brows, though I quickly try to straighten out my expression before he can notice, maintaining the apathetic mask I've perfected over the years.

Father told me that last night, a woman was found abandoned in a cornfield a few miles away from some sort of fight club with her neck snapped. When I asked if we were going to get involved, he laughed heartily and told me what he had just repeated now.

"We don't worry about matters that involve the humans."

I wonder if Father was too quick to dismiss the connection.

Two women killed on the same night at the same location? One human and one shifter? I don't normally believe in coincidences, only facts, but this is too strange for me to dismiss.

Of course, I don't dare voice my thoughts out loud. I may be training to take over my father's position on the esteemed Council, but I'm not in control yet. He'll beat me black and blue if I dare to contradict him, especially in front of his so-called "inferiors."

Father opens his mouth to respond to my question but immediately snaps it shut when a bright-orange Volkswagen barrels down the dirt driveway and squeals to a stop beside my father's SUV.

Father's lips purse as if he just ate something sour.

"Matthew," he greets as the driver's side door opens and a tall, balding man steps out.

As always, the twins' father wears a bright smile that causes the skin around his eyes to crinkle. His orange shirt is the exact same color as his car and looks almost tacky when matched with his black jeans.

Ethan and Emery file out of the car as well and move to stand beside their father.

"Gregor! How are you, my dear friend?" Matthew exclaims, leaning forward to pat my father on the shoulder.

Father stiffens and takes a minute step away from the jovial man.

"I don't think this is the time to play catch-up, do you?" Father asks stiffly, seemingly unmoved by the brilliant smile Matthew continues to aim his way.

"Ah. Yes. Of course." He clears his throat. "Do you have the details of the case?"

When my other fathers and mother died, Matthew and his pack were appointed temporary Council members. They had been the second most powerful pack in the area—after my parents' pack—and quickly filled the void my parents' deaths left behind.

Father, understandably, was infuriated by this change. Granted, he knew he couldn't rule alone, but he had never liked Matthew. They're too...different to ever see eye to eye on things. Not only are they polar opposites in appearance—Matthew has blond hair while Father's is as black as night; Matthew is tan while

Father is dark-skinned; Matthew is stocky while Father is lean—but they also have completely different viewpoints on how the wolf community should behave.

Father believes shifters should remain isolated from the humans.

Matthew thinks they should acclimate with them.

Father believes shifters are the superior species.

Matthew thinks they are both equal.

It's an intense tug-of-war whenever they are together.

There's never been any doubt, however, that my pack will rule the Council as soon as we graduate high school. We're the most powerful group of wolf shifters by far, even without a Heart to ground us. And now that the majority of shifters believe that we're going to take Desiree as a mate...

I shudder at just the reminder.

"Is Reid here?" Ethan whispers, sidling up beside me.

I frown. "No."

Not that I'm surprised. Reid would rather cut his own foot off than take part in this political game—even when this political game involves stopping murderous Hunters hellbent on destroying everything we've ever known.

"He wasn't at school either," Emery says from my other side, keeping his voice low.

"He's been skipping more and more often," Ethan says.

Shared worry for our brother permeates the air between us.

None of us like to discuss what happened to Reid, though the truth of it dangles above all of our heads like a guillotine just waiting to drop. I remember my best friend before everything went to hell—he had been vibrant and full of life, flirty and energetic, caring and funny.

And because of one scorned woman—and a pissed-off brother—all of that changed. The man standing in Reid's place is barely recognizable.

"I'll give him a call," I murmur, already sifting through the various tools I can use to either bribe or blackmail him to attend his afternoon classes.

"There's actually something we need to discuss with the two of you..." Ethan begins anxiously, but before he can finish his sentence, Father jerks his chin towards me haughtily.

"Ashton, why don't you discuss the case with Officer Lenny." He nods towards a tall, skinny man with bright-red hair and a goatee. "See if you can collect footage from the night Larissa was murdered."

"Yes, sir," I respond immediately, nodding.

With one last helpless glance at the twins, I go to do my father's bidding.

As always.

Seventeen

IZZY

Desiree, apparently, has second hour AP Literature and third hour Chemistry with me. She practically drags me from room to room, garnering more than a few stares along the way. Evidently, Desiree doesn't normally adopt anyone as a friend, hence the constant gawking from other students.

Now I just need to figure out *why* she decided to kidnap me...

We enter our third period class, and I look around anxiously, hoping to catch a glimpse of the twins. My heart sinks when I don't spot either of them.

"They're still gone," Desiree murmurs, as if she somehow has sensed the direction of my thoughts. She tosses a strand of perfectly curled hair over her shoulder. "But they'll probably be back by lunch."

Jealousy momentarily pierces my chest at how casually Desiree talks about the twins.

As if she knows them.

As if she's aware of everything they do and say.

The shock of such an irrational emotion makes me stumble a few steps forward. I bring a hand to my chest and begin to rub at the skin there, trying to will my rampant heartbeat back under control.

What the fuck?

I'm not the type of girl to get jealous, especially concerning guys I barely know. Grayson is the one and only exception I have to the whole "jealousy" rule, but in my defense, I've been in love with that fuck face for years now.

Desiree's watching me with unencumbered amusement, her eyes sparkling as if she's in on a secret that I don't yet know.

"We've already chosen our lab partners for the semester, but maybe the teacher will allow you to work with me and Mimi." She jerks her chin towards one of the beautiful girls I noticed before.

Mimi has long, cascading blonde hair that's so straight, I half wonder if she spends hours flat ironing it. There's not a single strand out of place. The gold is highlighted by white streaks that appear entirely natural—no hair dye to be seen.

She flashes a bright smile as soon as she sees us and moves to stand.

"Desie!" She waves enthusiastically before turning

her smile towards me. It's warm and surprisingly genuine on her pretty face.

I don't know what I expected when Dec and Jake referred to Desiree and her friends as the Queen Bees of the school, but it wasn't this. Aren't the popular girls usually bitchy bullies?

I've been reading way too many romance books.

"You must be Izzy," Mimi continues in her lilting, high-pitched voice. She throws her arms around me before I can say anything, bombarding me with her sugary-sweet perfume. "I'm Madeline, but everyone calls me Mimi." She pulls away to survey my face, and her smile broadens, unveiling perfect dimples on each of her cheeks. "You're so pretty!"

"Mimi, curb the enthusiasm," Desiree says dryly, but I hear the undercurrent of amusement and affection in her voice.

Mimi's cheeks pinken. "Sorry." She ducks her head forward until her shiny, straight hair curtains her face from view. "I just get a little excited sometimes."

I laugh softly. For some reason, I want to put this woman at ease. "You would get along great with my new foster sister. You guys are both..." I struggle to find an adequate word.

Mimi's head pops up, and she offers me a megawatt smile. "Awesome?"

Desiree snorts. "Really, Mims? Awesome? That's the word you choose to use?"

"What's wrong with awesome?" Mimi's lips push out in a teasing pout.

"It just sounds kind of...childish, you know? No one uses the word awesome anymore."

"How about on fleek?" Mimi winks conspiratori- ally. "Is that better?"

Desiree gives a full-body shudder. "I will disown you as my friend if you refer to yourself as that."

"Rad? Can I call myself rad?"

"No. That's not allowed either."

"Hot stuff?"

"Mimi, do you want to leave this classroom friend- less?" Desiree pops her hip out to the side and flutters her lashes innocently.

Mimi laughs out loud—the noise drawing atten- tion from more than one guy in the classroom—before turning towards me with a wink.

"You see what I have to deal with?" She playfully grabs my arm and pulls me away from Desiree. "Now, go ask Mr. Holter if you can be lab partners with me and Des." She gives the middle of my back a firm push that has me staggering forward a few steps. "Go!"

I chuckle wanly and go to do as she instructed. Yet my gaze can't help but flit to an empty table near the back of the room. For some inexplicable reason, I know this table is used by Ethan and Emery.

The throbbing in my heart intensifies, echoing between my ears and drowning out all other sounds, but I force my gaze away and step to the front of the classroom.

Mr. Holter glances up from the textbook he's currently skimming, one of his gray brows arched beneath his wire-framed glasses. He stares at me blankly, as if he doesn't realize I'm the new student in his class but also has no idea who I am.

"May I help you?"

"Hi." I fiddle with the strap of my backpack. "I'm the new student. Isabella. Izzy. Um…I wanted to ask you—"

"Oh right." He waves a hand in the air dismissively, cutting off my words.

I immediately clamp my lips together as he turns towards his computer and begins to type something in. A second later, the printer behind him rumbles to life, and he slides his chair backwards to grab the freshly printed sheet.

"Here are the chapters you missed so far," he says without preamble, handing both the paper and the textbook to me.

I actually stagger under the weight of the damn thing.

Do we have an additional textbook to the one I picked up earlier? Fuck.

"Okay…?"

"I expect you to do the reading on your own time and catch up enough to be able to take a test over the chapters you missed by next Friday."

"Next Friday?" My voice comes out a little higher pitched than I would've liked.

Mr. Holter doesn't even blink at my obvious distress. "You'll have to make up the labs you missed after school. Again, on your own time. I'll be here for an hour every day after the bell rings, but you'll need to schedule your makeup labs ahead of time."

He absently scratches at the whiskers on his chin, as if he's wondering if he forgot to mention anything. After a moment, he snaps his fingers together and jerks his chin towards a lab table near the front of the classroom. "You'll be partnered with Ansel for the remainder of the semester, as he is the only student here who doesn't have a lab partner."

"Um..."

Mr. Holter reclines in his seat and steeples his fingers together on his chest. "Now, if you don't mind, Ms. Isabella, I have a class to teach."

"Yeah. Of course. Yup." I wince inwardly when I realize that the entire class has bore witness to our awkward exchange.

Desiree and Mimi flash me sympathetic smiles. Well, Mimi's smile is sympathetic. Desiree is simply hurling daggers with her eyes at the back of a stranger's head.

Correction.

My new lab partner's head.

What's his name again? Ansel? Why does that name sound so damn familiar?

As I move through the aisle to claim my seat, I can't help but study him out of the corner of my eye. My breath actually catches in my throat, trapped there as if it's been vacuumed up.

My god.

Is it a rule that all of the men at this school have to be insanely good-looking? No, that can't be a requirement. The kid directly behind Ansel isn't going to be *America's Next Top Model*, if you know what I mean.

But Ansel...

To say he's been chiseled to perfection is not an understatement in the slightest. His face holds a perfect symmetry I don't think I've ever seen before, not even in models. His hazel eyes are framed by thick, dark lashes that could be on the front page of any makeup magazine. Light-brown hair, artfully tousled in a way that appears both immaculate and messy, hangs in loose curls at the top of his head. He doesn't wear glasses like Ethan does, but he's dressed in a tight sweater, brown khakis, and polished loafers—the epitome of a nerd if I've ever seen one.

A sexy, mouth-watering nerd...

But then I realize he's glaring at me with almost as much fury as Emery glared at Ethan.

"Are you just going to stand there ogling me, or are you going to take your seat?" he snaps. His voice is harsh and succulent, a bark of words that wheedles its way down my spine.

Instantly, my cheeks flush, even as indignation burns like hot coals in my stomach.

What the fuck is his problem?

Gritting my teeth together—and ignoring the chuckles of the classmates who overheard Ansel's comment—I claim the seat beside him.

Ansel immediately inches away from me on his stool as if he believes I have cooties or some shit.

Good fucking grief. Is he trying to pretend he's Edward Cullen sniffing my blood? I half expect him to inhale obnoxiously and then immediately clamp his hand over his nose to block out my scent.

But he doesn't do that. He simply remains as far away from me as the table will allow and focuses intently on Mr. Holter as the teacher wastes no time diving into the next lesson.

I push all thoughts of Ansel to the back of my mind as I take careful notes on the lesson. Chemistry has never been my strongest subject, but I'm hoping the chapters I missed will coincide with the ones I took in my old school. Fingers crossed, or I'll be shit out of luck.

Mr. Holter dismisses us fifteen minutes before class ends to work on homework or chat quietly amongst ourselves. The grumpy teacher may be a hard-ass, but I'm beginning to believe he may just become my favorite teacher at this school.

I look over the reading assignments he gave me and begin to consider a course of action.

If I can read two chapters today and two tomorrow, then that will give me over a week to make sure I understand the material before the test—

"If you think you can cheat off of me to get an A, you'll be wrong." Ansel's curt voice shatters my concentration like the crack of a whip.

I straighten in confusion and turn to glance at him, only to see his head lowered over one of his assignments. It appears to be Chemistry...but not from our current chapter. Is he really five chapters *ahead* of the class?

Then his words register, and I blink at him belatedly.

"Excuse me?"

His upper lip peels away from his teeth, and he quirks one perfect eyebrow, though he never looks up from his textbook. "I'm not going to allow you to hold my coattail in this class. If you want to pass, you'll have to do the work yourself."

What the fuck?

Anger bubbles in my stomach, white-hot and blistering, but Ansel continues on before I can get a word out.

"But you don't have to worry about partner projects," he continues in his slow, succulent voice. He finally pulls his attention off of his homework assignment to glare at me in disgust. "I'll do it. The last thing I need is for you to fuck things up and ruin my GPA."

"Excuse me?" I stare at him in disbelief, unable to

believe the audacity of this guy. "Did you just call me stupid?"

"Did you hear that word leave my mouth?" He rolls his eyes as if I'm being ridiculous.

Fucking asshole.

Why do all the pretty ones have to be raging dicks?

"It was heavily implied," I snap.

"Ahhh. So you're capable of reading between the lines." He taps his pencil against the edge of the lab table absently. "At least I know you won't be failing your English class."

What. The. Fuck?

My bloodstream sizzles. I suddenly want nothing more than to slam his stupid, perfect face against the table and make it not so perfect anymore. I wonder if he'll still be the pretty boy with broken teeth and a nose gushing blood.

"What the hell is your problem?" I hiss, trying my hardest not to raise my voice in case I'll be overheard.

He scoffs and ignores me, focusing back on his work.

For the longest time, I don't think he's going to answer me. I've just returned to my own assignments when his cruel voice reverberates through the room, loud enough that I wouldn't be surprised if the entire class hears him.

"I know exactly what you foster children are like." Disgust taints each word he says. He may have a beautiful voice…if it wasn't currently dripping in malice. "You always take things that don't belong to you." He sniffs and then adds, "And I'm sure all of that bouncing around doesn't make you the sharpest tool in the shed, either. Have you ever even passed a grade?"

Shame burns my cheeks, even as indignation ripples through me, settling on my tongue. I want to scream at the jackass, tell him to take his assumptions and shove them up his ass, but the bell rings before I can get a word out.

Ansel gracefully slides from the stool, shoves his journal, homework, and textbook into his bag, and then hurries out the door. I'm left gaping after him, unsure if I imagined the entire interaction.

But then Desiree and Mimi are there, the latter staring at me in sympathy while the former glares holes into the retreating asshole's back.

"We should've warned you about Ansel." Mimi sounds as if she's on the verge of tears. "But he hasn't had a lab partner in all the years I've known him, so I just assumed you wouldn't get paired up with him."

"What the fuck is his problem?" I murmur, aggressively shoving my own textbook into my bag.

Desiree cants her head to the side and studies the door Ansel exited out of with a curious expression. "Do you want me to kill him?"

"What?" I gape at her.

She blinks at me innocently. "What?" Then she

flashes a bright smile, links her arm with mine, and drags me out the door. "Come on. I'm fucking starving. We can discuss Ansel's painful demise at a different time, okay?"

Eighteen

IZZY

My stomach is growling by the time I enter the cafeteria.

It's crowded—much more so than it was this morning—and the line to the buffet twines around the perimeter of the room before exiting out one of the far doors.

As soon as we enter, Desiree and Mimi are pulled into a conversation with a group of burly football players. Mimi attempts to drag me along with them, but I stealthily move out of her reach and jerk my chin towards the long cafeteria line.

Food or hot guys? There's no contest.

Food for the win.

Unlike my previous schools, which had a thirty-minute lunch break, this school gives students forty-five minutes to get their food and eat. Which is fucking amazing, considering the fact that it takes me over twenty minutes just to get to the front of the line.

Note to future self—pack a lunch.

Once my tray is piled high with a salad, a piece of greasy pizza, sliced pears, and a cookie, I maneuver the sporadically placed tables and mingling students until I see a familiar blond head.

Jake.

He sits with a few of his football friends. One of the guys I recognize as Dec from this morning, but the other is a stranger.

Jake looks up when I slam my tray down beside him and offers me a smile. It causes the skin around his eyes to crinkle.

"Hey, new girl," he greets, scooting across the bench to make more room for me.

I notice that, unlike me, he packed a lunch today—a sandwich, an apple, and a bag of chips.

"You should've told me to pack a lunch," I say accusingly, wagging my fingers at his half-eaten food. "That line was ridiculous."

He snorts and takes another bite of his sandwich. "It's better to learn from experience. What's the saying? Better to learn and let live than to never live at all?"

To emphasize his point, he grabs a chip and tosses it at my face. It hits my forehead before dropping to the tray.

"Real mature," I say, picking off a pepperoni...and

then flicking it at his cheek. "And I never heard that saying in my life."

"You're just not as cultured as me." Jake hefts his chin into the air in mock superiority, seemingly unconcerned with the sauce now sticking to his skin.

The man I haven't been introduced to yet chuckles. "I like this one, Jake. Make sure to keep her."

Jake actually looks appalled by his friend's suggestion. "We're not together." His nose wrinkles like the idea of us hooking up actually repulses him.

I can't say I disagree. Jake is sweet, funny, and handsome, but I don't get that self-professed *spark* whenever I look at him. My feelings for him are strictly platonic, and I'm relieved to know he feels the same way.

"She's my new foster sister."

"Kinky." The stranger winks at Jake before turning towards me.

He's handsome, I suppose, with light-brown hair styled in spikes and chocolate eyes, but there's something about him that makes me uneasy. I can't put my finger on what it is.

"So if you're not dating that asshole, does that mean you're single?"

"Dude!" Jake throws a chip at the man's face with way more force than he did to me. "Knock it off."

"I was just teasing." The man flashes his perfectly white teeth at first Jake and then me. My skin instantly crawls. "I'm Kain, by the way."

"Izzy." I offer him an awkward, tight-lipped smile.

God, I don't know what it is about him that has ice skating down my spine. He seems nice enough, if not a little flirty, so there's no reason for my instinctive reaction to his presence.

Yet a tiny voice in the back of my head warns me to stay clear of him.

"Now that Kain has finished making a fool of himself..." Dec leans forward conspiratorially, his garnet hair flopping in front of his face and obscuring one of his eyes from view. He flashes me a boyish grin.

Like with Jake, I don't feel any sexual attraction towards him, but I also don't want to crawl out of my skin the way I do around Kain.

"Is it true that you befriended Desiree and her minions?" Dec asks.

I notice that Jake has gone very, very still beside me. Red climbs up his neck and settles in his cheeks, and he suddenly seems preoccupied with the food on his plate.

"Minions make it sound as if she's some sort of evil villain," I point out with a snort.

For some reason, I feel protective of the girl. She was one of the few people who has gone out of her way to befriend me since I arrived here. I don't understand why everyone is acting like she's the devil herself.

"If the shoe fits..." Kain murmurs.

Annoyance briefly flares inside of me. "She's been nothing but kind to me since I arrived."

"Probably because she wants something from you."

Kain seems unperturbed or oblivious to my ire. He stabs at his spaghetti with a little more aggression than necessary. "Trust me. You'll want to stay as far away from Desiree and her minions as possible. Come to think of it...stay away from all of her companions as well, including those damn twins people saw you talking to earlier today."

What the hell?

Is he stalking me or something?

Anger bubbles inside of me, white-hot and searing.

"Mimi's nice enough, but she doesn't have a brain to think for herself." Dec chuckles at his own joke, even as I internally fume. "And Emilia is just..." He struggles to find an adequate description.

"Scary," Kain finishes around a mouthful of pasta.

Dec nods seriously. "Yeah. Scary."

"But she has the best tits." Kain lifts his hands in the air and pantomimes squeezing two breasts. "I would love to see those things bounce while I fuck her."

Dec looks a little uncomfortable with the turn this conversation has gone. "Doesn't she like girls?"

"So?" Kain lifts an eyebrow sardonically. "Once she has a taste of my cock, she'll never want to go back to pussy." He licks his lips exaggeratedly. "I couldn't stop staring at her nipples when we had that swimming unit in gym class last year. They were so hard, and I just wanted to bite down—"

"You guys are being real dicks, you know that?" I snap, my frayed nerves finally snapping.

I don't know Desiree and Mimi that well, and I never even met Emilia, but I hate the way these guys are talking about them. It's condescending and rude and so fucking infuriating that I want to stab them with my plastic fork.

"Knock it off, guys," Jake agrees, finally lifting his head from his food. His eyes blaze with an emotion I can't quite name. "Izzy's right. You guys are being dicks."

"At least we're not *thinking* with our dick," Kain snaps back, which I find fucking ironic for him to say, considering he spent the last few minutes talking about some girl's breasts. "Speaking of dicks..."

His gaze homes in on something—or *someone* —over my shoulder, and his scowl deepens.

I follow the direction of his stare to see two familiar men walking towards us.

Ethan and Emery.

My heart skips a beat.

Behind them stands a man I never met before but who instantly makes my palms slick with sweat. As if he can feel the burn of my stare, the new guy's gaze focuses on me unerringly, his brows lifting in surprise.

Like Ethan and Emery, this guy is insanely good-looking, but unlike the twins, I wouldn't describe him as handsome or even pretty. His features are too rugged for such a descriptor.

He has dark-brown skin and tightly coiled black hair cut close to his scalp. His eyes, at first glance, are an unassuming shade of brown, but on closer inspection, I see specks of gold in those mesmerizing orbs. He's shorter than the twins but broader, his muscles compacted and chiseled beneath his dress shirt. Despite his smaller stature, he carries with him an aura of superiority and dominance that has heat rushing through my veins.

Aura of superiority and dominance?

Where the hell did that thought come from?

"It looks like Desiree's boy toys discovered we were talking about the Queen Bee," Kain murmurs with a chuckle.

His words have me spinning back around to face him.

"Boy toys?" For some inexplicable reason, the thought of any of those men with Desiree makes me feel sick to my stomach. It's a completely irrational reaction to three virtual strangers, yet one I feel regardless.

It seems as if I've been plagued by irrational reactions since I first arrived on campus today.

"Don't worry," a sultry voice murmurs from beside me. Desiree stands directly behind Jake with her hip cocked to the side and her blistering glare fixed on Kain's face. "Those three are *not* my boy toys."

Kain pulls his lip away from his teeth in what I

would almost describe as a snarl. "But you want them to be."

"You don't know what I want," Desiree replies flippantly before dismissing him without a backwards glance.

I notice, somewhat belatedly, that her hand is on Jake's shoulder, the touch almost absent-minded. She doesn't seem to notice she's even doing it.

But Jake surely *does* notice if his crimson face and rapidly blinking eyes are any indication.

"I would ask if you wanted to sit by me, Mimi, and Emilia," Desiree says to me, nodding her chin towards a table on the opposite end of the room.

Mimi and another girl sit there, deep in discussion. There are a few other people at the table—boys and girls alike—but I can't put names to faces yet.

"But I have a feeling *your* boy toys won't like it." A mischievous smirk curls up her lips.

I choke on my sip of water. "*My* boy toys?"

I glance at Jake in horror, who looks as if he wants the ground to open up and swallow him whole. What is up with people thinking I'm dating Jake? No offense to him...but eww.

"I'm not dating anyone at the table." And I don't *want* to date anyone at the table, though I don't say that part out loud.

Desiree's grin only broadens. "I'm not talking about the guys at the table." She flicks her gaze over my shoulder before refocusing on me, her eyes sparking with amusement. "See you later, Iz!" She waggles her fingers at me before sashaying back to her friends.

It's only then that I sense a presence behind me, the heat from his body burning through my sweater and warming me from the inside out. Lava burns in my lower belly before branching outwards in every direction.

What the fuck?

And then, behind me, comes a low, rumbly voice that makes my pulse spike and my throat close.

"*Mine.*"

Nineteen

IZZY

*M*ine?

What the fuck?

Tension thrums through my body like an electrical storm has just been unleashed, weighing down my muscles and causing my shoulders to stiffen. I can practically feel the heat from this stranger permeating the air around us and seeping into my skin.

"Umm... What he meant was...um..." Ethan moves to stand in front of me, agitatedly forking his fingers through his golden hair. He flicks his gaze from me to the stranger at my back and then back to me once more.

Emery moves to stand beside his twin with a sardonic smirk on his lips and his hands tucked into his front pockets. He bleeds nonchalance and arrogance, but there's a certain tightness to his jaw that belies his easy-going demeanor.

"What my eloquent little brother meant to say was that Ashton here thought that you were eating his lunch." Emery tsks his tongue disapprovingly. "And my friend is super protective and possessive of his lunch."

What the fuck?

His *lunch*?

I exchange a glance with Jake, who looks just as confused as I do. His brows are scrunched together, and his eyes are comically wide.

"Well, this is an interesting development." Kain folds his muscular arms over his chest and grins like the cat that ate the canary.

It's a smile that makes me decidedly uneasy. Then again, *everything* about Kain makes me uneasy.

"Fuck off, Kain," Emery growls, his cocky smirk momentarily fading, replaced by something infinitely darker. Dangerous. It transforms his angelic features entirely, making him almost unrecognizable.

Just as quickly, the darkness shrouding his face disperses, and while it doesn't lighten entirely, he no longer looks all "doom and gloom."

"How does Desiree feel about Ashton's...lunch?" Kain mocks, though I don't understand what, exactly, he's making fun of.

Still, everything he says is rubbing me the wrong way, and it infuriates me that I have no idea *why*.

What the hell am I missing?

And why do I have the irresistible urge to slap Kain across the face?

Jake must feel the same way I do because his eyes harden, the blue frosting over. "You're being such a jackass today. Just fucking leave, Kain."

Kain's devious smirk only broadens as he stands and reaches for his lunch. His eyes home in on me like two heat-seeking missiles. Then he winks.

And I swear I hear three growls reverberating through the cafeteria, audible even over all of the chatter and laughter coming from the other students.

"See you at practice, Jake. Dec. Emery. Ashton." He nods his chin at each man individually, skipping over Ethan—probably because Ethan isn't on the football team.

Kain walks away with a swagger to his steps that makes my eye twitch.

Why does he irritate me so damn much?

Jake watches his friend's retreating back before turning towards me and wincing.

"I'm sorry about..." He gesticulates wildly but doesn't finish his sentence.

Dec pipes up. "He's sorry Kain's a dick."

Jake nods decisively. "Yeah. That."

"What's his deal anyway?" I don't know who I'm directing the question at, but surprisingly, it's the stranger—Ashton—who answers.

He steps in front of me with a sort of lethal grace best reserved for predators in the wild.

It's the man I noticed before—the handsome man with dark skin, tightly curled hair, and golden-flecked eyes. This close, I can see the hardness of his jaw, almost as if he's constantly clenching it, and the keen intelligence radiating from his eyes. His no-nonsense stare examines me from head to toe, and I wonder what he's thinking.

Whatever it is has his jaw clenching even tighter—a feat I didn't think was possible. A vein in his temple pulsates.

"Jealousy," he answers gruffly, his eyes never leaving my own. "Isn't that what makes everyone a jackass nowadays?"

Emery takes over the conversation, coming to stand beside his friend. "Kain is our...neighbor, so to speak. And we've never really gotten along with him and his two brothers."

Ethan stands on Ashton's other side. "The three of us and Reid—who I don't think you met yet—have been friends for years. And Kain and his brothers always resented our friendship. Now that his brothers have graduated and left the school, Kain feels the need to overcompensate by being a complete ass to everyone."

He shifts slightly, and I see that he changed his clothes from when I last saw him. He now wears a *Legends of Zelda* T-shirt that clings to his muscular frame. Or maybe he just took off his sweatshirt. I try to remember what he had on before, but my mind comes up blank. I was a little too focused on...well...every-thing else.

Including his beautiful face.

Errr...not beautiful. Handsome.

Sexy?

Stop being a weirdo, Iz!

"Well..." I scratch at the back of my neck, suddenly unsure of what to say or do next.

I feel as if everyone in the cafeteria is staring at us, varying expressions of shock and disbelief on their faces. Not that I'm necessarily surprised—all three of these men have a magnetism that pulls people towards them.

And from what I gathered so far, they're not the type to befriend any new students. They seem to stick to themselves.

"I'm starving!" Emery groans dramatically and flops himself into the seat beside Dec, opposite me.

I flash him a grateful look, and he winks in response, causing my body to flush with heat.

"Somebody feed me before I perish," he says.

Ethan quickly claims the seat on the opposite side of me and also offers me a quick smile. Unlike Emery's, this one is tentative and almost shy, not a hint of arro-gance to be seen.

The third man, Ashton, remains standing, his jaw still clenched and his eyes narrowed on my face. The intensity of his glare makes me shift from side to side anxiously.

"Umm...did you want some of my food?" I ask, inwardly cringing at how awkward I sound.

Ashton blinks at me once, twice, three times...and then seems to come out of whatever trance that has gripped him. He shakes his head and moves closer, a hand extended.

"I apologize for my rudeness." He has a deep, almost raspy voice. It rumbles through me with the force of an earthquake. "I'm not usually so...laconic. My name is Ashton. And you are...?"

"Izzy." I give his hand a firm shake, trying to ignore the pinpricks of heat that migrate from where we connect. It isn't an unpleasant sensation by any means but still shocking enough to elicit a gasp from me.

Ashton pulls his hand away instantly, his lips firming.

Emery chuckles wanly. "I swear this school is full of static. I'm constantly getting shocked."

Jake, who has been mostly silent until now, gives his friend a bemused look before he forces a smile on his face. I don't know Jake that well yet, but I've determined he's a pretty chill guy, always willing to go with the flow. Not a lot seems to perturb him.

My foster brother pulls Emery and Dec into a conversation about the upcoming football game against a team called the Vipers. The two of them try to ask Ashton, who has finally sat down beside Emery, for his opinions—he must be a football player too—but Ashton doesn't answer.

He just keeps staring.

At me.

His features are utterly blank, almost impassive, as he regards me. He's no longer clenching his jaw, but there's a calculating glint to his dark gaze that makes me uneasy. It's not the same uneasy feeling I have around Kain. It's more as if I'm being sized up and rated, and I have to wonder if he finds me...lacking.

I've never been a self-conscious person before, but just then, I want to burrow my head in the sand and disappear. His penetrating gaze seems to see too much yet not enough.

It unnerves me.

And then Ashton speaks, his low, growly voice slashing through the air like the crack of a whip. His words cut Jake, Dec, and Emery's conversation off in mid-sentence.

"Why are you here, Izzy?" Ashton's eyes narrow nearly imperceptibly as he studies my face.

I blanch. "Excuse me?"

"Why are you here?" he repeats.

"Dude!" Ethan hisses, sounding mortified. His face has gone a dark shade of crimson.

"Ash..." Emery's voice holds a hint of warning and reproach.

"I'm a foster child," I say with a forced neutrality. What the hell is this dude's problem? "My newest placement is in this school district."

His lips thin further. "And this is the first time you've ever been here before?"

I try to chuckle, but the noise comes out harsh and guarded. I'm not sure if Ashton is simply trying to get to know me—and going about it in a way that borders on creepy—or if he's accusing me of something. It almost sounds like the latter, which is absolutely ridiculous. What could he possibly be accusing me of? I've never met him before in my life.

"First time," I say. "Is there anything else you want to know? My middle name? Address? Bra size?"

"Okay, enough with your weird-ass interrogation." Jake slings an arm over my shoulder, pulling me closer against his side. "You're scaring the new girl. She's going to think we're weird or something." He places his lips by my ear. "They're weird. I'm not. Obviously."

Across from me, Ashton and Emery go very, very still. Emery's eyes are fixated on where Jake's arm touches my shoulder, and Ashton's jaw has once again resumed its clenching. I glance towards Ethan to see that he isn't faring much better. There's a dark, predatory glint to his eyes that I've never seen before, and his hands are curled into fists.

Dec, obviously sensing the strange tension saturating the air, jumps to his feet and grabs his lunch.

"I'll see you guys at practice," he says to no one in particular. Then, almost as an afterthought, he turns to me and waves. "Bye, Izzy."

"See you later, Dec."

I swear Ashton actually growls.

What. The. Fuck?

Do they not like Jake? I thought Jake said they were friends. Is it Dec? Maybe they're not fans of him. It certainly has nothing to do with me—Emery and Ethan barely know me, and Ashton *doesn't* know me.

"So..." I try to change the subject, suddenly desperate to temper the animosity permeating the air. "The three of you are all friends? How long have you known each other?"

As I speak, I subtly shift out from underneath Jake's arm and resume eating.

The three men seem to relax as soon as I'm no longer touching Jake.

It's Emery who answers. I'm beginning to believe he's the most talkative of the bunch, though I don't get the sense he's the leader. His eyes constantly flick in Ashton's direction, as if asking the other man for permission.

Interesting.

He flashes me a large grin and reaches across the table to grab at one of my pepperonis. I half-heartedly swat at his hand, but my eyes are fixed to his mouth as he brings the stolen food to it. The piercing cutting through his bottom lip commandeers my attention.

I swallow.

"I've known Ethan since the womb days," he says lightly and bites down on the pepperoni. He chews quickly, swallows, and then says, "And I feel like I've known Ashton and Reid just as long."

"Not the same womb," Ethan interjects, fiddling with his glasses. He blushes when I turn to stare at him but continues babbling. "Obviously." He gestures between his own pale skin tone and Ashton's darker coloring. The red in his cheeks intensifies. "But we've been best friends since we were little kids. Our parents used to say that we share the same mind."

A fond, almost wistful smile touches the edges of his lips at whatever memory he just slipped into.

And I feel...

Jealous.

Not necessarily because of what he just said, but because I've never had anyone in my life who I could call my own. Not even Grayson could truly be described as mine. I don't have a "best friend" or a "soulmate" or anything as ridiculous as that. I'm that second-place friend. The people in my life always have someone they'll put above me.

Even Gray.

A leaden, miserable feeling settles in my gut at the reminder.

"And you have a fourth friend in this little bromance?" I tease, forcing myself out of my despondent state.

"Yeah, Reid." Emery nods, though the smile on his face gradually begins to dim.

Ashton, who has his phone out, quickly types

something into it and then places it face down on the table.

"You'll meet him today." His voice holds a no-nonsense quality that leaves no room for argument.

"I will?"

"I just texted him and told him to come to school," he replies cryptically. "He should be here by fifth period."

Ashton told this Reid person to come to school?

And he *listened*?

"Why isn't he at school already?" I volley my attention between the four men, including even Jake in my stare-down.

"He skips a lot." Emery smiles brightly, but it doesn't reach his eyes.

I don't know how I can tell, only that I do. His green eyes are dimmer than usual.

"Yeah, he's been different since the incident last year," Jake pipes in. "He doesn't even play football anymore."

Ashton looks annoyed by Jake's interruption, though I have no idea why. Yet again, it feels as if I'm missing something, something important...

"Let's not talk about Reid," Emery chirps, his pierced lips stretching into another forced smile. "I might develop a complex if *all* of the attention isn't on me."

I snort before I can stop myself, and Ashton

doesn't even bother to look away from me as he hits Emery on the back of the head.

The five of us spend the rest of the lunch period chatting about everything...and nothing. The conversations are entirely inconsequential, but I still feel a strange flutter in my chest just hearing Emery, Ethan, and Ashton talk.

I don't know why Emery hates Ethan, but I know that Emery has been playing football since he was in first grade, and Ashton and Reid joined a few years later.

I don't know why Ashton stares at me like I'm an insect he yearns to dissect, but I know he's taking only advanced placement classes. He could be in college right now if he didn't choose to remain at high school with his best friends.

I don't know why Ethan's eyes sometimes flash with melancholy, but I know he's a tech wizard and has half a dozen computers in his bedroom. He's also obsessed with video games, and the two of us spent almost ten minutes just discussing the newest *Zelda*.

It's not enough.

I want to know *everything*.

And that terrifies the shit out of me.

Twenty

IZZY

It's in art class that I finally meet the mysterious Reid.

He didn't show up for my fourth period class—the one I also share with Emery—and I could tell that irritated the handsome, flirty twin. He immediately whipped out his phone and began to text someone. I tried not to snoop, but I saw Ashton's name on the screen more times than I cared to admit.

So you can imagine my surprise when I sit at an easel near the back of the room and am immediately bombarded with whispers from my classmates.

"Can you believe it? Reid's actually here."

"I haven't seen him in this class since the first day of school."

"He used to be so fucking hot."

"What the hell happened to him?"

"I heard it has to do with his ex..."

I zone out the incessant gossiping, though not before I throw the three girls and one guy in front of me a withering glare. I don't even know this Reid person, yet I feel...protective of him, in some strange way. Or maybe I'm just protective of my new friends. Either way, irritation thrums through my veins at hearing them so blatantly gossip about a fellow classmate.

Where even is he? What does he look like? I pick my brain for any information I might've gathered about Reid but come up blank.

Straining my neck, I begin to scan the students entering the room, wondering if I'll somehow recognize him...

I quite literally *smell* him before I see him. The overwhelming stench of body odor barrages my senses, making me want to gag.

I don't know how I know that this stranger is Reid, only that I do. Heat spirals tight in my stomach, burning in preparation to strike, as I hold myself perfectly still.

A huge figure looms over me for only a fraction of a second before claiming the empty stool beside mine.

I don't dare even breathe—and not just because of the potent, stomach-churning smell permeating the air. I feel like a bunny caught at the end of a hunter's gun, and any sudden movement will determine my fate.

Live or die.

Prey or predator.

This is the elusive Reid who Ethan, Emery, and Ashton talk so highly about?

I try to study him inconspicuously out of the corner of my eye.

He's huge. That's the first descriptor I can think of to use. His arms are the size of tree trunks, and his entire body seems to be rippling with power and strength. I swear even his muscles have muscles. He has dark, auburn hair styled into a messy fauxhawk. The shorter strands on the sides of his head somehow emphasize his sharp facial structure and piercing blue eyes.

The gossiping girls—and one guy—in our class were right when they said he could be a heartthrob. He'd probably still be one if it weren't for the pungent smell emitting from him and the acne on his face. Lots and lots of acne. The bright red is a startling contrast to his pale skin, a mountain range of crimson and pink.

Wait...acne?

He looks like a man—a *huge* man—but that splatter of acne on his forehead and cheeks makes him look years younger.

On closer inspection, I see that his auburn hair is dark because it's *greasy*, not because it's naturally a shade of inky garnet.

Numerous stains cover his shirt as well, and I can't tell if they're from food, sweat, or something else.

He could be unbelievably sexy if he showered, put deodorant on, and changed his clothes. It's like he's trying to be as repulsive as possible, though I don't understand why. And of course, I don't want to assume anything. Perhaps he just doesn't give a shit about what he looks like or wears.

As if he can feel my eyes on him, the scowl on his face deepens even further, and his hands clench into fists on his lap. He holds himself perfectly still on the stool, almost rigid, his gaze fixed to the front of the classroom, where the teacher sits at her desk.

I want to introduce myself to him, but something about Reid...scares me. He's just so much bigger than me, and there's a sort of predatory intensity to his cold eyes that siphons the breath straight from my lungs. Ethan, Emery, and even Ashton radiate a welcoming countenance. Ethan's is warm, Emery's is playful, and Ashton's is authoritative.

But Reid?

Every muscle in my body locks together, urging me to run.

Run fast and run far, and never, ever look back.

The teacher finally begins her lecture, and I gratefully force my gaze off of Reid.

One of the girls in front of me dramatically plugs her nose, and her friends begin to giggle. I can practically feel Reid stiffen beside me, though he doesn't say a word. I wish I had laser vision capable of slicing through that girl's head. I narrow my eyes into slits, but of course, with her back towards me, she doesn't notice my ire.

Still, at least *I* feel better. A little less...stabby.

Mrs. Appleton drones on and on about shading before finally releasing us to grab supplies and try out what we learned.

I already know I'm going to fail this class. I can't draw a stick figure to save my life, let alone paint the way Mrs. Appleton can. Yet this school requires every student to take one art class, and it was either this or choir.

I'm not in the mood for anyone's ears to bleed, thank you very much.

The way the classroom is set up, there are two easels situated close together with a single table between them. An assortment of art supplies rests on the table—paintbrushes, paint, and a container of water. I also see some pastels, colored pencils, and other equipment I've never heard of or used before.

I reach for one of the paintbrushes at the same time Reid does.

Our hands meet.

Zings of electricity dance across my skin, and I instantly pull my hand away, stunned. Did I just get electrocuted? What the hell?

Reid misinterprets my hasty retreat and quickly looks away from me, muttering a noncommittal, gruff apology under his breath.

If I thought Ashton's voice was low, that's nothing compared to Reid's deep tenor. I suppose it's fitting. A man *that* large would most definitely not have a high-pitched, cutesy voice.

Unbidden, my mind conjures up images of Reid talking like a valley girl, and a tiny smirk curves up my lips.

Once again, Reid must interpret my smile as something more malicious and diabolical than it truly is. He inches his stool away from me as far as he's able to and focuses on his blank canvas. His jaw is clenched so tightly, I'll be surprised if he doesn't break a tooth.

Fuck, I'm being so rude. Unintentionally too.

What did Ethan say earlier? Something about not judging Reid by his appearance?

I shift uncomfortably on the tiny stool, take a deep breath—inwardly cringing when I inhale his body odor—and then force a smile on my face. I swivel on my stool so I can face him completely.

"Hi. My name's Izzy. And you're Reid, right?"

The giant man freezes, his hand tightening around his paintbrush, before he pivots slightly to face me. One of his eyebrows quirks in what appears to be disbelief. A strand of his greasy hair falls in front of his face, and he flicks it away with irritation.

"Yeah," he grunts out.

That's it. Nothing else.

Okaaaay, then.

He turns back towards his painting, effectively dismissing me, but for some reason, I don't want the conversation to end. Maybe it's because I'm a stubborn bitch on the best of days, but I hate the way he just banished me like an annoying stray dog begging for pets.

I try to keep my face friendly as I focus back on my own easel. I grab my paintbrush and dip it in the orange blob of paint. I have no idea what I'm going to paint—probably a sunset or some shit—but I find that I need to keep moving. The reckless energy skittering just beneath my skin doesn't allow for anything else.

"I met your friends today," I begin casually. "Ethan, Emery, and Ashton, right?"

He simply grunts in response, but I don't peel my gaze off of the canvas to see his reaction.

"They must've told you about the strange new girl." I chuckle as I begin to make tentative strokes over the canvas. "Is that why you're sitting next to me? To keep an eye on me?"

He doesn't respond, but that's okay. My best friend is Grayson, after all. Silence is his middle name.

Okay, that's a lie. It's Liam. But still.

We both focus on our work for the next few minutes, and I try my damnedest not to look over at him. I can feel his presence as keenly as I would a blade in my side, embedded just beneath my rib cage.

Think, Izzy. Think.

How can you get him to talk to you?

You can't force your friendship on him, a snide voice in my head remarks.

Um...have you met me? I most definitely can.

I decide I've been using way too much orange in my painting—it looks like a carrot had sex with slime and produced a deformed orange baby—and move to clean out my paintbrush. Perhaps I could add some red and yellow? Maybe blue?

"Damn," I murmur as I pull my paintbrush out of the water, only to see that it's still covered in dark paint.

We need clean water. Pronto.

I stand, reaching for the cup, when my foot catches on the edge of the easel. A surprised squeak escapes me as I begin to fall forward...

But just before I can become intimately familiar with the ground, arms grab me, keeping me on my feet. All I can see is a broad chest obscured by a gray, stained T-shirt. I move my gaze upwards, past the stubble lining his jawline, past the scars marring his face from old pimples, past the crook in his nose.

His blue eyes hold mine hostage for a fraction of a second before he pushes me away as if I'm toxic.

"Be more careful," he snaps, anger flaring in his eyes. "You can't expect me to always save your clumsy, dumb ass."

He gives me a scowl that would make a lesser woman piss herself.

I don't piss myself.

I just get pissed.

"Don't be an asshole," I snark back.

I want to say thank you for catching me...but I'm too freaking irritated to do anything but glare at him.

Why is he acting like my clumsiness is a personal affront to his well-being?

"Just watch where you're fucking going from now on," he barks, already reclaiming his seat in front of his easel.

His huge shoulders and back block his canvas from view as I stand there gaping at him.

What the *fuck* is his problem?

"You stupid, micro-penised, dick-faced, ass-munching, butt-sucking dildo," I growl under my breath.

He stiffens—having no doubt heard me—but remains silent.

For all of two seconds.

"Have you seen the size of me?" he rumbles, gesturing towards his huge body. "Do you really think I'll have a micro-penis?"

"You have to be compensating for something," I snap back, even as my thoughts stray to his dick.

If it's as big as the rest of him...

No. Not going there.

I shake myself out of my man-meat trance, my cock stupor, my penis daydream.

Fuck him.

No...no fucking him.

Gah.

I'm fuming with anger as I refill the water, reclaim my seat, and continue my work.

I know Ethan begged me to give Reid a chance, but

come the fuck on. Does Ethan not know that Reid is a bag of STD dildos?

I'm not vain. I wouldn't just dismiss him because he's not the most...erm...attractive man in the world.

But I also refuse to allow him to talk to me like that either.

Why did he even sit beside me if he was going to act like such a jerk?

Why did Ashton demand he return to school?

By the time the bell rings, signaling the end of class, I'm so lost in my thoughts that all I managed to paint was a few stripes of orange, red, and yellow on the canvas. I suppose you could call it a sunset...

Maybe.

Probably.

Okay, perhaps it's more of a school bus getting railed by a tomato, but it's the thought that counts.

"Please place your paintings on the drying rack before you leave!" Mrs. Appleton calls to us as the class begins to hurry out of the room.

Reid ignores our teacher and all but stomps away. The rest of the students give him a wide berth as he exits the classroom, his shoulders hunching in on themselves. The stench of his body odor trails after him like a damn wedding train. More than a few students turn away, their faces tinged green and disgust gripping their features.

It's only then that I see what he's been working on for the last forty minutes.

It appears to be a cornfield, the stalks so realistic I half expect to be able to lean forward and touch them. A tiny, desolate cabin sits at the very edge of the painting, with a twining road leading up to it. The sky is dark and riven with storm clouds, though Reid didn't draw any rain. The threat of a storm looms over the entire painting, though, and I can just imagine the sky opening up and releasing a heavy torrent of rainfall.

There's something so...despondent about the picture before me. I can't put my finger on why that is.

The seemingly abandoned building with cracked windows, broken doors, and fading wood? The empty field with not a soul—human or animal alike—in sight? The incoming storm that offers a darkness to the painting that wouldn't be there otherwise?

My heart feels like lead in my chest.

For the rest of the day, all I can think about is that damn painting.

And the reason why Reid drew it in the first place.

Twenty-One

REID

I want to slam my fist into someone's face and punch them until they fall unconscious. I want to tear out someone's organs and then force them to wear their small intestine as a noose. I want to claw out someone's eyes and then pour acid into the empty eye sockets.

I've never really considered myself a violent person before, but everything changed after the...*incident*.

The incident that irrevocably altered my life, and not for the better.

I angrily scratch at the inside of my wrist, uncaring that my fingernails catch on the pimples dotting my skin, causing them to bleed. The rest of the students give me a wide, noticeable berth, their features distorted in disgust.

This right here is why I choose not to go to school most days, why I've decided to take most of my classes online, why I lock myself away in my bedroom for days at a time.

Everybody used to stare at me with unfettered desire—the girls wanted me, and the guys wanted to be me.

Then, everything changed.

I know I probably stink to high heavens, but that can't be helped. I showered three times already today—twice in the morning and once during lunch—and slathered deodorant on my armpits. Hell, this is literally the fifth shirt I changed into, though it doesn't make a difference.

I'm a goddamn beast, but unlike the fairy tale, there's no magical cure for my predicament. No true love's kiss or any of that bullshit.

My hands ball into tight fists when I think about Michelle and her batshit crazy brother. I wonder how different my life would be now if I'd just fucked the bitch back then instead of refusing.

I scrub a hand through my auburn hair, inwardly cursing at the feel of greasy strands against my palm.

Shame floods me, potent and heady, at the thought of *her* seeing me this way.

My mate.

Why the fuck couldn't she have arrived last year, before everything went to shit?

Fuck this.

Fuck her.

Fuck my life.

My shame and self-deprecation are quickly replaced by a sweltering, incandescent anger that scorches my skin.

I *never* should've been blindsided like that.

When Ashton texted me, demanding I attend my afternoon classes to keep an eye on the new student, I thought it was because his father had managed to sneak a spy into the school. It wouldn't be the first time.

But this...

I didn't expect *this*.

Fucking hell.

The need for violence rages like wildfire in my chest.

And I find just the targets I'm looking for when Ashton and the twins step up to me.

"What. The. Fuck?" I growl, slamming my locker door shut, despite the fact I didn't actually grab anything out of it.

Ethan and Emery appear cautious—rightfully so—but Ashton maintains his impassive mask he's perfected over the years. I swear that man could be stabbed in the chest and wouldn't even bat an eye.

The bell rings overhead—signifying the beginning of sixth period—but the four of us don't move. The rest of the students, however, hurry into their respective classes, not willing to risk detention.

"You needed to know," Ashton says at last, once he's positive no one's in hearing distance.

There's not a single crack to his apathetic façade,

nothing to hint at the darkness I know lurks just underneath his seemingly perfect exterior.

Nothing to hint at how out of control he feels with this new development.

"Fuck you," I snap.

My wolf growls low in my chest and claws at the cage that contains him but is unable to break free. He is just as unhappy by this new development as I am.

Before Michelle and her brother, I never felt such anger and aggression. Yeah, I may have been a little bit of an asshole, but I never started fights for no reason, nor did I ever imagine hurting my brothers.

Now, that's all I can think about.

And these fuck faces thought it would be a good idea to introduce me to my mate? What the fucking hell were they thinking?

Izzy...

I've never given much thought to what I wanted my future mate to look like, but even I have to admit that Izzy is more perfect than I could've ever imagined. She's fucking gorgeous, with golden hair I ache to run my hands through, porcelain skin, and a heart-stopping smile. Even when she's snapping at me and calling me an asshole, she's beautiful. So fucking beautiful, it actually hurts.

But it doesn't matter. We can never be together. Not when I'm...me. The new me. The me Michelle and her brother cursed me to become.

Rage builds inside of me, white-hot and scalding,

and I twist my body so I don't accidentally take any of my ill-founded anger out on my brothers. I ram my fist into the locker hard enough to dent it and then stand there breathing heavily, my chest heaving.

Ashton takes a step closer, appearing in my periphery, and arches one elegant eyebrow. "Are you done with your temper tantrum yet?"

A growl reverberates through my chest. I don't know if it's me making that sound...or my caged wolf. "Fuck off."

Ashton merely flicks a piece of imaginary lint off his shoulder. "Can we please have a civil conversation without you...decimating school property?" His nose wrinkles in obvious distaste.

I sometimes wonder how I ever became friends with Ashton in the first place. We've always been so different from each other, even before the curse. He's meticulously clean; I'm sloppy. He prefers suits and ties; I wear T-shirts and jeans. He's currently the running back on the football team; I used to be the tight end. He handles any and all confrontations with blackmail and deceit; I solve my problems with my fists.

Yet here we are, years later, tied together by a primordial bond that the world can't even begin to comprehend.

I spin around and lean against the lockers, folding my arms over my chest. I try to mask my expression, to make it as impassive as Ashton's, but my perpetual scowl remains firmly in place.

"So we all agree, right? Izzy's our Heart, our mate." Ethan smiles broadly, either oblivious or choosing to ignore the bloated storm cloud hovering over us all, threatening torrents of rainfall. He actually sounds downright cheerful, which is completely ridiculous.

Fuck, a mate...

My mate...

Fear slides up my spine and knots in my throat.

I wanted a mate so fucking badly only a year ago—which is how everything went to shit in the first place—yet I feel nothing but horror now.

How can a woman like Izzy ever love or even care for a beast like me? I'm disgusting, both physically and even mentally. She tried to hide it, but I saw the way she flinched when I sat down beside her, her eyes churning with fear. Fear...and disgust.

And what if I lose my temper one of the times I'm around her? What if I accidentally hurt her?

Fuck.

"I can't be the only one who believes her timing is a little...convenient," Ashton murmurs, scratching at the stubble on his chin.

Ethan's brows furrow. "What do you mean?"

"Not everything is a fucking conspiracy, Ashton," Emery adds with a dramatic eye roll.

"You're telling me that you didn't notice Desiree and even Mimi cozying up to her?" Ashton counters with a look that suggests he thinks Emery's an idiot.

My stomach pitches. "Desiree and Mimi?"

The two of them have been sniffing around our pack for years now. And with everything going on with Desiree and her father...

"Desiree touched her and began acting really weird," Ethan confesses. He heaves out a breath and shifts his weight. "But Desiree's strangeness has nothing to do with Izzy."

He sounds almost defensive, as if he honestly believes we're going to storm into Izzy's sixth period class, pull her out, and then kill her.

Just the thought of any harm befalling Izzy makes my wolf open one slitted, yellow eye. I'm more aware of his presence than ever before as he peers through the bars of the cage he's locked in and growls, the sound low and haunting.

Emery levels a glare on Ashton. "You can't order us not to see our mate."

For once, Emery's in complete agreement with his twin. Hell, they're even mirroring each other, both standing on either side of Ashton with fury etched in every line of their scowls and their arms folded over their chests.

"I wasn't going to." Ashton begins to tap his fingers against the mark on his wrist, as he always does when he's attempting to compute an answer to a complex equation. "You know what they say—keep your friends close, but your enemies—"

"She's not our enemy," Ethan snaps, vitriol heavy in his voice. Red rises up his neck and splashes onto his cheeks. "She's our Heart."

"She's human," Ashton points out, his eyes glittering with cunning. "There's never been a case of a human being a Heart."

"What the fuck are you suggesting, Ash?" Emery sounds as if he's seconds away from completely losing his shit.

And I'll be the first to admit, I'm not that far behind him.

Fuck.

I don't even know the girl, yet she's already twisting me up inside. My heart stirs at just the thought of her, but my inexplicable anger is far from appeased. It tightens my chest and speeds my heart rate, even as butterflies simultaneously attack my stomach.

Fuck. Fuck. *Fuck.*

"We keep an eye on her. Befriend her." Ashton cants his head to the side, his eyes glazed and unfocused as he thinks things through. Two lines knit between his eyebrows. "But we don't tell her about wolves or packs or mates. And we don't pursue anything romantic with her—not while we're keeping these secrets."

"What the fuck?!" Emery roars. Rages colors his cheeks a dusky red. He curls his hands into fists. "She's our mate—"

"She's an unknown factor," Ashton counters calmly.

I know he's not trying to be a dick—this is just the way his brain operates—but even I can admit he sounds a little too...callous. Cruel. It causes my rage to move in riotous swirls deep within my chest.

He needs to shut the fuck up before I punch him unconscious.

My wolf howls in agreement, the noise muted and subdued, barely audible.

"So you want us to resist the mating bond? Deny it?" Ethan stares at our alpha in dawning horror, all color draining from his cheeks, turning them ashen.

"Not deny it." Ashton shakes his head quickly. "Just ignore it until we can figure things out."

"Mating bonds can't be faked, if that's what you're insinuating." Emery still sounds as if he wants to punch Ashton in the face. "You know that. Izzy's ours—"

"And she's also a human during a time of war," Ashton snaps back. "Are you really going to risk her life just so you can get your cock wet?"

"You motherfucker—" Emery lunges for Ashton, but I'm moving between them in seconds, shoving at Emery's chest to force him back a few steps.

"We're not getting anywhere by fighting amongst ourselves," I growl, already sick of this conversation. Sick of everything, really.

All I want to do is go home, hide away in my room, and forget this fucked-up day ever happened.

Forget *Izzy* ever happened.

Fuck, my head's pounding like an invasion of tiny drummers has taken up residence there. And the pain of knowing I can never be with my mate... It's so unbearable I half wonder if someone placed spikes against my soul.

"Ashton's right," I continue irritably. "Even if Izzy did know about wolves and the damn bond, you guys would still befriend her first, right? Before pursuing anything? Be the girl's damn friend, and we'll figure out everything from there."

For a long moment, all three of my friends gape at me. Ashton's mask cracks just a smidgen, and the twins appear stunned. I think this is the longest they've heard me speak in...how many months? Twelve? More? Fuck if I know anymore. Time's a strange, stagnant thing when you don't give a shit about what happens to you.

Something I said seems to shake Ethan out of his stupor.

He blinks at me, his green eyes wide, and says, "Why does it sound like you're not including yourself in this plan?"

"Because I'm not," I grunt with a scowl.

Emery matches my scowl with one of his own. "You can't even be the girl's friend, Reid? Our *mate's* friend?"

Something in my chest coils at his words.

"She seems to have enough damn friends," I bark.

And she doesn't need me.

She appears to be sweet and kind and beautiful. I'm the antithesis of everything she is. It would be best for both of us if I maintain my distance.

So why does the thought of staying away from her bring about a hurt that seems to chisel itself onto my heart?

Emery looks as if he wants to protest but instead clamps his lips together and turns away, almost as if it pains him to stare at me.

Ashton simply watches me with unnerving, soul-clenching intensity.

Fuck this.

I push off the lockers and begin to move down the hall.

"Where are you going?" Ethan calls to my retreating back.

"Away."

"Reid, she's our mate! You can't seriously—"

The rest of his words are cut off by the door to the school slamming shut behind me.

The sun immediately heats my skin, and I squeeze my eyelids shut and tilt my head towards the blistering rays. I used to love being outside...but that was before five seconds in the heat had sweat coating my pits and balls.

Reason number five hundred why I shouldn't involve myself with Isabella.

I move towards my motorcycle—a silver Ducati that I spent years saving up for—and grab the helmet I left on the seat. For a moment, I simply stare at my reflection in the visor and think about how fucked up my life has become.

Maybe the world would be a better place without me in it.

You're ugly.

Hideous.

Worthless.

Useless.

Disgusting.

A beast.

My wolf releases a soft, melancholic howl, but the noise barely reaches me, as if it's coming from miles away.

With a snarl, I throw the helmet as far as I can and watch it sail through the air before it lands on the hood of some poor fuck's car. Then, I straddle the bike and start the ignition.

A dark, rictus grin twitches the edges of my lips.

Without a backwards glance, I peel away from the parking lot, cranking the speed of my bike higher, higher, higher, higher...

And if I crash my bike, then so fucking what? No one will care if I die. Hell, I doubt anyone will even notice I'm gone.

At least when I'm staring the Grim Reaper down and giving him the middle finger, I feel free.

That's more than I can say for my wolf.

Twenty-Two

IZZY

I'm not surprised in the slightest to find Grayson No Last Name waiting for me in the parking lot after school.

And I say Grayson No Last Name because the bastard refuses to have one. Sure, on paper, his last name reads Grey—no fucking joke—but he hates being associated with his biological parents. And not just because they named their son Gray Grey. The last person who referred to him as Grayson Grey got punched in the face and then beaten into unconsciousness.

Which is why I immediately snap out, "Grayson Grey, what the fuck are you doing here?" I fold my arms over my chest and scowl.

I try to keep my angry façade up, but I can't quite hide the sliver of hurt that curdles in my chest. What makes this entire situation even more infuriating is the

213

fact that Grayson doesn't know *why* I'm mad at him. He doesn't know that I saw him with pretty, perfect Sydney. He doesn't know that jealousy swept over me in a wildfire, white-hot and painful. He doesn't know that I desperately wanted to grab the girl by the hair, tug her away from him, and then take her place in his arms.

Stupid, unreciprocated crushes.

Stupid, idiotic boys.

Stupid, annoyingly gorgeous Grayson.

His scowl deepens at the use of his full name, tiny lines materializing between his eyebrows, and he pushes off of his truck to stalk towards me. I hold my ground, refusing to be cowed, refusing to back away from the threat in his eyes. Grayson will never hurt me, not truly.

At least not physically.

Emotionally, on the other hand...

Did I mention it sucks being in love with a guy who looks at you like a little sister?

"Why the fuck are you ignoring me?" he rasps out, his voice breaking on the final word. He clears his throat, though that perpetual scowl never leaves his face.

Despite what a lot of people believe, Grayson *can* talk. He just doesn't like to. His voice is soft and almost husky, sounding as if he smoked over a thousand packs of cigarettes in his nineteen years on this earth. However, it wasn't *him* who smoked so religiously. It was his bio parents. The smoke fucked up his vocal cords when he was just a kid, and he hasn't been able to fix it, despite years of speech therapy.

"I don't have to explain myself to you," I snap, already stomping towards Jake's car.

He's at football practice for the next two hours, so technically, Hale will be picking Lissa and me up from school, but at least walking in the direction of Jake's car gives me something to do. I'm afraid if I remain standing there, I'll deck Grayson across the face.

The parking lot is still crowded, but no one pays us any mind. I imagine it's not the first time two students bickered.

Okay, maybe I need to rephrase that statement. No one pays *me* any mind. But Grayson? He gets a lot of mind. Err...people pay him a lot of mind.

He's too fucking sexy for his own good.

And combined with his sleek, leather jacket, the scruff on his jawline, and the bad-boy aura he seems to exude in tangible, heady waves? He's a walking wet dream.

My wet dream.

Ugh.

I quicken my pace, my gaze homed in on Jake's tiny red car, but Grayson's voice stops me in my tracks. Of fucking course he's been following me. Why would I expect anything different?

"Quit being a stubborn bitch, Iz, and talk to me."

I whirl around, heat already exploding in my

cheeks. I grit my teeth together and take deep, calming breaths in an attempt to appease the anger rioting in my gut. But...nope, it doesn't work. I still want to punch him just as hard as I did a minute ago.

"What the fuck did you just call me, asshole?"

The mischievous smirk that curls up the corners of his lips should be declared illegal. I momentarily lose my mind just looking at it, looking at *him*. He could decimate entire populations with that infuriating smile.

"So you can call me an asshole, but I can't call you a bitch?" He laughs, the noise mocking and just as raspy as his speaking voice.

A tiny kernel of electricity manifests in my lower belly and then flares outwards, engulfing me in a strange, prickling heat.

"You're acting like an asshole." I scowl at him, but some of my anger is already fading—a wave battering against the shoreline before retreating, returning to the more peaceful part of the ocean.

"And you're acting like a stubborn bitch," he retorts. "Now, are you going to tell me what has your panties in a bunch?"

"Stop thinking about my panties, perv," I say lamely, but secretly...I wish he would think about my panties a little more often.

Is that too much to ask?

But god help me, I feel the last of my ire recede. If anyone else were to call me a bitch or speak to me in such a manner, I'd stab them. But Grayson is... well... He's my best friend. He's probably the only person alive who can talk to me like that. He doesn't make it sound like an insult or a slur. It's more... teasing and lighthearted, almost reverent. He could swap out "bitch" with "baby," and I wouldn't even bat an eye.

It's just the way we work.

It's the way we've always worked.

I fork a hand through my blonde curls and puff out a breath. "Look, I'm sorry for being cranky. I'm hungry and about to start my period soon—"

"Same," he deadpans.

I snort on my laughter. "Yeah, well... You're right. I was being a stubborn bitch. I was just feeling..."

Insecure?

Helpless?

Pissed as hell that I'm in love with a guy who has a girlfriend?

All of the above?

I'd rather carve my own eyeballs out with a rusty spoon than admit any of that to Grayson.

"Why'd you leave?" he grunts out, shoving his hands into his front pockets and rocking back on his heels.

I know he's asking about why I left the barn last night without him, but the answer to that question is just another secret I'll take to my grave, thank you very much.

So instead, I settle on a half-truth. "I ran into Justin."

A dark, bloated storm cloud passes over his face, and that grumpy scowl returns with a vengeance. "You went home with him?"

He sounds almost...jealous. Insanely so. If I didn't know he had a girlfriend, I would've thought he was upset at the prospect of me having sex with another guy. But alas, reality is a cruel bitch, and I know he probably just wants to protect me from entitled rich boys the way an older brother might.

Either way, I can't help but ruffle his feathers.

I arch an arrogant eyebrow at him and cock my hip to the side. "Does it matter?"

His eyes narrow, turning to thin slits. "Izzy..." His voice is a low, rumbly growl that I swear reverberates through my entire body like an earthquake.

"Someone is feeling rather talkative today," I taunt, already reaching for my water bottle.

I hand it to him without a word, and he takes it and swallows quickly to soothe his frayed vocal cords. Still, his glower doesn't fade, doesn't dissipate.

"You need to tell me," he finally manages to bite out, though I notice his voice still sounds raspy and distorted.

"Why the fuck do I have to do that?"

"So I can kill him." He says that last statement without any inflection whatsoever, his stare hard on my face.

I scoff. "Yeah. Sure."

"Wanna test me, little bird?" He takes a single step forward like a predator advancing on its prey, and my heart does a strange jig in my chest at his use of my old nickname.

I can't remember the last time he referred to me as a little bird. Years ago, maybe.

I also can't forget the reason for that nickname in the first place.

I'm about to retort when a large body moves to my side, dwarfing me in shadow.

Startled, I turn to see our vice principal glaring at Grayson with an unreadable expression marring his handsome, aristocratic face. His dark hair is a little more mussed than I remember seeing it earlier today, but he still radiates power and confidence. His hard, streamlined muscles are just barely contained beneath his dress clothes.

"Is everything okay, Ms. Martin?" His tone is succulent and curt, though there's an undercurrent of steel that hardens each word he says. He doesn't pull his gaze away from Grayson, whose scowl has deepened to impossible levels.

"Yeah. Everything's fine."

Mr. Montgomery's lips firm into an unrelenting line, his eyes hard. "You don't appear to be a student here."

"You know every one of your students?" Grayson rasps, and takes another swig from my water bottle.

Mr. Montgomery's voice is dry when he responds. "I make it a habit to know my troubled students. And you, young man, reek of trouble."

I don't know what part I find funnier—the fact that Mr. Montgomery referred to Grayson as "young man" despite being only a year or two older than him, or the fact that he recognized Grayson as trouble.

Because he *is* trouble. Even I can admit that.

Grayson's eyes flare in irritation before they slide to me.

"Izzy, let's go," he growls out, already extending a hand for me to take.

"Ms. Martin, stay," Mr. Montgomery clips. He straightens the lapels of his jacket, the movement decidedly indolent and almost lazy, as if he hasn't a care in the world.

"I'm beginning to feel like a damn dog," I murmur to myself.

Montgomery's lips twitch in the beginnings of a smile, but Grayson looks as if he's seconds away from slicing the vice principal's neck with one of the daggers that I know he keeps on his person.

"Not a dog. Just a student who doesn't know how to fill out paperwork properly." Montgomery flashes me a smile to show he's only teasing before turning to face Grayson once more. The smile immediately slips from his face with enviable grace. "You may go now. Only students and guardians of students are allowed to be on campus during school hours."

Grayson folds his arms over his chest and smirks. "School hours ended a few minutes ago. Or do you not know your own school's schedule?"

Honestly, I'm not even surprised that Grayson knows that information. He probably researched it so he knew what time to arrive and confront me.

Wait.

How *did* Grayson even know what school I'm attending? I certainly didn't tell him. Not that there are a lot of options...

"Actually, young man—"

I snort, but Montgomery ignores me.

"—school hours technically continue for another three hours until all extracurriculars have left the premises."

I don't know if the smile Montgomery offers Grayson is patronizing, smug, or pitying. I also don't know if Montgomery is telling the truth about that— no doubt, it's utter bullshit—but then again, who am I to argue?

Montgomery turns away from Grayson as if he's an insignificant speck of dust, and my best friend's eyes ice over. His hands curl into fists by his sides, even as he attempts to keep his expression impassive and disinterested.

"Ms. Martin, if you may..." Montgomery gestures back towards the front of school, where I know the administrative offices are. "I can call your foster dad if you need a ride back home."

"Nah. I can just wait for Jake to finish football practice."

Grayson's brows furrow when I mention "Jake," and a strange flash of what I would almost describe as jealousy shoots across his face. The butterflies in my stomach suddenly seem to be tripping on acid.

"Come along, then." Montgomery doesn't bother to glance back at me as he moves towards the school, a single step from him equaling two of mine.

He doesn't bother to slow his pace, content for me to run along after him like the damn dog I joked about being.

Still, I don't want to make any waves on the first day of school, especially with the vice principal.

Even if he is one of the sexiest men I've ever seen before.

"I'll text you later," I murmur to Grayson, grabbing my water bottle from his hand and shoving it back into my backpack.

He snarls something noncommittally but doesn't protest.

However, I can feel his gaze on me as I step into the school and out of sight.

And that sensation of eyes caressing my skin doesn't fade, even as I step into the office to finish my paperwork.

One thing's for certain—this town is making me believe I'm losing my goddamn mind.

Twenty-Three

IZZY

"So how was your first day of school, Izzy?" Hale asks later that evening, as the five of us —me, Hale, Jake, Lissa, and Seth—sit around the table for dinner.

Hale has prepared an elaborate feast, complete with an entire chicken, salad, dinner rolls, sweet potatoes, cobs of corn, and a bowl of fresh fruit. According to Jake, Hale always whips together a huge dinner whenever a new foster kid starts school. He knows how stressful and terrifying it can be to leave the life you once knew without any warning, so he wants to do what he can to help alleviate the tension.

"It was great. Thanks for asking."

Jake flashes me a shit-eating grin from across the table. "She seems to be making a lot of new...friends."

He waggles his eyebrows suggestively as heat floods my cheeks.

I give him a glare, one that promises pain and death, and hiss, "Shut up."

In response, he blows me a kiss.

"Is it true that you're friends with Desiree?" Lissa all but squeals. She's been relatively silent so far—her cheeks stuffed with so much food she looks like a chipmunk—but apparently, she can only hold her tongue for so long. "She's soooo pretty. You have to introduce me to her! She's super popular and super gorgeous and super nice. I've also heard you befriended the Magnetic Four, and—"

"Magnetic Four?" I ask, wrinkling my nose.

Jake hides his smile behind his palm, though his eyes still glimmer with amusement.

Lissa turns bright red, the color contrasting with her pink clothing, and begins to stab at her salad aggressively. She's a vegetarian, apparently, but it's only because meat makes her gassy. Her words.

"Yeah...well...that's what me and my friends call them."

"Is that so?" Jake asks, his grin broadening.

Apparently, this is the first time he's heard of it, and I know he's pleased to have another weapon in his arsenal to tease her with.

She rolls her shoulders back, her embarrassment transforming into determination. I have to hand it to the girl—there isn't a lot that can ruffle her.

"That name fits them, don't you think? I mean,

they're just so…" She stares off into the distance with hearts in her eyes as I bite back a chuckle.

"I'm assuming you mean Emery, Ethan, Ashton, and Reid?" I ask, wanting to make sure we're on the same page.

She gives me a "duh" look and then begins squirting Italian dressing on her salad.

I glance inconspicuously towards Hale, but he seems to be preoccupied with Seth, reminding the other boy that it isn't appropriate to wear headphones at the dinner table. Knowing he's not listening to my conversation with Lissa, I finally get the nerve to ask her one of the many questions clamoring for attention in my mind.

I lean forward and whisper, "So what's up with the four of them?"

Lissa gives me a pleased, jovial look, as if she's been waiting her entire life for someone to ask her that. She opens her mouth, and I brace myself for Hurricane Lissa.

"Well, they've all been best friends since they were kids. They used to have a fifth bestie until they all sort of had a falling out. Don't ask me for the details—I don't know them. Ethan is *super* smart. Like, the smartest person in the entire school, except for maybe Ansel.

"And Emery is super athletic. He plays football and basketball and sometimes even baseball. Ashton is a mixture of both Ethan and Emery. He's smart, but not in a way that's super showy, you know? He doesn't really care if he gets straight As, but I know that if he were to try, he would beat out even Ethan for valedictorian. He's a little weird, though. He's almost always glued to his phone. Melissa James once told me it's because he's a member of the mafia, but I just think she's full of shit.

"Then there's Reid. He used to be the school's 'it boy,' so to speak. He was insanely handsome, smart, funny, and charismatic. Then something went down with his ex-girlfriend, and he sort of fell to pieces. No one knows the full story, though."

Lissa takes a long, exaggerated breath as if during that entire monologue, she didn't inhale once. Come to think of it, her cheeks had begun to look a little blue...

I process the information she just threw at me.

Most of it I already knew or could infer, but a few snippets surprise me. Like the mysterious fifth member, for example, and Reid's ex. She must've done a number on him to leave him so...disheveled.

"And have you heard any information about the vice principal? I'm surprised girls aren't flaunting to his office left and right."

Lissa's nose crinkles. "Mr. Hedgerows? He's, like, eighty and has a potbelly. And have you smelled him? Ewww."

Mr. Hedgerows must've been the vice principal before Mr. Montgomery took over.

"I can answer this one, new girl." Jake places his elbows on the table and leans forward so as to not be overheard by Hale, who's still arguing with a stone-faced Seth. "Apparently the new vice principal started at the beginning of the school year, but he hasn't been introduced to the student body yet. Probably because he's young. Really young. Much too young to be a vice principal. But apparently he's, like, a genius or some-thing who graduated high school when he was fourteen and got his degree in Educational Administration shortly after. Don't know how he got the job, though, when he doesn't have any experience—"

"His father's on the board," Hale interrupts, and my cheeks pinken at being caught gossiping about the new vice principal. "And there were...other circum-stances."

Hale focuses on his nearly empty plate of food.

"Other circumstances?" I furrow my brows.

Hale manages a weak chuckle. "Enough gossiping. We're worse than old ladies in a nursing home, giggling about cute nurses while knitting blankets for our grandchildren." He waves a negligent hand in the air. "Are you guys done? Jake, why don't you show Izzy the game room. Lissa and I will clean up."

I open my mouth to protest—after all, Hale spent all day making this fabulous dinner, and I want to show my appreciation—but Jake grabs me by the shoulders and steers me towards the hallway.

"Nope. No cleaning for you, missy. New girls don't

clean on their first day." A beatific smile lights up his face. "Now, do you know how to shoot a zombie in the face?"

* * *

The "game room" is large and spacious, located at the end of the hallway. I'm surprised we didn't visit it during the tour.

Then again, the tour did get kind of cut short when I flipped Jake and held a knife to his throat.

Oops.

Three leather couches face a flat-screen TV mounted to the wall. An assortment of gaming devices are connected to it. Behind the couches are a pool table, a closet full of board games, and what appears to be a toy chest for younger kids.

Before we entered the game room, I made a quick pit stop to change out of my fancy school clothes. I now wear a pair of leggings, an oversized sweatshirt, and a Yankees ball cap my baseball-loving foster dad bought me.

I curl my legs under my ass as I watch Jake grab two controllers for the PlayStation.

"Okay, we have some choices. We can play *Fortnite, Call of Duty, Resident Evil, Mario Kart*, or—"

"Anything's fine," I reply as my phone pings, signaling an incoming text.

I slide it out and smile when I see Emery's name flashing on the screen.

EMERY

You thinking about me yet?

IZZY

I'm not running away screaming in terror, so...no.

EMERY

sad face Don't be like that, doll.

EMERY

I really loved meeting you today.

IZZY

It was nice meeting you too.

EMERY

I think you'll like this town. Hale and Gerry are two of the best guys I know. And of course, there's me...

IZZY

I actually haven't met Gerry yet.

EMERY

Yeah. He's been away for work. But he should be back soon.

IZZY

How do you know that?

EMERY

A magician never reveals his secrets.

He then proceeds to send me a plethora of magician GIFs, each one more ridiculous than the last. I snort and roll my eyes, even as heat bursts to life in my stomach.

"Talking to one of your boy toys?" Jake asks teasingly, flopping down onto the couch beside me.

"Oh my gosh. Are you ever going to let me live that down?"

He pretends to think about it, tapping his finger against his chin in contemplation. "Hmmm. Probably not."

"You're the worst." I toss the nearest throw pillow at his head, but he stealthily ducks out of the way.

In retaliation, he grabs a different pillow and whacks me across the head with it. Hard.

"Jake!" I screech.

He snickers like a damn toddler. "Your hair's all messed up. You should maybe fix that."

He points towards my blonde curls, as if I didn't notice they're now a frizzy mess thanks to the pillow.

"Oh, should I?" Instead of reaching for the pillow —he'll expect that—I begin to rub his blond hair with my knuckles, causing the strands to stick up in every direction as if he stuck his finger into an electrical socket.

"TRUCE! TRUCE! Don't mess up my hair!" he all but whines, flopping backwards dramatically so he's out of reach. "I have a shift tonight."

"You have a job?" I ask incredulously.

I have no idea why I'm surprised. I suppose I just

don't know how he finds the time between school, football practice, and homework.

Jake attempts to pat down his hair as best he can, though the strands continue to stick up in every direction. "Yeah. At the local theater. It's pretty boring, but the boss is cool, and the pay is stellar." He glances at me consideringly out of the corner of his eye. "You know, I've heard that they're hiring…"

"Could you get me an interview?" I ask eagerly.

Don't get me wrong—I love fighting and the benefits that come with it, but that job isn't the most reliable source of income. And since I'm turning eighteen soon, I'll need to have a plan in case Hale throws me out on my ass.

Jake pouts. "I don't know. You messed up my hair."

"Pretty please." I clasp my hands together in the universal prayer position and offer him the best puppy-dog eyes I'm capable of.

"Don't make that face."

"Pleeeease."

"Izzy, I swear to God…" He flings an arm over his eyes as if it pains him to look at me.

"Pretty, pretty please."

"Ugh! Fine! But you owe me an apology for messing up my glorious mane." He dramatically tosses his head to the side, causing his blond hair to flop around.

"You messed up my hair first!" I protest.

Jake drops his gaze down to his phone, and a shit-eating grin erupts on his face. When his eyes meet mine again, they're sparkling with mischief. "I know how you can make it up to me…"

Instantly, I'm suspicious. "How?"

"Well, you see, I invited my friend over to play some video games…" That infuriating grin of his never leaves his face. If anything, it grows, transforming into a full-fledged smile. "But I completely forgot I had to work." He snaps his fingers in an "oh damn" motion. "I suppose you'll just have to hang out with him instead."

I narrow my eyes even further. "You *didn't*."

"Oh, I most definitely did." He flicks his gaze back to his phone again to read an incoming text. "Ethan should be here in about twenty minutes. You're welcome, by the way. Am I the best foster brother ever…or am I the best foster brother ever?"

The idiot gives himself a high five above his head as I fume.

Motherfucker.

Twenty-Four

ETHAN

*Y*ou're *just going to play video games, Ethan. Just video games. You're good at video games. Calm the fuck down.*

I repeat that mantra again and again in my head as I pace across Hale's front porch.

Gumballs in a candy store, it's just a single video game! Izzy probably won't even be there. Take a breath, man.

No one was more surprised than me when Jake texted and asked if I wanted to come over and play some games. We play together online a couple times a week, but I don't think I've been to his house in months.

If situations were different, I'd probably refuse the invitation—I'm a shy, introverted nugget who prefers to play games in the sanctuary of my own room, thank you very much, where I can eat all the junk food I want without judgment—but I found myself eagerly replying yes to his message.

I want to see Izzy.

Fuck, I can't get her out of my head, and it's driving me insane. I half wonder if I imagined her. Is her hair truly as golden as I remember it being? Does her nose really crinkle when she smiles? Does she have dimples, or was that just a trick of the light?

My wolf is almost pacing as restlessly as I am. He, too, wants to see her, smell her, taste her. The bastard repeatedly sends me images of her smiling face, as if to say, "You know what she looks like. Now go kidnap her."

It's futile to remind my wolf that kidnapping is a huge no-no. The furry predator just won't listen to me.

My nerves tingling with anticipation, I place my knuckles against the front door, prepared to knock. At the last second, I chicken out and resume my pacing.

You probably won't even see her. You got this. You're a strong, independent man who—

The front door swings open, and I screech louder than a motherfucking banshee. I bring a hand to my chest in a desperate attempt to calm my rampant heart.

Hale stands in the doorway, looking amused, his arms crossed over his chest and one brow cocked.

"Um...hello." I give an awkward wave and then, just because I can, the *Star Trek* Vulcan salute.

Oh. My. God.

I somehow bypassed "sexy nerd" and went straight

to "super nerd who will live in his parents' basement with cats forever."

"I heard you pacing for a good fifteen minutes." Hale's lips twitch upwards in a microscopic smile. "Everything okay?"

I shove my hands into the front pockets of my jeans and then rock back on my heels. This is the third time I changed clothes today, but I wanted to look nice, on the off chance that I do run into Izzy. My jeans have been freshly plucked from the dryer and do great things for my ass.

Yeah, yeah, yeah. I know how pathetic I sound.

But girls aren't the only ones who are self-conscious about their bodies.

I threw on a gray T-shirt and a plaid long-sleeve, currently unbuttoned. It hides my tattoos, but I found that girls really, really like it when I roll up the sleeves of my shirt to reveal my forearms. It's the equivalent of female cleavage.

I'll be the first to admit I'm attempting to make myself a little slutty to capture Izzy's attention. I almost pulled out the gray sweatpants but worried that would be trying too hard.

Next time, Ethan.

"Are you here to see Jake or Izzy?" Hale continues to offer me an amused, knowing smirk that makes my skin itch.

Or maybe that's just an anxious rash. Do wolves even get rashes?

"Iz— Jake," I blurt, forking my fingers through my golden hair. "We're here to play games."

Hale's smile broadens at my obvious fumble, but he moves to step aside, allowing me entrance.

It's pretty uncommon for wolves to visit the homes of other wolves not in their pack. It's a territory thing—probably something to do with scents.

But Hale and his partner, Gerry, have always been cool about allowing the four of us to visit their home. We used to come over all the time to watch games on TV and just chat, even before they began fostering children. Rumor has it that Gerry and Hale used to have a third member in their pack, but no one knows any more about it. He or she probably passed away long before they moved here.

Gerry's been away on Council business the last few weeks, and I can't imagine how badly Hale must be missing him, and vice versa. Fated mates are almost always inseparable, especially once the bond has been completed.

"Are you staying for dessert, Ethan? We already had dinner, but I plan to whip up something special in a little bit to celebrate Izzy's first day of school," Hale says kindly as he guides me down the hall, towards where I know the game room will be.

He doesn't need to. I've been to his house enough times to know where it is.

Yet I get the distinct impression he wants to ask me something.

Something more personal than, "Are you staying for dessert, Ethan?"

My heart catapults into my throat and becomes lodged there, this huge, fleshy ball that makes swallowing virtually impossible.

Does he know about Izzy?

Is that what he wants to talk to me about?

Hell, is that why he agreed to foster her in the first place?

But no...that's impossible. Nobody has the power to predict mates or see mating bonds, except for maybe Desiree, who's been gifted with premonition.

My hands are sweaty by my sides, and I hastily scrub them on my jeans.

We stop in front of the game room, where laughter emanates from inside. Izzy's twinkling, musical laughter.

And Jake's.

A strange, rumbly sound rattles my chest, and it takes me a second too long to realize it's a growl. I quickly try to smother the sound by biting my lower lip, but it continues regardless, my whole body shaking from the force of it.

Hale casts me a sharp, searching look, but I attempt to appear nonchalant, as if I'm *not* growling like a freaking maniac.

Dodododo. Nothing to see here. Just a teeny, tiny growl. Totally normal.

Hale opens his mouth, shuts it, and then immediately reopens it. He seems to be struggling to find words to say.

Finally, he blows out a haggard breath and barks, "Just be careful."

And that's that.

No threat to stay away from Izzy.

No questions about my random-ass growl.

No curiosity over my strange reaction to Izzy's and Jake's laughter.

He simply nods once, the slightest jerk of his head, and then turns towards the kitchen.

Just before he disappears out of sight, I call out to him, "I would love to stay for dessert. If you'd have me, of course."

Anything to stay here and not return home.

I don't want to hear my parents rave on and on about what a perfect son I am and how lucky we are as a pack to mate Desiree. I don't want to listen to my older sister giggle as she talks about her new boyfriend she's already desperately in love with. And I definitely don't want to see the derision, disgust, and loathing on my brother's face whenever he even glances in my direction.

Hale's smile turns soft, some of the rigid tension from moments ago melting away. "Of course. Brownies and ice cream sound good to you?"

"Sounds delicious."

Who can possibly say no to Hale's homemade brownies? I swear those fuckers melt in my mouth.

Even my wolf is salivating, and chocolate gives that asshole gas.

Hale smiles again and then disappears into the kitchen. I, on the other hand, take deep, calculated breaths as I work up the courage to step inside the room.

It's just video games.

So what if Izzy's here?

Remember what Ashton said—just be her friend.

You can do that, right?

My attempt to hype myself up is shattered when Izzy squeals with laughter, and jealousy ripples through my veins. I don't seem to have any control over my body. One second, I'm standing there, slapping my face and reminding myself that Izzy isn't the first girl I've ever talked to, and the next, I'm storming inside. My wolf howls ferociously in my head, the deafening noise drowning out everything else.

My claws lengthen and my canines elongate when I see Izzy lying on the couch, her hair flowing around her in a waterfall of golden silk. Jake hovers over her, a shit-eating grin on his face and his fucking dimples on full display. Izzy's shirt has risen up just enough for me to see her toned stomach...and Jake's fingers brushing the skin there.

A potent mixture of possessiveness and blinding rage weave themselves around the jealousy already present.

They don't seem to notice I'm even here, too focused on each other.

Izzy kicks out at Jake as another giggle escapes her. "Get off of me, you shit brain!"

Jake just continues to smile wickedly and tickle her sides. "Not until you confess the truth! Admit it!"

"Fuck off!"

"Admit that you're super thankful for me, and I'm the best big foster brother ever," he continues in a singsong voice.

"Eat shit and die!"

Jake catches sight of me first, and he seems to do a double take, blinking rapidly.

Oh...fuck. Fuck, fuck, fuck, fuck, fuck.

I quickly pivot on my heel so I'm now facing the doorway, trying to get my breathing under control.

Deep breath in.

Deep breath out.

Deep breath in.

Deep breath out.

Slowly, my claws recede, transforming back into normal fingers, and my teeth shrink. The spurts of fur that have haphazardly grown on my arms dissipate, leaving smooth, unblemished skin with a little bit of tattoos peeking out from just underneath my shirtsleeves.

Only when I'm positive that I have my wolf under control—and the fucker won't go on a murderous rampage—do I turn back around with a tentative smile.

Izzy and Jake are both sitting up on the couch, staring at me. Izzy appears confused, maybe even a little worried, but Jake's eyebrows are scrunched together so tightly that it looks like he's taking a shit.

Motherfucking ice-cream truck.

"Hey." I venture a step forward and then stop when Izzy's sweet scent permeates the air.

It's so potent and heady that I half want to close my eyes and inhale deeply like a creeper. But I don't. I do, however, allow just a little bit to trickle into my nostrils. Call me a glutton for punishment, but a twisted part of me wants to see if she's aroused by what she just did with Jake.

My shoulders actually sag with relief when I detect no difference between her scent at school and her scent now. Unless she's perpetually aroused, then there's no way she got hot and bothered by rolling around on the couch with Jake and—

What the fuck is wrong with me?

Shame instantly fills me, and I feel like a ripe piece of shit. I shouldn't have disrespected her privacy like that. So what if she's aroused by another man? She doesn't know about mates or werewolves—at least from what I can tell—so she has no reason to be faithful to me and my packmates.

I'm being a primitive, possessive asshole, and I can't

even blame my wolf for that. Yeah, he may be amplifying my emotions, but I'm the one in control.

You need to do better, Ethan.

I make a vow to myself—right then and there—that I'll be her friend first and foremost. If she wants to talk about guys and crushes, then so be it. I have absolutely no fucking right to place a claim on her.

Hell, I barely even know her.

My wolf growls sharply in denial, but I shush him.

"Ethan, hey!" Izzy smiles at me then, and I swear all coherent thoughts flee.

I forget about my vow and my anger and my jealousy and even my wolf. The way she smiles, her entire face shifting to accommodate it... It makes me feel like I'm the only guy in the world.

My heart begins to race even faster in my chest.

"I heard that there were...errr...games?" I blurt stupidly.

I instantly want to facepalm.

Way to be articulate.

"Actually..." Jake stretches dramatically and rolls his neck from side to side. "I need to start getting ready for work. Sorry, bro. I completely forgot I have a shift tonight."

"Oh." I try not to let my disappointment show on my face.

"But Izzy here loves games. Why don't you play with her?" He flashes my girl a winning smile, which she returns with a scowl.

But then Izzy turns towards me, and her expression turns warmer, the glower transforming into a timid smile. "Yeah, we can play games, if you want."

I probably look just a little bit desperate when I return her smile with a huge one of my own. "Yeah. That'd be awesome!"

I all but run towards the couch, as if a part of me is worried that she's going to change her mind and send me away as soon as Jake leaves.

Jake snorts. "How can a man as hot as you be such a fucking nerd?"

Both of us turn to stare at him incredulously, but he merely laughs louder.

"What?" He holds his hands up in a pacifying manner. "I'm confident enough in my sexuality to admit to myself that Ethan's smoking."

He fans himself with his hand. Izzy snorts and rolls her eyes, but I feel my cheeks turn bright red with embarrassment.

"Errr...thanks?"

"Anytime, man." Jake slaps me on the shoulder and then curses. "I actually do have to run. Will you guys be okay on your own?"

He directs the last question at Izzy, and for once, his tone is devoid of his usual humor. He looks completely serious.

"Yeah, we'll be fine." Izzy offers him a tiny smile.

"All right. Good." Jake grabs his phone off the coffee table and jumps to his feet.

He works at a local theater owned by a werewolf named Silas. Silas is a little intimidating, if I'm being completely honest, but Reid assured me that he's a good boss, even if he is a hard ass.

"Behave yourselves, kids." Jake waggles his eyebrows suggestively then races towards the door.

Just before he leaves, he fiddles with the fancy light controls on the wall. Almost instantly, the room dims, and "Sex on Fire" by Kings of Leon bursts through the speakers.

Izzy's cheeks turn almost as bright red as mine while Jake begins to laugh uproariously.

"You little shit!" Izzy screams, attempting to toss a pillow at his face.

But he stealthily dodges it and disappears down the hall, still snickering like a crazy person.

Oh. My. God. I think this... This is how I'm going to die.

Death by embarrassment. What a way to go.

Twenty-Five

IZZY

I am going to *murder* Jake.

No, that's too easy for the little shit-stirrer.

He deserves to suffer. Perhaps I'll rip out all of his internal organs and use them as tinsel next Christmas to decorate the tree. Or maybe I'll strangle him with his own intestines...

Ethan releases a strangled sound from beside me and then rushes towards the light controller—a tiny box mounted to the wall that allows you to control the lights and speakers in the room.

He incessantly begins to press buttons on the screen, and the lights finally turn back on.

Only to immediately dim even further, providing a salacious type of ambiance to the game room.

My cheeks feel as if they're on fire, and I'm just grateful that the darkness shrouds my red face.

Ethan mutters something under his breath—I hear

the words "gumballs" and "turkey leg"—before he pushes another button. This time, the artificial fireplace beneath the television flicks on, emitting an orange and red glow.

With a desperate battle cry, Ethan slams his hand against the controller. The fireplace shuts off, the music goes quiet, and the lights turn bright.

Ethan's face is just as red as my own.

Yup.

Jake is *so* going to die. I don't even have a choice on the matter anymore. It's truly a shame I have to kill him before he even turns twenty-one.

"Sorry about...him," I say, wiggling my fingers in the general direction of the doorway.

I swear, somewhere above, I can hear Jake laughing raucously, but it's probably just my imagination.

Ethan flashes me a timid smile and removes his glasses to rub at the bridge of his nose.

"Shouldn't I be the one apologizing for Jake?" He puts his glasses back on and crouches in front of the television to sift through the games there. "I've known him longer, and he used to be my friend."

I snort. "Used to be?"

Ethan shoots me a smirk over his shoulder. "He's certainly not anymore."

We decide to play *Mario Kart*, and Ethan tosses me a plastic steering wheel. He grabs one for himself and then perches on the couch...as far away from me as he can physically get.

As the game loads and we begin the tedious process of selecting our characters and cars, Ethan clears his throat and then says, "You and Jake seem to be close."

I choose Princess Peach as Ethan selects Mario. I'm not even surprised. He totally seems like a Mario type of guy. Emery? I have a feeling he would pick Bowser. And Reid and Ashton—

I shut that strange line of thinking down, fast, and focus on Ethan's words.

"Yeah. I don't really know how to explain it, but we clicked fast." I shrug. "He's like the annoying older brother I never wanted but now have."

Ethan's eyes flick to me before immediately focusing back on the screen. A blush creeps up his neck and stains his cheeks crimson. "So you guys aren't dating?"

"You think I'm dating Jake?" I stare at him incredulously before barking out a laugh. "No. It's not like that. Besides, I don't make a habit of dating guys I've only known for a couple of days." I flash him a pointed look, and the red in his cheeks deepens. "He's just a friend."

"I'm happy you have him," Ethan says, and I think he's being sincere. "He's a good man."

"He's a piece of shit," I counter with a scowl, thinking about the stunt he just pulled.

But even still, a tentative smile threatens to curl up my lips.

Yeah, Jake may be a piece of shit, but he's *my* piece of shit.

I never really had a brother or a close friend before —excluding Grayson, who doesn't count since I'm helplessly in love with him—but I think I could have something like that with Jake. I wasn't lying to Ethan when I said I clicked with Jake unreasonably fast. There's just something about the goofy quarterback that makes me trust him intrinsically.

"So are you ready to get your ass whooped?" I ask, reverting his attention back to the game.

"You wish."

Surprisingly, the two of us are evenly matched, always getting first or second place at the end of each race. As we play, we talk about school and our interests.

I already know Ethan plays baseball during the spring, but I'm shocked to learn that he's the team's pitcher. He tells me about his failed attempt to join the football team his freshman year and how he accidentally ran the ball in the wrong direction and then tackled the coach who he mistook for a player.

I regale him with stories of my failed gymnastics and dance career. I once stood on the balance beam for over ten minutes during a meet because I was too chickenshit to do a back handspring. I got last place that day.

Of course, I wouldn't have been able to stay in gymnastics, even if I wanted to. It's an expensive sport, and the second I got removed from that foster family and placed in another, they canceled my membership. I'm just thankful I never liked it that much to begin with.

As the two of us talk—conversation flowing freely and naturally between us—I can't help but think of ways I can beat him. Our scores are both even so far, and we only have two more races to go in this series.

I've never really considered myself a competitive person before, but I really, *really* want to beat him.

Ethan has moved closer to me subconsciously as we played and chatted, and he now sits only a few inches away. His tongue pokes out from between his lips as he concentrates on the race.

I shouldn't find that as cute as I do.

As we reach the final lap, I stealthily inch my fingers towards one of the throw pillows lying beside me.

Ethan's gaze remains intent on the screen as his character makes a sharp turn. I'm controlling my character one-handed, but that's okay. I know this course like the back of my hand, thanks to my last foster home.

Just as Ethan prepares to make another turn, I slap him across the face with the pillow. He's so startled that he actually drops his steering wheel and begins to blink rapidly at the screen. His glasses are askew, and the static from the pillow causes his hair to stand up at odd angles on his head.

I giggle madly as my character easily passes his motionless one and then zooms across the finish line.

"What the...?" Understanding dawns on him, and he turns to me with a feigned scowl, even as his eyes sparkle with amusement. "You little cheat!"

I bite my lip to keep from smirking and then shrug noncommittally. "I have no idea what you're talking about."

"Is that the way we're going to play this?" He cocks an eyebrow.

"The pillow slipped from my fingers," I respond innocently as the next race begins.

"Hmmm." Ethan's grin is positively wicked, almost lurid, and does strange things to my insides.

The first lap starts off relatively uneventful. I keep glancing at Ethan out of the corner of my eye, certain he's going to strike at any moment.

He never does.

My paranoia puts me in sixth place. Deciding he's bluffing and isn't actually going to do anything, I focus entirely on the game and swerve my car around the AI players until I reach second place.

I can see Ethan's red car right in front me. He's so close—

I scream when a blanket is tossed over my head, enveloping me in darkness.

"Ethan!" I screech as I attempt to free myself from the soft prison.

He laughs boisterously.

Oh, it's *so* on.

As soon as I'm finally able to get my head free, I dive at him. I begin to tickle his sides with my free hand as I steer my car with the other, swerving like mad and bumping into every wall.

Ethan laughs and attempts to swat my wiggling fingers away.

"Seriously?" he asks. "That's not going to work."

But even as he says that, he begins to squirm and laugh harder, especially when I find his sweet spot—the skin just above the waistband of his jeans, where his shirt has risen up slightly.

"It seems like it's working," I tease with a wink.

Ethan gives up on trying to push me off and instead grabs a second pillow, which he uses to whack me across the head. I laugh and attempt to shove him off the couch, but he's too heavy for me to move.

We end up in eleventh and twelfth place.

And I don't think I've ever been happier to lose in my life.

Twenty-Six

IZZY

The next few days are relatively uneventful. I'm so far behind in my coursework that I don't get a lot of opportunities to talk to any of my new friends during the day. Most class periods are spent with my head buried in a textbook, and during lunch, I use the time to catch up on all of my missing assignments.

I sit with Ethan, Emery, Ashton, Jake, Kain, and Dec during lunch. Desiree joined us one time, but when the conversation became awkward and stilted, she excused herself and promised to text me later. I don't know what everyone's deal is with her, but I also don't want to ask.

The thought that Ethan, Emery, or Ashton might have dated her once upon a time leaves a sour taste in my mouth. However, I can't ignore the fact that I first saw her standing by Emery, leaning against his locker.

But then I tell myself that I'm being stupid, that I barely know the guys, and Ashton only seems to semi-tolerate my presence. Any and all irrational feelings of jealousy dissipate like flaky ash in a breeze.

I haven't seen Reid since that very first day, and I don't dare ask anyone where he is. I have the distinct impression he's skipping school because of me, which makes me feel self-absorbed.

Yet I can't help but feel as if I offended him somehow.

I move through the hall towards my last period of the day—Yearbook. It's the only class I don't have with any of my new friends. Ansel—my asshole lab partner—is in that class, but so far, he's been acting as if I don't exist. Then again, he does that with everyone. I'm pretty sure the icy boy doesn't have any friends.

I'm surprised when I step inside the classroom to see an unfamiliar man sitting behind the teacher's desk. Our usual teacher—Mrs. Kingsley—is a mousy woman with light-brown hair, gray eyes, and a protruding pregnant belly.

I wonder if she has finally gone into labor, and I can't help but feel a tiny thrill at the thought. Mrs. Kingsley is one of the kindest teachers, and I know she's been counting down the days until she gives birth.

I eye the substitute inconspicuously as I take a seat behind one of the computer monitors.

The man appears to be in his mid-thirties and has sandy-colored hair that curls around his ears. A wide, open smile lights up his face as he reclines back in his seat. He's handsome, I suppose, for an older man. Behind him, written on the whiteboard in messy block letters, are the words *Mr. Remington.*

"Is it just me, or is the new teacher really hot?" KD claims the seat next to me and offers me a wide smile.

KD—or KayDianna—is a pretty girl with chestnut-colored skin and wavy black hair. What first drew me in were her kind eyes. I don't think this girl has a mean bone in her body. She's even nice to Ansel, even though he stares at her as if she's a piece of shit he stepped on.

KD's words finally register, and I turn to stare at the teacher once again. Yeah, he's handsome, but hot?

"He's old enough to be your dad," I murmur, wrinkling my nose.

She giggles. "You don't have a daddy kink?"

I actually laugh out loud at that. KD may be one of the sweetest people ever, but she has a supremely dirty mind.

I can't help but notice that Mr. Remington's nose has scrunched up in disgust, almost as if he heard our conversation. But that's impossible, considering we sit at the very back of the classroom while he remains at the front of it.

"What are you two giggling about?" Ashlinn, KD's best friend and fellow senior, moves to claim her seat on the opposite side of KD.

Ashlinn's pretty as well, but more in a prim, tradi-tional way. Her light-brown hair is perfectly straight and is cut to just below her chin. If KD has kind eyes, then Ashlinn has mischievous ones. She always looks as if she's seconds away from starting trouble.

"The hot teacher," KD answers with another giggle.

Ashlinn wrinkles her nose—the expression almost mirroring Mr. Remington's. "He's old enough to be your dad, KD."

"That's what I said!" I exclaim.

"Besides." Ashlinn folds her hands primly on top of her desk, just in front of her computer's keyboard. "His tits aren't large enough."

The three of us break into laughter.

Ashlinn has made it extremely clear where her pref-erences lie when it comes to sexual and romantic part-ners. She actually has something going on with Emilia, one of Desiree's best friends, who I still have yet to meet.

The bell rings, signaling the beginning of class, and Mr. Remington unfolds himself from his chair to smile at us all.

"Hello, everyone." He claps his hands together in excitement. "My name is Mr. Remington, and I'm going to be your sub for the next few weeks. As some of you know, Mrs. Kingsley gave birth earlier this morning and will be on maternity leave."

A few of the girls coo at that, happy for Mrs. Kingsley.

"Now, I'll be the first to admit that I never took a Yearbook class in my life." Mr. Remington winces apologetically. "But I'm going to do the best I can to help you all until Mrs. Kingsley returns." His gaze sweeps over the entire room, and I swear it stops on me a second longer than anyone else. His smile falters for a fraction of a second before he quickly forces it back into place. "Mrs. Kingsley told me in her teaching notes that an Ansel Whitmore will know what to do."

A plethora of groans ripples through the classroom. Apparently, I'm not the only one put off by Ansel's icy demeanor. The man in question rises from his seat in the front of the classroom—of fucking course he would sit up front—and he quickly surveys everyone present. I can't help but notice the hurt in his eyes before he masks it, and I instantly feel like a sack of shit.

God, what must it be like to have absolutely zero friends? No matter what school I went to, I at least had a few casual acquaintances I could sit with and talk to.

Ansel has no one, at least from what I can see.

I half wonder if the other students are just too intimidated by him. He's insanely good-looking, and you'd have to be blind not to notice. Even Ashlinn once confessed that he's a "sexy nerd with the attitude of a shit."

Ansel clears his throat and smooths a hand down

his carefully ironed shirt. There's not a single wrinkle that I can see. I'm pretty sure it's been custom tailored as well. It clings to his muscular frame like a dream.

"A lot of the roles have already been assigned for the semester," Ansel says.

That's true. When I arrived a few days ago, Mrs. Kingsley told me that she already handed out the majority of jobs. I was supposed to help where I could, bouncing from person to person. It's how I met KD. She's in charge of going through all of the photos the photographers took and choosing the best ones.

"However," Ansel continues, "I'll need some volunteers to help photograph the football game with me on Friday. Usually events as big as that require at least two photographers, but I seem to be the only one who signed up."

His pink lips press together, and I can't help but wonder if it's in irritation or hurt.

Normally when a signup is posted, the slots are filled within seconds, especially for the football games. Not only do you get into the game for free, but you're also able to be right on the field with the players. The guys like it because they get to talk to their friends, and the girls like it because they can flirt with the football players for school credit. It's also a very easy A.

But no one wants to work with Ansel, who apparently makes life a "living hell" for any photographers involved. At least according to KD and Ashlinn.

"He made a girl cry," Ashlinn once told me.

"It should be easy to avoid him," KD said. "But he's *everywhere*, and he's constantly yelling at you and snapping at you and making you feel like shit."

So you can imagine the class's collective disappointment when Ansel put his name down for the most important football game of the year.

"Any volunteers?" Ansel's fingers begin to tap against his khakis as red blossoms on his cheeks.

It takes me a second too long to realize he's embarrassed.

The room is so silent, you could hear a pin drop. Even Mr. Remington is beginning to look uncomfortable, that easy smile of his gradually sliding off his face.

Mother*fucker*.

Before I can second-guess my decision, I lift my hand into the air. KD and Ashlinn both gape at me.

Ansel turns in my direction, and I swear I see relief seep into his eyes before he forces his expression to harden. He nods once in acknowledgment before continuing on with his spiel.

Keep up the good work, blah blah blah.

Make sure you meet your deadlines, blah blah blah.

Check the board for any new openings of events that need to be photographed, blah blah blah.

By the time Ansel dismisses us to continue our projects, I'm afraid my brain is going to explode from boredom. Is that even a thing? I make a note to look it up as soon as I'm able to.

"I can't believe you're brave enough to risk working

with Ansel," KD whispers under her breath as she pulls up the file labeled CROSS COUNTRY and begins to scroll through the photos.

"He's terrifying," Ashlinn agrees as she leans over KD's shoulder to point at one of the pictures. "This one's good."

KD nods and moves the photo to a separate folder before continuing. "Aren't you scared he's going to murder you and hide your body?"

"Nah, he doesn't seem like the murdering type." Ashlinn waves a flippant hand in the air. "More of the 'yell at you until you want to curl into a ball and die type.'"

"I'll make sure to keep my voice down when I'm around you, then," a smooth voice remarks from directly behind us.

All three of us spin around to face Ansel, whose eyes are dark despite his carefully neutral expression.

KD's cheeks redden with shame—she truly is too good for this world—while Ashlinn merely cocks an eyebrow.

"You need something?" she asks.

Ansel turns towards me. "May I speak with you for a second, Isabella?"

I wince at the use of my full name before reluctantly agreeing.

Ansel leads me towards the supply closet we keep the cameras and other equipment in. I notice Mr. Remington watching us, and his eyes narrow into slits when Ansel leads me inside the musty room.

"I want to make sure you know how to use the equipment before the game tomorrow night," Ansel explains absently as he flicks on the light, bathing the room in a soft yellow glow.

When I step inside, the door automatically swings shut behind us, but I don't feel scared. Despite KD and Ashlinn's jokes, I know Ansel won't truly hurt me. He's just a rich boy with a superiority complex who doesn't know how to have a conversation with another person.

Besides, even if he tried something, I'm confident I can take him down.

Ansel thrusts a camera at my chest and then proceeds to teach me how to use it. It seems simple enough, though I know I'm going to forget all of the settings by the time of the game tomorrow.

Ansel must read something on my face because he blows out a breath and says, "We can practice tomorrow during class."

"Yeah, okay. Thanks." I turn the camera over in my hands and offer him an awkward smile.

He doesn't return my smile, but I swear his eyes soften. Just a bit. "No, thank *you* for volunteering—"

Before he can finish whatever he's trying to say, the door to the closet is flung open, and an angry Mr. Remington glares down at us. I thought the older man was perpetually happy—one of those guys who never gets bothered by anything.

Apparently, I was wrong.

"From now on, we keep the closet door *open* at all times. You hear me?" Mr. Remington snarls, his narrow-eyed stare never leaving Ansel's face.

Ansel only now seems to realize what this looked like—the two of us, alone in a closed closet...

His cheeks pinken, and he immediately lowers his gaze. "I'm sorry, sir. It won't happen again."

Mr. Remington bares his teeth. "See that it doesn't."

Ansel all but rushes around the teacher—the back of his neck bright red—and Mr. Remington finally turns to look at me. The anger fades, replaced by something resembling concern.

"Are you okay?" he asks.

"I'm fine." Suddenly worried for Ansel, I rush out, "He didn't touch me or anything like that. He was just showing me how to work the camera." I chuckle before I can stop myself. "I honestly don't think he noticed the door shut."

"Oh." Mr. Remington seems to be embarrassed about jumping to conclusions and forks his fingers through his shaggy hair. He clears his throat and then says, "Well, off with you."

He steps aside to let me pass.

KD and Ashlinn are laughing raucously when I

retake my seat, and I murmur a half-hearted, "Shut up."

Why do I have a feeling that news of my "closet rendezvous" with Ansel will be spreading through the hallways like wildfire before the school day even ends?

Ugh.

I never should've volunteered to work the football game in the first place.

Twenty-Seven

IZZY

I study my reflection one last time in the full-length mirror before grabbing my backpack off the bed.

It's the following morning, though I didn't sleep a wink the night before. I blame Ethan. We started playing Fortnite online, and I only retired to bed when Hale caught me and warned me that I had school tomorrow.

A strange thrill shoots through me at the thought of the shy, awkward twin. The two of us have been gaming together almost every day after school, though he hasn't come over again since the incident with Jake. I love getting to know him, and I can readily admit that I can see myself developing a crush on him.

I glance down on my phone to see new messages from both Emery and Grayson.

EMERY

I'm freaking out over the game
tonight.

IZZY

Does that mean you passed your
math test?

Emery told me that he was stressed over a test he took a few days prior. If he failed, he risked getting benched for this game and the next.

In response to my text, Emery sends me a picture of himself holding a sheet of paper. On the top is a bright-red C+.

My breath hitches, and it's not because of the grade.

No, it's because Emery is shirtless in the photo, his defined six-pack on display. I dart my gaze to the trail of golden hair leading down into the waistband of his sweatpants. He has so many tattoos that I can't help but zoom in and study each individual one.

On his arm, I spot a rose surrounded by prickly thorns. And lining the length of his chest are angel wings. They look so real and lifelike that I half want to stroke them like a creeper.

"Whatcha doing?"

I jump about a foot in the air, accidentally dropping my phone in the process.

"Fuck, Lissa!" I screech as I turn to face her.

She simply blinks at me innocently before her eyes

trail over my outfit for the day. A wide, beguiling smile tugs up her lips as she squeals.

"Ohmygawd! I can't believe you're showing your school spirit already! You look so pretty!!! The guys are going to go insane. You're going to find out that the students and teachers take the football games very seriously. Honestly, everyone wears school colors on game day. Just look at me!" She gestures to her Bulldog shirt. "OMG! Does Jake know you're wearing his number? That's amazing! Are you two dating? You're not dating, are you? That would be weird. But if you are, I'd be—"

"Lissa!" I have to physically place a hand over her mouth to stop her verbal diarrhea.

Even still, she tries yet again to talk, even with my hand muffling the sound.

"I'm not dating Jake. He just asked me to wear his number, and I accepted." I subtly study my reflection in the mirror yet again.

Unlike Lissa, who has a dozen or so shirts with the Bulldog logo on it, I don't own anything that showcases my "school spirit." Instead, I chose to wear a black skirt that stops just before my knees and swishes around me when I walk and a red, off-the-shoulder blouse—our school colors.

I kept my hair down, and the blonde curls tumble around my shoulders like a waterfall of silk. With black paint, I've written the number 32 on my right cheek. Jake's number. He practically begged me the day before to wear his number, claiming he's the only loser on the team who never has anyone supporting him.

"Besides, it'll make me look good to have a girl as pretty as you cheering me on," he said, knocking his shoulder against my own.

I reluctantly agreed, though it wasn't because I harbored any romantic feelings for my foster brother.

I said yes because he has quickly become one of my closest friends.

I check to make sure I have everything as Lissa prattles on and on about how wearing Jake's number is a public declaration that the two of us are in a relationship. I can't help but smirk.

I wonder if Jake asked me to wear his number to make a certain brunette ice queen jealous...

Desiree actually FaceTimed me earlier this morning, just to make sure I was planning on wearing school colors today. She's on the cheerleading squad, along with Mimi and Emilia, so she's required to wear her uniform. But she stressed over and over again that *everyone* dresses up on game day.

I swear people treat football like a religion over here.

Lissa follows me out of our room, and the two of us head to the kitchen, where Jake is already sitting at the counter, eating a bowl of cereal. His eyes light up when he sees me, and before I can get a word out, he's rushing towards me with a wide, enigmatic smile. He grabs me by the waist and spins me around.

"You seriously are the best foster sister-slash-best friend a guy could ask for," he tells me excitedly, putting me on my feet.

I snort and give a dramatic bow. "A pleasure to oblige."

I move to claim the seat beside Jake as Lissa hands me a bowl and spoon. I say my thanks and quickly pour myself some cereal. As I eat the sugary goodness, I open my phone once more and check the messages from Grayson.

GRAYSON

I miss you.

GRAYSON

I feel like we haven't been able to hang out in a while, just the two of us.

GRAYSON

There are always people around.

GRAYSON

Wanna do something tomorrow?

The butterflies in my chest turn radioactive as a ravenous heat burns through me. I swear my cheeks are just as hot.

A part of me—the part that always secretly harbored a crush on Grayson—yearns to say yes. But...

IZZY

What would your girlfriend think about that?

Three little dots appear beside Grayson's name, indicating that he's typing out a reply, before they disappear. No new messages appear.

With a sigh, I turn my phone face down on the counter and take another bite of my cereal.

Jake nudges me with his elbow, and when I turn to face him, one of his eyebrows is arched quizzically.

"Everything okay?" he mouths, and I offer him a feeble smile and shrug.

I haven't told anyone about my friendship with Grayson, and I'm not sure I want to. I can already imagine the pity I'll receive when people learn that I'm in love with a man who has a girlfriend.

Shame washes over me, and I begin to jab at my cereal bowl a little more aggressively.

I need to get over this stupid crush on Grayson, and soon. It's not fair to our friendship, him, or his girlfriend. And honestly, it's not fair to me either. I refuse to allow my heart to break any further than it already has because my feelings for him refuse to subside.

Jake clears his throat, drawing my attention to him. "So you're coming to the game tonight, right?"

"Yeah. I have to take pictures for Yearbook." I smirk at him conspiratorially. "So I better not see you picking your nose, or I promise those images will be on the front page."

Jake throws a hand against his chest in mock

offense. "There is nothing wrong with a little gold digging!"

"You're disgusting," Lissa interjects, throwing a piece of dry cereal at his face.

She's the only one of us not sitting at the counter. Instead, she stands on the opposite side, shoveling mouthfuls of cereal into her mouth as if she's in a cereal eating contest. Is she even swallowing between bites?

"I thought Ansel was in charge of photographing this football game," she says.

"Scary Ansel?" Jake asks, blinking.

"Oh, shut up." I roll my eyes, even as a grimace takes over my face. "And yeah, he is."

"Oh, dear god." Lissa stares up at me in wide-eyed horror. Then, unable to help herself from divulging the newest gossip, she leans forward to speak softly. "Apparently his last Yearbook partner transferred schools because he was such an ass to him."

"No way." Jake snorts. "That's just a rumor."

"It's the truth!" Lissa insists, pouting. She folds her arms over her chest. "I heard it from the guy's friend."

"What did I tell you about gossiping, Lissa?" Hale asks as he steps into the kitchen, Seth trailing along behind him.

The younger boy doesn't even glance up from his tablet, despite the conversation going on around him.

Lissa makes a face at me and rolls her eyes. "It's not gossiping if it's true."

"There's no fucking way that nerdy Ansel scared a guy all the way to a new school," Jake protests with a bark of laughter.

"Ansel..." Hale taps his finger against his chin contemplatively. "Ansel Harthorne?"

"I have no idea what his last name is, but probably." Jake shrugs. "Super smart, kind of an asshole, about this tall." He places his hand out to help Hale visualize the height.

"Oh please. He's definitely taller than four feet," I say around my laughter.

Jake suddenly sits upright on his stool, his eyes sparkling with amusement. "Oh! Speaking of four feet...I talked to Silas last night about hiring you."

Hale inserts himself into the conversation before I can respond. "How the heck did four feet remind you of Silas? That man is massive."

Jake waves a flippant hand in the air. "Don't judge the process. My mind works in mysterious ways. Anyway..." He swivels on his stool once more to face me. "He said that you can come in this weekend to interview! So bring a resume or whatever shit you need."

Excitement fills me at the prospect of actually getting a job. A real job, not one that involves my fists. It only solidifies the fact that I may stay here longer than a few months. I'm not saying this town will be my forever home, but...I like it here. I like the people and forest and community.

Almost as soon as my excitement arrives, it dissipates.

How can I have a job, when I don't even have a car or my license?

Hale interrupts my internal musings. "I'm proud of you, Izzy, for taking that initiative." He offers me a kind smile. "The theater isn't too far from the house. I'll be more than happy to drive you to and from work until you can get your own license. And if you get hired, we can even talk to Silas about aligning your shifts with Jake's so the two of you can ride with each other."

"Oh yeah!" Jake fist pumps the air like a total doofus. "We'll be work buddies!"

Lissa then proceeds to whine for the next half hour that she wants a job too, with Jake butting in every few minutes with remarks that only rile her up.

It's loud. It's chaotic. It's frenzied.

But it feels a little like home.

Twenty-Eight

EMERY

I fiddle with my lip ring for the one millionth time since I first entered the school—a nervous habit I've had ever since I got the damn thing. I keep my eyes pinned to the front of the school as I wait against the lockers with a feigned casualness I don't truly feel.

I'm both excited and anxious to see Izzy. We've been texting almost nonstop since I first met her, and I have to admit she's pretty cool. Even if I didn't feel the mating bond between us—potent and electric—I would still want to get to know her.

Not only is she ridiculously beautiful, but she's funny, witty, and insanely smart. I don't know a lot about her past, but the few things I've picked up from our text conversations hint that she may have had a rough time.

I can't even imagine what it would be like to be

bounced from foster home to foster home, never settling down, never staying in one place longer than a few months.

An almost blinding, incandescent rage courses through me at the prospect of *anyone* hurting Isabella. I'm not stupid. I've read about the horror stories some of those kids have to go through, and the thought of that happening to Izzy...

I inhale sharply, attempting to modulate my sudden erratic breathing, when I feel a presence behind me. I stiffen involuntarily, every muscle in my body locking together as Desiree's familiar perfume assaults my senses.

"What do you want, Desiree?" My words are a strange combination of a growl and a weary sigh.

I just don't have the strength to deal with Desiree and all of her shit today.

"I'm just here to remind you to remain calm," Desiree replies nonchalantly.

The words are strange enough to snap my head in her direction.

Like all the rest of the cheerleaders, she wears her uniform that leaves very little to the imagination—a frilly skirt that stops in the middle of her thighs and a skin-tight top that reveals her stomach. Her brown curls have been styled into an immaculate ponytail, not a single hair out of place. Some might say that she looks beautiful or sexy.

She just looks plain to me.

I've *seen* beautiful, and trying to compare Desiree to Izzy is like putting a candle against the sun. Both of them shine in their own right, but only one illuminates every darkened corner.

Desiree places a hand on her waist and uses the other one to gesture flippantly. "I'm just saying, if you freak out or get jealous, you're going to scare her away."

"What the fuck are you talking about?" I stare at her incredulously. "Did the gates to hell drop on your head when you tried to escape this morning?"

She gives me an annoyed look that speaks volumes for her disdain towards me—honestly, I'm pretty sure she hates me nearly as much as I hate her—before heaving out an exaggerated breath.

"I'm not doing this to help you, you pea-brained moron. I'm doing this for her."

"What cryptic bullshit is this?" I demand.

But Desiree simply stalks away without a backwards glance. I notice more than one person stare intently at her ass, but I'm not one of those people.

There's only one ass I want to stare at.

Thoughts of Izzy have a warm glow rushing through me, enveloping me in heat.

I smooth a hand down my red and black jersey and check the clock. Yet again, I begin to fiddle with my lip ring. I always have to take my piercings out when I play ball, but I love them too much to remove them for good. They were one of the first steps I took in differentiating myself from Ethan, to remind the world that we're *not* the same person, despite popular belief.

Even thinking about Ethan turns the warmth inside me to ice.

That bastard thinks he's being subtle, but I've caught him on the phone with Izzy more than once this week. Yes, they're only playing video games—and their conversations are usually casual and lighthearted—but it doesn't stop the jealousy from plowing me over.

I want to be the one to elicit such sweet giggles from her lips.

He doesn't fucking deserve her.

I press my forehead against my locker in an attempt to get my breathing under control. The cold metal is a surprisingly soothing balm to my volatile emotions.

I scent her before I see her.

All at once, the stress of the last few hours, my anger concerning Ethan, my fear of the future... Everything disappears until all that exists is her. Heat cascades through me in a burning torrent, and I relish the sensation.

I force a smile on my lips—cocky and carefree—and push myself away from the locker. I just want to see her. Set eyes on her. Listen to her laugh.

Spinning around, I open my mouth to call her name...only to immediately freeze. My blood runs cold, turning into sludgy cubes of ice in my veins.

Because Izzy's there, standing next to that fucker

Jake, wearing *his* number on her cheek, almost as if he's claiming her.

Or she's claiming him.

Jealousy fizzles in my bloodstream, acerbic and potent, and it takes every ounce of self-control I have not to run over there, wash away that damn number, and then surround her with my scent. This time, when I press my forehead against the locker, I'm doing it for a completely different reason.

My claws elongate, breaking through my fingers, and fur explodes on my arms.

Fuck. Fuck. Fuck. Fuck!

Calm the fuck down, Emery! I mentally chastise myself.

For some reason, Desiree's words from before pop to the forefront of my mind.

"I'm just saying, if you freak out or get jealous, you're going to scare her away."

Did Desiree somehow *know* this was going to happen? Did she have a vision?

Does she know that Izzy is my mate?

Our mate?

Question after question swirls around in my mind, and having something to focus on calms me down some. The rage bubbling in my chest turns to a low fizzle instead of an inferno of heat.

"Em?" Izzy's soft, worried voice trails across my skin like fingertips.

My body instantly relaxes just at the sound of it.

I glance down, grateful to see that my claws and fur have both receded, and then do a quick mental inventory. Confident I'm not going to wolf out and attack the entire school, I spin towards her with a cocksure grin.

"Hey, pretty girl." I try my damnedest not to look at the number painted on her cheek.

Fuck, she looks gorgeous. Her shirt hangs off one shoulder, revealing the dark strap of her bra, and her skirt moves like pools of ink around her thighs when she walks.

"You okay?" she asks with concern.

No doubt, I looked like a complete idiot with my forehead pressed to the locker and my hands curled into fists to hide my growing claws.

I sling an arm around her shoulders and begin to guide her towards her first class of the day.

Is it creepy to admit I have her schedule memorized?

Probably. But I'm not looking into that too closely.

"Of course." I roll my eyes as if to say she has no reason to worry and then flash her a toothy grin. "Just worried about the game tonight."

"Well, I'm sure you're going to kick ass." She pauses, tilts her head to the side, and then amends her previous statement. "Or is it tackle ass? Kiss ass? I'm not caught up on football lingo."

I actually laugh out loud at that. "I dare you to tell Ashton to kiss ass tonight."

I chuckle at the thought. He'd probably look at her in disbelief for a solid five minutes as he struggles to get his thoughts in order.

I've always wanted to see his brain put up an OUT OF ORDER sign and for smoke to billow out of his ears.

Izzy's nose wrinkles adorably. "Hell no. He already doesn't like me."

"That's not true," I counter immediately.

She quirks a golden eyebrow at me. "It's totally true. Ever since I arrived here, he stares at me like a bug he wants to squish."

I distractedly scratch at the nape of my neck as I debate what to say next. I desperately want Izzy to know that it's not her eliciting this reaction from Ashton. He's always been a paranoid fucker, and I can't even blame him. Losing his mom and the majority of his fathers shattered something in him, something he can't get back.

Ashton *likes* Izzy. I can see that in his eyes. He's intrigued by her, and maybe it's the way a scientist is intrigued by an endangered species, but it's better than his usual cold detachment he offers everyone else.

Instead of saying all that to Izzy, though, I change the subject. "You still coming to the game tonight?"

Last I heard, she signed up to take photographs on the sidelines with Ansel for the yearbook.

"Yup." She pops the P. "I'll be there taking photos."

"I'll try not to pick my wedgie too often," I dead-pan, and she laughs.

I have to bite down on my growing smile because that was exactly what I wanted to happen.

I love her laughter.

"No, please do. We need some candid shots for the spread." She smiles at me playfully.

"Have you ever worn a football uniform before? I swear I get my underwear so far up my ass crack that I can feel it in my mouth." I shudder dramatically.

"That's a sexy visual," she muses.

"Super sexy, I know."

We finally reach her first period class, and I'm not surprised in the slightest to see Ethan waiting by the door for her. His eyes light up instantly, something warm and gushy filling his expression, and I have to bite down on my lower lip to keep from scowling at him. Bitter, possessive energy radiates through me.

"I suppose this is where I leave you." I purposely position my body so I'm blocking Izzy's view of Ethan. Petty, I know, but I can't seem to stop myself. "I don't know how I'll survive without you, pretty girl."

She scoffs and rolls her eyes, even as an enticing redness creeps up her cheeks. "You'll see me in two hours."

"That's two hours too long." I'm only half teasing, but fortunately, she doesn't seem to hear the sincerity in my words.

Not that I blame her. She's a human who doesn't

understand that she has four wolf shifters at her beck and call, desperate to please her, care for her, and love her. The bond connecting our souls screams at me whenever we're away.

And my wolf isn't any better.

That fucker whines and sobs and cries until he sees her. Then, he begins to wag his tail like a damn puppy getting kisses from his owner.

Even now, my wolf releases a melancholic howl at the thought of being away from her, even if it is only for two class periods.

I reach for her cheek and cup it gently. Slowly, I rub my thumb back and forth across her tender flesh, reveling in the way she blushes.

"Oops." I flash her a flirty grin that doesn't quite match the rapid pounding of my heart. A strange sort of desperation rises inside of me. "I seemed to have smudged the paint on your cheek."

Lie.

It's still perfectly in place, thanks to the paint having dried earlier.

"Let me fix it," I tell her, wetting the tip of my thumb with my mouth.

Her eyes home in on my lip ring, and hunger fills her gaze.

Probably the same hunger I feel.

Carefully, giving her ample time to pull away, I brush my now wet thumb across her cheek, smearing the black paint until the number is no longer recognizable. I use the sleeve of my undershirt to clean the rest of it away, not even caring when the white fabric stains onyx. Only when Jake's number has been completely removed from her skin do I step back and smile smugly.

She's gaping at me, her eyes wide and her lips parted.

"Let me fix it for you. May I?" As I speak, I fumble in my backpack until I find a black Sharpie.

When she nods, apparently too stunned to speak, I grab her face gently—treating her the way I would invaluable porcelain—and write my number on her right cheek. Then I twist her face to the side and write Ashton's number on her left cheek.

Satisfied with my work, I recap my Sharpie and shove it into the closest pocket of my backpack I can reach.

"There!" I say with a shit-eating grin. "You look perfect."

The shock gradually fades from her face, replaced by narrow-eyed suspicion. "What did you do? You didn't draw a penis on my face, did you?"

She hesitantly reaches upwards, but I grab her wrist before she can smear the still-drying marker.

"Maybe I did... Maybe I didn't." I waggle my eyebrows at her suggestively.

"If you did, then I'll have to draw a dick on your own face when you're sleeping," she huffs.

"Are you already suggesting a sleepover, pretty girl?

After only a few texts?" I wink at her to let her know I'm just joking, even as a thrill shoots through me at the thought of sleeping over with Izzy.

Of her soft curves pressed against my hard muscles...

Of her breathy moans as I kiss her into oblivion...

Of her sweet taste on my tongue...

The bell rings overhead, and for once, I'm grateful for the interruption. I'm afraid of what I might have done if it hadn't rung when it did.

Like grab her, kiss her, and tell her I want her.

"See you in Chemistry," I say with a flirty grin.

She waves and then steps around me, heading towards Ethan who's still waiting for her, exhibiting a patience I'm not sure I'd possess if the situations were reversed. Still, despite my hatred for my twin, I feel marginally better when Izzy takes his hand and allows him to lead her into the classroom.

Despite his faults, I know he'll protect Izzy.

I head to my first hour, content with the knowledge that she's wearing *my* number on her cheek. Mine and Ashton's.

I just hope he won't freak the fuck out the second he sees it.

Twenty-Nine

IZZY

The day passes in a blur of red and black, pep rallies, and "go team, go."

I swear I'm having so much school spirit shoved down my throat, I'm going to be shitting it out for months to come.

Only Ethan joins me at the lunch table today, since the football players and cheerleaders are required to sit together as a show of support. Even still, I can feel Emery's eyes on me more often than not, and whenever I look up and catch his gaze, he winks.

My stomach flips over itself.

Ashton, on the other hand, ignores my existence the way he always does. It didn't escape my attention that Emery painted his football number on one cheek and Ashton's on the other, but I doubt the stoic man even notices. I don't know what I did to piss him off, but whatever it is has him pretending I don't exist.

I can't quite decide if that's a bad or a good thing.

By the time I need to arrive at the football game—an hour and a half before it begins—I'm a chaotic mess of nerves. And no, it's not because of Ashton.

It's because I'm terrified I'm going to mess everything up.

Ansel tried to teach me exactly what to do in class today, but most of his words went in one ear and immediately out the other.

"Use this setting at this time of day, blah blah blah."

"Only take photos from this angle, blah blah blah."

"Use the flash between this time and this time, but never this time, blah blah blah."

My plan? Aim the camera and press the button. At least I'll get an A for effort.

The man in question is waiting for me at the gate leading to the field when I arrive. His head is lowered as he fiddles with his own camera—a sophisticated monstrosity with more settings than I know what to do with. I have to clear my throat twice to garner his attention.

He glances up, confusion distorting his handsome face as if he doesn't understand why someone is interrupting him, before his cheeks tint crimson.

"Isabella. It's nice to see you on time," he tells me curtly, reaching for the extra camera bag slung over his shoulder and handing it to me.

I nearly drop the damn thing before I manage to get my bearings.

"I've been here for a little bit," I say as I unzip the bag and grab out the camera. I quickly turn it on, grateful that it's as easy as pressing a button. "I rode with Jake, and he had to be here a couple of hours before the game."

"Jake..." Ansel's elegant eyebrows arch inwards. "That's your foster brother, correct?"

"Yeah." I quickly run through the pre-checks Ansel taught me—checking the memory card storage, taking a few sample photos to make sure the lens isn't smudged, and fiddling with the lighting.

"How do you like living with Hale and Gerry?" Ansel's question is asked almost absently, but I can hear the genuine curiosity lacing it. When I glance up at him in surprise, he lowers his gaze back to his camera with a muttered, "I was a foster kid too. So I just wondered how you like this particular house and family."

"Oh." Out of everything he could've said, I didn't expect that.

Ansel—perfectly immaculate, put-together, meticulous Ansel—was once a foster kid?

I know not all foster stories are the same, but I can't help but look at him in a new light.

Ansel's cheeks are so dark they nearly blend in with the red of my sweater.

"I'm adopted now," he blurts. "I haven't been in the system for years, but I just thought... Never mind." He shakes his head quickly, clears his throat, and then adopts a careful mask. A poker face. "I'll have you take this side of the field, and I'll remain on the other. Try to focus mostly on our team and stands, but it's okay if you have a few pictures of the Vipers. They're our biggest rivals and..."

Ansel drones on. Apparently, our heart-to-heart is over. I listen attentively, nodding along whenever it's appropriate, before Ansel dismisses me with a flick of his wrist and a succinct, "Don't mess this up for us."

Geez. Thanks. Way to make a girl feel special.

There's not much else to do but wait for the game to begin.

The stadium is larger than any I've ever seen before, at least at the high school level. The bleachers are a few feet above me and are blocked off by a black-painted gate. A track curls around the inside of the stadium, giving me room to maneuver without stepping on the field. According to Jake, there are two concession stands, one on either side of the stadium near the end zones.

Even though there's still over an hour until the game begins, the stands are already beginning to fill up. I spot Hale and Lissa sitting near the fifty-yard line, and they wave to me when we make eye contact. More and more students, parents, teachers, and general townsfolk congregate on the bleachers until there's barely any room to sit. The school's marching band itself takes up almost an entire section.

Exactly an hour before the game begins, the cheerleaders rush onto the field to the audience's raucous applause. Mimi does a few back handsprings, and KD does a layout. When the girls rush past me, they stop to say hello.

Desiree all but pulls me into her arms and squeezes the daylights out of me, her rose-scented perfume permeating the air.

"You need to try out for the competitive cheer team in the spring!" she gushes, finally releasing me. "You'll do great."

"OMG! Yes!" Mimi jumps up and down excitedly.

A girl—who I assume is Emilia, though I haven't officially been introduced to her—offers me a tentative smile.

"I'm not really a cheerleading type of person." I wrinkle my nose. I have nothing against the sport—I think the things they can do with their bodies are incredible—but it's not for me.

Desiree pouts exaggeratedly. "What about the dance team? You can choose to do that for an elective next semester if you want—"

"Girls! No more chitchatting! Start your warmups!" a strident voice calls, the words punctuated by a handclap.

A college-aged woman with curly orange hair and a kind smile waves Desiree and the others towards her. She must be the coach.

"Think about it," Desiree urges as she begins to

walk backwards towards the team. "I think you'll be a great addition to the team."

"Who would be a great addition?" The coach eyes me suspiciously, and Desiree grins like the cat that ate the cream.

"The new girl, Izzy. I heard from a little birdie that she used to do dance and gymnastics." Desiree winks when I gape at her.

Where the hell did she hear that?

"Is that true?" The coach stares at me in a whole new light, her green eyes appraising. "Let's talk after the game. Izzy, was it?"

"I don't think—"

But the coach has already turned away to address the other girls.

Desiree cackles like a hyena, and when I give her the middle finger, she only laughs harder.

"Isabella!" a familiar voice calls, and I quickly drop my finger as if the air is made of fire and it's burning me.

Mr. Remington leans against the railing above me, grinning widely. An impassive Mr. Montgomery stands beside him, though his attention is fixed on his phone instead of me.

Shame.

"Mr. Remington," I squeak, my cheeks flaming at getting caught flipping someone the bird at school.

Mr. Remington chuckles and gives me a conspiratorial look. "I didn't see anything," he assures me.

I really like Mr. Remington as a teacher. Yes, some of the girls thirst after him like he's the only glass of water in the desert—cough, KD, cough—but I don't think of him like that. Admittedly, he's attractive, at least for an older man, but I don't want to see him naked or anything like that. Ew. No thanks. Hard pass.

But Mr. Montgomery, on the other hand…

I flick my gaze in the vice principal's direction before immediately lowering it to my feet. I know my crush is insanely inappropriate—and I'll never act on it —but I can't help the butterflies that go to war in my stomach whenever I lay eyes on him.

"Do you have everything you need to take…um… photographs?" Mr. Remington absently scratches at the back of his neck.

"You mean a camera?" I ask sardonically, waggling it in the air.

I swear he mutters something about smartass kids under his breath, but I could be mistaken.

"Well, if you have any questions or need anything, I'll be right over here with Christian—I mean, Mr. Montgomery." He flinches at his mistake. "I may not be the official Yearbook teacher, but while I'm filling in, I'm going to do the best I can."

"We should take our seats before it gets too crowded," Mr. Montgomery murmurs to Mr. Remington, finally glancing up from his phone.

His gaze slides to me for a fraction of a second before immediately turning away. Dismissing me.

It doesn't hurt necessarily—he's my vice principal, for fuck's sake, and I'm only his student—but I can't help but feel a pang of something in my chest. What that something is evades me.

"Were you able to get a hold of AJ?" Mr. Remington turns to face Mr. Montgomery completely, and I know the conversation is over.

I begin to walk away, but still, their conversation trickles back to me.

"Of course not." Mr. Montgomery scoffs. "He's ignoring all my texts, as usual. He doesn't even know I work at the school now, too lost in his head to care or notice."

Mr. Remington says something else, but they must've moved farther away because I can no longer hear them.

Who's AJ?

It doesn't matter, Izzy. It doesn't concern you.

I shove all thoughts of sexy vice principals aside and focus instead on the field. Any second now, the football players are going to race out of the locker room, and I'll need to be there capturing each and every moment. If I fail, I risk Ansel's wrath.

Yay me.

The only good thing that comes out of all of this is maybe, just maybe, I'll be able to catch the impenetrable and unflappable Ashton with his hand up his ass, rearranging the stick there.

The thought makes me smile.

Game on.

Thirty

IZZY

By halftime, the score is twenty-four to twenty-one. We're ahead by only one field goal, and the Vipers start with the ball next quarter.

Tensions have mounted on both sides of the stadium. More than one fight has broken out between fans of the rival teams, and two players from the Vipers got kicked out for bad sportsmanship.

Jesus Christ. This is high school football, not the NFL.

But I don't dare say any of that out loud. I just snap my pictures like a good little Yearbook student and stay out of the players' way.

I'll be the first to admit that, more often than not, my camera strays to Emery and Ashton. Jake is amazing as quarterback, but the other two men? They're phenomenal. Emery moves down the field like he owns it, his body nothing but liquid that dances and weaves through the opposing players.

And as annoying as Ashton is, even I can confess that he looks fan-fucking-tastic in his uniform. If I drool, it's only because I'm a warm-blooded female, not because I actually like him.

But who *wouldn't* drool at the sight of him?

More than one girl has his number painted on their shirts or cheeks.

Just like me.

I touch my left cheek instinctively, where the number sits predominantly on my skin.

"How's it going?" Ansel moves towards me, nearly getting punched in the face with a pompom in the process as the cheerleaders perform a routine to the screaming crowd.

"I'm a little disappointed in myself," I confess with an exaggerated sigh.

His eyebrows dip in concern. "Why is that?"

"Because I only got two pictures of the players picking their noses." I hold up my camera and begin to flick through the hundreds of photos I took before I settle on one. "This art piece I call *Finding the Gold*. As you see here, we have number fifty-five's entire finger up his nose.

"And in this picture, taken immediately after, he's giving Ashton a high five. Best moment of my life." I scroll through a few more photos until I stop on another one. "And here, we have player thirty-seven with his thumb up his nose. His *thumb*. I don't know what he's looking for up there. Diamonds, perhaps?"

I shake my head in feigned sadness.

Ansel stares at me in disbelief...before he throws his head back in laughter. The noise is startling enough to garner the attention of not only the nearest cheerleaders but a few people in the stands as well.

I'm not sure I've ever heard Ansel laugh like that.

Hell, I'm not sure I've ever seen him even *smile*.

He's handsome normally—a cold, icy sort of perfection that makes him appear unapproachable—but when his lips quirk upwards, showcasing his straight white teeth, he's otherworldly. Ethereal.

My breath catches.

"I have a few photographs I can add to your collection." Ansel's eyes glimmer with mirth as he holds out his camera for me to see. "Now, they're not picking their noses, but..."

"Oh my god. Is that Emery?" I ask, my voice high-pitched and breathless with excitement. "Is he actually picking out a wedgie? This is the best thing that ever happened to me. Please. Send it to me. I need it."

The two of us continue to compare photos until the players rush back onto the field to begin their second-half warmups. Just before Ansel can move to his side of the field, however, someone elbows him in the ribs hard enough to send him tumbling.

"Get out of the fucking way, you piece of shit."

Kain.

Of course.

Kain and his buddies laugh as they jog away.

"What a dick," I murmur, glaring after them even as I help Ansel back to his feet.

Ansel sighs, a tired sound I feel in the marrow of my bones. "Don't worry. I'm used to it."

"They do that shit often?" I stare at him in disbelief.

Yes, I hear about bullying in schools, but I can't really say I've ever been a victim of it before, nor have I seen it with my own two eyes. I may not have had a lot of friends, but people didn't hate me.

Not the way they seem to with Ansel.

"It's no big deal," Ansel murmurs, attempting to fix a strand of wayward hair that has fallen into his eyes.

"It is a big deal if they're physically touching you," I snap. An inexplicable wave of anger surges through me. "I've always known that Kain was a dick, but this is ridiculous. I'm going to punch him in the damn balls if he goes near you again."

Ansel stares at me with a strange expression. "Why would you do that for me?"

"Because we're friends, aren't we?" I shrug awkwardly. "At least, we sort of are."

Maybe acquaintances is a better word, but eh.

Ansel just continues to stare at me, and I can't quite read the emotions percolating in his fathomless eyes. After a long moment of tense silence, he clears his throat and jerks his head towards the camera in my hands.

"I'll let you get to it." Without another word, he walks briskly to his side of the stadium.

I honestly don't think I'll *ever* understand the inner workings of a guy's mind.

As I move back and forth across the track, snapping pictures left and right, I make eye contact with Emery, who's drinking from his water bottle. His helmet is off and tucked underneath his arm, allowing me to see his sweaty, mussed blond hair and red face.

Desire floods me at the sight of him.

Good lord...

Bad, Izzy! Bad! No lusting after bad-boy football players.

He offers me a flirty smile and a wink. "I'm winning this game for you, pretty girl."

"You're ridiculous." I roll my eyes, but I can't stop the stupid grin from forming on my face.

"Ridiculous for you."

"That doesn't make any sense."

"Senseless for you." He winks again.

The player beside him hits him across the back of his head, and it's only then I realize that he's standing next to Ashton.

Emery glowers at his friend and teammate but reluctantly shoves his helmet back on to focus on the game.

The third quarter begins.

I find myself just as invested as the rest of the crowd as both teams make a touchdown. We're still ahead by three points, but the Vipers have the ball and are in field goal range. I bounce on the tips of my toes in excitement as I snap a few more pictures of the players.

The Vipers' quarterback throws the ball, and their player catches it and races down the field. Someone from our team begins to chase him.

I continue to snap picture after picture as the visiting team goes wild with anticipation.

The Vipers' player skirts quickly to the side, but our defense is right there, shoving him towards the foul line. The player steps out of bounds, and the ref blows his whistle. But still, the player keeps running, not losing momentum.

Right towards me.

I attempt to race to the side, but I'm too slow, shock holding me immobile and freezing my joints in place.

The next thing I know, I'm being tackled by a two-hundred-pound player.

And my world explodes into shards of agony.

Thirty-One

ASHTON

I run through the play for the thirteenth time in my head.

Thirteen is my favorite number. I don't know why some people believe it's unlucky; it's only ever brought me good things.

I was born on the thirteenth of June.

I discovered Ethan, Emery, and Reid were a part of my pack on my thirteenth birthday.

My football jersey number is thirteen.

And I met my fated mate on September thirteenth.

I bounce on the tips of my toes in eager anticipation as our defense makes another incredible tackle. Emery roars like a Neanderthal, jumps into the air, and then tackles me from behind, wrapping his arms around my neck. I just barely stop myself from flipping him onto the ground.

He knows how I feel about unsanctioned touch.

"We have this game in the bag!" my best friend hollers, practically vibrating with excitement.

I grimace and am finally able to detangle myself from the human-sized koala. "Don't get cocky. That's when people start making mistakes."

He snorts and takes a step away from me. "*People*. You say that like you're not one of them."

I cock an eyebrow at him, something he's unable to see with my helmet firmly in place. "Aren't I?"

"I forget that you're perfect and infallible." Emery slaps me on the shoulder hard enough to send me staggering forward a few steps. Asshole. "Certainly more perfect than a certain blonde—"

"Shut the fuck up, Emery." Abruptly, my good mood from our impending win diminishes in an explosion of flaky ash.

Any mention of the elusive Isabella does that to me.

She's an enigma—one I'm not certain if I want to figure out or ignore. I don't believe in coincidences, and I'm sure even my smitten packmate can admit that her sudden appearance leaves a lot to be desired.

Why now?

Why here?

I wouldn't put it past my father to use her as a tool to manipulate me.

Is that why she's here? Did he bring her? Is she working for him?

I'm suddenly desperate to get out on the field and

abolish some of this restless, chaotic energy bursting to life inside of me. I'm afraid I'm going to implode and obliterate everyone in the immediate vicinity if I don't fucking *move*.

And it'll be Isabella's fault.

It doesn't help matters that my brothers turn into simpering fools when it comes to her. Ethan spends most of his nights talking to her on the phone or playing video games online. He doesn't even seem to care that he's no longer at the top of the class and is falling behind Ansel. And Emery hasn't even looked at another girl since she barreled her way into our lives.

Even *Reid* is intrigued by her. He'll never admit it, but I know he watches her house late at night, especially when he heard about the two murders. The man hates all women, yet he willingly curls himself around her tiny finger without a second thought.

It doesn't make a lick of sense.

Unbidden, my gaze slides to where she stands on the track. I despise how beautiful she is. How perfect. The wind blows back her blonde curls, allowing me a view of her cheeks. A strange, indecipherable feeling bubbles to life in my chest at the sight of my number on her smooth skin.

My number.

It takes me a second too long to realize this unnamed emotion is possessiveness. I immediately want to slap myself across the face.

Just who does she think she is?

She's a distraction, Ashton. Remember that.

I learned my lesson at an early age what happens when you let people into your life, what happens when you open your heart to others. It leads to nothing but bitter disappointment and loneliness. Everyone leaves you in the end. It's inevitable.

My mother left me.

Most of my fathers left me.

My brother left me.

I berate myself for allowing my thoughts to drift down such a morose direction and focus back on the game.

"It's fourth down," Emery murmurs, jogging in place. I know he's speaking more to himself than to me. "We need to make this fucking tackle. Come on, guys. Come on. Come on."

"Even after all these years, you *still* talk to yourself." I shake my head in wonderment. "Some things will never change."

"Yeah...well...I don't have my twin to talk to anymore. So why not do the second best thing?" Despite his light-hearted jesting, I can hear the undercurrent of pain he tries to hide.

I hate the distance growing between Emery and Ethan. They're brothers, for fuck's sake. Twins.

If I had a second chance with my brother...

But no. I can't think about the past. Only my future matters now.

The Vipers' quarterback throws the ball.

It spirals through the air and lands effortlessly in the waiting retriever's hands. He takes off down the field without a backwards glance.

Beside me, Emery curses colorfully.

Kain chases after the player, but I notice that he's jogging more than running. As a shifter, we have enhanced skills when it comes to certain things—speed being one of them. Of course, we can't use the full extent of our gifts around the oblivious humans, but we do add just a little bit of juice when we move to give us an edge on the field.

So why the fuck is Kain moving slower than my now-dead grandma, who had a walker and was partially blind?

"Does the fucker want us to lose?" Emery snaps, obviously noticing the same thing I did.

The Viper skirts towards the sidelines, and I blow out a breath of relief. At least he didn't make it all the way to the end zone—

But my relief is short-lived when I notice that the player isn't slowing down. He's running...

Directly at Isabella.

Emery takes off before I can even get my bearings, but he's too far away. *We're* too far away.

However, I'm close enough to see terror splay across Isabella's face a second before she's tackled to the ground.

Bones snap.

Blood wells.

I see red.

I can't think through the sudden roaring in my ears. No, not a roaring. It's too high-pitched to be that. I equate it to the whistling of a train.

Somebody grabs the back of the Viper's uniform and yanks him to his feet.

Emery.

I realize that fact almost belatedly.

A loud snarl reverberates through the air.

I need to stop him before he does something stupid.

I need to move.

I need to—

I can't pull my gaze off of Isabella's broken body.

People are running towards her, one of them Hale, but surprisingly, it's Ansel who reaches her first. He places his hands over her chest, and the red coating my vision darkens, becoming almost garnet in appearance.

I lunge forward, prepared to rip him limb from limb for touching my mate...

When I see a strange green mist emitting from his hands.

What the fuck?

As I watch, both horrified and transfixed, Isabella's arm snaps back into place. It looks as if it never broke to begin with. Her fingers begin to straighten out as well, and her leg no longer bends at an odd angle.

What. The. Fuck?

I need to go to her.

Hold her.

Save her.

Fur explodes on my arms, and I take a step forward...

When a familiar man steps in front of me.

A man I never thought I'd see again.

"What...?" I blink, certain I'm hallucinating.

My older brother's face is grave, and his eyes are clouded with fear.

Fear for me?

Emery?

Isabella?

Isabella...

The shock holding me immobile dissipates, and I find myself moving. I need to get to her. I need to touch her. I need to—

"We need to get you out of here," my brother tells me, guiding me away from my mate.

I feel as if I'm walking in the opposite direction of a current. Everyone is racing to get to Isabella.

My mate.

I need to get to her.

"No—" I attempt to break free of my brother's grip, but his hand simply tightens on my shoulder, turning into a vise.

"I'm sorry, AJ." His eyes darken as they flick towards something over my shoulder.

Or some*one*.

A needle pierces my neck.

Somewhere in the deepest recesses of my mind, I recognize it as a tranquilizer dart alphas use to control unruly, young pups.

My brother...just drugged me.

Isabella...

Her name plays on a continuous loop in my head.

But then darkness claims me, and I think of nothing at all.

Thirty-Two

IZZY

First, there was pain.

Unspeakable, agonizing pain as if my veins had been doused in gasoline and then lit on fire. Then that pain took on a numbing, icy quality.

And slowly, that numbness transformed into confusion when I blinked open my crusty eyelids to find Ansel kneeling before me, his features set in concentration and his tongue poking out between his lips.

And I must've hit my head, because I could've sworn I saw green light emanating from his hands.

Now, that confusion has been replaced by horror as everything comes back to me with a staggering intensity.

The football game.

The player tackling me.

The breaking of my bones.

Only...I must've imagined that audible crack. I'm able to move most of my limbs, and the pain I thought I felt is nothing but a distant memory.

Even still, I feel groggy and lightheaded, almost as if someone shoved a thousand wet cotton balls into my head, and now they're sticking to every available surface.

"An ambulance is on the way," a feminine voice says. "Don't move, sweetheart."

Huh?

What?

An ambulance?

Why do I need an ambulance?

I blink a few more times as I will the world to come back into focus. It does—slowly and painfully, almost like colored pixels congregating together to form blurry, indistinct images.

Blink.

I spot a few school officials attempting to corral the growing crowd. Their murmured words go in one ear and immediately out the other.

I hear the words, "She's going to be okay," more than once.

Who's going to be okay?

Me?

I want to scream to the world that I feel fine, but my lips don't part. My tongue resembles a lead weight in my mouth.

Blink.

Blink.

Blink.

Blink.

I see Emery being restrained by four football players as he attempts to attack the Viper who tackled me. The blond twin's helmet has been discarded, allowing me to see the red splotches on his cheeks and the scowl distorting his mouth.

Has his mouth always been that...strange-looking?

Blink.

I swear I see razor-sharp teeth for a fraction of a second as his jawline elongates. And is that *hair* on his neck? What the hell?

Blink.

Blink.

Blink.

I notice Ashton in the distance, talking to a frantic-looking Mr. Montgomery. Mr. Remington creeps up behind the pair and sticks something into Ashton's neck. The boy immediately droops, but Mr. Montgomery catches him before he can hit the ground. The three hurry away before anyone can see them—not that anyone is paying attention. All eyes are on me.

Blink.

Jake's there, squeezing my hand, promising me that I'll be okay. Telling me that I scared the shit out of him. Warning me not to do that ever again because he felt his balls shrivel into raisins when he saw me get tackled.

Blink.

Hale and Lissa join him on my other side. Hale argues with the pale-faced woman—the school nurse, I believe—but I can't hear what they're saying.

Blink.

Blink.

Blink.

I'm being lifted on a stretcher. Something hard wraps around my neck. A brace? I want to tell them that I'm fine, that I don't feel any pain, but words fail me.

Blink.

Ansel's there, on the sidelines, his eyes shadowed, his lips curled downwards, his hands balled into fists at his sides. As if he feels my gaze on him, he turns in my direction. His frown deepens, and he immediately focuses on his feet.

Blink.

Blink.

I swear I see Grayson in the stands, watching me. A heady combination of terror and anger radiates from his eyes. The girl next to him places a hand on his knee and says something to him that has his jaw clenching even tighter. He shifts slightly so her hand falls off of him.

Blink.

I allow myself to surrender to sleep.

After all, reality isn't making a lick of sense. Maybe my dreams will provide some clarity.

Thirty-Three

IZZY

"We want you to stay the night for observation. There's a good chance that you may have a concussion." The doctor—an older lady with brown and gray hair, compassionate green eyes, and a haggard face—flips through the chart she has on me. Her lips compress in a taut line when she finally glances up. "This could've been a lot worse, Isabella. You got lucky."

Hale's hand tightens around mine. "Thank you, Doctor. Anything else we should know?"

Doctor Brenda, as she introduced herself as, offers him a feeble smile. "If she does have a concussion, we're going to ask that Isabella refrain from doing any physical activities for a few days. But besides that, no. She seems to be in good health, considering the circumstances."

Hale walks the doctor out of the room and then

returns a second later. Dark shadows underscore each of his eyes and draw attention to the wrinkles on his face, making him look years older. He hasn't left my side since I was admitted to the hospital a few hours earlier.

The doctors were initially worried when I fell unconscious, believing I had a brain bleed. But after an MRI, they determined that I probably just have a mild concussion. They also took X-rays of my right arm and leg, where most of my bruising resides. But both of those came back clear.

I, miraculously, am okay.

The question is...*how* am I okay?

I feel like I'm losing my mind. I've been given five random puzzle pieces and have no idea how they fit together. No matter what I do, the picture isn't clear.

"How are you feeling, kid?" Hale's voice is tight with concern as he moves to reclaim his chair beside my hospital bed.

I try for a smile. "Like I've been tackled by a two-hundred-pound football player."

My foster dad winces. "Yeah...not your finest moment. If you wanted to join the football team, you could've just asked."

I snort before I can stop myself. "Do you think they'll put me in the starting lineup?"

"Most definitely." He lowers his voice to a conspiratorial whisper. "The school board will be too afraid that you'll sue if they don't."

I actually laugh out loud at that before immediately sobering. I begin to pick at a thread on my blanket, twirling it around my finger. "So...what happened, exactly?"

Hale heaves out a tired sigh and relaxes back in his chair. "What do you remember?"

I think back, trying to ignore the sudden throbbing in my head, like my brain is being stabbed by a thousand flaming needles. "Ummm...well, I remember a big football player running at me. And then..." Pain. Lots of pain. Only, I must've imagined that, because I seem to be in relatively good condition. "Everything after that is a blur."

Hale nods like my answer is what he expected, though I detect the slightest tightening of the skin around his eyes.

"The doctor was right. You got very lucky it wasn't more serious." He blows out a breath, his entire chest seeming to cave in with the motion, and then scratches at the stubble lining his jawline. "Scared the living daylights out of me. I swear my hair turned gray."

"Don't blame me for that," I say with a scoff. "It was already gray when I met you."

He half-heartedly swats at my thigh. "Brat," he teases affectionately. Then he frowns. "Gerry should be coming home soon. I called him after the incident, and he told me he's on his way."

Something akin to unease skitters across my skin. I've grown used to the makeshift family I created with

Hale, Lissa, Jake, and even Seth. A part of me is terrified of adding a new face to the mix. What will Gerry think of me? Is he pissed that I pulled him away from work?

What does he even do for a living? I know he travels a lot, hence why I haven't met him, but Hale has never gone into specifics.

I debate asking but quickly decide now isn't the time. My brain is too focused on everything that transpired during the football game.

Ansel, with his shimmering hands.

Emery's distorted face.

Ashton being dragged away by my substitute teacher and vice principal.

Grayson sitting in the bleachers with his new girlfriend.

Unless I imagined all of that...

My head feels like it's about to explode. I can't even say for certain if it's my own tumultuous thoughts or the possible concussion. All I know is that I'm exhausted, my body aches but doesn't hurt, and the world is a confusing and terrifying place.

* * *

The doctors tell me I only have a mild concussion—which, considering the circumstances, is a miracle. They release me the very next day.

I change into a pair of clothes Hale grabbed for me

—leggings and a sweater that slides down one shoulder—and attempt to turn on my phone for the first time since I was brought to the hospital.

But the screen remains black.

"Shit," I murmur, realizing my phone is dead.

I shove it into the waistband of my leggings and then hurry out of the bathroom.

Hale's waiting for me in the hall, and he smiles when he sees me. "Ready to go?"

"Yup."

So, so ready.

I would rather gouge out my eyes with a rusty spoon than spend another second in that damn hospital room.

The ride home is silent. I keep my cheek pressed against the window as I fight off my growing drowsiness. I wasn't able to sleep for longer than an hour or two at the hospital, and now it's catching up with me. My eyelids feel like lead weights, and my body is a clump of cement.

Hale's phone rings where it's sitting in the cup holder.

My foster dad's lips purse as his gaze flicks towards the phone before focusing back on the road.

"Do you need to get that?"

He shakes his head. "Not while I'm driving."

The phone stops ringing...and then immediately begins again.

And again.

And again.

And again.

When it rings for the seventh time, I quirk an eyebrow and ask, "Do you want me to answer it?"

"I know exactly who's calling me, and I'm not in the mood to talk to him right now."

The drive seems to go on forever—made even longer by the incessant ringing of Hale's phone. I swear I'm going to have nightmares about that ringtone.

"Can you please just turn off my phone?" Hale begs when it rings a-fucking-gain.

Nodding, I grab the phone out of the cup holder and quickly move to turn it off. Just before the screen turns dark, I catch the name of the caller.

Kyle.

Who the heck is Kyle?

Not your business.

I lower the phone and place my hands in my lap.

When we finally arrive at Hale's house, I'm surprised to see an unfamiliar vehicle in the driveway.

Gerry's, perhaps?

Before I can even voice my question out loud, the front door of the house is thrown open, and two familiar men race towards me. I catch a glimpse of tan skin, sun-kissed amber hair, and green eyes fireworked with gold.

Emery and Ethan.

Emery reaches the car first and all but yanks the

door open. Less than a second later, I'm in his arms, my head nestled just underneath his chin.

I immediately go still in his embrace, almost as if an electrical current shot through me. As a general rule, I don't like touch. At all.

Yet there's no denying the heat that envelops me as he holds me close. A feeling of calmness and serenity sweeps over me, and I find myself sagging against him, confident he'll be able to hold my weight.

"We've been so fucking worried," he growls in my ear.

I can't help but note his voice is a little deeper than normal. Unbidden, my mind travels back to that moment shortly after the accident, when I could've sworn Emery's face lengthened and transformed...

Emery pulls me out of the car, still keeping his arms wrapped around me, and begins to penguin-walk me to the front door, my feet dragging against the cement.

"We were in the waiting room, but our father said we couldn't hover," Ethan adds.

I feel him more than see him step up to my other side.

His hand lands on my shoulder, the softest of touches, before immediately retreating. "But Hale said we could stay at your house until you returned home."

"More like you threatened me until I gave in," Hale mutters under his breath as he swings his house keys around his finger.

"I'm fine," I assure the twins, awkwardly patting Emery's back.

I'm not used to having people...care about me. It's unnerving, to put it mildly.

And also exhilarating.

"I heard a crack." Emery's voice is muffled from where he has his mouth pressed against my neck. The feel of his lips causes goose bumps to pepper across my skin and my stomach to swirl with a strange heat. "I thought... Well, the only thing that kept me from losing my shit was Hale assuring me that you were okay. But I still needed to see for myself."

Ethan runs a hand through my hair, and I finally have enough. There's been too much touching for one day.

I may spontaneously combust if they keep this up. I'm sure my rising body temperature isn't healthy after the night I had.

I wiggle my body in an attempt to break free of Emery's hold. Reluctantly, he places me on my feet and steps away.

"I promise you, I'm fine." I volley my gaze between both brothers to emphasize my point. "I don't know how I'm fine...but I am. Only a few bruises and a mild concussion. I'll be good as new by school on Monday."

Ethan's lips thin. "You should take the week off. Rest. Relax."

"I don't need an entire week off." I laugh lightly, certain he's joking, but his face remains serious.

"Do you have bath bombs?" Emery pipes in.

What in the...?

"Bath bombs?"

I give Hale an incredulous look, asking him without words if he knows what's going on, but his attention is fixed on the twins. His eyes narrow nearly imperceptibly.

"Don't chicks use bath bombs to relax?" Emery asks, running a hand through his tousled blond hair. "We'll buy you some if you don't have any."

"We can also bring you chocolate," Ethan adds as he absently unzips his jacket.

What the heck is he doing?

My confusion grows when he shrugs out of the coat and then drapes it over my shoulders. He doesn't even seem to realize he's doing it, his movements almost mechanical. Robotic.

"Do you need anything else?" Emery asks with concern as he removes first one glove and then the next from his hands. "Movies? We have some subscriptions we can log you into. Or do you want some new video games?" As he speaks, he thrusts my hands into first one glove and then the next. "We can get you a new gaming device—"

"What the hell are you two doing?" I finally ask.

Ethan freezes, his hands raised where he's been tugging at his beanie, and Emery stares down at my wrist in his grasp. Both men appear confused for a fraction of a second before their cheeks tint crimson.

"Um..." Emery scratches at the nape of his neck.

"I-I don't..." Ethan sputters.

"Scent-marking," Hale breathes, sounding stunned.

I give him a confused look. "Scent-marking?"

Hale blinks repeatedly, then shakes his head as if coming out of a daze. He focuses on me and forces a tremulous smile.

"Why don't you kids come inside and play some video games while I get dinner started? Ethan, Emery, you're more than welcome to stay if you want to, but it is late. Make sure you call your parents first and let them know. I wouldn't normally allow you to stay here past eleven, but these are unusual circumstances."

Without another word, Hale hurries into the house, leaving me behind with the two blushing twins.

What the hell did Hale mean by scent-marking? Was he making a joke?

Ethan wrings his hands together, opens his mouth, closes it, frowns, and then hurries after Hale with a hollered, "I call being Mario!"

Emery scowls. "What if I wanted to be Mario?"

"When have you ever wanted to be Mario in your life?"

"Right this second."

Ethan sighs and spins around to face us. "You're arguing just to argue with me, aren't you?"

Emery rolls his eyes. "Fuck off."

Slinging an arm around my shoulder, he leads me

towards the front door. But just before we enter the house, movement in the forest garners my attention.

Is that a...wolf?

For just a second, I swear I see a wolf sitting in the tree line, its tail thumping against the ground and the cresting sun glimmering off its light coat. Or perhaps it's a very large dog.

But then I blink, and the animal is gone.

I wonder if I imagined it to begin with.

Thirty-Four

IZZY

I wake to the feeling of eyes on me.

It's that sensation you have when you're in a room full of people, yet the spotlight is only on you. Your skin begins to crawl, and your stomach collapses in on itself, folding over like a building in a hurricane.

Every muscle in my body locks together as I debate what to do. In the bed opposite mine, Lissa continues to sleep peacefully, utterly oblivious to the intruder in our room.

Is it Jake checking in on me? He's been hovering a little more than usual since I returned home from the hospital, but this is creepy, even for him.

Hale?

A large shadow moves by the window, and I ball my hand into a fist and open my mouth to scream.

Before any sound can escape, however, someone places a palm over my mouth, trapping the cry.

Familiar ice-blue eyes peer back at me, appearing almost silver in the ambient moonlight seeping in through the window.

"Grayson?" At least, I try to say his name, but with his hand still over my mouth, it comes out like "Rayzon."

He keeps his hand on my face a second longer, ensuring I'm not going to scream, before pulling away and placing a finger to his lips.

Questions settle on the tip of my tongue, but I hold them back. I quickly slip out of bed, throw on a sweatshirt, and follow Grayson out the window.

The forest is eerie at this time of night. Darkness creates ominous silhouettes, and the trees look like skeletal monsters. The moon and stars only add to the creepy atmosphere. The minimal light they provide creates even *more* shadows, more places for monsters to hide.

Crickets chirp, and somewhere in the distance, an owl hoots. Dying leaves and brittle grass crunch underneath my bare feet as Grayson leads me farther away from the house and closer to the forest edge.

"What the hell, Grayson?" I mumble, rubbing sleep from my eyes. "I'm not wearing any shoes, it's colder than Satan's asshole out here, and I have a job interview tomorrow. Why are you—"

My rant is interrupted by Grayson pulling me into his arms.

Grayson Grey is hugging me.

Hugging me.

I abhor touch, but that's nothing compared to Grayson. He once broke the fingers of a man who accidentally bumped into him at a party.

My body wilts against his instinctively. There's just something so familiar about Grayson, so comforting. I know him on a primal level, in a way that defies logic and reason. If I were to believe in soulmates, I would say he's mine. He understands me better than anyone else I know.

Which makes this entire situation even harder.

He's hugging someone he considers a little sister. A best friend. An obligation he promised to look after.

I'm hugging a man I've been in love with for years now.

I try to tell myself to pull away, to put distance between us, to laugh this off, but I can't seem to get myself to move. I remain limp and pliant in his embrace —a rag doll for him to use and discard. My pulse skitters in a way that's almost painful as I inhale his leather scent.

But then reality slaps me in the face like the bitch she is.

Grayson has a girlfriend, and though we're doing nothing but hugging, this isn't fair to her.

It takes every ounce of willpower I possess, but I

force myself to leave Grayson's arms. Almost instantly, I'm bombarded by the cold air, which slices at my skin like throwing stars. I miss his warmth.

"What was that for?" I try to keep my voice light and playful, even as the knots in my stomach weave themselves into a damn quilt the size of Texas.

Grayson swallows heavily. "I saw. At the game. I saw. And I thought…" Shadows create dark lines across his face, almost obscuring his features from view. "Fuck, Izzy."

I wrap my arms around myself. I'd like to say it's to ward off the chill, but that would be a lie. A part of me feels the need to protect myself from Grayson and his words.

Only the people you love most of all have the capacity to destroy you so irrevocably.

"Well, as you can see, I'm good as new." I try for a smile, but it flutters at the edges before dipping completely. "I'm fine, Grayson. I swear."

"I thought I lost you," he rasps.

"I'm too hard to get rid of. It'll take at least two football players to keep me down for good. Now, can we talk tomorrow? I'm freezing my tits off, and I swear my—" Once again, I'm cut off.

But this time, Grayson doesn't just hug me.

He kisses me.

Kisses. Me.

His lips are soft against my own, and his five

o'clock shadow abrades my skin in a way that has pleasure coursing through me.

How many times have I imagined kissing Grayson?

Way too many. I lost count after fifty.

One of his hands settles on my waist, while the other tangles in my hair, wrapping it around his wrist. He tugs, and the pleasure-pain combination sends arousal spiraling through me.

Oh. My. God.

Oh my god.

Grayson Grey is kissing me.

And...

He shouldn't be.

Common sense returns to me, and I place both of my hands on Grayson's chest. But instead of tugging him closer—as I so desperately want to—I push him away. As expected, Grayson moves without prodding, his eyes hooded with unfettered desire.

The sight lights me up inside.

No. Bad, Izzy! Stop this.

"You can't do this to me." My voice is practically a croak.

His eyebrows furrow. "What—?"

"You can't kiss me like you care for me. That's not fair." God help me, tears actually prick the backs of my eyes and spill over. I brush them away angrily.

Grayson appears confused as he takes a step closer. "I do care for you—"

"Not like that." I shake my head. "Not the way I want you to."

"I don't understand—"

"Grayson, you have a *girlfriend*. You can't kiss me when you're with someone else. It's not fair to her or to me. I'm not some fucking mistress—"

"I never said you were!" Grayson hurries towards me and grabs my biceps.

Despite the urgency in his tone, his touch remains gentle. Soft. He holds me like I'm something precious and delicate, something immensely valuable. I can't decide if I hate it or love it.

"Izzy, listen to me. I don't have a girlfriend—"

"Now you're lying to me?" I stare at him incredulously.

How can this be the same guy who once held me in his arms for hours, just so I could get to sleep and not be plagued by nightmares? The same guy who sat outside my bedroom door when I was afraid of what my foster brother would do to me? I don't recognize him now.

That Grayson would *never* lie to me.

"I'm not..." He runs a shaky hand through his dark hair. "Fuck! Okay, yes. I have a girlfriend, but it's not what you think. Izzy, you have to believe me. Things are more complicated than—"

"What's complicated about this?" I demand. "You have a girlfriend. And you can't kiss me when you're with someone else. Are you saying you're breaking up with her?"

His eyes darken with what appears to be anguish. "I can't. But as I said before, it's not what it seems. I want *you*."

"Oh, fuck off, Grayson." I slap his hands away from me.

"It's the truth," he says through clenched teeth. "You're the only girl I love—"

"Love?" I gape at him and then burst into slightly hysterical laughter. Every word he says is another knife being jammed into my heart. How many more can I take before I bleed to death? "What the fuck, Grayson?"

"It's the truth!" His hands ball into fists at his sides.

"So...what? You want me as your side piece as you go fuck your actual girlfriend—?"

"I'm not fucking her! I never even touched her!" Grayson snarls. "And don't you dare talk about yourself like that. Izzy, listen to me."

Abruptly, he grabs a hold of my arms again, only this time, I don't push him away. I have no idea why. Maybe a masochist part of me wants to hear what he has to say.

"Everything I do is to protect you."

"Are you really feeding me that BS excuse?" I blink at him.

I suddenly feel tired. No, not just tired. Exhausted.

It's the type of bone-deep weariness that weighs down my eyelids and slackens my muscles.

"There are things that you don't understand," he insists, his voice breaking on the final word. He clears his throat and tries again. "Not everything is as it seems."

"Grayson, I don't want to fight. I'm tired, and my feet hurt, and my head is pounding, and I just want to go to bed." I'm practically pleading now.

"Izzy…"

"Look, why don't we just forget this ever happened? Okay?" My heart batters against my rib cage.

I doubt I'll ever forget the feel of Grayson's lips against my own, but I'm giving him an out. We can still be friends, he can continue seeing Sydney, and everything will be right in the world.

Even if it feels as if my heart is being shredded into confetti-sized pieces.

Grayson looks as if he wants to argue, but whatever expression he sees on my face has him reconsidering.

He reluctantly nods.

"Yeah, okay." He shoves his hands into his pockets and walks me back to my bedroom window.

We don't speak, which I'm grateful for. Every word he said before twisted me up inside, and it'll take years for me to untangle the mess he left behind.

"I'm sorry," he whispers just before I can climb inside my room.

He leans forward, and at first, I think he's going to kiss me. Instead, his lips brush against my cheek in the softest of caresses.

Without another word, he's gone.

And so is a shattered piece of my heart.

Thirty-Five

IZZY

"**I**f you start feeling lightheaded or faint or sick, give me a call," Hale says for the one millionth time as he pulls the car to a stop in front of the ancient theater downtown.

"I will, Hale," I assure him...also for the one millionth time.

Hale wasn't pleased when I told him I still planned to show up for my job interview today. He tried to tell me he knew the owner and could get it rescheduled, but I refused. For one, I feel perfectly fine. For two, I don't want the owner to think I need special privileges.

I need this job.

My phone buzzes where I have it face down on my knee, and I pick it up with a smile. I have two new texts, one from Emery and one from Ethan.

And over two dozen messages from Grayson, but I'm pretending those don't exist.

Avoidance at its finest.

I click on Emery's name first, just because he happens to be at the top of the screen.

EMERY

Are you excited for your interview? You'll do great. Probably. Unless you suck. So…just don't suck.

And then I click on Ethan's text.

ETHAN

Good luck! Fingers crossed for you.

A giddy feeling unfurls in my chest as I shoot off responses to both guys. How can two completely different men make me feel so…happy? Buoyant? Airy?

Just as I hit send on the one to Ethan, a new message pops up on the screen.

UNKNOWN

How are you feeling?

I furrow my brows.

IZZY

Who is this?

I wait for a reply, but when I don't receive one right away, I shut my phone off and put it in my purse.

I chose to dress nice for the occasion in a sleek, black pencil skirt and white blouse. I styled my hair in an elegant chignon that rests at the base of my neck. A few loose curls tumble down to frame my face.

"You ready for this, kid?" Hale asks as I stare at my resume.

There's very little on it. I never actually had a job before, unless you count babysitting. Being bounced from home to home, town to town, didn't give me the luxury. Still, Hale helped me early this morning create one, putting himself as a reference.

"As ready as I'll ever be," I mutter as I push open the car door and step outside.

"I'll be at the coffee shop right across the street. Text me when you're done," he tells me, and I offer him a wobbly smile.

I can do this.

I can totally do this.

I totally can't do this.

I take a moment to study the theater.

It sits smack-dab between two buildings—a tiny clothing store and a candy shop, to be precise—and has a flat, red roof. The brick walls have begun to fade in color, appearing more umber than brown or red. The glass doors are opaque, not allowing me to see inside.

There's no parking in front of the building—unless you're able to find street parking—but there is a lot directly behind it. However, you'll have to walk around the block to enter the theater.

It's small and quaint and exactly what I pictured in this redneck town.

Pulling on my metaphorical big-girl panties, I take a deep breath, push back my shoulders, and then enter the theater.

The smell of buttery popcorn immediately assaults my senses, but it's not entirely unpleasant. Almost immediately, I home in on Jake, who stands behind the concession stand, handing a couple two sodas. When he sees me, a wide grin splits across his face, but he doesn't speak until the couple enters a theater and disappears from view.

Jake runs around the counter and pulls me into his arms, rocking me from side to side.

What is up with all of the men in my life *hugging* me? Ugh.

"Can't. Breathe," I puff out dramatically.

"Shit. Sorry." Jake pulls away and then immediately attempts to straighten a piece of my hair that his freaking chest messed up. "How are you feeling? Does your head hurt? Hale told me to keep an eye on you, so I want to make sure—"

I place my hand over his mouth. "I'm fine. Promise. Stop worrying."

Something wet brushes against my palm, and I pull my hand back, aghast.

"Did you just *lick* me?" I demand.

Jake flashes me a shit-eating grin. "Anything you put in front of my mouth, I'll lick. It's the new rule."

"So if I put a piece of dog shit in front of your mouth, you'll lick it?" I deadpan.

Jake doesn't even blink. "That's what I said, didn't I?"

"You're such a dork." I shove his shoulder and step farther into the lobby.

It's small, with wooden floorboards, cream-colored walls, and a single stand that seems to sell both concessions and tickets. Movie posters decorate the walls, though I don't spot any from this century. A hall to the right leads to the bathrooms and theater one. The opposite hallway has theaters two, three, and four, as well as what appears to be a closet.

"So, I'm here for the interview." I attempt to inject confidence into my voice. "Do you know where I need to go?"

I have to stop myself from shifting on the balls of my feet or fiddling with my hair—both of which are nervous habits I haven't gotten rid of, even after all these years.

"Yeah, one second." Jake practically skips to a door I hadn't noticed earlier directly behind the counter. He knocks on it twice. "Silas, Isabella's here for her interview."

There's no answer.

Oh god. Is this the wrong day? Is he not expecting me? Did Jake pull my leg when he said he got me an interview?

My stomach roils madly, and I fear I'm going to throw up.

I should just walk away before I can embarrass myself further.

Yup.

Leave.

Just leave.

Before my feet can catch up with my brain, the door swings open, revealing a scarily large man.

He isn't just tall but muscular. He looks as if he can bench press both me and Jake without breaking a sweat. His dark hair hangs in disheveled waves on the top of his head, the exact same shade as his trimmed beard. Tattoos cover both his arms and hands.

And where his left eye should be, there's now nothing but white, puckered scars.

He appears to be in his mid-thirties, early forties, though it's hard to guesstimate his age. There's something hardened and almost ancient about his scowl. That sounds cheesy as fuck, but it's the truth. He looks like a man who has been through some *shit*.

"Silas, Isabella's here for her interview," Jake says formally, and if I wasn't freaking the fuck out, I would've snorted.

I've never heard Jake sound so well-mannered in all the days I've known him.

Silas's gaze slides to me and sticks there. His jaw clenches, and he immediately turns away, almost as if it pains him to stare directly at me.

"Come on now." His voice is gruff. Low. A rich baritone. "I don't have all day."

He leaves the door to his office open, and after one parting glance at Jake, who gives me a thumbs-up, I hurry to follow after the scary theater owner.

The office is small and cluttered, with figurines lining the back shelf, comic books on the desk, and movie posters on the walls. It's almost comical to see such a nerdy setup. Silas is so...scary. Somehow, his geeky office demotes him from intimidating to approachable.

Silas waves a hand towards the seat opposite his desk, and I take it after only a moment of hesitation. Hands trembling, I give him my resume, which he takes without ever glancing in my direction. His jaw still seems to be clenched.

"So you're new to town and living with Hale." He doesn't phrase it as a question, yet I take it as one.

"Yeah. Just arrived a few days ago."

Has it only been a few days? It feels longer.

He nods once, still not meeting my gaze. His fingers begin to tap against the top of his desk. "Hale told me you were a foster kid beforehand."

"Um, yes, sir." I inwardly wince at how fucking awkward I sound.

Silas mutters something too low for me to hear and then gives me an assessing glare. Well, at least his one good eye narrows. "You can't wear fucking skirts here."

"Oh, yes, of course—"

"Next time, wear jeans or something." He wheels

his chair backwards, opens a box on the floor behind him, and grabs out a stack of shirts, all with the theater logo on them. "What size are you? Small?" He throws a shirt at my face. "Get changed in the bathroom, and then I'll have the assistant manager show you the ropes."

He crosses his arms over his chest and scowls at a spot over my shoulder.

Wait...

That's it? I got the job?

Elation wars with confusion in my chest.

"I...um...thank you, sir. I really appreciate the opportunity—"

Silas mumbles something—once again too quiet for me to hear—and then pushes his massive form out of the chair. He leaves the room without a second glance, presumably to get Jake.

I stare down at the shirt for a long moment as I bite down on the need to squeal at the top of my lungs.

I have a job.

I actually have a job.

Would it be weird if I hugged the shirt to my chest like those Victorian women do in movies when they get a fancy new Cinderella dress? Yes? No?

The door opens, and I turn towards it with a wide smile, expecting to see Jake.

But it's not Jake who steps inside.

Reid stares at me for a long moment—his garnet

hair tousled, his forehead dotted with perspiration, and his assistant manager name tag pinned prominently to his chest—and then mutters a quiet, "Fuck," under his breath.

Fuck is right.

Thirty-Six

IZZY

Reid can be very scary when he wants to be.

Which seems to be all the time.

I don't think I've ever seen him without his customary scowl firmly in place.

Today is no different.

As Reid gives me a brisk tour of the diminutive theater, that trademark glower never leaves his face. He looks as if he wants to murder someone.

Correction—he looks as if he wants to murder *me*.

And I very much prefer *not* to be murdered, thank you very much.

Everything he shows me is pretty self-explanatory. The four theaters. The ticket booth-slash-concession counter. The employee break room. Silas's office. The locked closet the staff keeps all cleaning materials.

If you're working the opening shift, you're required to arrive an hour before the theater opens to prepare for the day. The closing shift is responsible for the majority of cleanup, but the morning shift is supposed to start the popcorn machine, open the register, turn on the soda fountain, etc. And after every showing, a team of two will head into the theater and clean it.

"This seems simple enough," I tell Reid as I peer into the tiny closet at the very end of the hall. I spot a broom, dustpan, vacuum, window cleaner, and a duster.

Reid mumbles something noncommittally as he guides me back towards the front, where Jake is working the counter. My foster brother offers me a huge smile and a thumbs-up when he sees me.

Reid, I've come to notice, doesn't spend any time near the counter. I wonder if it's because of his...smell. I can't imagine patrons would be eager to buy popcorn from someone like Reid.

Before the large man can guide me back into Silas's office, I dig my heels in and turn towards the bathroom.

"Can I quickly change my shirt? I'll be quick."

Reid volleys his gaze between me, the shirt in my hands, and then my white blouse. His cheeks turn an enticing shade of red as he mutters a quick, "Yeah."

I hurry into the stall, unbutton my blouse, and then shove the shirt over my head. The damn material fits me like a glove, conforming to every curve. I try to tug it away from my chest unsuccessfully, but it continues to cling to my breasts and stomach.

I sigh.

Maybe I should lay off on all of those brownies...

Folding my blouse, I hurry out of the bathroom to find Reid waiting for me, his muscular arms crossed over his chest and a scowl firmly in place. He scratches absently at his forehead and then frowns when he accidentally makes himself bleed.

He drops his arms to his sides quickly.

"Is there a place I can put this?" I ask, holding the white shirt in the air.

Reid turns to stare at me, his frown growing...

And then he freezes.

Stares.

Gulps.

His gaze should feel unnerving or even slimy, but it doesn't. I'm surprised by that discovery myself. The weight of his eyes on me is almost a physical caress. It cascades over my body like rivulets of warm water on a freezing day.

We continue to stare at each other, and though his eyes never dip from my face, I swear I can feel his gaze everywhere. On my bare arms. Across my chest. Stroking my thighs.

I swallow heavily, and either the sound of it or the sight of my throat bobbing makes him straighten. He turns away from me as if it physically pains him to stare at me for too long.

"Come," he says briskly. Curtly.

After placing my folded blouse in the break room, I shoot a text off to Hale explaining the situation. Hale tells me to be careful and to text him when I'm done.

Reid turns and heads back towards the supply closet. Once there, he pushes open the door and says, "Grab disinfectant wipes and meet me in theater two."

Before I can say anything else, he stalks away, leaving me baffled. His scent still lingers long after he leaves, a pungent, musky smell that makes me crinkle my nose.

Okay, then.

One packet of disinfectant wipes, coming right up.

I glance around the closet quickly, certain I didn't see any during the initial tour. I push up on my tiptoes to see higher up, and...there! On the top shelf, I spot a yellow container of wipes.

I stand as tall as I can and extend my arms, but my fingers only graze the container.

Fuck.

Sometimes I hate being short.

Considering, I scan the room for something to step on.

My gaze snags on a tiny table.

Perfect.

I quickly climb onto the table—making sure my skirt is pressed down so I'm not flashing anyone who steps into the closet—and then reach for the wipes yet again. I tilt my body to the side, reaching, reaching, reaching—

"What the fuck are you doing?" a strident voice demands.

A second later, hands grip my waist and heft me off the table.

Reid.

"You could've fallen and gotten hurt," he scolds as he easily reaches for the wipes.

"From standing on that tiny table?" I ask incredulously.

He bares his teeth at me like a fucking animal and leans close—so close our noses almost touch.

"Next time, you ask for help," he snaps, anger flaring in his eyes.

They're a pretty color, I realize belatedly. A light shade of blue flecked here and there with darker spots.

"But I didn't need your help," I counter snarkily. "I had it handled."

"What if you had fallen and hit your fucking head?"

"Then I'd say that would hurt like a bitch."

His scowl deepens. "You just got *tackled* by a two-hundred-pound man. You're concussed. You can't be—"

"How do you know I'm concussed?" Wait. Emery and Ethan. I swear guys gossip more often than women do. "But I'm fine."

"You're not fucking fine."

"Are you a doctor now? Congratulations." I give him a slow, sardonic clap. "I would've gotten you a graduation present if I'd known."

"Are you always such a smart-ass?"

"Are you always such a hard-ass?"

The two of us continue to glare at each other. The tips of his shoes touch my own. This close, I can see the strands of gold in his tousled red hair and the acne dotting his crooked nose.

I remember Lissa telling me he had once been beautiful, and I can see it. There are hints of that beauty even now, in the sharp curve of his jaw and the plushness of his lips.

Wait...plush? Why the hell am I thinking of his lips?

Reid yanks the wipes out of my hands with a muttered curse and then stomps towards the theater.

"I thought you wanted me to clean it up!" I call to his retreating back.

"You fucking stay. Relax. Take a damn break!" he barks, as if I've been working ten days and not ten minutes.

"I'm not even tired—"

"Sit!" he orders, turning to face me. He jabs a finger in my direction. "Stay."

I stomp after him. "I'm not a dog. I know that's hard to believe—"

"I never said you were a dog." His brows bunch together. He seems genuinely confused by my comment.

"Sit. Stay. What's next? Come? Good girl?" I mean for my words to be scathing and teasing, but I know I made a mistake the second they leave my mouth. I wish desperately I could scoop them up and throw them away.

Come.

Good girl.

Reid growls something I can't hear, points a trembling finger at my face, and then drops it with a huff. Tiny red blotches unfurl on his cheeks.

"You're ridiculous," he snaps, throwing his hands up in the air. "Just take it fucking easy!"

"I am!" I give him the finger.

He opens his mouth to retort but immediately shuts it. His face drains of all color, and his gaze homes in on something behind me, directly over my shoulder.

I turn to look and come face-to-face with a gorgeous woman with light-brown skin, honey eyes, and glossy black hair.

She bites her lower lip demurely as she takes a step towards us.

"Hello, Reid." Her voice is soft. Lovely, even.

I hate it.

Reid looks as if he's going to be sick. "Michelle." He swallows. "What are you doing here?"

Thirty-Seven

IZZY

I thought I knew what it meant for Reid to hate someone on a visceral level. The scowls he hurls at me are capable of withering flowers and encasing freshly bloomed buds in ice.

But that glare is *nothing* compared to the one he's currently sporting now.

The girl—Michelle—shifts from foot to foot as she wrings her hands uneasily.

Why does that name sound so familiar?

She's certainly beautiful in a delicate, angelic sort of way. Her hair is so straight and smooth, I'm not sure even a single strand overlaps with another. Almond-shaped brown eyes are framed by long, dark lashes. She wears skinny jeans and a pink top that offsets her golden-brown skin.

"Reid, you haven't returned my calls..." She nibbles anxiously on her glossy lower lip.

I expect Reid to make a witty retort or an acerbic jab the way he just did with me. But he remains silent, glaring at her.

"We need to talk about this," she continues. "About us."

Michelle...

Wait a minute.

Didn't I hear that Reid has an ex-girlfriend with that name? And that he fell apart when they broke up?

Is this the girl?

A strange pit forms in my chest, accompanied by an exotic emotion I can't quite name. Every time I try to decipher what it is, it slips through my fingers like raindrops.

I inconspicuously glance at Reid out of the corner of my eye, wanting to gauge his reaction. Does he miss her? Is that why he's so silent? Is that why he's glaring so fiercely at her? I know from experience that it's often the ones you love the most that can hurt you more than anyone else.

If he loved her and they broke up, I imagine it'll be a shock to see her now.

"I miss you," Michelle continues earnestly, seemingly content to ignore my existence. She doesn't even glance in my direction. "I miss *us*."

Reid swallows, and this time when he stares at her, there's an expression of intense yearning and pain on his face.

My heart batters against my breastbone with a

frightening velocity as something strange and foreign unfurls in my chest.

Something akin to jealousy, as irrational as that emotion is.

He *does* miss her. There's no other explanation for the pain distorting his features.

But still, he doesn't speak. He doesn't even seem to be breathing.

When she steps forward and places her hand on his bicep—causing him to flinch—I can't hold my tongue a second longer.

"Reid, is everything okay?" I ask cautiously.

At the sound of my voice, Reid flinches again. Michelle slowly turns to stare at me, one of her perfectly plucked eyebrows arched. She gives me a tiny once-over, and her warm smile brightens, unveiling dimples on both of her cheeks. She truly is a beautiful girl, and a nonsensical part of me hates her for it.

"Hi! I'm Michelle. Reid's girlfriend..." She blushes prettily and places her fingertips to her lips, smothering a giggle. "Well, it's complicated."

I slide my gaze towards Reid, but he doesn't agree with or contradict her. He just continues to stare, his hands curling into fists and then uncurling by his sides. His face is abnormally pale, causing his acne to stand out starkly.

"Are you a new employee?" Michelle continues.

"Yeah. Today's my first day." I offer her a tentative smile, but I know it probably looks forced.

Something about this petite woman sets every alarm bell in my head off at once.

"And you know Reid?" Though she tries to sound casual and friendly, there's a hint of *something* in her voice that raises my hackles.

The tiny hairs on the back of my neck stand at attention, and the alarm bells transition into blinking red lights and a mechanical voice that says, "Warning! Proceed with caution!"

"We have a class together at school," I say briskly, wanting this conversation over with.

I don't bother admitting that Reid only attended said class once.

"Oh." Michelle's lips part in a perfect O, and she bats her abnormally long lashes at me. "How nice." She flashes me a sugary-sweet grin that threatens to give me a toothache. "It certainly was lovely to meet you, Izzy. I'm sure we'll be seeing a lot more of each other."

"Leave." Reid's voice is almost a growl. The sound of it lifts the hairs on my arms. "You need to leave. Now."

At first, I think he's talking to me, but when Michelle rolls her eyes, I realize he's addressing her.

"Reid..." She pouts.

"Leave!" he snarls, lowering his head so his shaggy red hair obscures his face from view. His entire body seems to tremble.

What the hell? Is he having a panic attack? Seizure?

Terror grips my throat in a chokehold and refuses

to let go. One of my friends at my old school had seizures. Her parents told me what to do if she were to start seizing, but God forbid I remember anything I was taught now.

But what if this is a panic attack, not a seizure? What the fuck do I do then?

"I'll see both of you later. Goodbye, Izzy. Goodbye, Reid." Michelle smiles first at me and then at Reid before sashaying down the hallway and into the lobby.

It's only when she has disappeared from view do I hurry towards Reid.

"Are you okay? What's going on?" I anxiously scan his body, searching him for injuries, but I don't see any.

Then again, if this is a panic attack or even a seizure, I wouldn't notice anything out of the blue.

I tentatively place a hand on his back, which is covered in sticky sweat, the liquid seeping through his shirt. I try not to cringe away as I offer him whatever comfort I can.

Reid continues to shake and convulse, his entire body locking together.

"Call. Ashton," he grunts out, letting loose a shaky breath. "Phone. In pocket."

His words are distorted, almost guttural.

"What's going on?"

"Call him!" he demands.

I quickly reach towards his front pocket, trying not to notice how hard his thigh is underneath my fingers, like chiseled granite. I'm grateful when my fingers close around the phone. The last thing I want to do is grope him longer than necessary.

"Passcode?"

He can barely speak. Whatever's happening to him seems to have impacted his ability to function.

"Five. Seven." He breaks off, gasping.

"Five, seven...?" I press when he doesn't immediately continue.

"Eight. Four." Sweat continues to soak my hand as he pants. "His name is under Dick Face."

I snort before I can stop myself.

Yeah. Dick Face seems like a fitting name for Ashton.

Fortunately, Ashton's number is Reid's most recent call, so it only takes me a second to click on it.

The ice prince himself picks up on the second ring.

"Is this important?" Ashton asks briskly. No hello. No greeting. "I'm with my father."

"It's me. Izzy," I say quickly.

The line turns silent. So silent, I actually fear that Ashton hung up on me. The only indication that he hasn't is his harrowed breathing.

I hurry to finish speaking before he can end the call. "It's Reid. There's something going on—"

"Explain!" Ashton demands, seemingly getting over his shock at having me call him from Reid's phone.

"He's breathing heavily, and he's shaking, and he's talking weird—"

"What the fuck did you do?" Ashton hisses.

Indignation burns white-hot inside of me, running through my blood in a ravenous inferno.

"I did jack shit. This girl named Michelle showed up, and they were talking. And then he just started freaking out—"

Ashton mutters something I can't hear, the words muffled as if he placed his hand over the speaker.

"Did you talk to her?" Ashton asks, his voice now clear.

The question is shocking and strange enough to give me pause.

"Isabella, answer me."

"I... Yes. I mean, not really, but—"

"Fuck. Okay. I'm on my way. Grab Silas and tell him about Reid. He'll know what to do before I get there."

"What's wrong—?"

"Now, Isabella!" Ashton snaps, and then there's nothing but dial tone.

Fucker hung up on me.

Reid's still shaking, trembling, convulsing. Strange raspy sounds emanate from his body.

"I'll be right back." I try to keep my voice low and soothing as I rub his sweaty back. "I'm going to grab Silas."

I turn to walk away, but his hand shoots out and grabs my wrist. The touch only lasts for a fraction of a second, but I swear my whole body bursts into flames at the contact.

What the hell?

Reid's hand drops back to his side as he falls to his knees on the ground, his head lowered, his greasy hair almost brown in the waning light.

His voice, a gentle hum, whispers, "Don't leave me," but I could just be imagining things.

Either way, my throat closes up, and my skin prickles.

It's only as I rush into Silas's office does something occur to me.

Michelle called me Izzy...but I never told her my name.

Thirty-Eight

REID

Who does that bitch think she is?

Threatening my mate?

Izzy may be oblivious, but I'm not. I could see the pure cunning and malice in Michelle's eyes as she feigned friendliness. The witch looked like a snake just waiting to pounce and bite down, infecting us all with her venom.

I attempt to grapple with my caged wolf, the creature howling despondently as he fights to break free. My eyes will currently be a bright shade of amber, and my hair will have begun to lengthen—though no matter how far my human form mutates, I won't shift.

Not after what Michelle and her brother did to me.

Bitter loathing rushes through my veins, amplifying my already turbulent emotions. I attempt to curl my hands into fists to keep my claws hidden. The last thing I want to do is terrify my mate.

Izzy.

My mate.

Threatened.

A growl emerges from my throat, reverberating through the hallway, and the hand tentatively patting my back freezes. Stops. Pulls away.

She says something too low for me to hear and then begins to retreat. Every step she takes away from me feels like a blade to the heart.

Don't leave me.

Please don't leave me.

I don't know if I say the words out loud or just in my head.

How dare Michelle come waltzing back into my life after what she did to me? The lies she told? How fucking dare she pretend that we're anything but bitter enemies?

I never dated her, despite the rumors floating around the school. I never even touched her.

Last year, I became aware that the witch harbored a crush on me. It started innocently enough—she would leave notes in my locker, smile shyly at me in the halls, and sit by me in class. I never returned her affection, but I also was never an outright asshole.

Then things started getting...weird. Looking back, I should've spotted the warning signs, but I'd been innocent and naïve, at least when it concerned her.

She would show up at all of my football games, even the away games, with my number painted on her cheek. She told everyone who would listen that we were dating. When I confronted her, she simply giggled and said that the gossip was getting out of hand and that she never said such a thing.

Then she would show up at my house uninvited with boxes of takeout and video games for us to play. When I told her to leave, she ignored me and shoved her way into my home. It got to the point where I had to get Ashton involved, and he threatened to put a restraining order on her if she didn't knock it off.

I thought things were better. She still left me creepy notes and flowers, but she no longer followed me around like a lost, besotted puppy.

However, on the night of junior year prom, she saw me talking to Rebecca Weasley in the hallway. Rebecca was merely asking me for a set of notes she missed out on when she got sick, but Michelle wrongly assumed I asked Rebecca to homecoming. The very next day, Rebecca's car crashed. No explanation of how it happened. The police were baffled.

But I knew the truth.

I knew it deep in my bones, the way I can tell you the sky is blue, the grass is green, and Michelle is batshit insane.

Fortunately, Rebecca survived, but the experience left her shaken enough to transfer schools. Thank fuck for that. I don't even want to think about what Michelle would've done to her if she remained.

Ashton, the twins, and I confronted Michelle, and she simply laughed it off, saying that if Rebecca had "stayed in her lane," she never would've crashed. It made me sick to my stomach to know that I'd inadvertently caused an innocent woman to be in an accident.

I told Michelle to fuck off.

And *she* told her brother—a powerful warlock—that I fucked her and then broke her heart.

Now, we're here.

Michelle may no longer go to the same school as me, having graduated a year prior, but she still finds ways to torment me. Her ghost lingers, and no matter how many times I attempt to banish her, she returns like a damn fungus.

What will she do to Izzy?

Will she hurt her?

I'll rip her apart piece by piece if she dares to even lay a finger on my mate.

Another deafening growl leaves me. I'm the embodiment of rage and wrath. Nothing can compare to the thunderous rate of my heart, pounding, pounding, pounding—

"You need to calm the fuck down," a strident voice demands.

Someone touches my shoulder and leads me down a hallway and into a small, cluttered room.

Silas's office.

The wolf himself stands in front of me, his arms

crossed over his chest and a stony expression on his scarred face. His one good eye is narrowed into a thin slit.

"I. Can't," I pant out as I struggle to control myself.

Silas's scowl deepens. "You could've hurt Isabella! What were you fucking thinking?"

The implication that I would ever hurt my mate rips a snarl from my throat. The noise is loud enough to make Silas stagger back a step.

"I would never hurt her," I growl, my voice more beast than man. "And neither would my wolf."

My wolf howls in agreement.

Silas's brows pinch together. "What the fuck are you—"

The door to his office is pushed open, and Ashton stalks inside, his phone already in his hand as he prepares to do damage control. Fortunately, the only person who saw me in this state was Izzy, and there are no video cameras in the immediate vicinity.

I ignore Silas entirely and turn towards my alpha. If anyone can fix this fucking mess, it's him.

"She. Threatened. Her," I rumble out, the words escaping through clenched teeth.

"Who threatened who?" Ashton barks, shutting the door behind him and stepping closer.

Silas moves to the side to make room for the other man.

"Michelle. Here. Izzy." Those are the only words I can get out, but they seem to be enough for Ashton.

His intelligent brown eyes immediately sharpen, and his lips firm.

Silas interjects before Ashton can get a word out. "Who the fuck is this Michelle chick? And what did she say about Isabella?"

Ashton turns towards the older man as if he honestly forgot his existence.

"This is between me and my pack, Silas," Ashton says curtly. Not coldly, per se, but with enough bite to his tone to let him know he means business.

Silas's glower could flay the skin off of a normal man. The air between the two of them practically crackles with electricity as they glare at each other. Silas is bigger and stronger, but Ashton has always been a dominant wolf. I don't know who would win in a fight between the two.

Silas opens his mouth to retort when a hesitant knock sounds on the office door.

"Is everything okay in there?" Izzy.

Her voice rushes over me like cool water on a blistering-hot day. Calming. Peaceful.

The rage festering deep within my chest begins to dwindle. It doesn't suddenly disappear or anything like that, and my anger doesn't entirely fade, but I'm able to breathe normally and regain a smidgen of control.

Before I can get a word out and assure her I'm fine,

Ashton wrenches the door open and stares down at her. I can't see his face, but I can tell by the way her shoulders bunch together and her hands clench that he's glaring.

"What the *fuck* are you doing here?" he demands.

And I lose it.

IZZY

"What the hell is your problem, asshole?" Reid roars, lunging at his friend.

Before anyone can stop him, Reid has Ashton pinned against the wall, one of his large arms held against the other man's neck.

"My problem"—Ashton's upper lip peels away from his teeth in a snarl—"is this *bitch*. We don't know anything about her, yet she thinks she can waltz in here like a damn hurricane and act like we're all one big happy family."

His absurd words actually make me laugh out loud, garnering both boys' attention.

Act like we're all one big happy family?

When the *fuck* did I do that?

All I did was ask if Reid was okay after his panic attack. How does that make me the villain? Or maybe Ashton's just so desperate to paint a target on someone's back—*my* back—that he's willing to overlook the truth.

My laughter starts off quiet before it transitions into a full-on belly laugh. I clutch my sides and keel over.

Ashton and Reid both stare at me in disbelief, the former looking seconds away from strangling me and the latter no doubt wondering if I lost my marbles. Silas, who moved closer to me when the boys started fighting, smirks.

"What the hell crawled up your ass and died?" I explode once my amusement finally subsides and anger takes its place.

I point an accusatory finger at Ashton, who's still being pinned against the wall by Reid. Reid reluctantly releases his friend, as if realizing that my verbal berating will do far more damage than his fists.

Ashton brushes at his shoulders like a pompous prick attempting to remove imaginary lint. But he doesn't respond. Hell, he doesn't even acknowledge me, his eyes intent on his shirtsleeve.

I take a step closer to the asshole, feeling inexplicable rage rush through me.

"I have done absolutely nothing to you, yet you use every opportunity to tear me down or act like I don't exist. I tried being nice to you, Ashton, but I'm done being a fucking doormat." Another step closer forces me to crane my neck to maintain eye contact with the prickly bastard. His brown eyes remind me of topsoil right after it rains, when the water darkens the color until it's almost black. "So if you want to pretend I don't exist, then fine. I can do the same to you."

And with that, I turn away, doing exactly as I said —pretending he doesn't exist.

Silas's tiny smirk has stretched into a full-blown smile that makes the skin around his good eye crinkle. He chuckles. "I knew I liked you, kid."

Reid just gapes at me.

"Isabella, we are not done—" Ashton begins.

"I apologize for my outburst," I tell Silas sincerely, feeling heat envelop my cheeks. "I hope this won't impact my employment here."

Curse my big fat mouth.

And curse Ashton.

Silas's smile reveals sparkly white teeth. "You just got a raise." He moves to exit the office, but just before he passes me, he clasps a hand down on my shoulder and gives it a squeeze. "I'll email you the work schedule tomorrow. Why don't you head home now, okay? Get some rest."

My face is still hot, but I smile timidly and nod. "Yeah. Okay."

With one last parting glance, Silas exits his office and shuts the door behind him, leaving me alone with Reid and the Ass.

I turn towards Reid. "Are you okay? After what happened with that girl? You don't have to answer if you don't feel comfortable..."

Reid's eyes soften slightly, though his lips remain compressed in a thin, unrelenting line. "I'm okay."

His voice is gruff and raspy, reminding me of all those times Grayson talked too much and couldn't speak right for days after.

"Isabella," Ass-ton begins, but I ignore him and offer Reid a tentative smile.

"I suppose I'll be seeing you around?"

He folds his arms over his chest and grunts something that could be a "yes" or a "fuck off." It's hard to tell with him. Just before I can leave the office, however, I hear him call my name. I turn back around to see him watching me with his brows furrowed.

"You have a ride home?"

"Hale's across the street," I explain.

And even if Hale wasn't around, Jake gets off of work in about an hour.

Not that I want to hang around here any longer than necessary...

"Good," Reid grunts. "Not safe at night."

Ass-ton curls his hands into fists. "Isabella Martin—"

With one last wave at Reid, I slip out of the office. Just before the door slams shut, I hear Ass-ton's muttered cursing. The sound of it makes me smile.

He thinks I'm a bitch? Then so be it.

I think it's time he sees how truly bitchy I can be.

Forty

IZZY

"**G**uys are stupid," Desiree laments as she shoves another spoonful of mint chocolate chip ice cream into her mouth.

"Tell me about it."

No one was more surprised than me to see the Queen Bee herself waiting at Hale's house when I arrived home from work. She held up a bag that she deemed held all of the "essentials"—which translates to ice cream, ice cream, and more ice cream.

When I asked her why she was here, she looked at me with a sly grin and declared, "I had a feeling you could use some girl time."

Now, the two of us sit on the couch in the basement while *Magic Mike* plays on the flatscreen TV before us. But even Channing Tatum's rippling muscles and gyrating hips can't elevate my sour mood.

"I can't believe Ashton called you a bitch," Desiree

says with a scowl. She begins to lick at her spoon, making sure to capture every last drop of ice cream. "I always knew he was an asshole, but that's too far, even for him." Abruptly, she smirks and nudges me with her shoulder. "Want me to kick his ass?"

I try to picture five-foot Desiree going against six-foot Ashton and can't help but chuckle. Mainly because I have the distinct feeling Desiree would win that fight.

"Tempting..." I take another huge mouthful of chocolate chip cookie dough—my favorite flavor, though Desiree couldn't have possibly known that.

"I wouldn't take Ashton's words too personally. He's had a tough life, and I think that makes him afraid of letting people in." Desiree doesn't even bother to glance up from her carton as she speaks.

Jealousy arrows through me at how casually she talks about Ashton. As if she knows him. As if she talks to him. As if they're more than just friends. As if they're—

What the fuck am I thinking?

Am I really jealous of Desiree and Ass-ton?

Nope. Definitely not. That's insane. I hate him.

Desiree continues on. "After his mother and fathers died, he kind of became a shell of his former self. He didn't really let a lot of people in, you know? And then his brother left—"

"Wait, wait, wait." I wave my spoon back and forth in the air to emphasize my point. "Back up. Did you say *fathers*? As in plural? Multiple? And Ashton has a brother?"

A mischievous grin tugs up Desiree's lips as she positions herself so she can sit more comfortably on the couch. "You didn't know? Ashton had one mom and multiple dads. They were in a poly relationship." She pauses, licks her lip, and then adds, "That dynamic is actually pretty common around here. Does that... interest you?"

"What?" My voice comes out as a high-pitched screech. I cough, clear my throat, and then try again, working to modulate my volume so I don't sound like a strangled hyena. "I mean...what? What?!"

Real articulate, Izzy.

Desiree's smirk only broadens, unveiling perfectly white teeth. "I see the way you look at Emery and Ethan..."

"What way? I don't look at them in any way. I don't even look at them." I can't seem to stop babbling. Flames engulf my cheeks, and I suddenly can't meet Desiree's all-knowing, penetrating gaze.

"So you never thought of being a meat in that twin sandwich?" Desiree asks candidly.

"DESIREE!" Oh my god. Kill me now.

Seriously.

Just kill me.

I'll even provide the knife.

Desiree begins to cackle like the evil Witch of the

West. I grab the nearest pillow and whack her across the face with it multiple times.

"Stop it," I plead, wanting the floor to swallow me whole.

Maybe I could just live underground. Become the Queen of the Worm People.

Career. Goals.

"I mean, I don't understand what you see in Tweedledum and Tweedledumber..." Desiree scratches at her wrist absently as her nose wrinkles.

"So you never pictured being with the two of them?" I don't know why I ask that. I don't want to know the answer.

Desiree is...beautiful. Funny. Smart. Popular. I'm not sure I'll stand a chance if she decides she wants to date the twins.

Wait...

Do *I* want to date the twins?

When the hell did that happen?

Desiree's appalled look pulls me out of my shocked spiral. "Me? And Ethan and Emery?" She pantomimes gagging. "Fuck no. I would honestly rather eat my own hair than touch one of them." She waves a flippant hand in the air. "Besides, even if I did like them like that—which I most definitely don't—they're not meant for me."

I stare at her in confusion. "Meant for you?"

"You know, like soulmates and all that shit."

"You believe in soulmates?" I wouldn't expect that

from Desiree. She doesn't seem like the "hopeless romantic" type of girl.

Then again, I don't really know her that well. This is the first time we ever hung out outside of school.

"Don't you?" Desiree cocks an eyebrow imperiously at me, but before I can respond, my phone buzzes for the millionth time that night.

Desiree grabs it before I can.

"Who's Grayson?" She wiggles her brows suggestively.

I bark out a harsh, humorless laugh. "How much time do you have?"

"Do I need to sneak you some alcohol?" she asks.

"Probably. That might be the only way I can talk about him."

Honestly, I'm not sure I even *want* to talk about Grayson Grey, the one wound that has never healed properly. What could I possibly say?

Oh, I know. How about... I'm in love with my childhood best friend who has a girlfriend. He kissed me and confessed his love to me, but I snapped at him for leading me on. Now, he's calling and texting me incessantly, demanding that we speak, but I'm not sure my heart can handle another moment in his presence.

"I already have a feeling I'll need to grab some garden shears after this conversation is over," Desiree says, her eyes narrowing. "Does this man deserve to have his balls still attached?"

"Debatable."

"IZZY!" Jake's enigmatic voice precedes the man himself running into the room, his hair damp from his shower. He wears a pair of *SpongeBob SquarePants* sleep pants and a T-shirt so holey it would fit in at church. "What the fuck happened at the theater? No one would tell me anything and—"

Jake cuts off abruptly when he catches sight of Desiree sitting beside me on the couch.

His cheeks turn bright crimson.

I hide my smirk behind my hand as I make the introductions. "Desiree, you know my foster brother Jake, correct? Jake, of course you know Desiree."

He flashes me a murderous stare, but I simply wink at him. Payback's a bitch.

"Desiree. Hi. You're here. In my house. Here. In my house. On my couch. Here." Jake runs a hand through his tousled blond hair...and then abruptly drops it when he realizes that the movement displays the holes beneath his armpits.

"Yes. I'm...here?" Desiree gives me a *"what the fuck?"* look.

"I'm just going to, um..." Jake jabs a finger over his shoulder as he begins to walk backwards, never taking his gaze off the two of us.

"There's a wall!" I call a split second before he runs into it.

He stealthily shifts a few feet to the side. Then, once he's out the door, he breaks into a run.

I wait until his footsteps disappear completely

before I break into laughter. After a few moments, Desiree joins in as well.

I know I'm going to pay for this later, but right now, I just allow myself to enjoy the moment—teasing someone I've come to think of as a brother and hanging out with a girl who could become a close friend. All thoughts of stupid, idiotic men leave my mind.

Maybe I should just swear off boys and live a life of chastity...

Or maybe I'll feel better once I beat the fuck out of someone in the fight ring.

I think I prefer option number two.

Forty-One

ETHAN

I jiggle my knee as I wait for this meeting to begin. Ashton called us over an hour earlier, yet the idiot has yet to arrive himself.

I don't want to be here.

What I want is to be with Izzy.

Maybe I can convince Jake to invite me over to play more video games...

Emery sits on the couch opposite me, purposely pretending that I don't exist. He stares intently at his phone as he plays some stupid game that most definitely does *not* require as much attention as he's giving it.

I try to ignore the strange pang in my chest—this tightening of muscles that threatens to make me physically ill.

I hate this silence between me and my brother. And more than that, I hate the animosity. If he just ignored my existence, I could deal with that. Yes, it would hurt like a bitch, but it wouldn't flay me open.

But Emery always stares at me as if he hates the ground I walk on. As if he doesn't want to even breathe the same air as me. Every time I speak, his upper lip curls away from his teeth and his eyes narrow into slits.

If he could, I have no doubt he would leave this pack and find a new one. He would willingly give up me, Reid, and Ashton.

Maybe even Izzy.

How could things have gone so wrong?

Because you fucked up, a bitter voice reminds me. *Because your decision nearly cost us everything.*

I scrub a hand through my hair.

No apologies will ever fix what I did, but maybe—

My thoughts cut off as Ashton and Reid storm into the room.

"About damn time," Emery mutters, scowling. He flicks his phone off and crosses his arms over his chest.

Ashton doesn't speak immediately. Instead, he moves towards the fridge, grabs a bottle of beer, and returns to the living room.

Ashton? Drinking? What the fuck is happening?

I exchange a wary glance with Emery...before the two of us seem to realize what we're doing and immediately look away.

Most of our pack meetings take place in Ashton's "room." And I say "room" with quotation marks because it's actually a small house on his father's property.

The tiny pool house has only two rooms. The main one is a combination of a bedroom, living room, dining room, and kitchen. All four blend in seamlessly with each other, the smooth tiles of the kitchen transitioning into lush carpeting and then the carpeting turning into bamboo floorboards on a slightly raised platform that holds Ashton's bed. The living area consists of two couches, a single armchair, and a flatscreen television connected to every single gaming device I can think of.

The only other room in the tiny home is a bathroom.

Ashton throws himself into his customary armchair, and immediately, Pepper moves to snuggle on his lap.

Pepper is Ashton's pure black cat he found years ago when she was just a kitten. Ashton worried initially that the tiny cat would be scared of the four of us— some animals can sense our wolves—but it proved to be the exact opposite. Pepper clings to the four of us with the steadfast devotion and love only a pet can emulate.

Who would've thought that the big, scary Ashton is secretly a cat lover?

Ashton strokes Pepper's fur as he waits for Reid to take his seat. However, the large man remains standing, his muscular arms folded over his chest and his scowl firmly in place. He glares at Ashton with an almost incandescent fury that makes me instantly cautious. And curious, if I'm being completely honest.

What the fuck did Ashton do?

"Is someone going to explain what's going on here?" Emery interjects, flicking his gaze between a brooding Ashton and a glowering Reid.

Ashton grits his teeth together. "Christian's back."

Out of everything I expected him to say…it wasn't that.

Even Reid seems taken aback by Ashton's announcement, like he thought the purpose of this meeting would be for an entirely different reason.

"Christian?" Emery asks in disbelief. "The fuck?"

I haven't seen Ashton's older brother in…well… Who the fuck knows how long? Years, maybe. The last time I saw him was on his eighteenth birthday, when it was officially revealed he was a lone wolf without a pack. Ashton always assumed he would join our pack, so to discover his beloved brother was fated to go feral? That destroyed him.

But what *obliterated* him was Christian's decision to leave town without a single goodbye to his brother. Ashton already lost his mom and most of his dads. And now his brother? It was a near fatal wound, one Ashton still hasn't healed from.

Ashton looks as if he's going to be sick. "I'm sure you all heard of the new vice principal, Mr. Montgomery."

"I hear the girls talking about him," Emery responds with a roll of his eyes. "But what does that have to do with Christ—" He cuts off with a sharp inhale. "Holy shit! Christian is Mr. Montgomery, isn't he?"

Ashton nods stiffly. "It appears as if he changed his last name."

"What the fuck is he even doing at our school?" Emery demands. "Why now? Do you think your father asked him to come? To spy on us?"

As the next pack slated to take over the Council, we've been under a microscope since we first came into power. Our dominance surpasses that of any other pack in the territory, and that makes people afraid.

Including Ashton's father.

Personally, I don't believe one pack should rule over all. That's a dictatorship waiting to happen. I'm firmly on team "democracy."

But my opinion doesn't matter. Not yet.

Not until I'm officially on the Council.

"Wouldn't put it past my father to add two spies to the school," Ashton mutters, his voice dripping with acerbic distaste.

Reid growls harshly. "Izzy isn't a damn spy!"

"No?" One of Ashton's eyebrows arches. "Then why is she here? Why now? Why did she arrive the exact same time Christian did? I don't believe in coincidences."

I have to ball my hands into fists to keep from

doing something stupid—like slapping him. Or choking him. Or clawing his eyes out.

Emery doesn't have the same restraint.

My hotheaded twin jumps to his feet and rounds on Ashton. "Why are you such an ass to her? What did she ever do to you?"

"Your dick is going to get you in trouble, Emery," Ashton responds coldly, not even bothering to move from his casual position on the armchair.

"Fuck you, Ashton." Emery jabs a finger in our pack brother's face, but Ashton simply stares at it as if it's a twig he could snap in the blink of an eye. "You're going to push Izzy away, and then, when you realize you were wrong, you'll regret every cruel word you ever said to her."

Ashton begins stroking Pepper faster, even as his eyes harden, turning to chips of obsidian, the darkness swallowing the golden brown. "Or I'll save my brothers from ruination."

Emery takes a step closer, and I quickly insert myself into the conversation before things can come to blows.

"Did you talk to Christian? What did he say?" I ask quickly.

Emery tosses me a look rife with betrayal—as if he's upset I didn't take his side—and the sight of it makes my stomach sink like a lead weight. An uncomfortable itchy sensation overtakes my skin.

Why can't I do anything right when it comes to him?

Ashton accepts the subject change with ease. "Christian said absolutely nothing. One second, I saw him at the football game. The next, I woke up at home and in bed. The asshole drugged me."

His lips purse, even as an agonizing silence settles over our group.

All of us are thinking of last night, when Izzy was tackled.

Has it only been a day since that happened?

God, I still remember sitting on the bleachers, watching her get swallowed by the body of a two-hundred-plus-pound man. Her tiny squeak of fright plays on a continuous loop in my head.

Reid growls and pushes himself off the wall. "That fucker Kain had a part to play in it. I'm fucking sure of it. He allowed that Viper to tackle Izzy."

"We don't know that," Ashton says, but his voice is calculating. Thoughtful, even.

When Ashton claims not to know something, it's only because he hasn't turned over every rock to discover the truth. I guarantee that by the end of the week, Ashton will know for sure if Kain had a part to play in what happened to Izzy.

He can bitch and moan all he wants, but Izzy is still our Heart. Our mate.

And we'll destroy anyone who dares to hurt her.

"That actually brings us to another topic of conversation." Ashton leans forward slightly, his eyes astute as they study each of us. "Ansel."

"Ansel?" Emery blinks. "The annoying fucker?"

I squirm uncomfortably.

Ansel and I have always had a bitter rivalry. We're both on track to be the top of the class, but only one of us will end up valedictorian. Admittedly, I've been a little preoccupied with other things as of late, but I still don't want Ansel to win.

"I saw him use magic."

Ashton's proclamation is the equivalent of an atomic bomb exploding in the room. My ears begin to ring, this high-pitched whistling noise that threatens to make my brain bleed.

"That's impossible," I say immediately. "All warlocks are required to register themselves as such."

I don't know a lot about the other supernatural species—most of us live independently of each other, and for good reason—but there is a large group of witches and warlocks in town. Probably due to the ley line running through the forest and providing magic to the land.

Warlocks and witches form covens, and all covens are required to register with the Unholy Trinity—the Maiden, Mother, and Crone who work closely with the wolf Council to instigate peace. From the day they're born, every witch and warlock must take part in some secretive ceremony with the Unholy Trinity where they're officially indoctrinated into the world of magic.

So how is it that none of us knew about Ansel?

Is he an illegal warlock in town?

"What exactly did you see?" Reid's voice is thunderous, and his face is slightly paler than normal.

He'll never admit it to anyone, but I suspect he's afraid of witches and warlocks after what happened with that bitch Michelle.

Ashton quickly explains what he saw at the football stadium.

Izzy falling.

Her bones breaking.

And then Ansel, his hands emitting a strange light...

"We need to keep an eye on him," Ashton finishes, leveling us all with a penetrating glare that dares us to argue. "An undocumented warlock could prove to be dangerous. Why is he here? Who is in his coven? Why didn't we know he was a warlock beforehand?"

"He *is* adopted," I point out, wondering if that has a part to play in it.

Perhaps his adoptive parents don't know the truth about him.

Hell, maybe he doesn't even know the truth about himself.

"So keep an eye on Christian and Ansel..." Emery lazily spreads his arms over the back of the couch. Despite his nonchalant posture, his eyes remain sharp. Piercing. He volleys his gaze between Reid and Ashton. "Anything else we need to discuss?"

I can't forget the way Reid was glaring at Ashton when they first stepped into the house. If something happened, we need to know.

But both Reid and Ashton stubbornly remain quiet.

I exchange a loaded look with Emery once more before the two of us immediately turn away from each other. Tension saturates the air, but I'm not sure where it's coming from. Me and Emery...or Ashton and Reid.

Mates are supposed to bring packmates closer together.

Yet, if things keep going the way they are, there won't be a pack for Izzy to unite.

How many times can something break before it's irreparable?

Forty-Two

IZZY

"Call me if those idiots don't get their heads out of their asses." Desiree gives me one last hug before stepping back. "I'm pretty good at castration."

"Noted."

She grins, wiggles her fingers in a wave, and then says, "Bye, Izzy." Louder, she calls out, "And bye, Jake!"

Jake, who's been hiding behind a pillar separating the living room from the entryway, pokes his head out with a decidedly sheepish expression at having been caught spying. "Bye, Desiree."

My new friend chuckles as she walks outside, and I gently shut the door behind her.

As soon as the latch catches, Jake points an accusatory finger at my face. "I hate you, and you're dead to me."

I stick my tongue out. "Turnabout is fair play."

Jake rakes his fingers through his blond hair with a dramatic groan. "I can't believe I embarrassed myself like that in front of her." He grabs a handful of his *SpongeBob* pants as if the fabric has personally offended him. "Damn you, SpongeBob. Damn you to the deepest pit of hell where you belong."

"It wasn't *that* bad," I reason, snorting. "At least you didn't have on your *My Little Pony* shirt."

Jake places a hand over his chest in mock horror. "How did you know about that?"

"I can't give away all my secrets, now can I?"

"I'll have you know, that was a gift from Lissa. What was I supposed to do? Burn it? You certainly haven't seen an angry or depressed Lissa yet." He shakes his head slowly.

Jake follows me into the kitchen and then heaves himself onto the countertop. I move to the cupboard and survey the food options. While ice cream was good for curing my shattered heart, it isn't a suitable dinner.

"You hungry?" I ask, grabbing out a box of spaghetti.

Usually, Hale makes us dinner, but he's been busy with work for the last few hours. I don't know what, exactly, he does, but I theorized it involves accounting and numbers. Ew.

And after everything he's done for me, the least I can do is make him some dinner.

"You trying to bribe my love?" Jake demands with a haughty sneer.

"Is it working?"

"Unfortunately, yes. I'm weak."

As I begin to boil water on the stove, Jake regales me with all of the latest gossip. Apparently, a lot can happen in a day.

"Your accident is all over social media," Jake tells me. He grabs an apple out of the fruit bowl and tosses it up into the air.

I make a face at him. "Really? Why?"

"Because we live in the middle of nowhere, and you getting injured is the most exciting thing that's ever happened to us," Jake deadpans. He bites down on the apple, and juices cascade down his chin. "People are also talking about the new vice principal. My TikTok is covered in fancams."

"Fancams?" I arch my eyebrows.

Jake chuckles and hands me his phone, which is pulled up to a TikTok video. I push play and am immediately bombarded by images of Christian Montgomery. Walking down the hallway. Talking to another teacher. Leaning against the receptionist's desk. Sitting down.

I snort before I can stop myself.

Scrolling down, I see that there are even *more* videos, all from different accounts.

"Really?"

"Read the captions."

MandyGirl06: This is one Christian that makes me want to sin. #sinforviceprincipal #canhebemydaddy? #punishme

T8teKole: Hot dayummm. Someone send me to the principal's office. Pronto. #onmykneesforyou #fatherforgiveme #daddygoals

Alish@James: Can I transfer schools? #thatass #harderdaddy #iamabadgirl

"Oh my god." I don't know whether to laugh or feel appalled. "Poor Mr. Montgomery."

Jake chuckles as he takes his phone back from me. "It seems as if his anonymity has ended."

I laugh awkwardly, but internally, I feel a sharp pinch in my chest. That familiar tendril of jealousy curls around my heart and squeezes.

I don't like all of these women thirsting over Christian Montgomery, but I know my reaction is irrational.

"Well, a man that gorgeous wouldn't stay secret for long," I say absently as I toss the pasta into the water.

I then move towards the fridge, yank it open, and study the contents. When I find ground beef and a can of sauce, I pull them out.

I'll make spaghetti with meat sauce.

Maybe a side salad to go with it?

Movement in my periphery captures my attention, and I turn, expecting to see Hale.

But it's not Hale standing in the doorway of the kitchen.

A large man smiles widely at first me and then Jake. He has long hair that cascades nearly to his waist, the strands a dark-red color. A leather jacket encases his broad shoulders, but the badass look is juxtaposed by his light-brown cowboy boots.

I don't think; I just react.

Without second-guessing myself, I grab the largest steak knife and hold it at the ready. Fear twists in my gut.

Who is this man?

What is he doing in the house?

"GERRY!" Lissa's high-pitched voice precedes the girl herself racing into the kitchen and throwing herself into the giant's arms.

He laughs boisterously and spins her around, quite literally taking her feet off the ground in the process.

"How's my little missy doing?" His voice is deeper than any I've ever heard before, a raspy baritone.

Lissa begins talking a mile a minute as Jake jumps from the counter and pulls Gerry into a hug. Gerry pats Jake on the shoulder and then pushes him back to get a good look at him.

"Damn, kid. You grew five inches since I last saw you. You're nearly as tall as me."

"Or maybe your old age is making you shrink," Jake retorts with a grin.

He steps away, and Gerry finally turns towards me.

He has smiling eyes. They crinkle at the corners and burn with a jovial light that has my muscles loosening and my tension receding.

"You must be Izzy!" Gerry extends his arms as if he's going to give me a hug, and I instantly tense again.

Fortunately, Hale arrives before I can do something I'll regret.

Like stab my foster dad.

"Ger!" The older man pulls Gerry down into a short but passionate kiss.

When he pulls away, there's so much love in his eyes—in *both* of their eyes—that I almost feel as if I'm intruding.

And it also reminds me that I'm still holding the kitchen knife.

Oops.

I sheepishly drop it back to the counter as Hale turns to me with a beaming, lovesick smile.

"Izzy, this is my husband, Gerry. Gerry, this is Izzy."

"Nice to meet you," Gerry says in that rough, grating voice of his.

But despite how terrifying he sounds, I sense nothing but sincerity from the older man. His smile is wide and genuine, and his eyes seem to twinkle with his amusement.

"Izzy started dinner for us," Jake interjects.

Hale beams at me as Gerry claps his hands together.

"Perfect! You guys can all catch me up on what the hell has been happening over dinner."

One thing I learn pretty quickly—Gerry is loud and boisterous. He laughs often and is always quick to tell a joke or a cheesy pun.

I like him. A lot.

As I retire to my room for the night, my phone begins to buzz in my back pocket.

I haven't checked the damn thing since I first left the theater, and there's already a plethora of unread messages from Emery, Ethan, and Grayson.

But it's the newest message that captures my attention.

> UNKNOWN
>
> This is Ansel.
>
> UNKNOWN
>
> I hope you don't mind that I got your number.
>
> UNKNOWN
>
> I just wanted to check in.

A myriad of butterflies bursts to life in my chest. The mysterious texter from this morning...is Ansel.

How did he even get my number?

I shake off the wayward thought and quickly type back a reply.

> IZZY
>
> I'm okay. Thank you for checking in on me.

I pause, considering, and then shoot him one final text.

IZZY

Good night, Ansel.

ANSEL

Good night.

Forty-Three

IZZY

Something startles me awake.

At first, I think it's Grayson sneaking into my room yet again. My muscles lock together as I think about all of the ways I can make him suffer. He *knows* that I'm ignoring him. My blatant disregard of all his texts should be indication enough.

But then I hear a whisper of fabric and the sound of the window opening. Cold air blows through the room, causing the tiny hairs on my arms to stand at attention.

What the...?

I twist slightly on the bed, and my confusion only grows when I spot Lissa's blankets strewn across the floor and the girl in question nowhere to be seen.

Huh?

I sit up and turn towards the window just in time to see a flurry of pink.

Lissa.

Where is she going at—I grab my phone and flick it on—two in the morning? Is she meeting someone? A guy?

I know I'm the last person who should be talking, let alone judging, but I don't like the idea of Lissa wandering around outside by herself late at night. And I hate the idea of her meeting up with some random guy even more.

Yeah, yeah, yeah, I'm a hypocritical bitch. Sue me. I can't help it that I've become protective of Lissa. She reminds me of the little sister I never got to have—someone who annoys the shit out of you but who you'd kill and die for.

And I have a feeling someone will die tonight.

Cursing under my breath, I throw back my covers and move towards my closet. I quickly shove a sweat-shirt over my head and slip on a pair of sneakers sans socks. Then, I grab my phone off the nightstand and a container of pepper spray Hale bought me after I started my job at the theater.

"Lissa?!" I whisper-hiss as I poke my head out of the window.

At first, I see nothing but darkness and skeletal, towering trees. I'm halfway out the window when movement captures my attention.

A flash of pink materializes between the branches.

Lissa.

I release a plethora of swear words and hurry after her.

Where the hell is she going?

She's not even headed in the direction of the road. Is she lost?

Unbidden, my mind travels back to the huge wolf I saw on our property line. I quicken my pace as fear creates a tangled mess of nerves in my stomach.

I use the flashlight on my phone for guidance as I maneuver the maze of fallen trees, buoyant branches, and large stumps. Leaves crackle beneath my shoes as I hurry.

I debate calling Hale, Gerry, or even Jake before deciding against it. I don't want to worry them or get Lissa in trouble for sneaking out. I want her to be able to confide in me, and she won't do that if she doesn't trust me to keep her secrets.

Still, I just wish her "secret" didn't involve a midnight stroll through wolf-infested woods.

I lose sight of her more than once and have to backtrack a few times. Every so often, I'll spot a pink shirt and hurry in that direction, but when I get there, Lissa's gone.

Terror strangles my airways, and I begin to second-guess my decision not to get my foster parents or brother involved.

What in the world is Lissa up to?

If she's meeting with a guy, I'm going to murder

him for allowing her to traverse these woods on her own.

I have Hale's number pulled up on my phone, but before I can press the call button, a large, decrepit building comes into view.

A barn.

It appears to be centuries old, the red-painted wood having faded to a dusky brown interspersed here and there with splotches of mold. Glass from the windows now rests on the ground, and the doorway is nothing but a gaping hole, eerily resembling the mouth of a ravenous monster.

Lissa steps inside the barn and disappears from sight.

"Lissa!" I call, now that I'm in hearing range.

There's no answer.

With my heart thundering in a strange mixture of trepidation and irritation, I race the final distance to the barn.

"Lissa! It's me! Izzy!" I hold my phone light steady as I sweep it over the immense room.

There are a few stalls that probably once held horses. Now, however, the doors are wide open, and there's nothing but hay and dirt on the ground.

Buckets, rakes, and shovels litter the area, and I train my flashlight on the straw-covered floor to not trip over anything.

"Lissa, where are you? You shouldn't be out here alone." God, she's probably terrified I'm going to tattle on her. I work to modulate my volume so I sound soothing instead of angry. "I won't tell Hale or Gerry. But you shouldn't be this far out in the woods. And whose barn is this?"

The floorboards beneath my feet squeak as I venture farther into the room. The noise is almost ominously loud in the eerie silence.

Shining my flashlight in both directions, I see that there's a loft directly in front of me, though I don't spot any ladder to climb up in order to reach it. Bales of hay line the far wall, and wooden boards have been stacked haphazardly against a thin pillar.

There's no other door that I can see, which means Lissa must still be in here. I would've seen her leave through the front door or windows.

"Lissa, I promise. I won't tell anyone. Are you meeting someone?"

I reach the very end of the barn and breathe a sigh of relief when I catch sight of Lissa's tangled brown hair and pink pajamas.

She stands in the far corner of the room, moonlight from the hole in the roof casting her in a preternatural white light. She doesn't flinch when I approach her, keeping her back to me.

"Lissa," I say, reaching for her shoulder. I spin her around.

Lissa stares at me blankly, not a single hint of recognition in her gaze. She sways unsteadily on her feet.

"Lissa?" I ask, instinctively waving my hand in front of her face.

She doesn't even blink.

Is she...sleepwalking?

That could explain why she didn't hear me calling for her earlier.

Concern for my foster sister eclipses my anger over her actions from only moments before.

"Shit, Lis," I murmur, knowing she can't hear me.

She's probably freezing. She may even need to get her feet cleaned and bandaged.

I study my foster sister's face intently before something over her shoulder captures my attention.

I frown and shine my flashlight in that direction.

A scream bubbles in my throat but refuses to erupt.

In the corner of the barn, directly where Lissa was standing, is a body.

A *dead* body.

All I can see is abnormally pale skin, blonde hair, and terrified, crystalline eyes. And there, on the center of her forehead, is a strange symbol painted in blood— a large circle with a triangle inside of it.

"Oh my god." I think I'm going to be sick.

Lissa moves closer to me until her shoulder touches my own, and she peers down once more at the body.

Then she opens her mouth wide and begins to scream.

Forty-Four

IZZY

The woman's name is Alixandra.

She's twenty-seven years old and was born only a few miles away from Hale and Gerry. She works as a barista at the local coffee shop and is engaged to be married.

But I suppose I should stop thinking about her in the present tense.

Because she's dead.

Murdered.

The last two weeks have been a whirlwind of police interviews and questions. It seems everybody who's anybody wants to know what Lissa and I saw.

Did we notice anyone else in the barn?

Did we hear anything suspicious?

Did we see anything unusual?

The answer to all of that—at least from me—is a resounding no.

Lissa doesn't have a response.

Mainly because she doesn't remember going there in the first place.

She only woke from her trance when she began to scream, and even then, she passed out shortly after. That was how the police found us less than a half hour later—Lissa unconscious on the ground while I stood over a dead body.

I'm beginning to worry about my foster sister. She hasn't talked about what transpired in the barn since the initial interview with the cops, and she's withdrawn from everyone. She barely leaves her room, and when she does, it's without that customary smile I've come to expect from her.

She's a shell of her former self, walking aimlessly through the halls, her eyes glossy and vacant and devoid of any spark. She hasn't even returned to school since the incident, and I heard whispers that Hale and Gerry are considering an online program for the remainder of the semester for her.

I don't know if I'm necessarily faring much better. I still go to school and work, but there's a constant weight on my shoulders that seems to be increasing by the day. It's a suffocating sensation. Every time I close my eyes, I see the young woman's face etched onto my eyelids, her expression twisted in fear and horror.

Did she feel any pain before she was murdered?

Do the police have any suspects?

Those questions reverberate through my head now as I head towards my Art class.

Recently, we've been working with acrylic paint, and though I definitely can't say I've improved as an artist, I happen to like the class. It's peaceful, and more than that, it's an easy A. All we have to do is show up and try our best.

As soon as I'm in the classroom, I take a seat behind my easel and pull out my phone. I know it's not healthy or even sane to fixate on the murder, but whenever I have spare time, I research everything I can about Alixandra. I'm becoming obsessed. I *need* to know what happened to her, and so far, I haven't received any news from the police.

Not that they would tell me even if they had an update.

I scan through article after article, most of which I've already read. But there's one, however, that causes me to pause.

It's a recent piece, posted only an hour ago, and discusses Alixandra's murder in gruesome detail. The author suspects it's the work of a serial killer, especially since her death resembles that of a different young woman killed a month or so back.

The article provides a picture of the second victim, and my blood runs cold at the sight before me.

I...

I recognize her.

I *know* her.

Not well, of course, but I've talked to her. Shook her hand. Fought her.

Larissa, the woman I fought and beat in the ring.

An indecipherable feeling arrows through me as I stare at her smiling, heart-shaped face. And that strange feeling intensifies when I read the date she was murdered.

The same night of our fight.

I know it's just a coincidence, but I can't help but feel sick to my stomach.

Was I the last person she saw?

Where did she go after the fight?

Oh god.

I scan the article for more information but come up blank.

My breaths are embarrassingly choppy as I slip my phone into my backpack.

Breathe, Izzy. You need to breathe.

But it's hard to get air into my closed lungs.

Two girls are dead. Murdered.

And I was there both times.

Tears scorch the backs of my eyes, but sheer determination keeps them at bay. I refuse to let them fall.

The class begins to fill up, and the teacher hustles into the room seconds later, her wire-framed glasses sliding down her nose and her hair in a frizzy bob.

"All right, class! You all should be finishing up your assignments for this week. You only have a few more days until it's due. I'll give you time—"

The door to the classroom is thrown open, and Reid steps inside. I swear every student releases a collective gasp at the huge man's presence.

His lanky, dark-red hair falls forward over one eye, and he sweeps it away with the back of his hand.

"Reid. Why don't you go take your seat?" The teacher smiles kindly at him, though I notice she grimaces a little as he passes.

Still, her reaction is better than most of the students in the classroom. Almost every single person stares at Reid with thinly veiled disgust and disdain.

I haven't talked with Reid since his panic attack a couple of weeks ago. For the most part, our work schedules don't seem to align.

I can't help but wonder if that's on purpose, especially once I figured out Reid is in charge of creating the shift schedule.

He can hate me all he wants, but that won't stop me from befriending him, dammit.

I smile at him as he takes the seat beside me, trying desperately to ignore the pungent scent that wafts off of him in almost tangible waves. I notice he looks crappier than usual today, which is saying something.

His skin is pale—so pale that his acne stands out starkly—and purple shadows underscore each of his eyes.

I can't help but compare *this* Reid to the one I saw a picture of from years before.

That Reid was lithe but muscular, with garnet-colored hair highlighted here and there with gold and tawny brown. He was so handsome it almost seemed unreal—the type of ethereal perfection only achieved by models and actors, not normal high school students.

Obviously, something horrible must've happened to him that caused him to fall apart.

I remember the beautiful girl from the theater—Michelle—and feel a pang of jealousy in the center of my chest. I can't imagine the heartbreak he must've felt when she left him.

Why doesn't he just get back together with her? It's apparent she wants to, despite his appearance now.

Or maybe they already have. Maybe that's why he hasn't been at school lately—

Rough fingers grab my wrist and then force me to release the death grip I have on the paintbrush.

I turn in surprise to see Reid scowling at me. Despite that, his touch is gentle as he runs his thumb back and forth over my pulse. Goose bumps flutter across my skin, and a strange tendril of warmth unfurls in my belly.

Staring into Reid's angry face—with the broad forehead, sharp cheekbones, and defined jawline—I can't help but think he looks...handsome. Maybe it's the way the sun is slanting through the blinds behind him, illuminating his features in a hazy sheen of gold. Maybe it's the keenness in his eyes that's in dichotomy to the softness of his touch. Maybe it's—

Reid releases me as if my skin burned him. And

with an angry grunt, he focuses once more on his art piece.

Well, then.

Huffing, I get to work on my own painting. I *tried* to paint a scenic landscape I saw on the internet, but I'm afraid the picture resembles a series of blobs and colors more than anything else. Trees can go fuck themselves. Every time I try to create one, I either make the trunk too thin or the branches too thick. The result is... well... Maybe I can claim that this is an alien planet?

I'm in the process of painting white waves on my ocean when I become aware of eyes on me.

I turn towards Reid with an arched eyebrow, but he simply narrows his eyes at my masterpiece of a painting.

"Why the *fuck* are you drawing little penises in your ocean?"

I gape at him. "I'm not drawing penises! They're waves!"

"Why do they have ball sacks?" He appears genuinely befuddled.

"There are no ball sacks... Oh wait." I frown as I consider the painting with fresh eyes.

Now that he mentioned it, my attempt to create waves cresting the shoreline does appear a little ball sacky.

Reid chuckles, a dark, delicious sound that amplifies the heat in my stomach, turning it into a raging inferno.

"And are those mutant aliens?" Reid continues, using his own paintbrush to point at my painting.

I huff indignantly. "Those are trees."

"Why do they have arms? And legs? And eyes?"

"Those are trunks and branches and little chipmunk holes," I declare with a pleased grin. "Now, let me see yours. It's only fair."

I swivel on my stool to get a look, but Reid very purposely tilts his canvas away from my line of sight.

"Nope," he grunts simply.

"Reid..." I stand and place my hands on my hips.

"Sit your cute ass down," he barks, already dismissing me.

No way in hell.

Wait...

He thinks my ass is cute?

Butterflies swarm in my belly.

Focus!

"Let me see it," I singsong.

"Nope."

"I'm going to see it no matter what you do." I shrug nonchalantly. "Might as well save us both the trouble and let me look at it now."

"Nope."

Quick as a whip, I move so I'm directly behind him, but he shoulders his way forward so he's blocking my view of his painting.

"Real mature," I huff.

"No means no."

"Reid…" I growl, though I can't help but think the noise sounds pathetic in comparison to his rumbly voice.

Whatever Reid says next is lost to the whispers of the three students sitting directly in front of us.

"Is she really flirting with him?" the boy asks, sounding incredulous.

A girl sniffs. "Of course not. He's disgusting."

"I heard that she's dating Emery," another girl interjects.

"She's probably cheating on him with Reid," the first girl retorts. "I heard she's a little bit of a whore."

"Not even a whore would lower their standards to sleep with Reid," the boy says with a chuckle.

"God, what happened to him? He used to be hot. Now, I can't stand being in the same room as him. His smell alone seriously makes me want to vomit."

All three of them laugh at that, and I see red. My hands curl into fists as fury races through me, scorching my veins.

"Hey, assholes," I whisper-hiss, immensely grateful that this is the one class where everyone can get away with chatting amongst themselves.

No one pays me or my outburst any attention.

No one, that is, except for the three idiots.

Slowly, almost warily, the three of them turn back to stare at me, almost as if they're shocked I'm addressing them directly. I don't recognize any of them, but that doesn't surprise me. I don't have a really big social circle yet. They may be the same assholes who talked shit about Reid that first day of school.

The boy flushes bright red, and one of the girls lowers her head in embarrassment. The other simply stares directly at me with arched eyebrows and flared nostrils.

"Yeah?" she asks, sounding annoyed at being interrupted.

"Why don't you guys stop gossiping about us and get back to work, okay? You don't know anything about me or Reid. Or Emery, for that matter. Besides, what you're saying is vile and completely untrue. So just kindly fuck off." I can barely speak through the rage percolating deep in my chest.

"It's not untrue when it's someone's opinion," the girl snaps.

God, I want to slap her across her smug face so badly right now.

"As I said before, you don't know either of us, so you have no place to judge or even have an opinion." I slowly work to unclench my hands, one finger at a time.

The girl looks at me for a second longer, her gaze assessing, before she rolls her eyes with a muttered, "Whatever," and focuses on her own canvas.

Her friends giggle guiltily and turn around as well.

It's only when they're no longer staring at me that I feel like I can breathe again. The pressure in my chest eases ever so slightly.

Until I turn to face Reid.

His jaw is clenched so tightly I'm surprised he doesn't chip a tooth. He keeps his glare pinned on the backs of the three students' heads. One of his hands balls into a fist while the other flexes by his side. He doesn't seem to realize I'm watching him, so I take the moment to study him unencumbered.

For a brief moment, I see a flash of vulnerability in his eyes. Pain. Grief. *Agony.* The sight of it steals the breath from my lungs all over again. Then Reid's mask slides back into place like a door being slammed shut.

"Reid," I say softly, but he's already slinging his backpack over his shoulder and ripping his canvas off the easel.

The teacher calls his name, but he ignores her as he stalks out of the classroom.

He doesn't look back.

And I don't see him again for another week.

Forty-Five

IZZY

"Izzy, we need to talk," Hale says almost as soon as I step through the door after my shift at the theater.

I smell like butter, hot dogs, and Coke—the latter courtesy of a little boy who "accidentally" threw it at me. And I say "accidentally" because I'm ninety percent sure the little shit did it on purpose after I told him he couldn't have a soft pretzel for free.

I hang up my coat and run my fingers through my knotted blonde hair.

Hale and Gerry sit in the living room on the couch, almost as if they've been waiting for me to return home the entire time I was out.

An uneasy feeling slithers through my stomach and settles in my chest, coiling around my heart.

Is this about the murders? Alixandra and Larissa? Something else entirely?

"What's up?" I ask a little cautiously as I move into the living room.

I don't sit despite the empty armchair that has clearly been left for me. I have too much energy skittering across my skin, almost as if I stuck my finger into an electrical socket.

Hale and Gerry exchange an unreadable look that sends my heart into palpitations.

While Hale is dressed comfortably in sweats and a T-shirt, Gerry still wears his signature leather jacket and cowboy boots. His long hair cascades down his shoulders with a single braid woven near the front.

"Don't look so terrified, kid," Gerry says with a chuckle.

The sound causes some of the tension riding my shoulders and neck to ease.

"What did you expect?" I throw my hands up in exasperation. "You can't just tell a girl 'we need to talk' and not expect her to freak out."

Hale rolls his eyes. "But we *do* need to talk."

"You could've started the conversation with something a little more light-hearted," Gerry teases. "Maybe you could've started the conversation with a song?"

"A song." Hale doesn't phrase it as a question as he blinks up at his husband.

"A ballad, maybe? Or a rap?" Gerry continues, running a hand over the beard on his jawline.

"What do we need to talk about?" I ask, getting the conversation back on track.

I've witnessed firsthand the way Gerry can rile Hale up with his teasing. The two love each other more than anything, but I swear Gerry's boisterous, jovial personality makes Hale want to go on a murder rampage.

Hale and Gerry exchange another one of those unreadable looks, and the room once again turns fraught with tension.

"You're going to be eighteen soon," Hale says kindly, and I swear my heart stops beating.

How often did I pray to turn eighteen and finally be free of the shackles foster care put on me?

Now, I'm dreading my upcoming birthday more than anything else in the world. It feels as if I'm staring up at the sparkly blade of a guillotine just waiting for it to drop. My heart doesn't just beat; it *pounds*. I wouldn't be surprised if the entire room could hear it.

Are they going to kick me out?

Where will I go?

Terror threatens to flay me open.

"Jesus Christ, Hale!" Gerry snaps. "Why did you have to phrase it like that?"

Hale blinks. "What did I do wrong?"

Gerry ignores his husband and turns towards me. "Kid, we're not kicking you out, so if that's what you're thinking, stop it."

Hale finally seems to grasp how his words could be construed, and he gapes at me in wide-eyed horror. "Oh no, sweetheart. No. We're not kicking you out. God, no."

"That's the whole purpose of this conversation," Gerry continues. "We want you to know that you have a home with us, always. *Mi casa es tu casa.*"

Hale's eyebrows scrunch together. "Isn't it *su casa?*"

"*Tu* means you, right?"

"Honey, I haven't spoken Spanish in over thirty years. Don't be asking me that."

"Whatever. *Su casa. Tu casa.*" Gerry waves a flippant hand in the air. "Our house is your house."

Unexpected tears scorch my eyes, but I quickly blink them away.

"I... I..." Swallowing, I clear my throat and try again. "Thank you."

"No need to thank us." Hale smiles gently at me, the movement causing the wrinkles around his eyes to deepen. "You're family and—" A frown touches his face as he focuses on something over my shoulder. "Lissa? Where are you going?"

I pivot on my heel just in time to see Lissa hurrying towards the front door.

Or at least, a version of Lissa.

She wears a black sweatshirt a few sizes too big for her—probably Jake's—and similarly colored leggings. When she turns to face us, I notice that her eyes are outlined in dark makeup and her lips are bloodred.

"What?" she snaps, folding her arms over her chest. "What the hell are you staring at?"

"Language," Hale chastises instantly.

Lissa rolls her heavily made-up eyes. "I've heard worse from you two over the years. Don't be hypocritical."

I bite my lower lip to keep from saying anything.

Since the night Lissa found the body in the barn, she's been...different. And not in a good way. I can't remember the last time I saw her in pink, and she only talks to us when she wants to insult us. I understand that what she saw was traumatizing, but I miss the old Lissa.

Even if she did talk a lot.

I hoped that she would revert to her old self as soon as she started hanging out with her friends again, but I was wrong.

So, so wrong.

She kicked all of her friends out of the house as soon as they arrived the other day and hasn't contacted them since.

"Izzy's birthday is coming up," Hale says, trying to infuse his voice with cheer.

Lissa gives him a droll look. "Yay," she deadpans. "Does that mean I'll finally have a room to myself again?"

I try really, really hard not to let hurt show on my face.

"Lissa!" Gerry snaps.

But my younger foster sister merely rolls her eyes. "Whatever. I'm going out."

"Not on a school night—" Hale begins, but Lissa

ignores him and quickly slips outside, the door slamming shut behind her. "Dammit," Hale mutters as he pushes himself off the couch and hurries after her.

I watch his retreating back as concern for Lissa twists my stomach into knots.

"She's going to be okay, Iz," Gerry says in his gruff voice. He moves to stand beside me and places a hand on my shoulder. "She's a tough kid."

"She sleepwalked straight to a dead body," I point out, nervously chewing on my nail. "That's fucked up."

Gerry rubs his palm down his face. "She's a tough kid," he repeats.

And this time, I don't know who he's trying to convince—me or himself.

Forty-Six

EMERY

"It smells like Mom's making pot roast today," Ethan says, shifting awkwardly on the chair across from me.

I don't even bother to glance up from my phone as I grunt something noncommittally in reply.

The dining room has been completely transformed, courtesy of my mother. A white tablecloth covers the mahogany table, and six place settings have been stationed. I see a basket of rolls, a glass bowl full of salad, a container of fresh corn, and a tray of Jell-O.

Mom and Dad only go all out when they have guests over. Usually, we all take our meals to go and eat in front of the television or in our bedrooms. Mom tries to make us have family dinners every week, but it's hard with our schedules. I have football every day after school, Ethan has his clubs, and our older sister works night shifts and doesn't even live at home anymore. Our weekly dinners have turned into monthly dinners.

Mom hums merrily under her breath as she emerges from the kitchen, carrying a pot full of beef, carrots, and potatoes. I inhale deeply and feel my stomach rumble in response.

"Am I not feeding you enough?" Mom teases as she lowers the final dish onto the table. She then stands back to survey her work.

"I'm a growing boy," I tease, placing a hand on my taut, muscular stomach. "I need calories."

"Have too much calories and you'll end up like your father," Mom says.

Dad chooses that exact moment to enter the room and gives his wife a playful glare. "Are you calling me chubby, darling?"

"I'm saying you can afford to cut back." Mom pecks Dad on the cheek, and he melts under her touch.

"Fat is just muscle for old men," he insists, brushing his fingers along the back of her cheek.

"You keep telling yourself that."

Even after all of this time, my parents are still so stupidly in love with each other. It makes me want to find something similar for myself.

With Izzy.

Warmth blossoms in my chest, and I glance back down at my phone, searching to see if I have any new texts from her. I try not to let my disappointment show when I realize I have no notifications.

She's probably at work, I tell myself. And I know she's not allowed to have her phone with her while on the clock.

Still, I wish she were here with me. My sister is bringing her boyfriend to dinner, so why can't I bring Izzy?

Not that she's my girlfriend.

Or anything to me besides a close friend.

It's been immensely difficult, but I've been trying to take it slow with her. She deserves to be romanced and wooed. Yet I can't help but feel as if I shoved myself firmly into a little area one calls the "friend zone."

Does she even think of me in a romantic way?

Fuck, when have I turned into such a sap? I'm not the type of guy to wax poetic or become obsessed with a girl. I'm not a player, but I'm certainly not the ideal candidate for a boyfriend either.

But with Izzy, everything's different. She's my first thought in the morning and my last one before I fall asleep at night. I'm actually *excited* to go to school because I know I'll get to see her beautiful face. I revel in her laughter—in the way her eyes crinkle and seem to shine with their own inner radiance. In the way her lips curl upwards. In the way her body shakes.

I could listen to her laugh forever.

Not that you'll be able to have a future with her if you don't solve the Desiree problem first.

A boulder settles in my gut.

Not every pack is fortunate enough to find their fated mate. Look at my father's pack, for example. My dad is mated to my mom, but the other two members of his pack aren't. It's immensely rare for a same-sex pack to not share a mate but not entirely unheard of. Most packs know almost immediately if they have the same mate. When their marks appear, they also get a secondary brand directly below it, so miniscule that it often goes unnoticed.

My pack symbol is a flame, but directly beneath it is a zigzagging line—the same line that mars the flesh of my brothers. It's how we knew from the beginning that we were fated to share a heart.

My mom and dad are mates, but their other two packmates—my "uncles"—aren't. My sister once told me that she heard our mom fucking our Uncle Ted when they thought we were all out of the house.

It's not uncommon for packs to share lovers, and it seems like my parents' mating status doesn't make them any different. Sometimes, unmated wolves will partake in a ceremony to connect them with their lover. It's not as potent or consuming as it would be if the person was their fated mate, but it's stronger than a mere marriage.

Binding.

Eternal.

What would I have done if Izzy wasn't my mate? If she belonged only to the others, not to me? Would I have been able to walk away?

No. I don't think so.

The clearing of Ethan's throat pulls me out of my reverie. My twin volleys his gaze between my phone and my father, and I get the unspoken message instantly.

Quickly, I slide my phone into my pocket.

Dad may not be as gung-ho about family dinners as Mom, but he has a strict "no phone" policy at the table. When my sister was younger, she once had her phone confiscated for an entire week because she was caught texting during dinner.

"Oh! I think I hear a car!" Mom says, canting her head to the side like a dog.

"Are you sure? I heard most people lose their hearing with old age…" Dad trails off when Mom whacks him in the bicep.

"You're so naughty!" she squeaks with a smile. "Now, finish setting the table while I go greet our daughter."

My sister lives in an apartment only a few miles away from the local community college, where she's taking a few of her prerequisite classes. She actually met her boyfriend on campus, though I don't think he's a student. Then again, what do I know? Her boyfriend is a grade-A asshole.

Mom hurries out of the kitchen to greet them while my father begins pouring wine into glasses. He even gives me a little bit, but he passes over Ethan, unsurprisingly. My twin stares wistfully at the red liquid, but when he notices me scowling at him, he looks away.

Ethan's been sober for over six months now. Logically, I *know* he's trying to right his wrongs. I *know* he's trying to better himself.

I know all that.

But it doesn't take the sting out of his betrayal.

I did everything for him. Supported him. Helped him. Cared for him. And what did I get in return?

Flashing red and blue lights.

Sirens echoing in the air.

Rubble.

Blood.

Crying.

"BABY BROTHER!" Thin arms wrap around me from behind, and I awkwardly pat my sister's hands.

"Hey, sis."

Sydney sashays into the room, practically dragging her boyfriend along behind her.

Grayson stares first at me and then at Ethan, his features unsurprisingly expressionless.

I don't know how I feel about the large, quiet man. Honestly, I'm not sure if I ever heard him talk before. Sydney says it's because he's "thoughtful" and "contemplative," but I think he's just a dick.

I have to give him credit, though. Syd's last boyfriend practically ate her face off whenever he got the chance. Grayson won't even give her a kiss in front of us.

Thank fuck.

There are some things you just don't need to see, and your older sister getting handsy with a guy is one of them.

"Why don't we all take our seats?" Dad smiles at all of us. "Your mother slaved away all day to create this feast."

Mom's cheeks pinken with pleasure. "I hope you enjoy."

And I settle myself in for a *long* evening, secretly wishing I were anywhere else.

Like with Izzy.

* * *

When dinner ends, Mom shoos all of us "kids" into the living room while she and Dad clean up. I try to protest —mainly because a part of me despises being referred to as a kid—but Mom simply gives me a glare and says, "Shoo."

That's how I find myself sitting in the living room on one of the armchairs, staring blankly at the roaring flames of the fire.

Dad chose years ago to decorate our house like a rustic cabin. No fucking idea why, considering we live in the middle of a bustling neighborhood. Still, wooden logs have been placed over the normal wall plaster, and the furniture pieces are bedecked in fur blankets. A faux animal rug rests on the floor directly in front of a stone hearth which features a mounted buck head.

Sydney and Grayson sit on the couch, and to my absolute horror, my sister stealthily places her hand on his upper thigh, inches from his crotch. Grayson immediately turns stiff and grabs her hand, forcing it away.

Probably feels uncomfortable being touched in front of his girlfriend's younger brothers.

At least one of them has some sense.

Ethan takes a sip from his water glass as Sydney turns her sparkling eyes onto him.

"Sooo…" She waggles her eyebrows suggestively. "Tell me about the girl."

He begins to choke on the water.

"W-what girl?" he stutters out, wiping at his mouth with the back of his hand.

My sister's shit-eating grin only widens.

"Mom said that you have a crush on some new girl at your school. That you've been talking on the phone with her almost every night."

The tips of Ethan's ears turn crimson as he ducks his head.

"I don't know what you're talking—"

"Her name is Isabella," I interject, smirking.

I'll never pass up on an opportunity to give my brother shit.

Besides, Sydney doesn't need to know that I have a crush on Isabella as well.

Grayson goes rigid beside Sydney, and he slides his ice-blue eyes in Ethan's direction.

What the fuck is his problem?

"Have you kissed her yet?" Sydney continues teasingly. "Or maybe gone further—"

"I need to piss." Grayson stands up abruptly, a frown tugging at the corners of his mouth. "Where's the bathroom?"

Sydney smiles sweetly. "Ethan will show you." She turns towards our brother. "And after, I was thinking you could show Grayson your new gaming system?"

Ethan's brows bunch together in confusion. "Errr...sure?"

Sydney claps her hands together. "Perfect." She leans forward to give Grayson a kiss, but just before their lips touch, he turns his face to the side and offers her his cheek instead.

"Not in front of your brothers," he murmurs in a low, husky voice.

Is this guy a fucking chain smoker? I swear it sounds like he just ate a handful of gravel.

Sydney seems disappointed but forces a smile on her face. That smile remains as she watches him follow Ethan down the hall. Only when he's completely out of sight does she turn towards me with a frown.

"I need your help."

"Yeah?" I arch an eyebrow.

Sydney glances in both directions, ensuring we're

alone, before she reaches into her pocket and holds out a tiny flip phone.

"What...?"

"It's Grayson's," she explains. "I stole it off of him."

Now I'm really confused.

"Why would you do that?"

Sydney's lower lip begins to wobble, and tears materialize in her eyes. "Because I think he's cheating on me."

For a moment, I only sit there in stunned silence. But then her words register, and a murderous rage courses through me.

That motherfucker!

I'll fucking cut off all of his toenails and then shove them up his ass if that's true. I'll skin his cock and then sew together his balls. I'll gouge his eyes out with a rusty spoon.

Sydney must see something in my expression because she quickly sniffles and wipes at her eyes. "I don't know for sure," she admits. "But..."

"But?" It takes every ounce of self-control I have to keep a leash on my anger.

"Okay, take this phone for example." Sydney waves the tiny device in the air. "What person nowadays owns a flip phone?"

"And you think he's cheating because of *that*?" Slowly, my anger begins to abate.

It's not as if I don't believe my sister, but she's been

known to create wild conspiracy theories, especially ones that concern the men she dates. She broke off with her ex because she was convinced he was secretly a part of the mafia after she overheard him talking to someone named Alessio, demanding his money back.

Spoiler alert—Alessio is the owner of the local pizza joint, and Sydney's ex wanted a refund after he received sausage on his vegetarian pizza.

My sister begins to spin the phone around in her hands. "I could've sworn I saw him with an iPhone once. So why would he have two phones?"

"Maybe that iPhone wasn't his—"

"And he has never kissed me. Not once."

I awkwardly scratch at the nape of my neck, wishing more than anything a flesh-eating monster will emerge from the ground and swallow me whole. "Errr, maybe you should tell Ethan this—"

"I practically throw myself at him," she continues, oblivious or choosing to ignore my unease, "but he always puts me down. Says that he wants to take things 'slow.'" She makes exaggerated air quotes around that last word.

"Why the fuck are you making me be the voice of reason?" I run a hand through my already spiked hair. "That's Ethan's department." I shake my head and then focus back on her. "Okay, look, there are logical explanations for all of that. He could have religious reasons for wanting to take things slow, or maybe he's just old-fashioned. You know how some guys are.

Besides,"—I give her a pointed look—"you shouldn't be getting attached to him. What would you do when you find your Heart?"

Sydney's in a pack with two other girls, but so far, they haven't come into contact with their fated mate. For the time being, all three of them have been playing the field, so to speak, in the hopes of forming a connection with someone.

"You're one to talk." She waves a disapproving finger in front of my face. "Don't think I didn't notice the way your eyes lit up when you talked about Isabella. You're going to be mated to Desiree at the end of the school year. Why put yourself through the heartbreak?"

Dread settles in my stomach like a clump of cement. I fucking hate the direction this conversation is going.

My family knows the truth about my pack's arrangement with Desiree, and though they don't approve, there's nothing they can do about it, despite Dad being a member of the Council.

And I'm certainly not going to think about my future mating to fucking Desiree. It won't happen. I refuse to allow it to. Now that I found Izzy—my Heart—there's no way in hell I'm going to tie myself to another girl.

My sister focuses once more on the flip phone. "And then there's the whole Gracie incident."

"Gracie?"

Her lips firm. "I arrived at his place early—oh, I forgot to mention that he *never* allows me into his apartment—and got bored waiting outside. So I went to his room and overheard him leaving a voicemail for someone named Gracie. He kept telling her to call him back, and he's sorry, and he meant what he said." She swallows heavily. "He talked more to this Gracie chick on the phone than he ever does to me."

Okay, yeah, that sounds pretty damning, but I try to put myself in Ethan's shoes. My brother would come up with a logical solution to explain away Grayson's odd behavior.

"Maybe Gracie's a relative. A sister, perhaps?"

"Yeah, maybe. But I guess we'll see for sure in a few seconds." Sydney tosses me a diabolical smile. "I watched him plug in his password."

"Syd, you really shouldn't be invading his privacy like this," I say gently, and my sister frowns.

"I went to you instead of Ethan because I thought you'd have my back."

I roll my eyes at her dramatics. "I do have your back, hence why I'm warning you to stop."

She waves away my words. "Just watch the door. Give me a shout if they're coming back."

Yeah, no thanks.

Instead of doing that, I flop down beside her on the couch. I totally don't think it's cool that she's going through his phone, but if he proves to be a lying cheater? Well, a brother's got to know these things.

"There's literally nothing on the phone." Sydney's brows furrow. "No apps or games or even messages."

Okay, that *is* pretty damn suspicious.

"Click on his photos," I suggest, pointing.

It takes Sydney a few seconds—we're so used to touch screens that it's strange to click on buttons—but she's finally able to access the photo icon.

Nothing.

"Maybe check recently deleted?"

Sydney nods and does as I suggest.

"WHAT THE HELL?" Sydney screeches, red splotches erupting on her cheekbones in her rage. "That cheating son of a bitch."

"Let me see," I say, feeling a strange ball of yarn congregate in my throat.

Grayson's phone is full of pictures.

Pictures of females.

Pictures of females who don't seem aware they're being watched in the first place.

I recognize both of them, even if Sydney doesn't.

I saw both of their bodies. Studied the crime scene. Talked with the police officers.

Larissa and Alixandra.

The two wolves who were murdered.

My heart feels like a mound of cement in my chest. There's a strange roaring sound between my ears as I scroll through all of the recently deleted photos.

There are *hundreds* of them, all dating back to a couple of months ago and ending the days they died.

Holy fuck.

Holy. Fuck.

Is Grayson...?

Could he possibly be...?

I don't want to believe it, but the truth is quite literally staring at me in the face.

Footsteps sound in the hallway, and I exit out of the photos and then drop the phone between the sofa cushions. Quickly, I move to reclaim my seat in the armchair.

Ethan and Grayson enter the living room once more.

"I showed him my PlayStation, as requested," Ethan says lightly, scratching at one of his tattoos. "Kind of awkward because Grayson doesn't even like video games, but whatever."

"You don't?" Sydney blinks up at him innocently, not a hint of the sorrow or rage I saw in her expression only moments before. "I'm sorry, Gray. I thought you did." She pats the sofa cushion beside her and then frowns, reaching down to grab out his phone. "What's this? Grayson, I think your phone fell out of your pocket."

She extends the device to him with a sweet smile, and he takes it without a word.

I can't seem to get my heartbeat under control. It's erratic. Loud. Deafening.

I don't know what the fuck to do.

My sister's boyfriend may be the werewolf hunter we've been looking for this entire time.

And if that's the case...

Rage rushes through me, almost staggering in its intensity.

I'll make Grayson pay for every life he took.

Larissa.

Alixandra.

Two innocent werewolves who didn't deserve to die.

I meet Grayson's gaze from across the room.

You think you can hurt my people and get away with it? Use my sister for your malicious games?

Once I find the evidence I need, I won't turn you into the current Council.

I'll kill you myself.

Game on.

Forty-Seven

IZZY

"Isabella Martin, please report to the main office. I repeat, Isabella Martin, please report to the main office. Thank you."

The intercom crackles once with static before going silent.

"Ohhh." KD leans forward with a salacious wag of her eyebrows. "Someone's in trouble."

"What did you do this time? Get tackled by a basketball player?" Ashlinn teases, brushing at a strand of her short brown hair.

"You guys are hilarious," I deadpan, dragging my attention to Mr. Remington, who frowns in my direction.

The substitute teacher nods his head once and says, "Take your stuff with you. It's nearing the end of class, and I'm not sure you'll make it back before school lets out."

As I throw my backpack over my shoulder, I can't help but wonder what this could be about.

My eighteenth birthday? No, that's insane. Why would anyone care about that?

Did I do something wrong?

Questions tumble around and around in my head like a leaf in a hurricane as I hurry out of my Yearbook class and towards the office.

When I finally arrive, Olive—the sweet secretary—jerks her chin towards Christian Montgomery's closed door.

"He's waiting for you, sweetie," she tells me kindly, already turning back to her computer. The only sound in the room is the clack of her nails against the keyboard.

Wait...

Christian is the one who wants to see me?

Christian Montgomery, the sexiest man I've ever seen?

A zing of excitement sizzles along my nerves, but I attempt to squash the feeling before it can intensify. I have to remind myself that he's significantly older than me and my vice principal. This stupid school-girl crush needs to go. Now.

Still, my heart beats almost painfully fast as I rap my knuckles against his closed door. There's silence for a moment, and I almost think that Olive was wrong and he didn't wish to see me, when the door is thrown open.

And there Mr. Montgomery stands, in all his hot glory.

Today, he wears a teal-colored shirt that does wonders for his eyes. The stubble on his chin has been recently trimmed, giving him a sophisticated, elegant look.

Am I drooling?

Please tell me I'm not drooling.

That would be fucking embarrassing.

Christian steps aside and gestures for me to enter.

"Thank you for meeting me, Ms. Martin," he tells me politely, gently shutting the door behind us.

I jump at the sound, unable to ignore the sudden surge of goose bumps that pebble on my arms or the delicious heat that spurs to life in my belly. With the door closed, the room suddenly seems ten sizes smaller. I swear his body emanates an almost palpable heat that caresses my skin like the whiskers on a paintbrush. His cinnamon scent permeates the air, and a part of me wants to inhale deeply and capture the fragrance.

But then I remind myself that that would be insanely creepy, and instead of giving in to my baser instincts, I perch on the chair in front of his desk and fold my hands in my lap.

Christian moves with an almost predatorial grace, his shirtsleeves pushed up to his forearms and his tie loosened. He scrubs a hand through his spiked black hair before claiming the seat opposite me and forcing a smile.

"Sorry for the impromptu meeting." He reaches under his desk and grabs out a can of Coke. "Drink?" When I nod, he tosses it to me, his eyes sparkling. "Just don't tell on me, okay? I don't want to get in trouble."

"Ha. Ha. Very funny," I tell him dryly, feeling my cheeks burn with embarrassment. "You know, you could've told me that you were the vice principal."

His smile broadens, and I swear for a fraction of a second a dimple appears in his cheek. Then he compresses his lips into a straight line and leans forward, resting his elbows on the table. "I wanted to check in with you. See how you're handling things."

I slide my backpack off my shoulders and place it by my feet as I think over Mr. Montgomery's question. Is he asking about my personal life? Or does he want to know how I'm handling the course work?

Before I can give voice to my questions, he continues, his voice low and earnest. "I know you've been making friends with some of the other students here, and that's good." He seems to consider something and then adds, "Including my brother."

My eyebrows crawl to my hairline. "Your brother?"

His lips twitch, but he doesn't allow them to stretch into a full-fledged smile. "Yes. Ashton. Ashton James."

Ashton?!

Ashton is Mr. Montgomery's brother?

I study my vice principal carefully, searching for any similarities to the asshole, but find none.

Is he pulling my leg?

"Half brother, technically," Mr. Montgomery continues, obviously seeing the confusion on my face. "Same mom. Different dads."

"Oh." I debate what to say next but decide it'd be a dick move to tell him, "I'm sorry your brother is an asshole."

"I also heard that you're turning eighteen soon." Mr. Montgomery's eyes sharpen on my face, becoming unreadable. His fingers begin to tap against the desk repeatedly. "Has my brother or his friends talked to you about that yet?"

My brows bunch together. "Talk to me about what?"

Irritation flickers across his face, there and gone before I can comment on it. "They haven't said anything to you?"

"About what?" Now, *I'm* the one getting irritated.

What is this about?

"Nothing." Mr. Montgomery shakes his head. "It's nothing. They just...love birthdays." He absently scratches at his jawline, which I'm beginning to think is a nervous habit of his. "But I want you to know, Isabella, that you can come to me with any questions or concerns."

His earnest eyes ensnare my own, and I feel the strangest sensation of falling, tumbling, spinning head over heels. Heat rushes through me and congregates in my stomach.

"Um...yeah. Sure. Okay." I quickly look away, unable to hold eye contact for a second longer.

His penetrating gaze seems to burrow its way beneath my defenses in a way that terrifies me.

I remind myself for the one millionth time that he's my vice principal, not some high school boy for me to crush on.

The bell rings overhead, signaling the end of classes for the day. The noise seems to startle Mr. Montgomery, who jumps about a foot in the air, brought out of his internal musings.

He shuffles some papers on his desk and clears his throat. "I think that's all I needed to discuss with you. You're free to leave."

I reach down to grab my backpack and then head towards the door.

Just before I exit the office, however, Mr. Montgomery's raspy voice reaches me. "Remember, Isabella. You can come to me with any questions. The others may be hesitant to answer them, but I don't agree with leaving you in the dark."

As I step out of the office and into the hallway, I can't help but replay Mr. Montgomery's last words over and over in my head.

What did he mean?

Why does he think I'm in the dark?

And who, exactly, are the people keeping secrets from me?

Forty-Eight

ANSEL

I don't like using the word "crush." It sounds so... inconsequential, so trivial, so tame. People in my school throw that word around so often that it has begun to lose its meaning.

Brittany has a crush on Tyler.

Tyler has a crush on Abbie.

Abbie has a crush on Paul.

And so on and so on.

I never really understood the point of such a term before. What does it mean to have a crush on someone? Why do people even refer to it as such? Couldn't there be other, more potent words in the English dictionary to describe such an emotion?

Yet, whenever I stare at Isabella Martin, I finally understand the meaning of such a crude term.

There's a heavy weight on my chest, and it's growing in size every damn day. The pressure cuts off my air supply until all I can do is suck in ragged breaths. That pressure... Is that what it means to have a crush on someone?

Panic claws at my guts, even as zings of excitement sizzle along my nerves.

When did these feelings even develop? I try to think back to the first moment I saw the golden-haired beauty but remember only feeling growing irritation and annoyance. Most women like her don't give me the time of day. I'm too nerdy, too cold, too strange to be taken seriously. They see me only as someone they can use to copy test answers off of.

But not Izzy.

I glance inconspicuously at the girl out of the corner of my eye as she takes notes, her brows knitted in concentration and her pink lips pursed. I should be paying attention to the teacher droning on and on and on, but I'm not. I can't. It seems I'm incapable of tearing my gaze away from the enchanting beauty when she's in the vicinity.

Science is my easiest subject by far, so I know I won't miss anything by zoning out this class. Besides, the only competition I have is from the blond-haired idiot sitting a little bit behind me—Ethan.

And heaven only knows Ethan isn't paying a lick of attention to the teacher either.

More than once, I've seen him and his brother watching Isabella with a predatory lethality, a keen intensity, that makes my hackles rise. I don't know what it is about the two brothers that twists my stomach into knots...

Honestly, it's not just them, though admitting that even to myself makes me feel insane. A lot of these students give me the creeps. Ethan and Emery, for starters, but also their friends Reid and Ashton. Desiree and her crew. Kain.

I begin to tap the edge of my pencil against the black countertop as I once again glance at Isabella.

Izzy.

My heart pounds against my breastbone the longer I study her.

God, how could I have been so stupid?

I'm not the type of guy to develop crushes on pretty females.

And I'm certainly not the type of guy to use my powers out in the open.

I divert my attention away from her profile and study my hand, my knuckles bleached white from how tightly I grip the pencil.

What exactly did Izzy see?

She was halfway unconscious—and certainly delirious—so I'm hopeful she dismissed everything that happened as a product of her imagination.

But what if she didn't?

What if she demands answers?

What will I tell her?

My mother has always told me to keep my gifts a secret. And that's how she referred to them—as gifts.

"No one can ever know what you do, baby boy," she would say, her eyes wide and frantic in her oval face. *"They'll take you away from me."*

So I kept my mouth shut and refused to befriend anyone in this godforsaken town. It was the only way I could protect myself.

But Izzy's a drop of ink in water, spreading quickly and consuming everything in its path.

I'm sure there's a name for what I am and what I can do, but my research has proved inconclusive. Maybe I'm a superhero who was bitten by a radioactive spider. Or maybe I'm a wizard just waiting for his acceptance into Hogwarts. Hell, I could even be a vampire who somehow missed the memo that I'm supposed to sparkle in the sunlight.

I suppose it doesn't matter. As long as no one knows the truth about my powers, I can be whatever I want.

And what I want is to be a normal teenager.

"Okay, class." Our teacher claps his hands together once. "Why don't you guys take the remainder of class to go over the lesson with your lab partner? There should be practice quiz questions on page one hundred and three in your textbook."

I let loose a shaky breath as I swivel in my seat to face Izzy fully. I can't help but note that her bone structure is delicate, almost elfin-like, while her lips are contrastingly full. The overall effect is candescent.

Ethereal. Lust runs through my blood in a ravenous inferno.

I force my lips into a straight line and turn away from her, focusing on the textbook.

However, no matter how hard I try, I can't read a single damn word on the page. The letters blur together, turning distorted and indistinct.

"What question do you want to start on?" she asks sweetly.

I open my mouth to respond just as the intercom above crackles and our secretary's voice filters through the room.

"Mr. Holter, please send Ansel Harthorne to the office. I repeat, Mr. Holter, please send Ansel Harthorne to the main office. Thank you." There's a click and then silence.

Mr. Holter glances up from where he's been grading our homework. Wordlessly, he jerks his chin towards the door, and I quickly gather up my supplies, knowing I won't make it back here before the class ends. Izzy glances at me with concern, but I ignore her inquiring gaze as I hurry out of the classroom and down the long corridor.

Is this about my grades?

I try to think through my most recent assignments.

I may not have gotten one hundred percent on all of them—I've been a little preoccupied with thoughts of golden-haired angels—but I definitely aced them. Maybe this is about valedictorian...

My lungs stall alongside my feet when I reach the end of the hallway and see a familiar figure waiting for me, attempting to ward off the two men on either side of her.

"Don't come any closer to me!" My mom's voice is halfway between a screech and a cry.

Her blotchy face—a testament to how little sleep she's been getting—swivels in both directions anxiously.

Shit.

"Mrs. Harthorne," Mr. Montgomery begins in a soft, soothing voice, "no one here will hurt you."

"You need to calm down," adds Mr. Remington, frowning.

My mother shakes her head, strands of graying hair flying free of her braid.

"No. No. No. No." She whacks her palms against her forehead with an agonized cry.

The sound of it forces my legs forward, and I run the remaining distance.

"Mom, what's going on?" I throw my backpack on the ground and hurry towards her. She's so much tinier than me that she barely reaches my chest. "Where is your nurse?"

"She just showed up here," Mr. Montgomery explains as he runs a hand through his tousled black hair.

"We need to go, baby boy. We need to go." Mom

begins to tug at my sleeve, desperation carved into every frigid line of her face.

"Mom, what's going on?" I repeat. I place my hands on her shoulders—ignoring how bony they feel, how thin—and push her back so I can see her face clearly. "Why are you here? Where is Shelby?"

Shelby has been my mom's nurse for years now, ever since my father died. My mother... She didn't take it well. She seems to believe that my father's death was an accident and that the murderers were actually going after me.

And she's right about one thing. My father's death *was* an accident. The roads were icy, and he was driving too fast. End of story. There were no other cars involved, no one near the crash site, no sign of foul play.

Try telling that to my mother, though.

She seems convinced that someone is after me, hence why we moved here to the middle of Butt Fuck, Nowhere.

"Mom..." I try not to let my embarrassment seep into my tone.

I hate the fact that Mr. Montgomery and Mr. Remington are here, watching the exchange. What must they think of me? Of her?

"We need to go. They're here. They found you." Mom trembles like a leaf in the wind.

With an almost blistering speed, she lunges forward and grabs my wrist. Her grip is a manacle around me.

The bell rings overhead, and I inwardly curse as the halls begin to fill with students. Heat fills my cheeks.

"Mom, let's go into the office—"

She gives my arm a shake. "They're going to take you from me, baby boy. They're going to hurt you. Hurt me. We need to go. We need to run. We need to—"

Mom stops talking abruptly, and her eyes zero in on something just over my shoulder.

No, not something.

Someone.

Fuck. No.

Nononononono.

"Ansel?" Izzy asks, concern evident in her voice. "Are you all right?"

She moves to stand beside me, and my mother's eyes home in on her like two heat-seeking missiles. And, to my absolute horror, they harden and frost over, dripping with pure malice.

"*You*," my mother hisses, releasing me. She takes a lumbering step towards Izzy and jabs a bony finger at the other girl's chest. "It's your fault! You stupid bitch."

She lifts her hand, and I'm too slow to do anything, my feet glued to the ground.

Just before her palm can connect with Izzy's cheek, Mr. Montgomery and Mr. Remington are there, stopping her. Remington grabs her wrist, his grip surprisingly gentle despite his thunderous expression, and

Montgomery shoulders his way between the two women. He gives Izzy a cautious once-over, as if ensuring she's all right, before focusing on my mother.

Shame threatens to swallow me whole.

"Mrs. Harthorne, I'm afraid we're going to have to ask you to leave." Montgomery's voice is steady, though his eyes are hard. Icy.

He moves to stand protectively in front of Izzy with his arms crossed over his chest.

"This bitch killed my husband, and she's going to get my son killed too!" Mom screams, spittle flying from her mouth.

Most of the students have stopped now, and there's a large crowd surrounding the five of us.

I want the ground to open up beneath me.

I've never been ashamed of my mother before, knowing that her mood swings stem from mental illness, but just then...I hate her.

I fucking despise her.

I can't meet anyone's gaze.

"I'll take her home," I tell Montgomery quietly, already grabbing my mom's arm to drag her away.

She fights me, her heels digging into the linoleum tiles, and screams over her shoulder, "Stay away from my son!"

"Mom," I whisper-hiss, quickening my pace, heat filling my cheeks, embarrassment inflating me like a balloon.

I want to tell Izzy I'm sorry, but that word seems

too inconsequential. Besides, I doubt she'll accept my apology.

She'll probably never talk to me again after this.

Not that I blame her.

I all but drag my mother outside, and it's only when we turn the corner does she sag slightly, the fight seeping out of her. I stop walking, and she leans against me with a muffled sob.

"I'm so sorry," she whispers, crying. "I'm so sorry."

I keep my arms limp by my sides, unsure of what to do.

After a moment, I hesitantly hug her back, stroking her snarled hair away from her face. "It's okay, Mom. It's okay."

"I'm so sorry. I'm so sorry." And then she dissolves into sobs.

She doesn't stop crying until the following morning.

Forty-Nine

EMERY

The prick doesn't even glance up from his phone as he maneuvers the backstreets. He's completely oblivious to the predator stalking his every move.

Watching him. Waiting for him to fuck up. Hoping he does.

I have my hood pulled up, obscuring my blond hair and hiding the majority of my tattoos from view, and I keep my face lowered. I'm nothing but a shadow traversing the streets.

A phantom.

I've been trailing Grayson for over a week now, and so far, he hasn't done anything too exciting. He only left his apartment a few times, and that was to go shopping and pick up Chinese. It seems as if he spends the majority of his time at home.

Which means I need to break into his apartment.

I spotted him on the phone earlier this evening, though there was too much traffic for me to hear who he was talking to. I did, however, hear Grayson tell a stranger that he'll meet up with him or her tonight.

I just need to be patient.

Grayson ducks inside his apartment complex—a nondescript, five-story building with peeling paint and row after row of unwashed windows—and I wait a few moments before rushing forward with my wolf speed and catch the door before it can shut and lock. I step into the lobby and survey the room.

No Grayson.

Taking a deep breath, I press my senses outwards until I hear what sounds like footsteps on a staircase. Grayson must be climbing the stairs to a higher floor— which makes sense, considering the fact that the elevator has a huge OUT OF ORDER sign taped to the front.

I count each step he takes before deciding his apartment must be on the third floor. Only when his footsteps retreat do I race up the stairs as well, my feet feather-light on the cement steps. The door to the third floor creaks when I open it, and I inwardly wince, freezing in the entryway. When no one barges out of their apartment and demands to know why I'm here, I begin to relax.

Once again, I utilize my enhanced senses to listen.

A couple is fighting in one of the apartments, and a

baby cries farther down the hall. In another, I hear a door slam and muffled cursing.

I close my eyes, willing myself to concentrate, and finally pick up on a gruff, raspy voice saying, "Gracie."

I zero in on that one-sided conversation.

"Gracie, please pick up the damn phone. We need to talk." There's a pause and then, "I'm so fucking sorry. Just let me explain. I'm coming over whether you like it or not."

Gracie...

A leaden feeling settles in my gut at the revelation that my sister's right. He *is* cheating on her. I don't want to jump to conclusions, but only a man in love would sound that desperate and heartbroken over a girl not speaking to him.

So he's a crazed murderer *and* a cheater.

My hatred for him grows.

Now, I just need to find proof, and then I can show it to my father and the other Council members.

Or I'll just kill him myself.

Grayson remains in his apartment for another hour —the most awkward and uncomfortable hour of my life, while I remain crouched near the end of the hall- way, hiding behind a potted plant like some fucking creeper—before he finally leaves.

I heave out a breath as I watch the large, intimi- dating man move towards the stairs. I wait another fifteen minutes, ensuring he's gone for good, before I slink out of my piss-poor hiding spot and hurry towards his door.

Belatedly, I realize this is fucking insanity. I shouldn't break in to some murderer's apartment on my own, yet I can't find it within me to care. Who the hell would I even tell? Ethan? The mere thought is laughable.

No, I can't tell my packmates. They would insist on coming with me, and I don't need them. Not now. Not ever.

I can do this one job on my own.

I grab my credit card out of my wallet and then slide it through the door crack, attempting to catch it on the latch. It only takes a few tries for the lock to click, and I quickly push the door open and step inside.

The apartment is tiny and sparsely furnished. If I hadn't seen Grayson enter and exit this place for over a week, I would've assumed that no one lives here. Yes, there's furniture, but it's the type of furniture you'll see in a staged home, not that of a teenager. There's only a bed and a nightstand. Not even a fucking TV.

What nineteen-year-old doesn't have a fucking TV?

I check the nightstand first, though I don't expect to actually find anything there. That would be too simple, and Grayson appears to be anything but. I don't even know what the hell I'm looking for.

Body parts?

A diary where he goes into extensive detail about his murders?

Photographs?

I move from the nightstand to the bed, then the bed to the kitchen. The fridge is full of pizza boxes, beers, and fast-food bags. The cupboards are nearly empty. I even check the goddamn oven.

Once I'm confident there are no hidden secrets in the kitchen, I move on to the bathroom. This appears to be the most lived-in part of the house, with a toothbrush and toothpaste near the sink, a razor blade, a comb, a tube of deodorant, and shampoo and body wash in the shower.

But no damning evidence.

The only place I haven't checked yet is the closet, though I feel as if Grayson is too smart to hide something there. After all, evil masterminds *always* place things underneath some floorboards in the closet. It's in the rule book.

And Grayson doesn't strike me as the type of guy to play by the rules.

I've just placed my hand on the doorknob when footsteps sound from directly outside the apartment.

I freeze, every muscle in my body locking together.

Fuck.

Desperation fueling my movements, I dive towards the bed and stealthily roll underneath it, trying to ignore the feel of dust and other unsavory substances clinging to my skin. A cough bubbles in my throat, but sheer determination keeps it contained.

The door to the apartment clicks open, and Grayson steps inside. I can't see what he's doing, but his footsteps head in the direction of the bathroom.

If he's taking a piss, then maybe I'll be able to escape. I just need to be quiet and fast—

But I don't hear the telltale thunk of the door shutting.

Grayson shuffles around in the bathroom for a few moments, and I shift slightly so I can see out from underneath the bed.

What the fuck is he doing?

His back is to me, but he stands in the entryway of the bathroom, fixated on the mirrored medicine cabinet. I try to recall what's in there, but I think it's only a few toiletries. Certainly not anything interesting enough to capture his attention.

His raspy voice echoes through the room, and I go still yet again.

"Gracie, something came up, but I'll stop by your place after. We need to talk. There are some things I need to tell you." He pauses and then adds, almost reluctantly, "I love you."

Gracie...

Who the fuck is Gracie?

Knowing her identity may be the smoking gun I'm looking for.

Is she Grayson's mistress, like Sydney seems to

believe, or a relative? I'm leaning towards the former, but I can't quite rule out the latter.

Silence permeates the air, broken only by the clicking of keys. Then Grayson steps out of the bathroom with his flip phone held to his ear. A scowl mars his face.

"Where do you want to meet?" Grayson's voice is curt and angry, laced with an edge of sharpened violence.

It's certainly not the soft way he talked to this Gracie chick.

I strain my ears to hear the person's response.

"The usual spot. Five minutes." The masculine voice sounds familiar, but I can't pinpoint where I know it from.

School, perhaps? Maybe...

"Fuck." Grayson scrubs a hand through his dark hair. "This is the last time, you hear me? No more. I'm done."

The other man chuckles. "You're done when I say you're done. You know what will happen if you disobey."

Grayson's jaw clenches, and his free hand forms a tight fist. "Leave her the fuck alone."

Her?

Sydney?

Gracie?

Questions race around in my head.

"Five minutes." And then the phone goes dead.

Grayson heaves out a breath, and I swear I can practically see the tension pulsating just beneath his skin. He lowers his head and closes his eyes as his chest rises and falls rapidly. For a long moment, he doesn't move, remaining perfectly still.

I don't dare to even breathe, afraid that the slightest hitch would garner his attention. The silence is too fragile—a frayed string a single tug away from snapping.

Grayson seems to regain control of himself, and he straightens and grabs his keys out of his pocket. Without another word, he stomps out of the apartment and slams the door shut.

I count to thirty—each consecutive second feeling like a death knell—and then slide out from underneath the bed. I frown down at the dust and dirt staining my jeans and try ineffectually to wipe it all away. When that proves futile, I stand and move to the bathroom.

Why was he so interested in the mirrored cabinet?

Hesitantly, my heart in my throat, I pull it open. But just like before, I only see a few toiletries. Nothing incriminating.

I place my finger along the outer edge and trail it down, frowning when it catches on something. I apply the slightest amount of pressure and the shelf opens, revealing a secondary shelf behind the first.

A hidden compartment.

Bingo.

I grab the iPhone—the only item I can see—and

frown at the keypad. What are the odds that the passcode would be the same for both this phone and the flip phone?

"Gotcha, fucker," I murmur with a grin as the phone opens.

I click on his messaging app first and find a slew of messages from Sydney. I click on her name instinctively...and then instantly dry-heave when I see a half-naked photo of my sister sent a day ago. It doesn't appear as if he responded.

"Fuck no. Ugh." I back out of that text thread and will myself not to vomit. "I need goddamn bleach for my eyes."

The only other conversation is with—you guessed it—Gracie. However, when I click on it, I realize that the messages must've recently been deleted. There's only a single message from the girl in question.

GRACIE

Fine. We can talk. Tonight.

Does his talk with Gracie have anything to do with the strange call he took just before he left the apartment?

I navigate to the photo app.

And instantly feel my blood go cold.

"No," I breathe in horror, the phone shaking in my hand.

Just like on the flip phone, there are hundreds, if not thousands, of pictures. All of them seem to have been taken when the subject wasn't paying any attention. In one, she's turned away, talking to someone just off camera. In another, her head is bent over a book, and a pane of glass separates her from the photographer. In a third, she's on the opposite side of the street, staring at her phone, utterly oblivious to her stalker.

Izzy.

My Izzy.

"Fuck." The phone drops from my hand and hits the ground with an audible thump.

But that barely registers.

The last time Grayson took pictures of girls, they ended up dead.

Bile scorches my throat like fingers of fire.

Izzy is Grayson's next target.

And if I don't do something soon, she'll end up like Larissa and Alixandra.

Dead.

Fifty

IZZY

I check my phone for the fiftieth time, my heart thundering rampant in my chest.

Grayson is coming over.

Frowning, I study my reflection in the mirror yet again. What do I wear around the man who claimed to be in love with me while having a girlfriend? The best friend I've secretly been crushing on for years now, with no hope of it ever being reciprocated?

I chose to dress casually in an off-the-shoulder, beige sweater paired with blue jeans. I've left my blonde curls down but applied just a little bit of product so they bounce.

Am I trying to impress him? Maybe.

Am I trying to show him what he's missing? Most definitely.

I won't be the other woman. I refuse to. I'm a lot of things, but a home-wrecker isn't one of them. If he wants to continue to date Sydney, then he can't make false promises and confessions to me.

Does Grayson even know what love is? I'm not sure. He hasn't really received a lot of it in his life. His parents were abusive assholes, and his foster parents weren't much better. I'm one of the only people who opened my heart to him—and look where that got me.

A broken heart, an unreciprocated crush, and this feeling of inadequacy that refuses to go away.

With a huff, I turn away from my reflection and focus back on my Chemistry homework. However, no matter how long I stare at the words on the page, they don't compute in my brain. I'd have more success reading a book in a foreign language.

I can't help but think about my Chemistry class a couple of days earlier, when Ansel was called down to the office. When class ended, I was surprised to see him standing at the end of the hall, attempting to console a frail, frantic-eyed woman.

She looked nothing like him, and it took me a solid minute to remember he's adopted. He has light-brown hair, while hers is black as pitch. His features are strong and angular, and his skin is pale. Hers are petite and elfin, shaded a coppery brown. He towers over her at six feet, hewn from solid stone. Even his muscles have muscles. She looks as if the slightest breeze could carry her away.

A chill works its way down my spine when I

remember her cold, acerbic words, notched back and then released like an arrow aimed at its target.

And that target happened to be me.

Poor Ansel.

I still remember the shame distorting his features as he herded his mother outside, his hand on the small of her back. He wouldn't meet my gaze...and he hasn't since. I want to tell him that it's okay, that I understand, that I'm not mad, but I'm not sure if he'll even believe me.

Besides, does he even want my sympathy? We're not truly friends, are we?

I rub a hand down my face, suddenly feeling exhausted.

Maybe it isn't a good idea to meet up with Grayson tonight.

Heaven only knows the mistakes I'll make because I'm sleep-deprived and upset.

"Knock. Knock." Jake's cheerful voice precedes the man himself entering my bedroom.

He's dressed in a pair of low-slung sweats and a white T-shirt that clings to his muscular physique. His blond hair is wildly tousled, almost as if he has run his hands through it one too many times, but his smile is infectious. I feel an answering one tug up my own lips.

"Most people actually knock on the door instead of just saying the words," I point out dryly.

He waves a flippant hand in the air. "Semantics."

He moves farther into the room and throws

himself onto my bed, his ankles crossed and his hands behind his head. The movement pulls up the hem of his shirt, revealing a sliver of toned stomach. I have to admit that Jake is hot, in the stereotypical, boy-next-door type of way. It's a shame that I don't feel that way about him. He's certainly better boyfriend material than Grayson or any of my other prospects.

Ugh.

Guys are dumb.

"Why are you dressed so nice?" He waggles his eyebrows suggestively. A shit-eating grin curls up his lips. "Do you have a date? Is it with Ethan? Please tell me it's with Ethan. I ship it."

"You *ship* it?" I place a hand on my hip and cock it to the side. "What are you? Twelve?"

"Mentally? Yes." He doesn't even blink. "But seriously, is it with Ethan?"

I tap at his legs, indicating for him to move them, and he pulls them back, allowing me enough space to sit down.

I cross my legs and blow out a breath. "No, it's not a date. And it's not with Ethan. I'm...meeting someone tonight."

A surge of heat floods my cheeks.

"Sounds mysterious. Who is it?" He sits upright and rests his chin on his pulled-up knees, a picture of innocence.

A part of me wants to tell Jake about Grayson and everything that's going on with him. I know Jake will have my back. However, another part of me is afraid of what he'll say. More than likely, he'll tell me to let Grayson go, and I'm not sure I'm strong enough to. Grayson has been a part of my life since I was a young girl, and losing him would be the equivalent of severing a limb.

Can I survive without a leg? Yes. Do I want to? No. No, I don't.

Grayson's a part of me. He's wiggled his way past my defenses and carved a niche for himself in my soul. I can't comprehend a future without him, and I don't know if I want to.

"Can we talk about something else?" I plead, shoving my hands together in the universal prayer position. I bat my lashes for added effect. "Pretty please?"

He eyes me suspiciously but relents. "Okay, fine. I actually came to your room for a reason, and it wasn't just to bug you about your dating life." He smirks mischievously, and a sliver of unease skates down my back. "What are you going to do for your birthday tomorrow?"

My mouth drops open. "Wh-what?"

"Oh please. You didn't think I'd find out?" He leans towards me so he can knock his shoulder against my own. "I know everything...including the fact that tomorrow is your eighteenth birthday."

"Jake..." I swear my cheeks are on fire. I place my hands to them to make sure they're not actually being consumed by literal flames. "I don't really want to make a big fuss about it."

It's why I didn't tell anyone that my birthday is approaching. Hale and Gerry know, of course, but they agreed to keep it low-key.

I've never really had the best track record when it comes to birthdays. My last few have been...

I shiver.

"Are we going to have a party this weekend?" He taps a finger to his chin in contemplation. "It sucks that your birthday falls on a Wednesday. Oh! Maybe we can have a party after the game on Friday. You haven't really been to a game since the incident."

"You mean the time I was tackled to the ground and nearly died?"

He scoffs. "You didn't nearly die. Don't be dramatic. But this Friday is senior night. Ashton always throws a huge party after the game."

"Ashton?" I wrinkle my nose. "And why would I want to go to a party thrown by the great Ashton James?" I tilt my head to the side and then ask, "What is his last name anyway? Is it James? Or is his middle name James? Or is that a part of his first name?"

Jake chuckles darkly. "You seem awfully interested for someone who claims she's not interested."

"Know your enemies and all that." I wave a hand in the air dismissively. "Now, proceed. You were talking about senior night and parties."

He rolls his eyes but continues. "Anyway, I'm sure

if we ask him, we could make it a birthday party as well."

A laugh bubbles in my throat. "Really? You think Ashton would want to throw me a birthday party? You think I'd want him to? You do realize we hate each other, right?"

And that's not even an exaggeration. Ashton likes to pretend I don't exist during the day. Even when I sit at his table at lunch, he very purposely ignores me.

"I see the way he looks at you," Jake says cryptically.

"Like a fart that he wants to swat away?"

"No, that's the way you look at him, not the other way around." He grabs my hand and gives it a squeeze. "But if you don't want a big birthday party, that's cool too. We can just watch a movie or something with Lissa and the others." His lips purse as he flicks his gaze towards the empty bed on the opposite side of the room. "Or maybe just the others."

"Do you think Lissa will be okay?" I ask softly.

I barely see her anymore. She'll stay in the recreation room until one or two in the morning—or until Hale and Gerry order her up to bed—then she'll sneak out at first light. When she is around, she's quiet and sullen.

I never in a million years thought I would miss her incessant chatting.

"I heard Hale and Gerry talking about putting her into therapy. I think that'd be good for her." He casts me a glance out of the corner of his eye. "What about you?"

"What about me?"

"Are you okay?" He rubs the pad of his thumb across my knuckles. "You saw the same thing Lissa did, yet all of our focus is on her."

I shrug helplessly and swallow down the lump in my throat.

How do I explain to Jake that, while upsetting, seeing the corpse didn't destroy me?

How do I tell him that Alixandra wasn't the first dead body I've ever seen?

Fortunately—or unfortunately, depending on how you look at it—I'm saved from responding by a loud, domineering voice barking, "Let us see her!"

Emery?

I exchange a glance with Jake, and as one, the two of us hurry downstairs.

Hale and Gerry stand in the foyer, facing off against Ethan, Emery, Reid, and Ashton.

Emery, surprisingly, seems to be leading the charge, his features twisted in rage and his cocksure smile nowhere to be seen.

"You don't understand—" Emery begins.

"No, *you* don't understand," Hale hisses.

I don't think I've ever seen my foster dad so angry before. It's written in every line of his visage, from the wrinkles bracketing his eyes to his pursed lips.

"Now isn't the time—"

"He's going to hurt her, just like he did the others!" Emery explodes.

Hurt her?

What is he talking about?

What others?

"That's a serious accusation," Gerry says calmly, folding his arms over his chest. His leather jacket creaks with the movement.

Ashton notices me first, though I'm not surprised. Despite his obvious hatred towards me, he seems attuned to every little move I make. When I shift in the cafeteria, his eyes zero in on me, and a pucker manifests between his brows. When I walk down the hallway with Desiree and the others, he stops whatever conversation he's having to just...stare at me, his dark gaze cold and assessing. I feel as if I'm on display—a butterfly pinned between two slides and shoved beneath a microscope.

He clears his throat, and Emery stops talking almost immediately, his chest heaving and a red flush crawling up his neck.

"Emery? Ethan? Reid? What are you guys doing here?" I give Ashton a passing glance. "And why did you bring *him*?"

Ashton rolls his eyes at my childish antics but doesn't comment. Good.

Emery's entire body seems to sag when he sees me, and he races forward, all but shoving Jake out of the way in the process. He pulls me into his arms and rests his cheek on top of my head. I don't know what to do, so I leave my arms limp by my sides.

"You're okay. Thank fuck," he breathes.

"Um...yes? Why wouldn't I be?"

"I'd like to know that as well," Ass-ton says dryly. "Emery seems to believe that your life is in danger, but he wouldn't give us more information than that."

Wait...what?

"My life is in danger?" I push Emery back just enough to search his arresting green eyes. "What are you talking about?"

"Look, I don't really know how to explain this without giving you all the details..." Emery gives my shoulders a squeeze that borders on painful.

"Maybe you should give her *all* the details," Hale murmurs, but his voice is soft, almost as if he didn't mean for me to hear that errant comment.

"Or maybe it'll be better for everyone if we left Isabella alone," Anal Bleach says in a bored, almost indolent tone.

Ethan spins to face their fearless leader. "Do you have to be such an asshole?"

Cum Stain's eyes narrow. "This is exactly what I'm talking about. She's tearing us apart."

"Or maybe *you're* tearing *us* apart," Ethan bites out. "We don't even feel like a pack anymore, let alone a family!"

"Can someone please explain to me what the fuck is going on and why you think I'm involved?" All I can focus on is the whole "your life is in danger" spiel Emery just gave me.

That deserves my attention, not all of this goddamn bickering.

Emery opens his mouth to answer, but I never get to hear what he has to say.

Somewhere above us, a window creaks open, and footsteps echo.

What the fuck is happening?

Fifty-One

REID

Must protect mate.

Mate. Protect. Yes. My wolf paws ineffectually at his cage, and for once, we're in agreement.

Nothing matters but protecting Izzy.

I wouldn't be able to explain the terror I felt when Emery called a pack meeting an hour earlier and told us that Izzy is in danger. Ethan and Ashton are still a little cautious—the latter doesn't believe that anything is ever this simple, and he won't act until he gets all the facts—but I don't give a shit if this is a false alarm.

I'll protect Izzy, no matter the cost.

I take the stairs three at a time, my mind consumed by one thing and one thing alone.

The hunt.

Blood. Need blood. My wolf salivates.

Somebody calls my name, but I'm too lost to my rage to respond.

Someone is in the house.

Near my mate.

Must protect.

The unfamiliar smell gets stronger the farther away from the stairs I go. Soon, it blends in with the enticing, sweet aroma of Izzy's floral scent.

Bedroom.

He's in her bedroom.

With a roar, I throw open the door, not even caring when it cracks and splinters. My chest heaves with the force of my unencumbered rage, and I'm sure my eyes flash amber in the darkened room.

There, near the window, is a tall, muscular figure dressed entirely in black.

Intruder.

Must protect.

I can't even differentiate my thoughts from my wolf's at this moment.

I lower my head like a charging bull and rush the stranger, forcing him to the ground. One sniff confirms that he's not a wolf, but I don't get the sense that he's completely human either. There's something about his scent that tickles the edges of my subconscious…

"Reid!" Ashton barks, and footsteps thunder behind me.

The light flicks on, and the room is instantly engulfed in soft, golden light.

"Oh my god. Grayson!" Izzy.

The man beneath me—Grayson—tenses at the sound and instantly throws a punch at my jaw. Pain reverberates through my face, but I maintain my position overtop of him. There's no way in hell I'm releasing him.

"Gracie, get out of here!" The man's voice is low and raspy, almost sickeningly so. He coughs as if those few words cost him.

"Gracie?" Emery asks.

"What the hell is happening?" Izzy demands. "Reid, get off of him!"

"Reid." A gentle hand rests on my shoulder, and Hale's unique, woodsy scent permeates the air. "Get off of him so we all can talk."

Threat! My wolf paces relentlessly behind his cage. *Must eliminate.*

We don't want to scare Izzy, I tell him, and a boulder lodges in my throat at the realization that I already have.

Fuck.

I can't even begin to imagine what I must look like to her right now. Feral. Out of control.

A monster.

Exactly like Michelle intended.

With great reluctance, I jump off of Grayson, though I never let my eyes stray from him. There's something about him that lifts my hackles. Something primordial and predatory in his piercing blue eyes...

Eyes that are currently fixed on Izzy as if she's the only thing in the world.

I follow the direction of his gaze to see Izzy standing in Ethan's arms, her cheeks pale, her eyes wide. Ethan whispers something to her softly, and she collapses against him, allowing him to support her weight.

A surge of jealousy rushes through me.

I want to be the one to hold her, comfort her, take care of her.

But she'll never allow me to.

I take a step away from the fucker on the ground and curl my hands into fists. I'm not sure if it's to curb the desire I have to punch him in the face...or to ignore the nagging voice in my head demanding I go to Izzy, pull her into my arms, and promise her that everything will be okay.

I scowl and force myself to turn away from her. She'll never care for a beast like me, and I wouldn't want her to. It's why I decided to keep my distance from her in the first place.

I can protect her from the shadows just as well as I can in the light.

"Hello, Grayson." Emery kneels down so he can stare into the other man's face. "Surprised to see me?"

Grayson doesn't respond, but his expression shutters and closes over, turning unreadable.

"You guys know each other?" Izzy asks from the safety of Ethan's arms.

"He's dating our sister. Sydney," Emery explains, his voice rife with cold malice.

Both Izzy and Grayson flinch at his words.

"Wait. Your sister is Sydney?" Izzy volleys her gaze between the twins and Grayson. "You're dating their sister?"

A look of absolute heartbreak crosses her face, and I want nothing more than to rip Grayson's still-beating heart out of his chest. No one is allowed to hurt Izzy.

Absolutely no one.

Not even me.

"Can someone please explain to me what's going on?" Hale's voice sounds deceptively calm, despite the tenseness in his posture.

I don't see Jake or Gerry anywhere, but I imagine that's intentional. This is wolf business, and I'm not sure how much Jake knows about us.

Emery kicks at Grayson's ribs, and Izzy gasps in surprise.

"Emery!" she cries.

He ignores her, his face twisted in a scowl. "Why don't you tell them?" He flicks his gaze to Izzy before refocusing on Grayson. "Tell your precious Gracie what you've been up to."

Gracie?

I frown in confusion, but no one rushes to fill me in.

Emery seems too lost to his rage to pay us any

attention. He kicks at Grayson's ribs again, ignoring Izzy's cry and Hale's demand for him to stop.

"You used my sister." Kick. "Hurt innocent females." Kick. "Tried to hurt my mate." Kick. Kick. Kick.

I don't even think he's aware of what he's saying.

Ethan's arms tighten nearly imperceptibly at Emery's use of mate, and Grayson's eyes widen at the term before darkening in anger. Hale appears shocked, his lips parted to form a silent O.

Ashton's face remains expressionless as he steps forward, places a hand on Emery's shoulder, and pushes him back. It appears as if he's had enough of Emery taking control.

"If what you're saying is true, then we need to get Grayson to my father." Ashton's voice is calm and collected.

If I didn't know him as well as I do, I'd say he was impassive, but I can see the undercurrent of anger shimmering in his apathetic brown eyes.

"If what is true?" Izzy demands, breaking free of Ethan's embrace to crouch beside Grayson. "What the hell is happening?"

Hale pulls Izzy backwards before she can touch Grayson—which is smart, considering the four of us are seconds away from breaking. Seeing our mate touch a potential murderer may send us over the edge.

Actually, there's no "may" about it. I know that I

will kill him without remorse if he even places one finger on my mate.

"Hale!" Izzy snaps indignantly.

Hale keeps one hand on Izzy's shoulder while rubbing the other down his face. He looks as if he's aged years in a span of seconds, the shadows beneath his eyes impossibly pronounced.

"Ashton, call your dad. Reid, help me with Grayson."

I nod once to tell him I understand.

Hale turns Izzy so she can face him. Tears stream down her cheeks, and the sight of it breaks my cold, dead heart.

"Izzy, stay here with Jake and Gerry. We'll be back in a little bit."

She angrily rubs at her face with the back of her hand. "What the hell did Grayson even do? I don't understand. Is this because he came to visit me?"

He gives her shoulder a squeeze and then turns towards us. "We'll explain everything tomorrow. I promise."

There's a warning and a threat in his voice, one we'd do well to heed.

Ashton's jaw clenches, but he doesn't refute, despite the denial I can see brewing in his eyes.

"Just stay inside, little hurricane," Ashton tells Izzy.

"Fuck off, Ass-ton!" she snaps. She sniffs and spins towards us. "This is just a misunderstanding. I don't know what you think Grayson did—"

"We'll explain everything tomorrow." Emery reaches out to touch her, but she flinches away. His face falls, and hurt seeps into his eyes. "But we need to go."

"With Grayson?" She sounds incredulous, and I don't even blame her.

From what little I gathered, it appears as if she knows Grayson. Cares for him. Maybe even loves him.

And if what Emery believes is true...

This will destroy her.

"Grayson will be okay," Hale assures her, and Ashton actually has the nerve to scoff at those words.

Because we all fucking know that if Grayson is who we think he is, he won't survive the encounter with the Council. We don't tolerate Hunters.

He'll be killed to teach a lesson to all those who think they can harm us.

I just pray Izzy will understand when all of this is over.

Because if she doesn't...

We may just lose her before we ever truly have her.

Fifty-Two

IZZY

What the fuck just happened?

My mind races as I shakily sit on the very edge of my bed, tears of indignation and fear pricking the backs of my eyes.

Seriously. What the *fuck* just happened?

Why did Hale and the others cart off Grayson as if he's...as if he's a criminal? Is this because he snuck into my room? Maybe I just need to explain myself better, tell them that this isn't what it looks like, that Grayson is my friend.

Yet, for some reason, I fear that my words will do more harm than good.

Now, I'm all alone in the room, staring forlornly at the spot I last saw Grayson, my mind unable to piece together this confusing puzzle.

What did Emery mean?

And how did I not know that the twins have a sister? A sister that Grayson is dating?

I think I'm going to be sick.

I don't know where Jake and Gerry are. They haven't returned since the others left, but I can't say I mind the solitude. It gives my brain a chance to rest.

I need to think.

Throwing myself onto my back, I place an arm over my eyes, shielding them the best I can from the bright artificial lighting.

Is this what Mr. Montgomery meant when he claimed others were keeping secrets from me?

My head pounds fiercely, threatening to explode at any second, as more tears well in my eyes. They don't fall, though. Instead, they just sit there, suspended, crystalline droplets that hover at the edges of my periphery.

Maybe I need to leave. My eighteenth birthday is tomorrow. I'll no longer have to stay with Gerry and Hale. I'll be free to explore the world at large. Live where I want to. Do what I want to. Be who I want to be.

And yet...

The thought of never seeing my foster parents again leaves an ache in my chest. And what about Lissa and Jake and even Seth? I can't leave them, can I?

Unbidden, my thoughts drift to a group of guys I have no right thinking about as often as I do. The pulsating ache transforms into a hollow feeling, like my heart has been physically removed from my body.

Can I leave them?

I blindly reach towards my bedside table and fumble until my searching fingers find my phone. With a huff, I remove my arm from my eyes and scroll through my messages, hoping for a new one from Grayson or Emery or any of the others. Hell, I'll even take a text from the King Prick himself.

Nothing.

Not that I'm even surprised.

They only just left the house.

Is Hale going to get Grayson arrested? For sneaking into the house?

Or is there something else going on, something I'm not privy to?

I toss my phone down beside me with enough force for it to careen off my bedding and land on the floor with a thunk. Wincing, I drag myself towards the edge of the bed and lean over it. I close my fingers around the phone just as my gaze homes in on a tiny box. It looks to have been kicked slightly underneath my bed.

It's black, velvety, and has a silk ribbon tied into a neat bow at the top.

My heart pounding erratically, I reach for the box and tug it up to my chest. A note card dangles from the side, and I turn it over to read the chicken-scratched words.

Happy birthday, Gracie

The pounding turns into a thundering as I untie the bow. Butterflies spin drunkenly in my stomach, and a surge of warmth radiates through me.

Grayson.

He must've dropped this in the scuffle.

I slowly open the lid.

A gasp slips free at the sight of the necklace nestled in the center of the box.

It's gorgeous—unlike anything I've ever seen before. The chain is long and silver, knotted in a way that seems almost intricate. A strange crystal dangles at the bottom. It's half the size of my pinkie and is curved on one end. There appears to be a red liquid in the crystal that sluices around when I twist the necklace to and fro.

It's beautiful.

I swallow heavily and hope the fire burning in my chest cremates the lump in my throat.

With shaky fingers, I clasp the necklace around my neck and feel the comforting weight of the crystal between my breasts. It's almost...warm to the touch, and trails of heat burn through me.

"You can't leave, you know."

The voice startles me enough to elicit a screech of fright.

I spin, my heart racing, one hand coming up to clutch at my new piece of jewelry.

Seth stands in the doorway of my room with an indecipherable expression on his young face. His headphones still rest around his neck, but for the first time since I've met him, his eyes are focused on me. Almost unerringly so.

"What?" I will my heartbeat to settle down.

Seth's eyes dart away from mine and focus on the wall. Or, more specifically, on one of Lissa's posters. It's some rockstar I've never heard about until I met her.

"You can't leave. Not yet." He cants his head to the side, as if listening to a voice I can't hear. "They need you. *We* need you."

My brows scrunch together. "I don't understand."

A tentative smile touches the edges of his lips. "You will. You're like me, and I'm like you, but we're not the same." He frowns. "You can't leave until the dead stay dead and the living thrive."

What the hell?

I open my mouth to say just that when Seth tugs his headphones over his ears, effectively ending the conversation. He slips out of my room and disappears into his own, the door shutting softly behind him.

Leaving me alone once again.

With more questions than I have answers to and a burning need to ask them all.

Fifty-Three

ASHTON

"You know why you're all here." My father stands in the center of the room, his arms outstretched, a sadistic smile on his face as he revels in the attention.

The pompous prick loves commanding an audience.

Matthew—the twins' dad—shifts uncomfortably on the couch and then places a hand on his mate's knee. Her sobs fill the room as she struggles to control herself. Their other two packmates stand behind the sofa, matching scowls on their faces and their arms crossed over their chests.

I allow my gaze to flick from person to person. Taking everything in. Assessing the situation. It's what I'm good at, after all, and what will make me a valuable Council member as soon as I take over for my father.

Emery and Ethan stand on either side of me, the

former practically trembling with unbridled rage while the latter just appears confused. Reid remains on the opposite side of the room, hovering over our esteemed guest.

Grayson Grey.

Raw fury threatens to plow me over, but I work to keep it adequately contained. I didn't rise through the ranks by giving in to my emotions. I can't afford to be irrational or erratic. I need to think with my brain, not my heart or even my cock. It's the only way to survive this bloodthirsty world.

My brothers refuse to, so the responsibility falls on me.

I purse my lips as I study the prisoner with a keen eye.

So far, he hasn't said much, keeping his head down and his shoulders slumped. I try to determine how much of that is an act and how much of it is resignation. I'll be surprised if he's already given in. And a little disappointed too.

Grayson fucking Grey.

Who is this man that thrust himself into my world and uprooted it? He seems to be important to Isabella, but why?

Is he the murderer Emery suspects him to be?

I don't rush to judgments like my impulsive packmates. That's not who I am. If I don't have all the pieces, then I won't even attempt to put the puzzle together.

It's why I'm staying clear of Isabella.

She's an enigma. A mystery.

I hate mysteries.

But that's not the only reason I'm staying away from her.

It'll be better for everyone if she hates me.

Even as I think that, a searing fire blazes through my chest and down my sternum.

Well, if you want her to hate you, then mission accomplished.

I rub at the ache building there and inwardly curse my pesky, wayward emotions. Somehow, they've gotten away from me without my consent, and it'll take an eternity to reel them back in and get them under control.

My father clears his throat, garnering the room's attention once more.

We're in the main Council building, which is nothing but a tiny brick building disguised as an office complex. The interior, however, doesn't have offices or cubicles. Instead, it leads to a spacious room with a lit hearth, a few couches, and a wooden table that serves refreshments.

My mother was the one who designed this space, actually. She wanted it to be cozy in order to make the visiting packs and wolves more comfortable. I'm sure my father would prefer to have a throne to lord over the others, but he doesn't have the heart to change anything. This was the last project my mother worked on before she…

A lump materializes in my throat. Swallowing proves to be impossible.

"Grayson Grey. You stand accused of being a Hunter responsible for the murders of Alixandra Laffey and Larissa Clarke." Even my father, in all his apathetic glory, can't hide the darkness seeping into his voice.

My mother—his fated mate—was killed by Hunters, after all.

Grayson doesn't respond, choosing instead to keep his head lowered.

Emery mumbles something under his breath, practically fuming with anger.

"Let me paint a picture of what I think happened," my father continues, his eyes sparking with wicked glee. Malice. "You began dating Sydney in the hopes of getting an in with some of the local wolves. Is that correct?"

The twins' mom begins to cry even harder, and Matthew shushes her, stroking her hair.

I don't know if she's crying because she cares about Grayson or because she's hurt on behalf of her daughter. Either way, the sound of her sobs tightens my stomach muscles.

Has anyone ever cried for me like that?

I'm not even sure my packmates would if something were to happen to me. Yes, they care about me and even love me, but our relationship has been strained for years now, even before everything happened with Reid and Ethan. I'd like to say that those events were the two catalysts that destroyed our pack, but I know that's not the case.

We were broken long before that.

It's why Isabella should run as far away from us as she can. As far away from this world as she can. She's human. Innocent. Sweet. Good. Assholes like us will only tarnish and destroy her, vaporizing everything that makes her...her.

My father clasps his hands behind his back and begins to pace in front of Grayson, practically preening from the attention.

"You were able to get close to Larissa and Alixandra through your relationship with Sydney, correct? Perhaps she introduced you to them, and you made the connection that they were also wolves. Or maybe you somehow found documents detailing as such." My father lifts a shoulder as if the answer to that question doesn't particularly concern him, but his eyes burn with curiosity. "You would stalk these girls for months, gathering as much intel as you could, and then strike when they were least expecting it. Is that true?"

Even before my father finishes speaking, Grayson's shaking his head. His raspy voice reaches my ears—soft, as if he hasn't spoken in a while.

"No. That's not true."

"Then why do you have pictures of Larissa and

Alixandra on your phone?" My father dangles the flip phone in front of Grayson's face, but Grayson doesn't even react.

His expression remains impassive. Aloof. His mask is almost as good as mine.

"Did you plan to kill Sydney next? Was that your plan? Or did you intend to fuck her for more information?"

"Gregor—" Matthew's voice is harder than I ever remember hearing it before. His eyes flare yellow as his wolf surfaces. "That's my daughter you're talking about."

"A daughter you should feel lucky is still alive," Dad snaps, and taut lines appear around his mouth and eyes.

I wonder who he's thinking of. My mother and other fathers, perhaps?

Or is it Christian, the son he'll have to watch go insane and then inevitably die?

My heart thumps harder at the thought of my older brother, but then I remind myself that now isn't the time to feel such pesky emotions.

I need to focus.

Learn what I can.

Because something about all of this isn't adding up.

"You were caught visiting that girl tonight, weren't you? Isabella?" My father tries to keep his voice neutral, but there's a sinister undertone to his words that lifts the hairs on the back of my neck.

I don't want my father to even think Isabella's name, let alone speak it.

Reid growls sharply, and the twins go rigid on either side of me. Matthew looks uncomfortable with this turn of conversation, but then again, it wouldn't surprise me if the twins told their father the truth about who Isabella is to us. Even if they didn't explicitly come out and tell him she's our fated mate, I wouldn't put it past them to hint at their growing feelings for her.

My father's either oblivious to the sudden tension saturating the room or chooses to ignore it. He continues to pace back and forth in front of Grayson, that smug grin of his never dissolving from his face.

The first sign of life has seeped into Grayson's eyes. They harden, turning cold, and his teeth grit together.

A strange feeling arrows through me at his obvious protectiveness towards her.

Just who is Isabella to Grayson? And who is he to her?

Why am I so consumed by the answers to those questions?

That foreign sensation swirls in my stomach like a whirlpool. I want to claw Grayson's eyes out, shred his tongue into confetti-sized pieces, and stab a knife through his skull.

It takes me a moment too long to realize the emotion I feel is jealousy.

Jealousy and anger, because if this asshole is the one behind the murders, then Isabella will be destroyed.

"Perhaps I should pay Isabella a visit and see if she has any answers for me," my father continues, and Reid lunges forward before I can even think to stop him.

Not that I want to. It takes every ounce of self-control I possess not to show my hand and react to my father's threat.

Matthew jumps up from the couch and places a hand on Reid's shoulder, stopping him. Reid trembles as he struggles to control his mounting rage. His eyes alternate between amber and their normal green-brown color.

"Interesting," my dad murmurs, studying Reid like he's a rare and exotic specimen he yearns to study beneath a microscope.

My stomach bottoms out, but outwardly, I keep my expression calm and collected, a skill I'm grateful I possess, especially when my father turns in my direction. His cold, calculating eyes travel first over me before focusing on Ethan and then Emery. I wish I could see the twins' faces, but I don't dare look in either of their directions. I can't give us away.

Whatever he sees seems to satisfy him—which may be good or bad—and he turns back towards Grayson.

"I don't know anything," the other male hisses through clenched teeth.

My father crouches until he's directly in front of Grayson. Even though it's nearing the middle of the night, my father looks as immaculate as always in his three-piece suit, cuff links, and red tie. He's a devil come to claim a soul, with or without a deal.

"For your sake, I hope that's the truth." He smiles, baring his teeth. "Because it would be a shame if I have to pay a visit to that pretty little blonde."

Grayson—who so far has remained pliant and submissive—lunges forward, his hands extended as if he wishes to wrap them around my father's neck. Ted and Nolan, the two other members of Matthew's pack, reach for him at the same time, pulling him back.

"Don't you fucking touch her," he hisses, his raspy voice breaking on the last word. "I swear to fuck—"

"Lock him away for the night." My father waves a flippant hand in the air. "We'll see if he's more willing to talk in the morning."

Ted and Nolan all but drag a struggling Grayson out of the room, but even a six-foot-plus man is no match for two adult wolf shifters. Only when the door slams shut behind them do I feel like I can breathe.

The room explodes into activity at once.

Ethan moves until he's standing beside Reid, offering him words of comfort. Reid still looks a single second away from destroying everyone in the vicinity. But if anyone can calm him down, it'll be calm, level-headed Ethan.

Emery is pacing in front of his parents, his hand

repeatedly running through his blond hair. I'm able to pick up a few words here and there as he mutters.

"She's going to hate me. She's going to fucking hate me."

Isabella.

Once again, I push all of my emotions into a tiny box and think of tonight's events from an analytical perspective. I try to see it from Isabella's point of view.

All she knows is that the four of us came barreling into her house like men possessed and threw cryptic accusations Grayson's way. Then we left with Grayson.

And now she may never see him again.

Emery is right. She'll hate him forever.

Hate *us* forever.

But how can we explain to her the truth?

Do I even want her to know what we are?

The answer to that last question is a resounding no.

Isabella needs to stay far, far away from the paranormal world. For her own safety.

And if I have to be the bad guy to ensure that happens, then so be it.

Maybe this is why the universe gave her to me as a mate—because I'm the only one heartless enough to do what needs to be done.

The ache in my chest spreads, turning unbearable, and I place my fist over my heart.

Yes, I'll cut her loose, make her hate us...

Even if it kills me in the process.

Fifty-Four

IZZY

Fifty-seven texts later, and still no response from Grayson or the others.

I walk through the school hallway in a daze, my mind adrift, my gaze sightless.

Where are they?

Why aren't they returning my texts?

Why won't Hale and Gerry tell me what happened to Grayson last night?

Happy fucking birthday to me.

Only Jake has been semi-normal, waking me up by jumping on my bed and thrusting a "birthday pancake" into my hands. Well, it was actually just a chocolate chip pancake on a plate with a candle in it, but it's the thought that counts.

I've never had anyone sing me "Happy Birthday" before.

Not like Jake did.

Still, even my foster brother's earlier exuberance hasn't been able to dispel my rapidly sinking mood. I'm desperate to set eyes on Emery, Ethan, Reid, or even Ashton and demand answers. They know more than they're letting on, and I'm sick of being left in the dark.

"So a little birdy told me it's your birthday today!" Desiree materializes before me with a bright smile on her face.

I try to match her enthusiasm, but I just don't have the energy.

Desiree, unperturbed by my feeble smile, balances a polka-dot party hat on my head. It tilts precariously to the side but doesn't fall off.

"Happy eighteenth birthday," Desiree singsongs as she links her arm with mine and begins to lead us down the hall.

In the distance, I can see Mimi, Emilia, KD, and Ashlinn waiting in front of my locker. Behind them is what appears to be a huge banner with the words HAPPY BIRTHDAY written across it.

My cheeks flush, and I dig my heels in.

"Oh no. Fuck that." I try to get Desiree to stop, but she's unnaturally strong for a girl her size.

She laughs evilly and forces me forward. "You don't get to hide on your birthday. This is the one day a year your friends are allowed to embarrass the shit out of you."

"Shouldn't a person's birthday be the one day free of any embarrassment?" I dig my heels in again.

"Hmmm." Desiree taps her chin with a manicured finger. "Let me think about it for a second." She pretends to ponder. "Yeah. No. I don't think so." She quickens her pace, practically bouncing with excitement, forcing me to jog in order to keep up. "We have to do something tonight to celebrate your birthday. We can have your actual birthday party on Friday, but we should do something small tonight. Just us girls. No dicks allowed." She waggles a finger in front of my face. "Not even your harem. Ohhh. Maybe we could go ice skating! I've always wanted to go but—"

The rest of Desiree's words get lost in a blaze of heat sweeping through my insides.

What the fuck?

The pain is sudden and intense enough to stop me in mid-stride. This time, Desiree doesn't continue walking but stops and turns towards me.

Her brows furrow in concern. "Izzy?"

But I can't answer her through the agony ripping me apart and rearranging my insides like a wooden spoon in a bowl of soup. A whimper of pain slips past my lips as my fingers tighten around her arm, my nails digging into her skin. I'm probably drawing blood, but I don't care.

Can't she see that I'm on fire?

That I'm being burned alive?

Why isn't anyone stopping this? Helping me?

A scream lodges in my throat as my skin continues to burn and burn and burn.

Oh god.

Make it stop.

Please.

"Come on, Izzy." Desiree's voice is low and urgent as she slings one of my arms around her shoulders. She wraps her own arm around my waist and supports my weight as we stumble towards the office. "We're almost there. You'll be okay."

All I can do is sob.

I don't care that we're garnering attention.

I don't care that some of the students are whispering behind their hands.

I don't care that people are staring at me in confusion, concern, and amusement.

Nothing matters but the pain ripping me apart.

I'm going to die.

I can feel it in my bones.

"A few more steps. You're doing good, babe. We're almost there," Desiree soothes. A door is pushed open, and she yells, "Montgomery!"

"What is the meaning— Izzy?" Mr. Montgomery's voice is rife with disbelief. Silence stretches for only a second before he immediately takes charge. "Bring her to my office. Now."

Another door opens, and I'm half dragged, half walked into the vice principal's office. Desiree releases me, and I all but fall into the armchair opposite Montgomery's desk.

"What the fuck happened?" he demands, moving to stand in front of me.

Through the pain, I can't help but think he's so handsome. So, so handsome. Sexy.

I want to touch him. Feel him. Run my fingers through the stubble on his chin.

"I don't know." Desiree sounds frantic. "It's her eighteenth birthday, and she just started crying."

Montgomery leans even closer to me, and some of the pain recedes. The flames are still there, still eating away at my skin, but the heat is now...pleasant. A strange fire bursts to life in my lower belly.

A halfway delirious laugh escapes me.

"What is happening?" Desiree asks.

Montgomery's eyes shadow, turning unreadable.

"Desiree, you need to leave."

"I'm not leaving her—"

"Desiree!" For a moment, I swear Montgomery's eyes flash...red.

But then I blink, and the strange color fades.

There's a beat, and then the door opens and shuts. I don't even have to look to know that Christian and I are now alone.

"Isabella," he whispers, and there's a hint of a warning in his voice.

"You're mine," I breathe, grazing my fingers along his jawline. I don't know where those words come from.

What the hell is wrong with me?

Am I drunk?

But I don't feel drunk.

My arm begins to tingle beneath my sweater as I grab a hold of Christian's dark hair and tug his lips down to mine. But I don't kiss him. Instead, I just hold his head there, our lips a hair's breadth away, his warm breath fanning across my face. Goose bumps ripple down my arms at the sheer rightness of this moment. Of him.

"Isabella," he says again as I slowly stand, never taking my eyes off of his.

I take a step closer until my chest brushes against his, my nipples beaded. I can feel his cock through his trousers, hard and wanting.

Our breaths mix.

Each exhale has my breasts brushing his abs, supplying delicious friction to my aching nipples.

I'm on fire.

The flames are everywhere.

And only Christian Montgomery can ease the ache.

"What's happening to me?" I whisper, wanting to taste him, touch him, feel him against me.

I shouldn't want that. He's my vice principal. It's wrong, taboo, twisted.

Christian swallows heavily. "We can't do this. Not until you know everything."

"Know what?" My heart pounds against my breastbone as liquid heat traverses my veins.

I want to close my eyes and surrender to the warmth enveloping me. Surrender to him.

I remember our conversation from only a few days earlier, when he promised to answer any questions I may have.

Will he finally tell me the truth?

With surprising tenderness, Christian grabs my arm and pushes up my sweater sleeve. I'm so confused that I don't move for a solid minute as I study the arresting man before me, with the blue-black hair, shadowed jaw, and penetrating eyes. It's only when I follow the direction of his gaze do I realize he's staring at something on my arm.

Something that most definitely wasn't there this morning.

"What the fuck?" I breathe as I trace the strange brand on my bicep. It resembles a flame, and directly below it is a diminutive, zigzagging line. "What is this?" My voice trembles.

Christian pushes up his own sleeve to reveal his strong, muscular bicep. His skin is darker than mine but lighter than Ashton's. The color contrasts beautifully with his dark hair and midnight-blue eyes.

He traces a mark on his own skin, and I lean in closer to see it.

It's not the flame I have on my arm, but it is the zigzagging line.

"I don't understand," I whisper, hovering my finger over the puckered skin.

"It's a mark. A mate mark." His eyes ensnare my own, and I get lost in them. Lost in him.

"A mate mark?"

"It means you're mine, little human." His eyes flare red with possessiveness and heat. "It means you belong to the wolves."

Fifty-Five

GRAYSON

I don't know why I assumed that the "cell" they'd put me in would be anything but a prison. Maybe because the Council chamber was cozy and comfortable, exuding an aura of homeliness.

Instead, I found myself moderately surprised when they shoved me into a dank, ten-by-ten cell with steel bars, a smelly cot, and a single toilet pressed against the wall.

It's only been half a day, but it's half a day too long.

I need to be with Izzy. My Gracie.

Hearing that asshole threaten her...

Rage pulsates through me, and the only thing capable of calming my internal turmoil is knowing she's safe. Alive.

I didn't know if she would find her birthday present, but I hoped she would. With it, I'll always be able to know where she is, and I can feel her heartbeat pound as if it's my own.

I close my eyes and rest my head against the wall as I allow my thoughts to drift.

Everything I've done has been to protect the woman I love. When the Hunters came to me a year prior and demanded I work with them, I initially refused. I'm a lot of things—most of them psychotic— but I don't hurt people who don't deserve it.

But then they threatened the one thing in the world I give a damn about.

Izzy.

My job was supposed to be simple. Date Sydney. Get information. Send the information back to my contact. No one was supposed to get hurt.

Those girls...

Guilt threatens to swallow me whole, eating away at me like moths devouring a blanket. Yet, beneath the guilt is something akin to resolve.

If I didn't do what they said, what would've happened to Izzy? Would she be one of the bodies in the morgue?

I'll kill the entire goddamn world if it means keeping her safe and alive. Maybe that makes me a psychopath, but I don't care. Izzy is the only thing that matters.

Where is she now?

What is she thinking about?

I reach for the crystal hanging around my neck and give it a squeeze.

It cost a pretty penny, but I was able to hire a witch to create these necklaces for me. With my blood inside each of them, I'm able to feel Izzy in a way that defies logic. Right now, I get a vague sense of her location—the school—and I can feel her heartbeat through the crystal. It's slightly erratic, but that doesn't surprise me. She's probably terrified and confused.

I should've told her everything when I had the chance.

That monsters roam this world and I'm one of them.

But would she believe me if I told her I'm a vampire?

Even as I have that thought, my fangs descend, desperate for a neck to sink into. I'm starving.

But starving myself was necessary for this mission.

I needed for the wolves to think I was nothing but a weak human. Only then would they lower their defenses enough for me to slip through the cracks.

I squeeze the crystal tighter and take comfort in Izzy's heartbeat. The repetitive thump-thump-thump serves as white noise that drowns out all other sounds. My eyelids begin to droop as the events of the past day overwhelm me.

But just before sleep can claim me, footsteps sound right outside my cell.

"I thought I told you to be more careful, Grayson."

I blink open my eyes and jump upright, gripping the bars of my cell tightly.

"What the fuck are you doing here?" I whisper, staring at my contact in growing horror.

He's a Hunter, and I suspect he's the one who killed those two girls.

So how the fuck is he in wolf territory?

No, the bigger question is—*why* the fuck is he in wolf territory?

He grins maliciously and leans against the wall, crossing his ankles and arms simultaneously. Amusement glimmers in his eyes.

"I should be asking you the same question." He tsks his tongue in mock disapproval. "I didn't pay you to get caught."

"You didn't pay me at all." I bare my teeth.

We both know I'm not doing this for money. He blackmailed the woman I love and didn't give me a choice in the matter.

"True." He shrugs nonchalantly as he peers around me, taking in my prison. He whistles mockingly. "Sweet digs. I've always wondered where you lived."

I don't have the time or the patience for this. The wolves will be back soon and will demand answers—answers I can't give them. I'm damned if I do and damned if I don't. Either way, Isabella's life is on the line.

But what side will be willing to protect her?

"Are you going to let me out? How the fuck did you even get past their security?"

His grin widens. "It was easy, believe it or not. They'll never suspect one of their own."

"One of their own?" My brows furrow.

My contact's eyes flash yellow, and two canines protrude downwards, cutting into his lower lip. He blinks, and his features return to normal, that smug smirk still plastered on his face.

I gape at him in stunned disbelief, unsure of what I just saw. "You're a...wolf."

He gives me a slow, sardonic clap. "Ding, ding, ding. We have a winner."

This doesn't make any sense.

"You're also a Hunter," I feel the need to point out, my voice cracking. "You kill wolves."

Kain's smile sharpens, and I feel as if I'm looking into the eyes of a predator who isn't just out for the hunt...but for the kill.

He takes a single step closer until only the steel bars separate us. His smirk sends chills down my spine. "Who said I can't be both?"

Epilogue

HALE

I blow out a breath before biting down on my nail. It's an anxious habit of mine that Gerry has been trying to get me to quit for years. Still, I can't stop. Not now. I need an outlet for all of this restless energy skittering just beneath my skin.

Silas crosses his arms over his chest and scowls. His one good eye surveys the room with that keen intensity he's perfected over the years.

Our group decided to meet in Silas's apartment. He's such a paranoid fucker that he checks for bugs and video cameras on the regular.

Which is good, considering their topic of conversation.

"It's her eighteenth birthday today." Gerry rubs his hands down his jean-clad legs from where he sits on the couch beside me.

He looks particularly handsome today, with his

long hair cascading loose around his shoulders and his leather jacket clinging to his shoulders. Then again, Gerry always looks handsome to me, even after all of these years together.

Kyle moves to stand by the window, shoving aside the curtain so he can peer out.

"We need to talk to her. Soon. We don't know what's going to happen today," Kyle says, frowning.

"We don't know for sure that anything will happen," Gerry assures him. Always the voice of reason, even amongst opposing packs.

Kyle begins to fidget, and Silas blows out a heavy breath.

"Sit the fuck down, Remington, before you give me a damn headache," Silas warns him.

Kyle tosses Silas a frosty glare but does as his pack-mate says, claiming the armchair on the opposite end of the room.

When Amanda Highland reached out to Gerry and me about another "special" child, we didn't hesitate to take her in. But I knew within seconds of seeing Izzy that she's different from the others.

After all, the resemblance Izzy has to her mother is uncanny.

Kyle scrubs both of his hands down his face and rocks in the chair. "I can't believe she's here. I can't believe she's alive."

His voice cracks on that final word, and Silas's expression softens slightly.

"You two need to be the ones to talk to her. Explain." I try to adopt a no-nonsense expression, but I'm not as good at it as Gerry is. I'm too soft, too lenient. A bleeding heart.

Silas absently scratches at the scars marring his eye. "What the fuck can we even say to her?"

"The truth?" Gerry drawls sarcastically, reclining backwards on the couch.

Silas's lips purse. "She won't believe it."

"She's stronger than you think she is," I say gently.

For a brief moment, Silas's expression twists with something akin to jealousy before he forces his features into a mask of indifference.

"If you don't talk to her, we will," Gerry warns, and I nod resolutely.

I have come to care about Isabella immensely.

I care about all of my foster kids, which is why the events of the last few weeks have been troubling, to put it mildly.

A Hunter is in town...if not multiple Hunters.

Isabella turned eighteen today.

Jake is beginning to ask questions.

And Lissa and Seth...

I scrub a hand down my face. Fuck, it's hard being a parent to teenagers.

Especially supernatural ones.

"We need to discuss something else," Gerry pipes up. He waits until he has all of our attention before he focuses on Silas—the unofficial leader of his and Kyle's pack. "Has anyone talked to Travan?"

A cold chill skates down my spine just hearing that name.

Silas tenses, and Kyle's mouth purses as if he just ate something sour.

For a long moment, nobody speaks, and I wonder if it's because everybody had the same reaction I did to hearing Travan's name or if it's because Silas and Kyle are trying to get their thoughts in order.

"No. Not yet." Silas and Kyle exchange an unreadable glance before Silas returns his attention to Gerry. "And I don't think we're going to."

"Is that a smart idea?" I interject, biting down on my nail.

Gerry grabs my wrist and tugs my hand away from my mouth. I frown at my mate but don't protest.

"Do you think it's a smart idea for him to know about Izzy?" Kyle counters immediately, and I don't have a response to that.

Because Kyle's right.

"Besides, last I checked, he was in Italy. I can't see him returning here anytime soon," Silas adds gruffly.

"He's going to recognize Izzy as soon as he sees her," Gerry points out.

I can't help but agree.

Silas's good eye darkens. "Let's hope it doesn't come to that."

We already have Hunters to deal with.

Adding Travan Zarrow to the mix is just a recipe for disaster.

But that's a problem that we'll, hopefully, never have to face. For now, we just need to decide what to say to Izzy to make her understand.

I will do whatever is necessary to protect my foster children from the horrors of this world.

Even if that means protecting them from themselves.

Afterword

Thank you all so much for reading! Book two is already written and being released on Ream and Kindle Vella. Don't feel like waiting? You can check out book two on Vella (start on Episode 58) and Ream and be a part of the writing process! It should release on Amazon KU later this year, followed closely by book three.

Acknowledgments

Thank you to my incredible team who made this book possible!

First, I would like to thank everyone who read Burning Embers on Ream and Vella. I absolutely loved your input. A special thank you to Elena and Tami! I love you ladies to death.

Next, I would like to thank my editor Lindsey and my cover designer Laura. You guys are the best. Thank you for bringing my vision to life.

And finally, I would like to thank you, the reader, for picking up this book. I hope you enjoyed reading it as much as I enjoyed writing it.

About the Author

Katie May is a reverse harem author, a KDP All-Star winner, and an *USA Today* Bestselling Author. She lives in West Michigan with her family, cat, and adorable puppy. When not writing, she can be found reading a good book, listening to broadway musicals, or playing games. Join Katie's Gang to stay updated on all her releases! And did you know she has a TikTok? Yeah, me neither. Follow her here! But be warned... she's an awkward noodle.

Together We Fall (Apocalyptic Reverse Harem, COMPLETED)

1. The Darkness We Crave

2. The Light We Seek

3. The Storm We Face

4. The Monsters We Hunt

Beyond the Shadows (Horror Reverse Harem, COMPLETED)

1. Gangs and Ghosts

2. Guns and Graveyards

3. Gallows and Ghouls

Out of Sight (Prison Reverse Harem, COMPLETED)

1. Blindly Indicted

2. Blindly Acquitted

Kingdom of Wolves (Shifter Reverse Harem Duet, COMPLETED)

1. Torn to Bits

2. Ripped to Shreds

Tory's School for the Trouble (Bully Horror Academy
Reverse Harem, COMPLETED)

1. Between

2. Beyond

3. Beneath

The Damning (Fantasy Paranormal Reverse Harem)

1. Greed

2. Envy

3. Gluttony

4. Sloth

5. Pride

6. Lust

7. Wrath

Prodigium Academy (Horror Comedy Academy Reverse
Harem, COMPLETED)

1. Monsters

2. Roaring

3. Venom

4. Fangs

5. Blood

Kings of Grove Academy (Contemporary Academy Reverse
Harem)

1. Mania

2. Psychotic

3. Pandemonium

4. Delirium

The Death Whisper (Fantasy Reverse Harem)

1. Of Rain and Wrath

2. Of Heat and Obsession

Supernaturalette (Interactive Reverse Harem)

1. Introductions

2. First Dates

3. Group Outing

4. Game Night

5. Exes

6. Truth or Dare

7. Scavenger Hunt

8. Reveals

CO-WRITES

Afterworld Academy with Loxley Savage (Academy Fantasy Reverse Harem, COMPLETED)

1. Dearly Departed

2. Darkness Deceives

3. Defying Destiny

Darkest Flames with Ann Denton (Paranormal Reverse Harem, COMPLETED)

1. Demon Kissed

1.5. Demon Stalked

2. Demon Loved

3. Demon Sworn

Darkest Queen with Ann Denton (Paranormal Reverse Harem)

1. For Whom the Bell Tolls

Dark Temptations with Ann Denton (Monster Reverse Harem)

1. Ravaged by Monsters

2. Devoured by Monsters

3. Worshipped by Monsters

Fae Revealed with Quinn Arthurs (Paranormal Reverse Harem)

1. Courting Darkness

2. Seducing Shadows

3. Loving Demons

STAND-ALONES

Toxicity (Contemporary Reverse Harem)

Not All Heroes Wear Capes (Just Dresses) (Short Comedic Reverse Harem)

Charming Devils (Bully/Revenge Reverse Harem)

Goddess of Pain (Fantasy Reverse Harem)

Demon's Joy (Holiday Reverse Harem)

Broken Howl (Wolf Shifter Reverse Harem)

Dark Paradise (Paranormal Motorcycle Club Reverse Harm)

Ruthless as a Cheetah (Paranormal Romantic Comedy Reverse Harem)

BOXSETS

Together We Fall